T
KEE
of
FEI
WH

The
KEEPER
of the
FERRIS
WHEEL

A Novel

JACK McBRIDE WHITE

DONALD I. FINE, INC.

New York

To Jack White and Anne McBride, my parents.

With special thanks to Andrea Reid for too
many reasons to say.

1

It just about broke my heart the way that chewed-up cat on her shoulder reminded me of Whitey. Whitey was a black dog with a white circle around each eye. The cat was a gray and gnarled ball of soaked fur with a scrinched-up face, two glowing eyeballs, and only one ear, but it reminded me of Whitey, and Whitey reminded me of Patrick. Everything reminded me of Patrick. It had only been a couple weeks since the funeral, and I wasn't used to it yet. Even after five years I'm not used to it yet, but back then it was worse than ever.

That was '67, back before Johnson quit, before the Tet Offensive and the siege of Khe Sanh, before Robert Kennedy and Martin Luther King got shot down a few weeks from one another, back when we were just noticing what a big war they'd slipped us into, and it never occurred to anybody we could lose the thing.

The woman with the cat draped over her shoulder was Robin Debussy. She owned the hotel. She stood in the smoke at the back of her apartment on the fourteenth floor and talked to us. It was July, but a cool breeze circled through the windows and swirled the marijuana smoke around her. She was tiny.

"I guess you people know there's a war going on," she said. "And I guess you know a guy from this town came home in a box not too long ago, and they couldn't even open it so his family could have a look at him."

I took a deep breath. I wanted to shout at her, this little woman with the screwed-up accent, this freak with the glass eye and wire glasses like your great grandfather in some old picture, this raggedy puppet in men's clothes and no shoes, standing there in a pair of argyle socks, yapping about my brother like some know-it-all.

What did she know about Patrick? What did she know about anything? One day she was a maid in the Roosevelt Hotel, the best in Deadwhale, New Jersey, which wasn't saying much, and the next day she owned the place.

She inherited everything when Margaret Ditzlow died in '65— the collection of old eyeglasses and ancient bicycles, the bar and doughnut shop on the strip, the twenty-three thousand in cash in the safe behind the framed photo of Franklin Roosevelt.

The place had barely scraped by since the forties, and when Robin kept it going, the rumors started about her being Margaret's lover, or illegitimate daughter, or a prostitute who took in whole football teams to pay the bills. They called her a heroin addict and a vampire, but nobody knew for sure, and Robin ran the place quietly, coming out once a day to walk the beach with her cat at sunup.

But that summer she took to the streets, shoeless in those argyle socks, wearing suspenders and neckties, and shouting at strangers about bombs. Soon they were throwing things at her and calling her a communist. She threw them right back. Her language got so bad, people wouldn't let their kids near her, and now I was in her living room listening to her talk about my brother, and I hated her.

"But I only get thirty people from the whole town," she said. "I had a conference room laid out and enough food and booze to feed Westmoreland's army, and I get thirty people."

"Don't get all bent about it, Robin, baby. I'll drink the wine."

It came from a huge, hulking character who stood in her shadow a few feet from one of the candles. He was bearded and balding and wearing a long coat in July, an overcoat with a ripped pocket, and when he smiled wide at Robin, a cigarette hung there like magic.

"I'd be glad to lend a hand with the food, too," he said, and he pulled a bottle from the ripped pocket and took a long swallow. He had an accent like James Bond, but reminded me more of a street fighter than a secret agent. I could picture him in an alley slamming some loser against a brick wall then stepping on the guy's hand when he tried to pick a knife off the ground.

When Robin looked at him, her face turned all sour like maybe she'd just choked down a fish that hadn't stopped kicking yet.

"Nigel," she asked, "shouldn't you be out biting the heads off chickens?"

"Not at the moment, love."

He blew smoke at her and winked. The candle on a table beside Robin danced and sent her shadow up and down the wall. She looked at the crowd and started up again, and the man in the dark kept smoking and smiling and drinking.

Robin's voice was soft and scratchy. She had a funny way of talking, like maybe she was from New York or up far in Jersey, maybe Newark or some other place way north of Deadwhale, but she sounded southern, too. It was the weirdest blend of east-coast thug and southern drawl, like some Mafia cowboy.

It was hard guessing her age. She had the voice of an old woman who'd smoked filthy cigarettes all her life, but she had a young body, and it was hard to tell about her face because her glasses made her eyes swell up huge, but once I'd seen her up close without the glasses down by the wharf. She was there every morning, stiff as a flagpole, with her hair and clothes flapping all around her, and she looked beautiful that morning with a slight Oriental slant to her eyes, a red lump on her nose, blonde hair hanging in a mess on her shoulders, and tears dripping on her cat. I figured she was twenty-five, but found out later I was five years low.

"But I guess it ain't too bad," she said. "You might've been Nazis. I guess all the Nazis are up in King's Port shining their boots."

They laughed. They didn't look like Nazis. Most had been smoking pot the past hour, tapping the ashes into the plants between the records and books all along the walls. They were a new type we were seeing around town. They had long hair and jeans and sweatshirts and beat-up track shoes. They were stoned, with pink eyes and droopy lids, and full of things to say.

"They're protesting all over the country," Robin said. "What the hell's happening here? You waiting for an invitation?"

Some guy with a ponytail shouted, "What are we supposed to do?"

"You tell me," she said. "I'm from Waxahachie, Texas. Don't know much about fucking Jersey."

My eyes popped wide open. She'd been saying "fuck" all over town, but I couldn't get used to it. Girls didn't say "fuck" in those days. Even I didn't say it. Never once.

She put her hands on her hips and stared over us all, but nobody said anything.

"All right, I'll get to the point," she said. "What's Deadwhale been providing the war?"

"Bodies," one said.

"What else?"

"Machine guns," another shouted.

"Bingo," Nigel said from his dark corner.

"Nigel, go find a chicken," she said.

"Sorry, love, I didn't mean to spoil your momentum."

"Then quit interrupting."

"Okay, love, so machine guns it is. Carry on."

It went that way. Robin suggested we close down the machine gun factory where my father worked. Nigel cut in with wisecracks. She told him to chew off a chicken head, and he told her he wasn't quite hungry at the moment. It got funny, like they'd been rehearsing, and even I laughed a time or two, and then she stopped talking, opened some wine, and suggested we get to know one another.

"Talk about the factory," she said. "And how we can shut it down."

The joints lit up. Robin put Louis Armstrong on, and while the cool people in the room talked about the war and this crazy idea about shutting down the factory, I stood in a corner in a sweater vest and khaki pants, wishing I had long hair and great opinions, wishing they would gather around while I explained how messing with the factory would ruin the town, but no one seemed too interested in my opinions, and I was pretty sure they all pointed at me and laughed whenever I turned my head. In twenty minutes I was roaring drunk and whispering fuck to a plant. I felt liberated.

I paged through some vegetarian cookbooks. I was astonished by the potential of beans and some of the miracles you could work with a few spices I couldn't pronounce. I considered learning to cook, but not very long, before I got interested in her crazy collection of albums and her gigantic plants and forgot all about beans.

I spilled wine in the plant I was whispering fuck to. I could never pass one without watering it. Patrick had a cactus once that I'd watered until it turned to jelly and fell on the floor. I hated thinking of Patrick, so I kept pouring down wine. It was supposed to make you forget, but I kept remembering Patrick's cactus and how hard he laughed when he found it all mushy on the floor.

"I think I gave it too much water," I told him.

Patrick raised both eyebrows as high as he could.

"Yeah, Itchy," he said. "It's a cactus, not a swimming pool."

"It's Jell-O now," I said, and Patrick must have laughed five minutes.

When Suzanne Waters came over, I was remembering the night Whitey escaped. I hadn't thought about it in a long time, but that cat reminded me. Whitey was my dog, and he got loose, in a sense, when I was fourteen. There was no Vietnam War then, or at least not one that we knew about. President Kennedy had just died. The mayor of Deadwhale had washed up on the beach two months before that.

I was a sickly kid with two healthy brothers. Patrick was two years older than me. Charlie was thirteen months younger. The doctors never decided what was wrong, and by '67 I was fine, but when we first got the dog, I was sick all the time. I stayed in bed a lot, dreaming about silver streaks in the sky and mushroom clouds rising over the edge of town, and only Patrick could calm me when I woke up soaked and screaming and flopping from side to side in bed.

I begged my father to build a bomb shelter. I used my allowance to buy canned goods. I filled a box with Campbell's clam chowder and chicken noodle and stored it in the cellar with the dust and dried-out cockroaches on their backs along the walls. When the air-raid whistles shrieked at noon on Wednesdays, I climbed under my desk at school, or ran into the cellar to count the soup if I was home.

Patrick talked my father into a dog to keep me company. I named the dog Whitey, but he was mostly black, some kind of spaniel, with a white tail and those circles around his eyes. I taught him to beg and roll over. He was a smart dog, maybe smarter than Charlie, but there was no way to tell for sure.

I read him *The Call of the Wild*. I talked to him about the Russians and Red Chinese, and sometimes he moaned in his sleep or moved his legs like he was running, and I wondered what nightmares a dog would have and woke him with a slap on the snout.

We had Whitey for seven years before he walked downstairs late one night and died in the kitchen by his bowl. Patrick discovered him. I heard him come in and whisper something to Charlie. Later I heard the kitchen door that led out to the yard. The yard was small. There was a green fence with paint that peeled off every summer. There were some rosebushes my mother took care of. There was a rusted mower in a patch of grass the size of the mound at Connie Mack Stadium, where my dad took us to watch the Phillies lose a baseball game once a summer, and there was a huge tree.

I climbed into the top bunk and watched my brothers through the branches that clacked and moaned when the wind blew. It blew that night, but it wasn't vicious. I'd seen a lot worse in February. We weren't far from the ocean or Deadwhale Bay, and sometimes there'd be a breeze full of sand and salt air that could tear through you. It wasn't one of those nights, though, just a freezing air that barely shook the tree.

I started crying when I saw the dog in Charlie's arms. Patrick had a shovel, and they took turns banging at the frozen earth. I didn't know why they didn't wait till morning. I watched till they were finished. By then, they'd both taken off their coats and rolled up their sleeves. I could see their breath in a light that came in from the alley behind the yard. I could hear the shovel banging and one of my brothers huffing, while the other hopped up and down with his hands in his pockets. I could hear their quiet voices.

It took two hours to dig the hole. Then Patrick jumped in, and Charlie handed Whitey down. It took another hour to cover it over, fix the grass back the way it was, and tromp it down so no one could notice. They stood by the hole for a while before they came inside. They bowed their heads, and Patrick said something I couldn't make out.

In the morning, Patrick told me that Whitey had escaped during the night.

"Probably headed for the beach," Charlie said. "Crazy dog thinks he's a dolphin, or something."

"Probably swimming to England," Patrick said.

Charlie was about to cry, and they both looked tired, with droopy eyes and dirt ground into their fingers.

"Someday he'll come back," Patrick said.

"The call of the wild," I said, and Charlie ran out of the room. That's when I knew I could live without Whitey, but I couldn't imagine not having Charlie and Patrick around. I couldn't imagine this war coming up.

2

And then someone touched my hand, and I was in a room of smoke and people. Louis Armstrong blasted his trumpet, all scratched and distorted, and cool beach air blew through the open windows. The candles flickered, and I stared at Suzanne Waters' beautiful eyes in the darkness.

She was the only dressed-up person in the room, as if she was on her way to church in her pretty blue dress. She'd gotten awfully close. She could have kissed me with a little tilt of the neck. She was famous and easily the most beautiful girl in Deadwhale, and I couldn't imagine why she would want to kiss me.

"I saw your picture in the paper," she said. She hugged me. She was taller than me, close to six feet, and she smelled beautiful, and I let her hold on as long as she liked.

"I'm sorry," she said. "They call you Itchy, don't they?"

"Yeah, when I was six I had this rash for about ten months. Stupid thing nearly killed me, and my brothers stuck that name on me. They thought it was funnier than I did."

"Well, I'm really sorry."

"It cleared up."

"What?"

"My rash."

"I'm talking about your brother, not your rash."

"Oh, yeah."

I was embarrassed. I didn't know what to do when people said how sorry they were, but I figured she knew how I felt. Her father'd

been mayor once, and he'd died when Suzanne was only fourteen or
so. Now she was eighteen, a little older than me.

"He was brave," she said.

"Yeah, lot of good it does him now."

Patrick died fighting for a hill. A marine and Father Joel came to
the house in their crew cuts and best solemn faces. They looked like
twins. Father Joel smelled like mothballs. The marine smelled like
old booze and English Leather, and his finger trembled when he
pointed to the hill on a map. He explained how the hill didn't have
a name, but had a number, something to do with altitude, but he
didn't explain why Patrick's unit abandoned it three days after
twenty-three guys died taking it. I had to figure that out myself,
except I couldn't.

"So you're a genius," she said. "In *The Lighthouse*, it said one
brother was the best football player in the state and one was the
smartest kid in the history of Deadwhale High."

"I'm the football player," I said.

"Funny, you looked a lot bigger in the paper." She smiled. "Is it a
good school?"

"Compared to the other ones I've been to."

"What other ones you been to?"

"None."

"You're pretty funny."

"Thanks."

She lived in the northeast part of town, up in King's Port, where
the houses were huge stone things that stood in lines on a hill and
looked down over their private beach. It was officially part of Deadwhale, but they had their own schools, and it was a lot different
from Fishtown in West Deadwhale where I lived. They called us
Whales. We called them Kings. They didn't go to Vietnam.

She hadn't let go yet. Her eyes were deep and dark, and there was
something strange about them. People said she'd never gotten over
her father's death. She'd dropped out of high school when she was
sixteen and taken a job in a frame shop on Nineteenth Street. She
stood in the back chopping wood with a framing tool, smoking like
a fiend, and whispering to herself all day. People said she talked to
the paintings of famous artists. She was kind of a tourist attraction.

"Once I had this dream," she said. "There were all these soldiers
waiting for a bus to some war, but you were the one who smiled at
me like we were old friends, and when I saw you in the paper, I
couldn't believe it."

"But I wasn't a soldier. That was Patrick," I said.

Her face was still against mine, but she wasn't holding so tight anymore. She had a face that was long finished being a girl's, but not quite a woman's, and her left eye was swollen as if someone had punched her. I wanted to touch her face. There was something delicate about it, as if some artist had made it up with a skinny pencil and a couple thin lines. He'd put her lips crooked. He'd made the head too thin and the cheeks kind of gaunt, but somehow it all just made her too beautiful.

"It was in one of your past lives."

"I don't remember any past lives."

"No one does. That would interfere with this one."

"Oh. So was it like the French army in World War One? Did you ever read *The Guns of August*? It's the greatest book."

"No," she said. "You spoke English."

"The Civil War?"

"I don't think they had buses at the Civil War, Itchy, and it doesn't matter which war. The point is you're here now drinking wine like a lush, and a few years from now your brother will be doing the same thing, and he won't have a clue he died in Vietnam."

She sipped from a cup of wine and lit a cigarette and sucked streams of smoke into her lungs.

"I knew you'd be here," she said.

"You were looking for me?"

She brushed the hair off her forehead. Every so often a strand fell over her eyes. It was pure black, and her face was pale underneath it, with just a few wisps of color, as if the artist were saving on lead or had used it all up on her hair and her black eye.

"Our brothers were friends," she said.

"Yeah. Joe's a nice guy. Patrick used to say what a great mechanic he is."

"Yeah, wonderful, except he should be running the city, or something, instead of oiling mufflers or whatever the hell he does."

"I don't think you oil mufflers."

"Oh, who cares? Dirty stinking cars. A raindrop hits mine, and a piece falls off. Joe says it has leprosy." She blew smoke in the air. "He says I should shoot it, like a horse, before it infects whole parking lots."

The smoke kept getting thicker. The music was loud. The door opened a crack, and someone peeked in.

"Hey, he's here," I said. "Right on cue."

Suzanne followed my eyes toward her brother.

"Oh great," she said, but it wasn't happy how she said it, and she looked nervous all of a sudden.

"Want to call him over?"

"Just be quiet. This anti-war stuff drives him crazy, and he's liable to make an ugly scene. Joe loves making ugly scenes."

She bit into a finger and watched him.

"He came to the funeral," I said. "Nobody else from King's Port would do that. No Donaghy would."

"Donaghys aren't human," she said. "They don't see the same world we do, you know, like how dogs can smell so good and hear things we don't hear, but maybe don't see colors."

Douglas Donaghy was mayor. His son, Stewart, ran the machine gun factory and dated Suzanne. He was nearly ten years older, and people said he hit her, but there were always rumors about the Waters and Donaghys, especially after Mayor Waters' widow married Douglas Donaghy for a while.

Joe was already laughing with some girl, and Suzanne slipped behind me, peering around me now and then, like a kid staring out behind a tree.

"Why's he here if he hates this stuff?" I asked.

"Who knows? Reconnaissance work, maybe."

"What's he looking for?"

"Wild Indians, Germans, communists. Joe's temporarily insane most of the time," she said.

She bent her neck forward. She'd been crouching all along, as if she was ashamed of her height, but now it seemed like she wanted to stick her head in a hole.

"Did you ever talk to Joe?" she asked.

"Yeah, he used to visit Patrick."

"Will you talk to him again? I thought you and your brother could talk some sense into him."

"What do you want us to say?"

Joe saw her. I could tell by how she got stiff all over and dropped her cigarette in her wine. It hissed. She handed me the cup.

"Pretend it's yours. Joe hates if I smoke or drink or breathe air."

Joe worked his way over. He acted like the tallest guy there, but he was nice about it, just grabbing people by the shoulders and gently pushing them aside until he had his arm around Suzanne. She smiled, but she'd slipped further into the darkness and turned the left side of her face away from him. The nearest candle had burnt low, but it lit her face orange.

He winked at me and stuck out his hand.

"These freaks," he said. "Now they're talking about closing up the factory. What'll your dad do then, Itchy?"

"Beats me," I said. "I don't know if he's good at anything, except yelling a lot. Can you get a job yelling?"

"Maybe he could do auctions," Suzanne said. "I think they call them barkers."

Joe pointed to the two cups of wine. "A two-fisted drinker, huh?"

"Joe, how come you're here?" Suzanne asked. "Isn't this your night to get drunk and beat-up?"

"I can get drunk and beat-up here," he said.

"But there's not as much opportunity," she said.

"You make your own opportunities."

He took a long drink from a bottle of Budweiser he'd brought in. He took her cup from my hand and looked inside.

"Smoking, too, huh?"

"Just a little," she said.

He picked the cigarette out of the cup. "Salem?" A drop of wine rolled off his fingers.

"I'm eighteen," she whispered.

"Lucky you," Joe said. He wiped the fingers on his pants. "How's that car?"

"It's dead. I think it's the muffler."

Joe laughed. "Yeah, probably, or the steering wheel."

"Can't you come look at it?" she asked. "Put in some new hoses or something?"

Joe had the same black hair as Suzanne, but he was shorter with much brighter eyes, gray eyes, and didn't look much like her.

"Take it to a museum," he said.

"It's a perfectly good car, and if I could get a decent mechanic..."

"I told you to bring it over, but I'm not coming to King's Port."

"How am I going to get it to your place, carry it on my back?"

"There's an idea." Joe turned to me. "You know this Robin?"

"I see her on the beach."

"What's she do on the beach?"

"She fishes for sharks," Suzanne said. "Sometimes she surfs."

"She stares at the wharf," I said. "I see her when I run by."

"I hear she's a communist," he said.

"Maybe she's signaling Russian subs with a piece of glass," Suzanne said. "I think they park off the coast to gather intelligence."

"They wouldn't gather much around here," Joe said.

"There's some intelligent lifeguards," Suzanne said.

Joe dipped his fingers in my wine, then splashed some on Suzanne. She blinked.

"I hear she's a vegetarian," he said, "and that she's got a glass eye."

"They should lock her up," Suzanne said.

"You're a funny girl," Joe said.

"How many one-eyed vegetarian communists you slept with?" Suzanne asked.

"Every one in town except her."

"Is that why you're here?"

"I've seen her on the street. You know I'm attracted to the lunatic fringe."

"You are the lunatic fringe," Suzanne said.

Joe laughed and tugged at his jacket. It was a nice thing, wool with useless patches sewn to the elbows. He always wore a sports coat and kept his hands clean, even his fingernails. Patrick could never get all the grease out of his nails.

Joe was twenty and just into his junior year at Princeton when his father died, and after the funeral, he drove a car into the surf and sat there drinking whiskey until the tide came in the open windows. Suzanne had to wade out and get him.

Later he set himself on fire. He didn't douse himself in gasoline, like those monks in Vietnam, and it was probably an accident, but he looked weird going around with no eyebrows and a burnt spot in his hair. He quit school after that and took to drinking and playing poker till the sun came up.

A few days after his eyebrows grew in, he attacked Douglas Donaghy outside city hall. Donaghy wasn't mayor yet, but he was already the most powerful man in the city. Joe walked up to him on a Friday afternoon. Donaghy didn't defend himself, and by the time Joe stopped hitting him, most of the bones in his face were broken, and he was crying on his knees with his hands raised up to Joe like someone begging, or worshipping God.

Joe walked away, but the cops found him sitting in a puddle on the beach, sucking fumes from a bag of glue. They put him in jail, but Donaghy never pressed charges, and Joe got out with a couple broken ribs and some heel marks on his side. Cop heels.

After that he moved into a neighborhood full of boarded windows and pissy-smelling dogs in Southwest Deadwhale, what we called the southwest slums, where the black people lived. He never set foot in King's Port again, not even to visit his family. Sometimes he would take trips to Europe, traveling all around with a pack on bikes and trains, sleeping in graveyards behind old churches in Germany and France, but he always came home and went back to work fixing cars for black people in the worst part of town.

"What's this?" he asked, touching her eye.

"Sloppy make-up," she said.

"You seeing that prick again?"

"Stewart?"

"Don't make me say his name."

"I wouldn't tell you if I was."

Joe pulled her toward him. He stared into her eyes, then twisted her arm and forced her toward another part of the room. I watched them arguing over there a long time before they stopped talking, and Joe started pouring down wine.

I remembered when their father died, the most popular mayor we'd ever had. They'd found him on the beach in the morning with waves lapping against his face and hundreds of sea gulls fighting over his leaking skull. His eyes were gone.

The cops said he'd fallen off the wharf during the storm the night before and split his head on the boards, but they never explained why he was on that rickety wharf that terrible night. There were rumors about women and booze and maybe even suicide or murder, but the case was closed.

I remembered Suzanne at the funeral, fainting at the grave and hitting her head on the coffin, and Joe lifting her from the grass and carrying her to the car with hundreds of people watching. I remembered Patrick whispering how pretty she was. It was worse than when Kennedy died.

The evening spun on. It had turned into a party, and I didn't want to go home, so I slumped against a pile of books while a scratchy saxophone wailed and honked some horrible melody. I got so drunk I had to close one eye to read the titles of the books. I saw one called *The Naked Lunch* and wondered if it was some new way of eating.

I wanted to tell some of the cool guests my theories about the war, but was pretty sure they were all laughing at my sweater and my short hair. So I decided they were all jerks and stayed in my corner, looking through piles of beat-up jazz albums and some Patsy Cline with a terrible haircut like someone's older sister would have. I couldn't believe she didn't have any Beatles.

By midnight, there were only about ten of us. Suzanne sat with Joe across the room at a table full of chopped vegetables. She picked at carrots and sipped on wine, while he drank. They didn't say a word. It was like they enjoyed hating each other.

I moved toward the group around Robin. She had her glasses off and dark make-up circling her eyes. Men gathered around her. They argued and passed joints. Robin's cat watched from her shoulder, and Robin watched, too. Robin watched Joe.

Nigel was talking. He stood real close to Robin, and every time she backed away, he would get close again, so that the whole group was slowly moving across the room. It reminded me of something I'd read about the gradual erosion of our beaches.

"You don't work in increments," he said. "You work in bold strokes. We're not talking painting, love, little dabs at the canvas. We're talking revolution. We're not impressionists, we're anarchists. So we'll shut them both down, the chemical place, too. It's disgusting how it fouls the filthy air."

"Donaghy runs them," Robin said. She looked toward Joe. He'd just touched Suzanne's wrist, smiled, and walked toward the center of the room.

"All the more reason," Nigel said. "He's using the bloody war to get rich."

And they all talked in a hurry, until Joe cut in. His voice was clear and loud.

"So you're going to do like the communists and decide what's good for the workers, right?"

Robin spilled wine on her wrist. She started to say something, but Nigel cut her off.

"So who have we here?"

"My name's Joe. Who are you? Trotsky?"

Nigel laughed. "Good. Trotsky, I like that. No, actually my man, the name's Nigel. Nigel Ross. I'm Robin's husband."

Robin got that look again, as if the fish she'd swallowed was working its way back up her throat.

"Jesus, Nigel. Quit telling people that," she said.

"Well, it's true, love, isn't it? I distinctly remember the wedding. It rained, and we drank champagne from your bloody boot."

Robin put her glasses on and focused on Joe. "Nigel and I were married in London thirteen years ago. I was seventeen."

She looked at Nigel, whose bulging eyes were fixed on hers. His lips, with the cigarette glued between them, were caught somewhere between a smile and a sneer.

"And we've lived happily ever after," he said.

"And I left him when I was eighteen, shortly after he bit the ear off my cat and washed it down with a bottle of wine."

Nigel laughed. "Ah, don't exaggerate, love. It was scissors and beer. You should have seen her, Joe. I'm a photographer, and those were classic shots. The fucking cat gushing blood. Robin kissing the poor thing. Its claws ripping at her eyes. And me snapping pictures with a cat's furry fucking ear in my bloody stomach. Ah, it was a sight. I'll show you the collection someday."

He reached for the cat, but Robin snatched it against her. She tried to kill Nigel with a look, but he just laughed.

"Great story," Joe said. He backed up a step.

"And he's been following me ever since," Robin said. "Like a plague."

"And it hasn't been easy, love, with you and the one-eared monkey slinking out of cities in the middle of the night. Lord knows how you found this dreadful hole."

"And now you've decided to close down our machine gun factory," Joe said.

"Ah, now isn't that a great idea?" Nigel asked.

"No," Joe said. "They're only guns for Christ's sake, not H-bombs. You'll just put people out of work."

"Let them eat the fucking bullets," Nigel said.

Robin stared at Joe, but whenever Nigel spoke, she closed her eyes like she was waiting for some deep pain to pass. The others had gotten awfully quiet. Everyone in Deadwhale knew Joe, and they were afraid of him.

"So how do you propose we end the war?" Robin asked.

"Winning it," Joe said.

Nigel let out a big laugh. "Ah, the genius," he said. "Why hasn't the military thought of that? Just win the bloody thing and have it over."

"It's not so funny," Joe said. "I had a friend..."

Nigel cut him off. "Don't tell us about your friend, Joe. We've all had unfortunate friends." He stepped too close to Joe. He was much taller. His shoulders were huge. His eyes were gigantic things, blazing and spread too far from his nose. He was ugly and handsome and a lot older than Joe, in his late forties, with a bald spot on the right and hair from the other side combed over it and little nicks and scars all over the parts of his face that weren't covered with beard.

"It's a lousy fucking war, and that's a crummy little factory," Nigel said. "And Robin and I intend to blow it to hell."

"So now you're blowing it up. Well who the hell put you and Robin in charge of Deadwhale?" Joe asked.

"Nigel doesn't speak for me," Robin said. "I'm not fixing to destroy anything."

Nigel smiled. "Blow it to hell."

"I'd like to hear Joe's position," she said. "If you could calm your enthusiasm for a second, Nigel."

"Ah," Nigel said. "But anarchy, blood, death, explosions, the thought makes me tingle."

Joe looked at Robin. "Your husband's crazy," he said. "I can understand that, but what about you? Are you crazy, too, or do you just want to close the factory to give a little meaning to your life?"

"I hate the war," she said.

"What's wrong with the war?" Joe asked.

"It's brutal," Robin said. "You can't ignore that."

Joe nodded. "Not half as brutal as communism."

"They just want to run their own country," some girl said. She wore a beanie and a sleeveless shirt, and there was hair all black and matted under her arms.

"Who?" Joe asked. "The Vietcong? How do the Vietcong rule when they get the chance, or let's not say rule. Let's say influence."

His right hand kept folding into a fist, unfolding, then folding again. He banged the fist against his pants.

"You know how, don't you? Crawl into the village at night, stuff the mayor's balls down his throat. A little education for the peasantry." He swallowed some wine and kept talking.

"Come on. They're killers with a little ideology spread over the top. They quote Marx and slit throats for the workers, but they don't give a fuck about the workers. They want power. They take it by terror, they rule by terror, and once they win, the country's fucked, and all that nice talk about peasants and workers is shit."

He stared around the room. The record had finished, and I heard the ocean through the window. I heard Joe breathing. Everyone watched him. Suzanne held a hand over her mouth. Nigel kept smiling. Robin stared at Joe, and everything blurred and echoed in my drunken skull.

"So we give in here," Joe said. "We give in the next time, and every time a group of thugs wants a country, they call themselves communists, get some guns from Russia, and we're sunk, and your ideals, if that's what you're professing here, are shit."

"And how come you're not in Vietnam, my friend?" Nigel asked.

Suzanne dropped her cigarette. It glowed on the floor. I picked it up before it burned the oldest hotel in Deadwhale to the ground. She stepped between Joe and Nigel.

"Come on, Joe," she said. "Ignore this sarcastic moron."

"Joe's a bloody hypocrite, sweets," Nigel said.

"Don't call me that," Joe said.

Suzanne had Joe's arm, but she couldn't budge him.

"Don't listen, Joe. He thinks he's smart 'cause he's got an accent, but I'll bet it's phony. He probably sent away for some tapes."

Nigel looked at Suzanne. "Joe's a hypocrite, a lot of talk about fighting communists, but here he is in Deadwhale, probably some King's Port college boy, drinking wine and making speeches, while the Whales do the fighting."

She snapped back at him. "What do you know about the Whales? Where the hell you from, anyway, New Zealand?"

"That's my business, love," he said.

Joe broke free of Suzanne. He tossed his jacket on the floor.

"Joe please," Suzanne said. "This guy's a loser. A gigantic one."

"Some people called my father a hypocrite," Joe said.

"So who the hell's your father?" Nigel asked.

"Robert Waters," Joe said.

Something hissed out of Robin then, and her hand rose to her mouth. She tripped backward a step, and her glasses fell on the floor. She reached for them, but Nigel crushed them under his foot.

"I've heard about your father," Nigel said. "He's the fucking hypocrite who turned the factory into a..."

Joe hit him so hard that a line of bloody spit flew from Nigel's mouth. He blinked, took a few more shots straight on, then knocked Joe on the floor with one swipe of his arm.

"We'll blow your factory to fucking dust," Nigel shouted, and he tried to kick Joe, but Suzanne got in the way, and when he threw her off, I dove on his back. I was drunk and furious, and it was like diving onto a wall of brick. I don't know if he hit me with his elbow or a fist, but everything turned green and red, and I remember stumbling, not so much in pain as shock, drunk and lost, and feeling my way along a wall, and I heard Suzanne shout. I heard Robin shout. I heard more punching and glass breaking, and then I heard nothing.

3

I was in the yard with Charlie. It was hot summer, blinding white. We were digging, sweating and digging and wiping our faces. My parents were there. Whitey was there. A zipped bag with U.S. Marines written across it in huge black letters lay beside the hole. Patrick cried inside the plastic, but no one else heard him. I begged my father to open the bag, but he just shouted.

"Dig. Dig."

We dug a long time in the blazing sun, and when we dropped the bag into the hole, it smacked the earth, kicked up some dust, then split, and a million bloody worms gushed into the dirt, twisting and squirming over one another, and from underneath them, my brother choked on blood and maggots and gurgled out my name.

I tried to scream, and then I felt the cool hands on my face. I heard the voices, and I was sprawled against the wall, soaked and confused in Robin's room.

"Grab a towel in the bathroom, a dirty one." It was Robin.

Joe answered. "Don't worry, I won't bleed on your linen."

Her fingers felt good. "This kid a friend of yours?"

I tried to talk, but I was too drunk and halfway lost in dreams. I wanted to tell her about the worms and Patrick and how they'd zipped him in a bag and sent him home, but he couldn't be dead. He was twenty years old. He was my best friend. He thought the war would be like in the movies. He didn't know. Who could have known?

"That's Dennis Shovlin," Joe said.

Her fingers brushed through my hair. Water ran in the bathroom, and Joe's voice shouted over it.

"His brother's Pat Shovlin, the one..."

"I know," she said, and she sounded sad and a little bitter. "Our first hero in Vietnam. The paper said we're lucky it's only one so far. They said Deadwhale has a fine tradition of giving up men for..."

"I read it." Joe was back in the room. His voice was soft. "I cut it out. Pat was my friend down at the garage. Good mechanic. We were the only white guys."

He touched my shoulder. "Itchy, you in there?"

I couldn't get anything out. She lowered my head onto a pillow and dropped a blanket over me. I opened my eyes. Robin stared down at me, just inches away in the darkness. She smiled.

"Hi," she said. "Having a bad day?"

I tried to answer, but I kept fading in and out, and then she was across the room.

"You're okay," she said. "It's close to your eye, but I suppose you'll survive. I wouldn't mess with Nigel."

"Yeah," Joe said. "He could bite my ear off. Must make a great husband."

"He's not my husband."

"That's not what he says."

"I don't care. I'd push him off a bridge if I could."

"Why'd he hurt your cat? Bad mood?"

"All his moods were bad. We lived in this freezing loft in Soho with no rugs or furniture and Nigel's pictures of naked teenage girls and mutilated animals all over the walls. I told him to quit fucking his models. He didn't, so I broke his best camera, and he swallowed Vincent's ear. Three weeks later I married him."

"It makes your hands shake to remember?"

"What?"

"Your hand. It's shaking," he said.

"Isn't your girlfriend waiting?"

"She's my sister. I sent her home. You've been shaking since I mentioned my father."

"You're imagining things."

"I saw your face when I said it."

I tried to follow their talk, but then I was dreaming again. Patrick was on the Ferris wheel with Mayor Waters. We had a huge Ferris wheel on the beach. It wasn't running anymore. Mayor Waters said he would fix it, just like he'd promised to build us a boardwalk and turn Deadwhale into a great resort.

But the wheel only turned in my dreams. It went around and around, and the night glowed with spinning lights, and Patrick and the mayor waved from way up high. I woke up shivering and tried to remember where I was. I kept hearing carnival music, and God I was thirsty.

A candle burned on Robin's bureau. It was an antique, and that and the bed were the only furniture in the room. Two gigantic shadows filled the wall. A hand from one dabbed at the face of the other. The room was full of marijuana smoke. I heard Joe.

"Careful. It stings."

She sat beside him on the bed.

"That's what you get, swinging at giants."

"He's an asshole."

"Obviously. A giant asshole. Have some wine."

She dabbed at the side of his head.

"I've been drinking all night," he said.

"I hope you feel like shit in the morning."

"I'll call and let you know."

"You don't take me seriously," she said. "But we'll close that factory."

"You're dreaming," he said.

"I don't think so."

"I have to go."

Her voice went low, almost to a whisper, and when she said it, it wasn't like she was talking to Joe. It was like she was whispering it to herself, or to God, like a sad prayer. "We're going to close it."

"You ever consider the consequences?"

"Some people lose their jobs. They die in the war."

"It won't stop the war," he said.

"It will stop our part in it, and we're going to do it. Don't hate me for it."

"I don't hate you. I just hate all this stuff, the long hair, the Beatles, the stupid clothes, all this protesting."

"People are sick of things," she said.

Joe got up. She stayed on the bed. He looked down on her.

"You're one of them, aren't you?" he said.

"One of who?"

"One of his women. Aren't you?"

"What are you talking about?"

"When I mentioned his name," Joe said, "it was like I slapped you.

They made him a saint around here, and maybe he was, but my mother, what's left of her, claims he had lots of women, that he was probably with one the night he died, and you're one of them."

"All I know's what I read in the paper."

Her voice cracked when she said it.

"You're lying."

"Get out of here," she said. "You're not hurt. You planned it to get me alone and accuse me of this shit."

"I've been watching you on the streets," he said.

"I've seen you."

I watched the shadows. I could barely see her on the bed. Joe stood over her.

"You know why?" he asked.

"Yeah," she said. There was a long silence.

"And you were watching me," he said.

"You scared me."

"No," he said. "You were wondering, too, wondering how it would be to fuck Mayor Waters' son. Wondering if it would be like fucking him."

She smacked him. His head snapped backward, but he let her get away with it. He headed toward the door. He looked back, then whispered, "Did he hurt you?"

"Good-bye," she said. "It's been interesting."

"Good-bye," he said. He turned, but she ran off the bed. She grabbed his arm.

"Yes," she said. "I want to know. I saw you. You looked so determined and smart, and like you wanted me so bad, but I didn't know who you were."

Robin let out some air. The flame swayed and almost died, then came on strong, and their shadows shrank and expanded with the flickering flame.

"I'm very high," she said.

"You're beautiful."

"Don't think bad of me."

He lifted her face by the chin. He kissed her eyes, her nose, her cheeks. He pushed her against the wall. They hit hard.

"The bed," she whispered.

He lifted her against him, turned, and came down on top of her into the bed. He found her mouth and pushed her into the mattress.

"It's been long," she whispered.

I watched their shadows on the wall, one shadow now.

"Baby," she said. "Take off your shirt."

I groped along the floor. My head spun. They were wrapped together on the bed. Robin kept making these sounds, these soft moans, these gasps. I tried to walk. I took a last look. Just this shadow on the bed, black within black, swaying and pushing together, slamming the frame, just this dark thing in the night.

I stumbled out of there, through the stale cloud in the living room, over the broken glass and toppled plants. The cat watched from the window sill, arching its back a bit, and soon I was outside in the cool air that blew in off the beach.

Suzanne sat on a bench across the street. She rooted around inside a huge bag. Her face almost disappeared into it, just this monstrous and battered suede bag with fringe hanging all around it, like something you'd expect an Indian to carry, instead of this girl in the nice dress.

I sat beside her, but she didn't take her face out of the bag.

"Imagine closing that factory?" she said. "Stewart would have them slaughtered. Oh hell. I know it's in here."

"What?"

"That astrology book and the wine glass, too. I wanted to give you a glass. I'm a good hostess."

She pointed to the bottle by her feet. There was a couple inches.

"You all right?" I asked.

She took her face out of the bag and stared at the sky.

"I'm cold," she said. "Do you know when that girl was born?"

"No. You waiting for Joe?"

"He told me to walk home so he could seduce that girl, but I waited, and I was wondering about her sign. Astrology's very inexact, but it's fun sometimes when things come out. Isn't she great, a little person like that thinking she can close factories and stop wars? I'm amazed if I can get my car started."

"He told you he was going to seduce her?"

"Of course not, but I know. I hate him, but I wanted to talk to him. He never visits, and I have to go to those awful slums to see him. Is he going to sleep with that girl?"

"They're talking about the factory."

"She said she'd fix him up, but they just wanted to get rid of me. They were shouting and pushing after she got that Nigel character out of there, but I could tell they wanted to be alone, and now it's been an hour. I'm going in there."

I grabbed her wrist before she could get up.

"Don't," I said.

She didn't fight. "Then it's true, isn't it?"

"Yeah, I guess."

"Shit." She drained the wine and threw the bottle over her head. A second later, it shattered.

My head hurt. My throat was dry, and I felt so tired I could hardly move. I remembered Robin moaning, and I wanted to touch Suzanne. I was awfully drunk, and my left hand slid up the back of the bench until it found her neck. I bent toward her. All her smells filled up my nose, her perfume, her skin, the cigarette and wine. I imagined us kissing like some passionate couple in a movie, and Suzanne moaning like Robin.

I moved my mouth toward her. I felt her breath on my face. I almost touched her lips, but she grabbed my neck and forced my head onto her lap.

"Will you help me?" she whispered.

It just about broke my heart not to kiss her. I thought I would choke or burst into tears. Her fingers ran through my hair, and I closed my eyes.

"How?" I asked.

The fingers felt so good. I wished my stomach didn't hurt. I wished time would stop at that spot forever, or just pass on by and leave us there, like a couple who missed a bus, just me and her, with her fingers in my hair and my head on her lap.

"Don't miss your brother," she said. "I missed my father so much that sometimes I couldn't move. I stared at the ceiling till everything was blurry. I made sounds, too, like a dog whimpering, and I couldn't move my fingers, but then I read how the soul lives on, and life's just a war we put ourselves through, and we're all the soldiers, like you in my dream, and then it was okay, except sometimes I hear his voice when I'm falling asleep, and I know he's drowning."

She stuck her face in her bag again, and reached in to her elbow.

"I'd show you some of these books, but everything's so disorganized in here. Have you ever seen the man on the Ferris wheel?"

"What man?"

"The one who sits up top late at night."

"You can't get up top. Nobody could climb that high."

"I should have known. I guess no one's ever seen him but me."

"It's impossible."

"Yeah, well, of course it is, because you know why? Because his eyes are tiny fires, and his hair's white like the moon, and sometimes, when you're real quiet, if you know how to listen, you can hear him howling like a million hungry wolves, and then you can't help but cry."

"Is it a dream you have?"

"It's no dream."

"Then who's he supposed to be?"

"I don't know, just the keeper of the Ferris wheel, I guess."

She closed up the bag, sprang to her feet, and started walking fast, as if someone had fired a gun, and she was off.

"Walk me home."

And soon we were in King's Port where the houses were huge and the trees cast long black shadows over the streets. I knew the neighborhood from delivering papers up there. I got good tips, but they never brought me in when I collected, except once near Christmas when a drunk old man gave me a glass of milk and seventeen dollars in nickels. One had a buffalo on it.

We didn't walk fast for long because Suzanne's shoes bothered her, and she'd thrown them in her bag, and now she was hobbling along barefoot, finding every rock and piece of glass in Deadwhale, and cursing and muttering and hopping. She was furious and graceful, and when the streetlight caught her face, it was hard not to stare.

We didn't say much. It was a long walk. It was cool, and she let me put my arm around her to keep us warm. She rested her head on my shoulder, and I felt all weak and happy inside, and kind of nervous, too, and I wanted to hear more about the man on the Ferris wheel, but decided not to bring it up. I figured it was just something she'd imagined or made up, or that maybe she was pulling my leg, but it was neat how she'd described him, how her voice had gotten soft and her eyes glowed and how when I listened, I could almost see him up there with the fire in his eyes.

When we came to a streetlight near her house, she pulled out a picture of her and Mayor Waters on the beach a couple weeks before he died, and we bent over it together. I felt her breath on my face.

"Photography's an amazing thing," she said. "Just some light and some chemicals, and look, here's a dead man with his little girl. Wasn't he handsome?"

"He was great," I said. "All the Whales loved him. We thought he'd do all that stuff, you know, the boardwalk and all."

"He would have. He was a Whale, you know, not like my mother. He grew up in Fishtown."

"I know. My dad remembers him from high school. He said people followed him around."

The picture fell and floated to the street. I picked it up, but when I tried to hand it back, she was facing over the hill toward the ocean. There were a few lights out near the horizon, but the water was blacker than the night, and I could hear it.

"They had him killed," she said.

"What?"

"Sure, and then they paid everybody off to keep quiet. Mayor Donaghy and my mother planned the whole thing."

"How do you know?"

"They got married right after, didn't they? I mean it doesn't take a detective."

"But the paper said..."

"Who cares what the stupid paper said? I've got evidence."

"What evidence?"

"Oh, never mind. Listen." She grabbed my arm. "You and the football player have to talk to Joe. Both of you. Please? Tell him how deep it hurt when they told you about your brother. Please? If you help, I'll remember forever and do anything I can, as long as I live and after, but you got to help keep him from that war."

"Joe's going to Vietnam?"

"He says probably."

She squeezed my arm. Her eyes burned into my face.

"You wanted to kiss me. Didn't you, at that bench?"

"I guess it crossed my mind."

"Promise you'll help me."

"Yeah, I'll help you."

"I cried when I read about your brother," she said. "He looked so handsome in the picture. Maybe he's watching. Maybe I can kiss him right through you, you know, like a good-bye kiss from the living."

And then her lips pressed into mine, and I tasted her tongue, warm and full of wine and cigarettes. She kissed me softly and slowly and for a long time, and it only took that long for me to fall in love with her in a way that would never stop hurting.

"Thank you," she whispered. "Isn't kissing amazing? I hope your brother felt it. I'll be in touch."

And she left me there under a street lamp in King's Port, the taste of her lips still fresh on my mouth, and my heart pounding so hard in the night, I thought it might break through my chest and go running after her.

4

But halfway through Mass next morning, Suzanne's kiss was already an old memory that I could hardly believe happened, and I was staring toward the giant crucifix over Father Joel's head and moving my lips with the prayers, so people wouldn't notice they were trembling. It wasn't even one yet, but already that day, Charlie'd banged my chest with his fist, my father had slapped me, and I'd had a gun pointed at my head. If only Sunday mornings were always so exciting, I might not have dreaded them like I did.

I hated twelve-fifteen Mass. When you got out it was late, and the day was half-shot. I hated any Mass. The church was old and cool with great windows of stained glass and lots of pretty girls in dresses, but Mass was boring, and my back ached from all the kneeling. I didn't believe any of it, and it was hard to mumble the prayers and the rest after all that happened.

They would say a prayer for Patrick. My father would bow his head. My mother would cry some more. I dreaded it. I figured if God wanted to do something for Patrick, he would have done it on that hill. It was too late now.

Charlie knelt beside me. I could tell he felt guilty about slamming me in the chest. Up on the altar the priest read his old lines, like some bad actor who'd played his part too many times and didn't care anymore. The altar boys knelt in their white outfits, and Charlie kept nudging me and pointing out girls. I tried to ignore him. My head hurt. My stomach ached. My mind was full of Suzanne and Patrick. It was good to see Charlie acting like his old self, being a jerk, but I couldn't even humor him.

He'd found me first thing that morning on the bathroom floor. I could see his feet in the doorway and hear him laughing. Charlie loved to see me suffer.

"Do they know?" I barely got it out.

"Not yet," he said. "Try puking louder. His ears are kind of dead from work." He came in and shut the door.

"Did she wait up?"

"Naa. She was snoring like crazy. I thought a train was coming through the house."

"Geez. I thought she'd keep a candlelight vigil."

"She's not as worried about you," Charlie said. He turned on the spigot and splashed his face. "She's got guys in trench coats on me."

"When I get in?"

"Must have been three. Lucky you beat fatso home."

Charlie started brushing his teeth. He was afraid they would fall out like our grandfather's and make it hard to get girls if he didn't brush them a few hundred times a day. He brushed them as hard as he could, like he hated them all for some reason.

"Think he heard me?" I asked.

He answered with the brush sticking out the side of his face. It sounded like his tongue was stapled to his lip.

"I don't know, man. He sleeps like a dead guy, but you could've closed the door."

"I didn't have time to plan it out, Charlie."

He spit into the sink and let out a big laugh. I was sprawled over the toilet.

"It's good to see you fucking up now and then," he said. "It stinks having the most boring guy in the world for a brother. What you get out of all them books, anyway? You get little tingles in your brain?"

"Yeah, Charlie, it's great. You should learn to read."

"I can read fast, man. It just ain't my whole life."

He left, shutting the door behind him, and I was at it again, reading the cracks at the bottom of the bowl until the water smeared over. A few seconds later, "Satisfaction" blared out of our bedroom. Charlie played it three or four times a day. He jumped around and banged his chest. He pushed out his lips like Mick Jagger and shouted the words in my face if I accidentally got near him.

I heard my father's voice through the door. "Turn that junk down."

Charlie answered. "All right. I forgot you were sleeping."

"What am I usually doing this time of day, bowling?"

"It's Sunday," Charlie said.

"I've been working Sunday mornings for months. They're going through more guns than they used to, or hadn't you heard? Where the hell's Itchy? Your mother said he was out late."

"Not too late. He's brushing his teeth. He wants to look handsome during Mass."

"Tell him I want to talk to him."

"He'll be happy to hear that."

I heard it, but I wasn't happy. He'd been in a terrible mood. Maybe he just wanted me to get a haircut before it got too close to my ears. He wanted me to look like a marine or a Buddhist monk.

He was sleeping when I passed. I got into our room and closed the door. Charlie lay in the top bunk with his shirt off, pressing his penknife against his chest to see how much pain he could take. He smiled.

"Feeling better?"

"What are you, nuts?" I said. "You expect him to sleep through 'Satisfaction'?"

"Hey, man. You sounded like a rocket taking off. I thought I'd drown it out."

I fell into bed, and he looked over the side at me.

"You better go out awhile," he said. "You look like shit. Father Joel's going to kick you out of Mass."

"I don't want to go to Mass," I said.

"You'll go to hell. All the girls are ugly there."

"So what? It probably beats Deadwhale."

"Man, I can smell your breath up here."

He hopped out of bed, hit the floor with a loud tromp, and bent over me like a doctor. He opened my eye.

"Looks like a hangover, young man."

"Cut it out, Charlie."

I swatted at him. He sat on the edge of the bed. He looked weird. He'd cut his hair really short with a piece of hacksaw after Patrick died, leaving his head all gouged and scabbed. He called it his killer cut.

Patrick went to Vietnam because he was patriotic. Charlie wanted to go kill communists. He read comic books full of war characters. He read real books, too, books about the Battle of the Bulge and the Normandy invasion. He'd been training for war all his life, or at least football, which he claimed was the same thing. He dropped to the ground without any provocation to knock out tons of push-ups. He lifted weights four times a week. He had huge shoulders and perfect arms with intricate muscles like a sculpture. They rippled when he moved a finger.

He didn't speak for a week after Patrick died. Some nights I heard him crying under his pillow. Other times he stared out the window and dug his knife into his arm until I heard a drop or two of blood splat onto the floor.

I wanted to take over as Charlie's big brother, but I didn't know how. He wasn't much younger than me. He outweighed me by sixty pounds, and he was four inches taller than I would ever be. I wasn't someone he could look up to, not like Patrick.

Patrick had been the leader, my best friend, and Charlie's idol. Both of us would do anything he said, even when it was stupid. Lots of his ideas were stupid, but they were always fun, and Charlie was usually the one who ended up falling out of a tree. Nothing ever hurt Charlie. Every time we figured he'd broken his neck, he would jump up and pound his chest like an ape.

I slept some, and when I woke, Charlie was doing push-ups. He whispered, "How many?" His circle of nubby hair rose above my bed, then down, then up again. "Thirty-three," he said. "Thirty-four."

"Seventy," I said.

"Oh, man," he said. "Be reasonable."

"Seventy."

Charlie huffed out some air and went even faster. He crossed forty without a letup, then fifty, but by fifty-eight he was slowing, and by sixty-five he was taking huge breaths between them, with his head all red and full of purple veins. When he hit seventy, he collapsed on the floor, wheezed out a few breaths, then threw himself up and raised his arms in the air.

"Charlie meets any challenge," he shouted, and he puffed out his lips like Mick Jagger and started strutting around the room like some kind of chicken. "Charlie meets any challenge."

I tried ignoring him. I figured next time I would try eighty. Sooner or later I'd stump him. He fell back on the floor and wheezed awhile and kept whispering, "Charlie meets any challenge."

I wanted to tell him about Suzanne. I could still taste her smoky tongue. Charlie liked her. He went by the frame shop a few times a week and stared through the window. He claimed every time he saw her, his life flashed before his eyes. I figured it might kill him if I mentioned kissing her. It was killing me, and I could hardly think about anything else.

"Are they up yet?" I asked.

His breathing was back to normal in no time.

"He's not. She's been up for hours, crying on the phone to Grand-mom. Sounds like a vacuum cleaner."

"I'm getting out of here," I said.

"We got Mass," Charlie said.

"Who cares?"

"You'll go to hell."

I headed up the street. The air stank. The fumes from the chemical factory blew around in the wind. The sun was bright, but it was a cool summer morning. Charlie caught me, and we walked to the corner. I wanted to be alone. I wanted to think about Suzanne and the things I'd seen and heard in Robin's bedroom, but Charlie hated being alone.

"So where'd you go?" he asked. He had his penknife out, and he worked at his fingernails while he walked. I couldn't get used to his haircut. I leaned against some wreck of a Ford. Herds of buffalo kicked up dust in my skull.

"You look like a space alien with that haircut."

"I am, man. I'm the tight end from Mars. So where'd you go?"

"The Roosevelt," I said.

"Oh, yeah?" His eyes narrowed. He snapped the knife shut. "Did you go to that chick's thing?"

"What chick?"

"You know what chick. The freak with the messed-up cat."

"Her name's Robin Debussy."

"Who gives a fuck? Did you go there?"

"Yeah. So what?"

"What do you mean, so what? She was having some stop-the-war meeting. I saw her, that weird little freak with the cat on her shoul-der, handing out papers and stuff. Why'd you go there, man?"

"I wanted to hear."

"That's great, Itch. These fuckers kill Patrick, and you want to make peace."

"You expect me to join up?"

"What do you think I'm doing, man? The day I hit eighteen."

"You do that, Charlie. But I'll make up my own mind."

"You traitor," he said, and he smashed my chest with the side of his fist. It knocked the wind out of me. I dropped to my knees for a long time. When I looked up, Charlie was far up the street, staring back my way with his hands in his pockets.

When I figured he was out of punching distance, I headed up to King's Port. I wouldn't have, but I was wearing the same clothes from the night before, and I found Suzanne's picture in my pocket. She looked so young in it, standing on the beach and smiling up at her father. Her teeth were too big, and I hid behind a pole and kissed the picture. It wasn't any fun, not like kissing her mouth, and it made me kind of ache inside.

The picture was black and white and smudged and bent. Robert Waters wore a tie and a white shirt with the sleeves rolled to his elbows. He looked happy and very handsome. He'd been dead four years, but I remembered all his promises. I remembered the posters of his face on telephone poles and walls, or going by on a bus, his dark hair parted on the side, and I couldn't imagine anybody wanting to kill him.

King's Port was wide open and clean. There were no row houses, no trash cans rolling in the streets, no alleys where seafood scraps rotted under swarms of flies behind restaurants and bars. Hedges were perfect, with all the branches the same height like my father's crew cut. There was still the hint of chemicals in the breeze, but there was more ocean and the smell of gas mowers and fresh-cut grass.

Suzanne's house hid off the road behind two gloomy willows. I could hardly see the place until I fought through the trees onto a path of rocks and weeds. The grass grew wild. There were no sprinklers or flowers, just these trees that drooped along like prisoners with big balls chained to their legs. The drain spout clung to the side of the house by a bent sliver of rust. A flat football lay on the grass beside a sea gull with dirty feathers.

The bird's eyes were blank dots. I kicked it over. It was open underneath and full of bugs. I remembered the story about the sea gulls and Mayor Waters and how the people at the hospital couldn't recognize his face. I kicked the bird. It rolled a few feet then stopped by a garden tool, some claw-like thing that had rusted away.

The bell didn't work, so I knocked. I was nervous. It seemed like a dream, her tongue in my mouth, her breath on my face. Maybe I'd imagined it. I'd been awfully drunk. So had she. She might be embarrassed. She might tell me to get lost, or maybe she was in love with me now. Maybe my kisses were like magic, and she would faint into my arms. I wasn't counting on it.

I was about to give up, when something scraped at the other side. There were scratches and locks clicking. The knob wiggled, and the door opened an inch. I saw darkness and a bloodshot eye.

"Is Suzanne home?"

The eye just stared.

"I have her picture." I waved the photograph.

The eye never blinked.

"We met last night."

The door opened in. Suzanne's mother stood there in a bathrobe with strings hanging from the bottom. Beautiful black hair hung far down her back. Her face was yellow, with those blood streaks in her eyes and the pupils wide open. Her gums showed too much teeth, and a thick rim of lipstick covered her mouth. She reminded me of someone in a movie Charlie would watch at two in the morning, someone who'd just crawled out of a grave with dirt caked in her ears.

I smelled smoke and medicine, but mainly I smelled booze. I imagined the fumes forming into a crooked hand and wrapping around my neck.

"Is Suzanne in, Mrs. Waters? I have a picture."

She snatched the picture out of my hand, ripped it to little pieces, then slammed the door.

"Nice meeting you," I said, and I scooped all the pieces of Suzanne and her dad together and put them in my pocket.

I felt worse. I'd come for Suzanne and seen the shipwreck of her mother instead. Eleanor Waters had been as famous as her husband once. Some people said she'd made him, that if he hadn't married into one of the best families in King's Port, he would never have gotten out of Fishtown, but I didn't believe that. He'd graduated from Princeton, served as a navy officer during the war, then gone to Columbia for his law degree.

Seven months after he died, she married Douglas Donaghy. People said they'd plotted Mayor Waters' death, that they'd had him pushed off the wharf, and rigged it to look accidental, but there was no proof that I knew about, and the marriage hardly lasted a year before they rushed the new mayor to the hospital with a towel against his neck.

I walked fast, and just when the houses were getting small and I could taste the ruined air of Deadwhale again, that mix of factory, marsh, seafood, and ocean, a car slammed on its brakes and skidded past. A miniature machine gun swung and squeaked from the bumper.

The passenger door popped open. The Beach Boys blared out. They were singing "Barbara Ann." Suzanne stepped into the street, and my heart went crazy again.

"Just a minute, Stewart," she shouted over the music.

He backed it in front of me and rolled down the window.

"Can I help you, kid?"

I hated looking at him. He was twenty-seven and perfect, with a well-groomed mustache and one of those square, tan, all-American faces you wanted to punch in the jaw.

"I was looking for Suzanne," I said.

The car stalled out. The door flew open, and Stewart Donaghy jumped into the street. He was a six-foot former track star who ran the mile and did the pole vault and went to Columbia on a scholarship. Now he ran the machine gun factory where my father and thousands of other men from Deadwhale made their living. He wore leather driving gloves, and his hair was stiff and short. I wanted to mess it up.

"Looking for Suzanne, huh?"

"Yeah." I shrugged. "You forgot your picture."

"Oh," she said. "Do you have it?" She tried to sound casual, but a kind of panic crossed her face.

"Sorta."

"Exchanging pictures with Whales?" he asked. He got so close I could smell the Colgate and hair lotion and all the other antiseptic crap he doused himself in. He reeked of cleanliness.

"He's one of the boys from last night," Suzanne said. "I showed him a picture and forgot it."

Stewart laughed. "Oh, yeah? One of the peace freaks?"

"That's right, Stewart. Are you going to hang him from a pole?"

Then his eyes lit up. "You're Shovlin. I saw your picture. Your brother was a good runner. It won't be any fun racing without him anymore."

He looked at Suzanne. "His brother could run, but he couldn't beat me."

"He beat you one year," I said.

"I had a bad ankle. I won seven out of eight, and I'll win the next ten."

Suzanne smiled at me. "Isn't he charming?"

"He's a jerk," I said, and before I saw him move, Donaghy had hold of my shirt. I tried breaking loose, but he was twice as strong.

Then a voice came from my right. "Let go, or you're dead."

Donaghy took one look and let go.

"Who the hell are you?" Donaghy asked. "His guardian angel?"

And I heard Charlie say, "His brother."

"Oh, yeah? Scrawny and I were talking about how I'm going to miss your other brother. He was fun to beat."

"You ain't winning next year," Charlie said.

"Oh, yeah? Why not?"

"Because I am."

Donaghy smiled. "No Fishtown Whale's beating me again in that race."

And he was probably right. We held a big race every year on the Fourth. Patrick won in '65, but Donaghy won most years before that, and killed Patrick in '66. Donaghy got better every year, and no one could touch him.

"Come on," Suzanne said. She took his arm. "Now that you've made some new friends, let's go."

"Shut up, Suzanne." He raised his hand, like he would smack her. She closed her eyes, but didn't back off. He looked at me.

"I hear that slut wants to close my factory. Your dad works there, right?"

"Yeah," I said.

"I'd hate to see him out of work."

"He'd get by."

"Nobody's closing any factory," Charlie said. "It's just a lot of stupid talk."

"Glad to hear it," Donaghy said. "And they'd better not try. I've got power around here, and I'm not letting some little freak screw it up. You tell her that, Itchy, 'cause if she tries, she'll pay. Now give Suzanne her picture, and get out of here."

"Her mother tore it up," I said. "You want the pieces, Suzanne?"

Her shoulders dropped, and she looked at the sky.

"She answered the door," I said. "She was in a pretty bad mood. She got a cold or something?"

Donaghy laughed. "A cold. Yeah. She's had that goddamned cold since the old man kicked the bucket. Drink enough booze..."

Suzanne snapped at him. "Shut up, Stewart."

He laughed. "Get in the car, Suzanne." He gave Charlie a look. "See you, pal."

Suzanne asked me for the pieces, and I handed them over. She stuffed them in her bag, and Charlie just stared. Donaghy brushed by us and got in the car. Suzanne looked at me like she wanted to say something. She looked at Charlie, then back at me, then got in. The engine roared. They drove halfway up the block before the brakes slammed. They came streaking back toward us in reverse.

He rolled down the window. Suzanne shouted, but I couldn't make it out. He gave us a big smile, then stuck a gun out, some long silver thing with one of those round chambers full of bullets, like you see in westerns. Charlie stepped in front of me and held me back with a huge arm.

"Hey, Charlie, nice haircut," Donaghy said. He smiled and waved the gun a few times. Charlie's right arm got real tight, locking me behind him. I couldn't move if I wanted to. Everything got quiet for a second, with Donaghy staring at Charlie, and Charlie stiff in front of me and probably staring back. I could hear my heart.

And then Donaghy laughed and drove away. Suzanne looked back once, and they were gone. Charlie let go of me. He stared at the street a long time. He was breathing heavy, and his huge chest rose up and down.

"Fuck, man," he said. "What are you doing up here?"

My heart beat so hard I couldn't even talk.

"First you're hanging out with protesters, now you're knocking on doors in King's Port. What's going on, Itchy?"

He yanked out his penknife, flicked out the blade, and slashed at the sky.

"I went to her house," I said.

"I know, I followed."

"She was there last night. She showed me a picture of her and the mayor, and I wanted to give it back."

Charlie took deep breaths and kicked at the ground.

"You believe that guy?" he said. "Pointing a gun. What's she see in him, a beautiful girl like her? You see that lump under her eye? Man, if she were mine, she wouldn't have no lump under her eye."

I told him about our talk and how she wanted us to see Joe. Charlie poked his palm with his penknife.

"I'd help her," he said. "But shit, these communists want to take over the world, and in case you forgot, they killed our brother. We couldn't even open the fucking coffin."

He jammed his knife further into his hand than he wanted. Blood rolled from a hole in the center of his palm.

"Yeah, Charlie. They killed him with a claymore mine, one of our own weapons that shoots out a million little balls and rips you to pieces."

"You don't want to go, don't go," Charlie said. "You want to talk Joe out of it, you try, but when the time comes, I'm going. Okay?"

"Great, Charlie." I tried to get away, but he pulled me back.

"I'm going, Itchy."

I started crying. I cried and shivered and threw up in the middle of the street. Charlie walked away, but then he rushed back. He put his arm around my shoulders and held me until I stopped.

"You're shaking all over."

"They tore him to a million pieces," I said. "He never meant any harm, and there's other guys, half a million, and they could die for nothing, too, and I don't want this war anymore, and I'm going to help her. I don't care if Dad loses his job. I'm going to help shut the factory."

"Itchy. Itchy, come on, man."

"He could've shot you," I said. I barely hacked it out. "You shouldn't have stood in front of me. He's crazy. He could've shot you."

"Better me than you," he said.

"Charlie?" I said. "Do you have to go?"

"Yeah, but not till after I beat that asshole next Fourth."

"You can't even beat me."

"We'll practice," he said. "Harder than ever, soon as you get over this little sickness."

I got sick some more, and he patted my back.

"Ah, Charlie. So many colleges want you."

"Come on. We got Mass. You need it, man. You're a sinner. What you drink, anyway, turpentine?"

5

When I got back from King's Port, I couldn't stop shaking, so I got under the covers and tried to sleep it off. I might've been sleeping ten minutes when my father barged in and stamped out my dreams.

He was the biggest member of the family, even bigger than Charlie, but without the muscles. He weighed about three hundred, but didn't really look fat, just out of proportion. I'd never seen him without a crew cut. He had it done every other week. There was a lot of gray in it now, especially near the front.

He worked every night from ten or eleven to anywhere from five or even noon the next day. He was usually home pretty early on Sundays, though, and up in time for late Mass.

"What are you doing?" he said.

"Trying to sleep," I said. "What's it look like?"

"Sleep it off most likely."

"Please, Nick, don't start." It was my mother. Her name was Anna. She walked in behind him and sat in the only chair in the room, this black rocker with a painting of fruit on it. She was barely Robin's size and looked like a midget compared to Nick Shovlin. She ate cottage cheese and sardines for lunch and grapefruit with sugar on it for breakfast. She exercised every morning with Gloria, a television exercise lady. She was always worrying about getting fat, but her face was pinched in and wrinkled and thin, and she couldn't have gotten fat in a million years without concentrating on it awfully hard.

She wore pink glasses and read novels by Agatha Christie or

abridged Reader's Digest versions of the classics. She looked a lot older than forty-two and not very pretty anymore, but in the old pictures, she was. Now she looked older than ever, and since Patrick's death, I hadn't even seen her eating cottage cheese and sardines. I hadn't seen her eat anything or read a book or exercise with Gloria. She just stared at the television. Charlie said it was sucking her brains out.

"You need a haircut," my dad said.

I tried to ignore him. I was tired of pointing out that, besides for Charlie, I had the shortest hair for my age in Deadwhale. I sat at the edge of the bed and looked at the dusty wood of the floor. He paced back and forth. There wasn't much room in there, just enough for the bunk beds, a bureau with a globe on it, and some Beatles pictures on the wall.

"Did you hear me?"

"Uh huh."

"So get one."

"What's the big deal?" I asked. "I do good in school. I already got a scholarship to one of the best schools around."

"Just get the haircut. We ain't arguing about it."

My dad stopped and hovered over the bed, while my mother rocked back and forth with her eyes on me. Sweat started tingling at the roots of my hair, and I remembered something I'd read about our angry dinosaur brains and how we couldn't control them.

"You understand, right?"

"Yeah, Dad. I just don't understand why. It grows out of my stinking head. Every hair's connected to a nerve. George Washington and them had long hair."

"I don't care about George Washington. Besides, it wasn't even hair. It was powdered wigs, and I ain't raising the founding fathers."

"What do you want?"

"I want you to get a haircut."

"For Christ's sake, Nick, leave him alone. You made your point."

I could have kissed her. He shut up, opened his mouth like he might snap at her, but got control of himself and fixed his eyes on me. He paced back and forth like some huge bear in a cage.

"Where were you last night?" he asked. "I'll bet I know. I'll bet you were at that Debussy woman's hotel. Well I heard a rumor she was going to stage some kind of protest against the factory, so you make sure you stay away from her, Itchy. I don't want a bunch of kids losing my job for me. There's something wrong with that woman, and she's going to cause trouble. Stay away from her. Understand?"

I just stared at him. I had a feeling he wasn't going to listen to reason.

"Now, your mother wants me to talk to you about Charlie."

"We're worried about Charlie," she said. "He hangs around with those boys from Little Brooklyn, and..."

"Lots are from Fishtown," I said.

"It don't matter," he said. "And that ain't what we're discussing. Your brother wants me to sign a paper when he turns seventeen in November, something he needs to get in the marines. I said no. I figure he's too young."

"Good," I said.

"When he turns eighteen," my mother said, "he won't need our permission."

"In another year or so, that kid turns eighteen," my father said. "Your mother don't want him to..."

She cut in. "You don't want him to, either."

"All right," he said. "I don't, either."

"You didn't stop Patrick," I said. "You were all for it."

"That was different," he said.

"Why?"

"Because I didn't think it through."

"So tell Charlie yourself."

"Charlie hates me," he said.

"He don't hate you," my mother said. "He just don't understand you. He's hotheaded and not so smart."

"He's stupid," I said.

"He hates me," my father said. "And so do you."

"I don't hate anybody," I said. "I just hate having hair like a freak."

"Is that all you care about?" he asked. "We're talking about Charlie's life."

My mother started rocking. I could hear the squeaking of the wood and the way her slacks swished together when she pushed the rocker back and forth. The slacks were ugly, with balls of lint stuck all over them.

"It don't matter," he said. "You can all hate me if you want, but I couldn't stop Patrick. He was the right age. They would've drafted him."

"That's right," she said.

"He could have joined the navy or something," I said.

"He didn't," my father said. "Now we're stopping Charlie."

"What happened to all that stuff about fighting communists, Dad? When Patrick asked, you told him to join."

"Shut up, Itchy."

The rocker squeaked faster.

"They'll draft him anyway," I said. "They suck up anybody who can't get in college, like they own us all. What am I supposed to do?"

"Talk to him," my father said. "You're the only one who can get through to him. He's All-State for Christ's sake. He can get scholarships."

"His grades stink," I said.

"Then make them better. Take his tests. Do his homework, but get him in college."

"He won't cooperate. He wants to go to the war."

"You stop him," he said. "We'll do whatever you think's right. Now get ready for church. Charlie's waiting downstairs."

"I'm not going."

"What?"

"I'm not going anymore."

"Yeah, you are."

"No."

He fixed his tiny gray eyes on me. He smoked a lot, and I could hear him breathing. The cigarettes had ruined his lungs. Now the cigarettes and fat were working on his heart.

"Itchy, don't start trouble," my mother said. "It's only an hour a week."

"An hour for what? Sitting in a bench pretending I care about stuff I hate. It's all shit," I said.

My father hit me in the jaw. I stared at the ceiling. I could hear the rocker going faster and my father wheezing.

"Okay," he said. "Your brother died. Okay. It hurt, and you can blame me if you want, but it ain't going to change things. This family's not falling apart, and you're not going to disobey me. Understand?"

I stared back at him. "Patrick was an altar boy. What good it do him standing up there with Father Joel and God?"

"You want Charlie to die, too?"

"No, but going to church..."

"We got to stick together."

He was panting, and his face was soaked and red. My mother cried quietly.

"Get ready for church." He walked toward the door, stopped, and said, "Grow the damned hair. Grow it to your knees, but you want to stay in this house, you go to church on Sunday, and you stay away from any protests against my factory. I need that job, Itchy. We all need them jobs."

He walked out. I sat on the edge of the bed and waited for the stampedes in my skull to slow down. My mother touched my hair.

"He hardly sleeps anymore," she said. "Just a couple hours real deep. He hardly talks to me."

She sat beside me and whispered.

"What about this woman? Is she really after the factory?"

"Yeah."

"You were there last night?"

"Yeah, and I want to help her. I don't care what he says."

She squeezed my hand between hers. "Denny, I don't know anything about this war, why we're fighting or anything, except what I hear from Daddy about a treaty and about stopping the Russians, so maybe I'm wrong.

"But if I didn't have you and Charlie, losing Patrick would've been the end of me. These politicians, maybe they know what they're doing. They have information we don't, and they're smart, or they wouldn't be where they are, but they're rich, too, and their boys go to college, and they don't lose sons in Vietnam, so maybe they don't know how it hurts, and maybe not knowing, they're not thinking straight."

Tears landed on my hand, but her voice was steady and determined.

"But I know, and maybe lots of other people are starting to understand, that if we're going to make kids die, it has to be a good reason, and everybody has to do it, not just poor people who can't get to college, not just boys who ain't so smart.

"I'm glad you got the scholarship and get to stay home, but it's not fair, and if you can stop Charlie, you do it, but even more important, use your mind. You have a gift. Use your mind somehow to help stop this thing, even if it means stuff like closing factories and losing people's jobs, but don't do it out of spite or because your heart's broke. Only do it if you're sure it's smart."

She talked fast, squeezing my hand until the bone hurt. Her hands were soaked. The tears kept falling on my wrists.

"I'll never see Patrick again, and I don't want other mothers to feel like me, and if I have to feel this way again, I couldn't."

6

Father Joel gave a rousing sermon about how women should keep their heads covered in church to show respect. Some of the girls weren't covering their heads, and Father Joel was fuming about it. He banged the pulpit and talked about respect and humility and the greatness of God, all of which were connected with women keeping their heads covered in church.

I tried not to think about him and that marine coming to the house and how Father Joel said we should be proud because Patrick died for a just cause, and God would reward him. I wondered why God would reward him for killing a lot of men on a hill.

Mass went on, but I hardly noticed. The altar boy rang the bell. Father Joel held the flat bread up, and everybody mumbled prayers. When they filed out for Communion, I got out in front of my father. His heavy breath tickled my neck, but I lost him in the aisle. Instead of turning right for the altar, I turned left, dabbing some holy water on my fingers and blessing myself in case it might do some good, then broke through the door, down the steps, and out into the warm sun with holy water rolling down my forehead.

As soon as I hit the steps, I ran. I heard my father shouting after me, like a man falling off a cliff, but I never looked back. I ran in my wing-tipped shoes. I threw my tie into the street. I didn't know where I was going, but I wanted to get there fast, and I knew I would never go home. I would never go to church. I was free.

I ran a long time. It felt so good to get my heart pounding and sweat the filthy alcohol from my system. I wanted to run forever. I cut down out of Fishtown and through Little Brooklyn, where all the Italians lived, and through there to downtown Deadwhale where the tourists stayed and the beach always splashed in the background. I headed for the library.

The library was the only place in Deadwhale I really liked, except the beach late at night and the tree behind our house in fall when the leaves changed and filled the yard so thick you could bury yourself in them.

I was starving and panting. My church clothes stuck to my back. My head hurt, and I had a mouth full of stomach acid, but it would be cool in the library, and I could use the toilet and get water from a fountain and maybe get lost in some book.

Patrick used to ride the bus to the library with me. He liked books about baseball, biographies of Joe DiMaggio, or anything about the '50 Phillies. Our father was from Philadelphia. His parents still lived there, and Patrick and I loved the Phillies. Patrick was obsessed with the "Whiz Kids" from 1950 and the '64 Phillies, too. The '64 Phillies had broken our hearts.

I would read through old magazines down in the basement. I read whole issues of *Life* from the Second World War. I read the ads and studied the pictures of people walking through rubble in foreign cities. I tried to imagine when the ads were new and the whole world was at war, when countries fell and thousands died every day, but it was so hard to imagine, just like trying to imagine big American jets dropping bombs on that little country full of rice paddies and people with weird cone hats.

I loved history and science and anything to do with the Beatles, and I would walk through every section, geography, art, literature, and pick a book at random. I would read for ten minutes in one row, then on to another. I thought I could learn everything.

But I felt bad when I saw the library that afternoon. It was one of the oldest buildings in Deadwhale, with pillars and white marble all black from the cars. It looked like something in the old parts of Philadelphia where my grandfather used to take me walking. There were words carved into the stone, things Plato had said, things from Shakespeare and the bible, and graffiti, too, hearts painted in black with initials inside, and *DOORS* in dripping red right over the main entrance.

I was just about there when I heard the shouting. I recognized the voice. It was Robin Debussy, and she was hollering so much, she had to stop for air.

Papers blew down the steps and piled on one another in the street. Her ragged cat arched its back, spread out on a step, and licked at its paws. There was a table with a cracked-off leg, and Robin waved the leg in the air. Nigel stood facing her with his hands buried in the pockets of his long coat. I couldn't tell for sure, but since I could see his pale legs where the coat ended beneath his knees, I figured he was either naked or wearing shorts.

"I'll do it my way," she shouted.

"Your way, Robin? Who taught you?" His English accent was gone.

"You gave me some books and talked a lot of shit, but all you wanted was to get laid."

"I could have left you in Amsterdam. It was awfully cold that night. What you have left, six marks?"

"Yeah, but you couldn't pass up a teenage blonde in distress."

Her face was red. Her glasses teetered at the end of her nose. On one side, her shirt was out too far, and on the other, it seemed to be pulled all the way down to her knee, and she kept waving that leg in the air.

"But you love me really, don't you, Robin?"

"I despise you."

"You don't understand your emotions," he said. "You love me. I've taught you how to think. Life is hard and ugly, and I've shown you that, and deny it as you will, Robin, I've made you." And with his English accent, he said, "Good day, love."

He pulled a banana out of his coat, peeled it as slowly as he could, and walked away. Robin just watched him, with that leg hanging in her limp arm. She strutted back and forth on the steps, waved the leg once or twice, moved her lips like she would shout at him, but just watched Nigel stroll casually away.

I didn't mean to laugh, but I couldn't help it. Her clothes flapped in every direction. Her argyle socks flapped at the end of her toes. Hair kept falling over her eyes, and her cat just lay there licking its paws. She noticed me then.

"Think it's funny?"

I shrugged. "Yeah. Sorry, but you do look kind of funny."

"You look kind of funny yourself. What they do, chase you out of church?" Her eyes were huge behind her glasses.

"I got bored," I said. "Somebody break your table?"

"Yes, somebody broke my table. That gorilla. He doesn't approve of my pamphlets or my methods. He wants revolution and blood.

He thinks he can piss me off."

"You're not pissed off?"

"Of course I'm fucking pissed off. He thinks he can, and he's right."

"What happened to his British accent?"

"He had an American father and a British mother. He can talk anyway he likes."

She whacked the leg against her palm and said everything with her mixed Texas and Jersey accent.

"He comes around in a turtleneck and shorts in that ridiculous coat and expects me to take advice from him. I'll close that factory, but I'm not fixing to light the damned thing on fire. He's crazy."

The table leaned over, three legs up and a corner down, like some crippled ship going under. Her cat swatted at papers that lifted off on the breeze, papers full of smeared blue about how we should close the gun factory.

"You look familiar," she said.

"I was on your floor last night."

"Oh." She dropped the leg. "You look terrible, and you smell like vomit. Is that vomit?"

"It's cologne. Girls love it."

"Girls are stupid. Carry the table. Come on, Vincent. Let's take this boy home."

I didn't have anywhere else to go, so I carried Robin's table the three blocks over to First and Sunrise where the Roosevelt Hotel shot into the sky and stared over the beach and the old Ferris wheel. The scrawny cat followed beside Robin, like a miniature bodyguard. It never strayed far from her heel, and it watched my every move, like it would jump at my throat if I touched her.

Most of Deadwhale's hotels stood along the ocean. They were the beach type, with neon flashing No Vacancy in red or green during the good summer weeks, the kind with names like The Bolero and The One-Eyed Jack. They had one or two floors and a pool and fat maids with cigarettes in their mouths pulling carts full of sheets and toilet paper from room to room. Most of the maids were black and from the southwest slums where Joe Waters lived among the swamps, the crumbling and boarded row houses, and thousands of black people. About thirty percent of the population was black, but you didn't see much of them outside their part of town.

Robin's hotel wasn't one of those. The Roosevelt was a monster that climbed into the sky and made the other buildings in Dead-whale, except city hall and the library, look sleazy and small. It had a black fire escape draped down the side and balconies with iron rail-ings and an aerial on top with a red light that spun in the night and showed far out at sea. It was originally called the Royal Swan, but after the war it became the Franklin Delano Roosevelt Hotel.

Thomas Ditzlow, from New York, had it built in 1919 for the rich people who flocked to town in those days, the same people who developed King's Port in the twenties and tried to form their own city because they didn't like the name Deadwhale.

The Roosevelt never did well, and by 1933, Ditzlow had lost everything and jumped off the top floor from the apartment Robin lived in with a set of wings strapped to his arms. They say he flapped like crazy all the way, then slammed into Sunrise Boulevard. His wings are still there in the Deadwhale Historic Museum beside a pic-ture of Deadwhale in the thirties and a photograph of Ditzlow in wire-framed glasses. The glasses looked just like Robin's, and later I found out they were. Ditzlow's old glasses were just right for her, and he'd left a huge collection behind.

His daughter, Margaret, inherited the hotel, and when she died, everything went to Robin. Robin was in charge of the maids by then, but she had no idea Margaret was fond of her or that she would get anything in the will.

Robin's apartment looked nice. Daylight streaked through the windows and turned the plants bright green. The smell of booze and rotten smoke lingered, despite all the open windows, but there were no other signs of the night before.

"Margaret's father jumped there," she said. She led me toward the living room window. Vincent rubbed against my legs every time I stopped moving. I didn't know if he liked me, if he had an itch, or if maybe he was jealous, but he made sounds when he rubbed against me, like some old toy with the batteries running low.

"They found four pairs of wings on the bed, all different sizes. The newspaper was open to the weather."

"Probably checking wind conditions," I said. "Probably picked the right wings for the weather."

"Margaret said there was a copy of the Bible on the mattress and *The Descent of Man* and that she found three birds wrapped in news-paper under his bed. He'd cut them up."

"Studying their anatomy," I said.

"I see you're a psychologist." She picked up her cat and kissed his face. He closed his eyes and made his noise.

She pulled me by the sleeve, and we looked over Sunrise Boulevard, the last street before the sand. The Ferris wheel stood to our left, creaking and rocking in the breeze, and far past that, with the water washing up underneath it, stood the rickety wharf.

We watched for a while before she dragged me into the other room and threw some pillows on the floor. We sat on the pillows, shiny, silk-like Oriental things, and drank tea that she boiled in a pot and filled with honey. We ate a box of Oreos and listened to weird jazz and argued about music.

I told her how every new Beatles record was a major event, and she told me the Beatles stunk.

"It's better than a bunch of guys playing horns," I said.

"Oh, bullshit," she said. "The Beatles are cute, but jazz is art, man, and you got to live before you can understand it. Do you smoke grass?"

"I never tried."

"I've been smoking a lot. One of the maids gets it. I think I'll promote her."

She lit a joint, sucked on it a few times, then took one long breath. The paper crackled. She offered it to me, but I shook my head. She sucked on the joint. Her right eye was red from the smoke. That was the deep brown one, the real one. The other was blue and dead and reminded me of some scuffed-up marble. She looked left and right, then behind her, moving her neck in quick jerks, like a bird.

She kissed the cat again. He kept staring at me. I figured if he was a lion, I'd already be one of those ripped-up carcasses you see on educational TV.

"Vincent's a communist," she said. "He thinks we should close the factory."

"He looks kind of beat," I said.

"He's sick." She rubbed noses with him and sucked on the joint. "I love this stuff. It beats those hangovers, waking up and wondering where the fuck you've been, who the fuck with."

Without the glasses, she was more beautiful than I'd imagined, exotic in a way, with the slant to her eyes and the high bones in her cheeks. Even the bump in the middle of her nose was nice. She let her hair do what it wanted. She wore the clothes of unknown men, stuff she picked up at Goodwill. She wore dangling earrings made of shells and dull tin, and all sorts of beads and medals that clanged around her necktie. Her eye liner was thick and crooked, and there was blush on her cheeks. Her make-up reminded me of some modern art I'd seen in a magazine.

"The vet said it's a tumor in his throat," she said. "He said it's slow and maybe Vincent has a year. Know how he got his name?"

"Probably Vincent van Gogh," I said. "Because of his ear."

"Very good," she said. Her face beamed at me.

"I read a book once, these letters he wrote his brother," I said.

"*Dear Theo*," she said. "It made me miserable."

"His brother died right after him from a broken heart or something."

She laid Vincent in her lap, stroked him once, then touched my face.

"You're afraid you'll die right after yours?"

"I feel kind of dead this morning."

"You'll be okay." She put her glasses on. "You're innocent, but very smart. I read about you in the paper, but that stuff about the highest grades in the history of Deadwhale and the best college boards in the state and your scholarship to Penn don't mean shit.

"I barely finished two years of high school. I learned from books, or traveling the streets without a buck, but I know what's right, and I saw in that picture in the paper you're smart, and I see it now. You'll suffer, but you'll do good things, and the first thing you'll do is help shut that fucking factory."

She stubbed the joint in a sea shell and dropped it in the shell with a pile of dead matches, the ends of other joints, and a coating of ash.

"I know," she said. "You're thinking, why believe this weird chick. She talks like some truck driver from Texas, or some fucking private at Fort Dix, and somebody said she was a communist. Well, what if I am, man?"

"I never met a communist before."

"You going to turn me in?"

"It's not illegal."

She laughed. Her eyes closed when she laughed, and all her teeth showed. They were straight and shining. The front two were chipped where they met, but just a little.

"I hate communists," she said.

She laughed, and I felt happy. She was pretty, and the cookies cured my hangover. The jazz sounded good. The pot smelled great, but mainly I was happy because I liked Robin and didn't want her to be a communist. They'd been the enemy all my life. They'd killed my brother. They dropped the bombs in my dreams.

"You'd be a big help," she said. "Your brother's the first, and you could tell about the pain. People would believe you. We need to bring the war home, you see, 'cause we're not getting bombed here, and they don't feel the pain. We got to make them feel the pain."

"Yeah," I said. "Suzanne Waters had the same idea. She wants me to talk to Joe."

When I mentioned Joe, everything about Robin changed. Her face seemed to shrink. All the muscles clamped tight, and she wasn't happy anymore.

"You know him?"

"Yeah, Joe and Patrick worked on cars together."

"He told me."

"That's right. I heard him when I was on your floor."

"You were awake?" She stood up.

"Just a little."

"I'm not a whore."

"Huh?"

"Oh, come on. You know I slept with the guy. I met him, then I fucked him. That makes me a whore, right?"

I shrugged.

"Well, I'm not. I was drunk, you see?"

"I didn't say anything."

"What do you know about the guy?"

"Well, he lives in the southwest slums and fixes cars."

"I mean is he on the level, or some kind of phony?"

"He's not phony."

"But is he honest?"

She tossed her black tie on the floor and picked up Vincent. She planted him on her shoulder and headed for the window that looked down over the beach.

"Yeah, he's honest, a lot like his father."

"You knew his father?" She sounded tired and kind of sad.

"Of course. He was mayor and came from Fishtown and went to school with my father. He was great."

"I read it in the paper."

"He was a Whale," I said. "He was going to fix the Ferris wheel and build a boardwalk. You ever been on the boardwalk? There were going to be rides and games and all, like Atlantic City and Wildwood, but after he died, all the money dried up."

"They started making guns his first year in office."

"He didn't know where it would lead," I said.

"What are you doing anyway? Were you at church?"

"I kind of ran away from home."

She crouched in front of me. She let Vincent loose. He walked over my legs and gave me a long stare. He seemed to be threatening me.

"Why?" she asked.

"I don't know."

"What are you fixing to do?"

"I don't know."

"Okay," she said. "You can stay here, you see, but only if you're serious, only if there's no way you're going home, and only if you tell your parents. You don't have to tell them where you are, but you got to tell them you're safe. Are you eighteen?"

"Not till September 23."

"I was seventeen when I left my father," she said.

"I could give you some money."

"No, but you got to help close the factory. Okay? I'm serious. Not like Nigel. I don't want to destroy the damned thing, but I want to shut it down or force them to make something useful, and I need help. You're smart, and you'll make for good propaganda."

The sunlight blazed on her skin. There were wrinkles around her eyes and tiny broken veins on her cheeks and nose.

"We won't have to burn any flags, will we? The flag reminds me of Patrick, and I don't want to burn any."

"Well hell. We ain't burning any flags. Not if it's going to bug you. Besides, I kind of like it. It's some of the slimy fuckers wrapping themselves in it I can't stand."

She gave me a wink.

"Okay," I said. "It will only be for a while."

"Stay as long as you like, but call home, so I don't get arrested for corrupting a minor or something."

"Are you going to corrupt me?"

"You want me to?"

"Yeah, I'm pretty bored with the way I am now."

7

Robin set me up in a tiny room that was practically a closet and gave me claustrophobia. There were no windows and just a candle in a wine bottle for light. Then she made me call home on a telephone that looked like it might have been the first one ever invented. My mother answered.

"Itchy, where are you?"

My father cut in. "Itchy, where the hell you at?"

"Russia."

"Don't get smart with me."

"All right, I'm not in Russia. What's it matter?"

I had to hold the phone away from my ear. "You left before Communion. That's a mortal sin."

Robin walked out of the room. Vincent followed her, but he gave me a long last look, just to make sure I didn't try anything funny.

"I want you home," he said.

"I'm not coming home."

"The hell you're not. I said you could grow the hair. What more you want? Maybe you'd like the master bedroom. I'm sure your mother won't mind sleeping in a bunk bed."

Then the sarcasm went out of his voice. "You can have Patrick's room if you want. I just didn't think either of you would..."

"No. Leave Patrick's room alone."

"Then what?"

"I just want to be alone."

"I'll call the cops," he said. "Are you in Fishtown?"

"I'm downtown. I'm fine."

"Where?"

"I'm not telling you. In a couple months I'll be eighteen, old enough for Vietnam. Then I'll tell you."

He nearly blew out my eardrum.

"Itchy, you're not going over there. Are you crazy?"

"Dad, will you shut up and listen? I'm not going anywhere."

"Where the hell are you?"

"Dad, if you don't quit shouting, I'm going to hang up, and you're not going to hear from me for a long time."

He stopped. I pictured him, all hot, wheezing, and sweaty, running his hand over that crew cut. I heard my mother whispering.

"When you coming home?" he asked.

"When I turn eighteen, I'll stop by."

"Why you doing this?" His voice was softer now.

"Because when I walk by Patrick's room, I want to kill somebody."

The line crackled. I waited. I kept the receiver far from my ear.

"You'll go to school this fall, won't you?"

"Yeah, Dad."

"Don't get mixed up in anything stupid," he said. "Everything's falling apart. I don't...be careful."

Robin had a wicker table in her kitchen, white with a glass top and a vase of dried flowers in the middle, and I sat there, and she touched my hand, and then someone banged at the door. She flinched.

"Who the hell? Frankie's supposed to call before he lets anyone up here. I'll have his skin if it's Nigel, in that stupid turtleneck, or some jerk selling vacuums."

"I don't think you can sell vacuums," I said. It wasn't a very good joke, and she didn't try to pretend it was. She yanked the door open, and I heard Joe.

"Hello, miss. Could I interest you in a vacuum cleaner?"

"Very funny," she said. "Did you have your ear pressed to the door, and who let you in, anyway?"

"I climbed the fire escape. How about life insurance?"

"You're a riot. Maybe you can get on television." She laughed, but it was nervous.

She showed him to the kitchen. "I've got company," she said, and pointed to me. "You know each other."

Joe winked. "Could I interest you in a vacuum, young man?"

I thought of trying my vacuum joke out again, but was afraid Joe wouldn't think it was funny, either, so I just smiled at him.

"How about some encyclopedias?" he said.

"I already read them all," I said.

"I'll bet you have," Joe said.

He handed a bottle of wine to Robin. His hair was wet, and there were a couple bruises on his face and a Band-Aid, but he looked good anyway. He was the kind of guy who looked good beat-up. It was easy to picture him all bloody in some movie with Indians in it.

I couldn't touch the stuff, but they drank the wine and then more wine, and by sundown they were drunk. Robin stared at his face every chance she got, but whenever he looked up, she looked down. Then he would stare at her. She got awfully drunk before her fingers stopped shaking and she could talk without stopping for breaths in the middle of sentences.

But then she was too drunk and started talking about Nigel. She told us about the night he found her huddled up in the rain in Amsterdam, listening to some black guys from America play jazz. She was too young to get in the bar. She'd just run away from her father, who was stationed in Ulm in Germany, the town where Einstein was born, and hitchhiked north and west on the autobahns with a few marks in her pocket. So she pressed her ear against the door, and Nigel found her soaked and freezing and took her back to London to model for him.

She talked about his cold loft and the dead goats he brought home to photograph and about the parties full of drug addicts and drunk artists who tried to seduce her and all the girls Nigel slept with while Robin drank wine in a corner all night long.

And then she talked about the peanut incident. It was hard to follow with Robin doing Nigel's accents and stopping every few words to call him a name, but apparently, they were drinking wine and sucking on some gas one night. She never explained about the gas. Maybe one of Nigel's friends was a dentist or a balloon salesman, but they had a contest to see who could blow a peanut farthest by loading it into one nostril, closing the other with a finger, then blowing.

She showed us. She crouched like somebody ready to take off in a race and shot an imaginary peanut out her nose.

"But the fucking thing was stuck," she said. "Fucking Nigel tried a paintbrush, tweezers, a pencil, anything to get at it, but the peanut kept climbing up my nose. He even wrapped his smelly lips around my nose and tried sucking it out. It's practically in my brain, and Nigel's laughing and snapping pictures. He tells me, 'Don't worry, love, it'll dissolve.' Dissolve, Jesus. He expects me to cheer up because this peanut's about to dissolve in my nasal passage."

She pointed to her left nostril. "See this little scar? Some British doctor did that cutting the peanut out. He called it an obstruction. I said, 'It's not an obstruction, it's a fucking peanut.' He must have thought I was awful, all slurring my words and my American accent, and Nigel out of his mind, and God what an awful peanut it was. You should have seen when it came out."

"You should have saved it in a jar," I said. "In formaldehyde, like a baby with two heads."

Robin smiled and focused on something sad and far away. "Fucking Nigel," she whispered. "That peanut nearly reached my eyeball."

Later they got into a fight about the factory, and she broke a glass against Joe's face. I ended up shaking like crazy on top of the sleeping bag, kind of wishing I could go home after all, and then Joe came in. He sat on the floor beside me. He'd drunk an awful lot, but his voice was steady. The room was pitch-black, and I couldn't see him, but I wasn't scared or nervous like I usually got in the dark. Joe had a nice voice, and it made me feel safe.

"Itchy, why don't you go home?"

"I get lonely there. For Patrick, I mean."

Joe let out some air. It was a sad sound.

"Yeah," he said. "It's like that at work. Why'd he go?"

"Because he was patriotic," I said. "It was reflexes, like when the doctor whacks your knee with a hammer."

"I think he wanted to be a hero," Joe said.

"But he already was to me and Charlie."

"He didn't realize. You were the genius of Deadwhale, and Charlie was a great football player, and Patrick was just a mechanic, you know. He wanted to make you guys proud of him."

"He tell you that?"

"I just figured it out."

"Ah, Joe that can't be true."

"Maybe not."

I felt sick again. I didn't want Joe to leave. They'd been friends a couple years, and sparks of Patrick flickered off him.

"You aren't joining, are you?" I asked.

"Maybe it depends on Robin. She's half crazy, but I guess I'm drunk, because it seems like I never liked anybody so much."

"Joe, don't go to Vietnam."

"You been talking to Suzanne?"

"A little," I said.

"I wish she'd do something. Ever since our father died, she's never been able to concentrate on anything. She used to be reading about art and psychology and making up little poems. Now she worries about past lives and conspiracy theories about our father's death, like the KGB plotted the whole thing with my mother."

He touched my shoulder, and I knew he was leaving.

"I'm going to help close the factory," I said. "Don't be mad at me."

"Okay," he said. "But don't forget where your father works, and you know, if I don't go to Vietnam, I'll fight you."

"You'll be on Donaghy's side."

"I'd just as soon kill him as help him, but it's not him I'm worried about. It's guys like your dad, and the principle of the damned thing. We need those guns."

He touched my hair.

"You sound like Pat," he said.

And then he was gone, and I was afraid of the dark, and soon I heard the bed shaking and the moans and her shouts and her deep voice crying out his name. At first I thought he was hurting her, but when I put my ear against the wall, the sounds were long and slow and from deep in her throat, and I knew he wasn't hurting her at all.

I put the pillow over my head. I wanted to talk to Patrick. I wanted to talk to Charlie. I thought about Suzanne until I couldn't stand it anymore, and then I imagined Robin with a peanut up her nose and everything felt a little better.

"You can't sell a vacuum," I whispered. And nobody laughed.

8

Then one night Joe disappeared. He came over with some wine and flowers, and they went into her room, and about an hour later he walked out. He passed me on his way to the door. He didn't say anything, but he smiled. The rims of his eyes were wet, and I knew something was wrong, but before I could ask, he was gone.

Months passed without a word. He never said anything to Suzanne, never called or sent a letter. Suzanne had a key to his apartment, and I went over there with her. His closet was full of clothes. There was a pot on the stove, a few books open on his bed. Rent came to the landlord, but Joe had vanished.

Suzanne and Robin got to be friends after that. They drank in Robin's living room and listened to music and tumbled to bed late at night, drunk out of their minds. Sometimes I would stare in, and Suzanne would be curled close to Robin. Their hair would be all messed together and their clothes scattered on the floor. Sometimes the covers would be half-off, and I would see the dark outlines of their naked bodies. My heart would pound, and I would feel so lonely and jealous. And Suzanne whimpered in her sleep.

I loved her. Every minute she sat drinking with Robin, I stared at her eyes and remembered kissing her under the streetlight. I wrote love letters to her, then threw them in the ocean in little pieces. When I ran like a madman on the beach, practicing for the big race, I ran for her. I pounded barefoot through the water wheezing out her name until I fell into the sand exhausted, and sometimes I stared into the mirror and said all the things I would like to say to her, things I knew I would never say.

It hurt loving her, and it just about broke my heart how sad she was now with Joe gone and how being around Robin was making her rough. She wore battered sweat shirts now and a pair of old red sneaks instead of her dresses and high heels. She wore eye liner thick and dark, and earrings like Robin's, and necklaces and bracelets. She jingled and clanked, like a tin can blowing across the road, whenever she turned her head. She smoked one cigarette after another and stared into space all the time, and she'd started saying "fuck" now. It sounded a lot worse coming from her than Robin.

I figured Joe'd gone to Vietnam. It was scary, especially that January of '68 when the Vietcong launched the Tet Offensive and infiltrated our embassy in Saigon. It looked like we weren't winning after all. The North Vietnamese captured Hue, and brave marines in uniforms like my brother's died in street-to-street fighting to take it back, and other marines died under siege defending the worthless dirt at Khe Sanh, and the war seemed to turn against us, and Westmoreland kept asking for more boys, and I would curse at the television and ache for Joe to come home.

I pleaded with Robin to start protesting again, but she wouldn't talk about the factory or Joe or the war. Nigel marched all over town with a band of radicals who went everywhere with him, and they were always fighting the cops, trying to get on the factory grounds, getting arrested and squirted with hoses and tear gas. Robin would bail him out of jail. He would say, "Thanks, love," and beg her to join the cause, but she would send him off again and sit staring at the television, drinking wine and smoking pot, just counting her money, or playing jazz for Suzanne. While Nigel hit the streets for another round of war and protest, Robin didn't seem to want to do anything, except drink and work.

She took the hotel seriously and put a lot of work into reviving her places on Deadwhale's nightclub strip, the doughnut shop and bar Margaret Ditzlow left her. The Strip was full of run-down joints on Sunrise Boulevard. Hot 'n Crispy Doughnuts stood between the Club Flamingo, where bleached blondes with tassels glued to their nipples danced to rock and roll, and Robin's bar, where drugged-up rock bands shook the walls with over-amped Stones and Doors.

Robin renamed the bar The Dead Whale and had a sign hung above the front door that said, The World Famous Dead Whale. It was hard not to laugh when you looked at it.

It was a dangerous part of town, but the murders and brawls I'd been reading about all my life, the kind of thing Mayor Waters was going to end, usually took place in the summer heat, and it was only March when Robin made me the manager of her doughnut shop and raised my salary to one hundred and fifty bucks a week.

All of a sudden I was rich, but it was hard work. Sometimes I worked midnight to seven and still made school. I ran on the beach every chance I got. I studied at work and kept my grades highest in school, but I was awfully tired, and sometimes I slept in class.

My customers were mostly night workers, homeless old men, perverts from the club, and drunks from the world famous Dead Whale. Sometimes Nigel stopped by, smelling of smoke and tear gas with lots of radical literature and all kinds of strange women, but Irv was my most steady customer.

Irv wore a flat baseball glove with all the webbing torn out on his left hand. He had a head full of dead leaves. His tongue was gigantic and gray and usually drooped on the counter, and he was always decked out with a paisley tie, dungarees, cowboy boots, and a sports coat with no elbows and the collar chewed off.

All he ever said was, "Hey, what are you driving?" He would shout that with this gruff voice. I would bend over to tie my shoe, and as soon as I came up, he would shout, "Hey, what are you driving?" And his tongue would hang there like a dead fish.

"A hard bargain," I would say.

"I used to drive a hard bargain myself."

He would sip his coffee, look up, and say, "Still driving that hard bargain?"

He would doze with his head on the counter. Once I found him sleeping with his nose gurgling in his coffee. After I rescued him, he coughed, got his wits together, and said, "Hey, what are you driving?"

"I should have let you drown," I said.

Robin wouldn't let me kick him out. She said he gave the place character. Sometimes she would sit with him, give him doughnuts, and actually answer his questions.

Charlie visited work in early April, just a few days after Johnson bailed out and threw the Democratic race wide open. It was great. Johnson couldn't end the war, but McCarthy or Kennedy sure could, and my hopes were high that it would end soon, and Joe would come home, and maybe we could forget it all. Of course, I would never forget the one part.

I hadn't seen much of Charlie lately. He was missing a lot of school. We were both seniors because I'd started first grade a year late, but we didn't have any of the same classes.

He hung out with some guys down on the wharf. A lot of them were dropouts. They were from Fishtown and Little Brooklyn mostly. They used to hate one another and fight all the time, but after they played tackle on the beach a few times, they got tired of beating each other up and became friends, and Charlie drank with them every night. I didn't see him until Irv shouted.

"Hey, what are you driving, bub?"

"A blimp, you idiot."

"Used to drive a blimp myself."

"That's great," Charlie said.

He slammed the counter, and Irv sucked in his tongue.

"What are you doing here?" I asked.

"Hey, Itch. Want to get high?"

"You're kidding." I'd started smoking the stuff awhile ago, but I figured Charlie never touched it.

"Hey, I like it," Charlie said. "I thought it was hippie shit, but I've seen the light, man."

"I'm going to quit," I said.

"You should," Charlie said, "but I ain't no rocket scientist like you, and it's no great loss for humanity if I fuck up my brain."

"You better ask the clientele," I said. "And put it out fast if anybody comes in, especially Robin. See that door back there?" I pointed to a side door that was all splintered and gray. "It connects to her bar. If that door moves, get it out."

"She's got you scared, huh?"

"She's nuts," I said. "She's always yelling at me. Yesterday she was going to kill me 'cause she found one of my toenails on her stinking toilet seat cover."

"So what was your toenail doing on her toilet seat, Itchy?"

"I put my foot up to cut them, but I couldn't tell her 'cause she'd yell at me for getting footprints on her toilet. She's always bugging me about keeping things clean. If I sit still too long, she dusts me off. It's like having this crazy wife without any of the benefits."

"You mean you're not humping her?"

"No, Charlie, I'm not humping her. She's about thirteen years older than me, man."

"So what, man? The older the better. If I was in your shoes, I'd be making the most of it."

"I don't know why I even talk to you," I said. "I've got a serious problem here."

"So move out."

"I can't. I swear she needs me around. That weird Nigel's always trying to get at her, and she's lonely, and besides, where would I go?"

"Come home, man. I miss watching Dad yell at you. It's neat watching all the hairs stick up on his neck, like a porcupine."

He stood, pulled his hair straight up on his head, pushed out his stomach, and did his imitation of our father. "Itchy, turn that shit down. You want to go deaf or something? You want to hear some good music, put on some Mantovani."

He sounded just like him. It was impossible not to laugh.

Charlie looked at Irv. "Hey, potato face. Mind if I smoke grass?"

"I'm driving a Packard now," Irv said.

"You don't say? Mind if I get high?" Charlie asked.

"I used to get high myself," Irv said.

"This guy's got some loose screws," Charlie said.

"He's got a hardware store in his skull," I said.

Charlie sat in a revolving chair that was red, with the yellow stuffing popping out through the vinyl. He lit the joint and took a long drag.

"Hey, Itchy, what are you driving?" Charlie asked. He laughed out the smoke. His eyes were pink, and I smelled beer. I pushed him an ashtray and a cup of coffee.

His hair had grown in and gotten sloppy. He looked kind of beat and a little skinny, but he still looked powerful. He kept sniffling and rubbing his eyes. His clothes were wrinkled. His fingers were dirty, with all the nails chewed down.

The back of his left arm was scarred from his elbow to his wrist. I'd seen it before, this mound of gray and purple flesh. It had healed some, and the scabs had gone away, but I still couldn't get used to it. He'd done it with his penknife, holding the knife over a fire then carving and burning the letters into his skin. The scar said PATRICK.

I didn't smoke. I liked the stuff. It made things clear and funny and took a lot of the sting off, but the race was coming in July, and I wanted to be at my best. I was shaving a second off my time a week, and I'd come within twenty seconds of Donaghy's record.

"You practicing for the race?" I asked.

Charlie blew out some smoke. "Of course. Charlie meets any challenge, man. I'm going to kick Donaghy's ass. How about you?"

"A little."

"Shit, Itchy, you should practice every night. You got skinny legs, but you're fast, like Patrick. Not as fast as me maybe, but fast enough. Wouldn't it be cool if we both beat him?"

"He's pretty fast," I said. "And he knows what he's doing."

"I know what I'm doing, too. I'll just get out front and hold on. Hey, did Suzanne ever say anything about me?"

My throat got tight. "No. Why should she?"

"Because, you know, I go see her a lot."

"What?"

"Well, I heard she broke up with Donaghy, right?"

"Yeah, she says, but she still comes over with bruises on her face and all, and I don't think she's falling down the stairs."

"Yeah, I started stopping in at that frame shop. She shows me all these pictures by them dead artist guys, you know, Pablo Rembrandt, and all, and I was wondering if she ever mentioned me."

"It's Pablo Picasso, Charlie, and no, she didn't mention you. Maybe it's not a real big event in her life when you stop by."

"I do that to her, too," he said. "Mix up the names on purpose, like I'll say Vincent Picasso. It drives her crazy. She gets real frustrated, and I don't know, maybe it's only a tiny event in her life, but she always seems glad when I come in. She touches me and all when she shows me things."

"Where?"

"Where what?"

"Does she touch you?"

"In the frame shop."

"Where on your body?"

"You know, the hands, the shoulder and stuff."

"She does that to everybody."

"Yeah, well I didn't say she was yanking down my zipper."

He sucked the joint. He kept coughing, and the place had that sweet smell. When it was half gone, he stubbed it out in the ashtray and dropped the end in his shirt pocket.

"Sometimes I think she's crazy," he said. "Like she's always trying to convince me there's some guy with fireballs for eyes, or something, who sits on top of the Ferris wheel. Half the time, I think she believes it."

"Maybe she does."

"Yeah. Look, man, you think she'd go out with me if I asked?"

I couldn't look at him. I cleaned the counter with a dirty rag. I wanted to stuff it down his throat, but I restrained myself.

"I don't know, Charlie. She's older than you."

"I'll be eighteen in November."

"Yeah, well, she's older, and she's mature for her age, you know. I mean, except for that Ferris wheel stuff, and all that reincarnation crap. Is that why you came, to bug me about her?"

"I was hoping maybe I could have a doughnut, too."

"What kind you want?"

"How about them white jobs with the cream in the middle?"

"How many you want?"

"How many you got?"

I counted. "Fourteen."

"Okay."

"Okay, what?"

"I'll take them."

"Charlie, I said, 'fourteen.' "

Charlie closed his eyes and started counting on his fingers. It was painful to watch. Then he smiled and said, "Five minutes."

"Five minutes, what?"

"I'll bet you a buck I can eat all fourteen in five minutes."

"Four minutes," I said.

"You're on."

I laid fourteen cream doughnuts in front of Charlie. I'd done some math, too. I figured he would have to eat one every seventeen seconds to make it. I pointed to the clock behind us. When the second hand came around, I said, "Go," and Charlie jumped at the doughnuts.

"Charlie, nobody eats fourteen cream doughnuts in four minutes." I laughed. Charlie stuffed a whole doughnut in his mouth. Three seconds later, he swallowed it, like a boa constrictor.

"You're going to kill yourself," I said, and I laughed some more. It was funny watching Charlie jam doughnuts down his throat. I got out my wallet, and made room for his money. I just kept laughing, and three minutes and forty nine seconds later, I stopped laughing, fished out a dollar, and tossed it across the counter. Charlie tromped around the place with his arms raised and powder all over his face, shouting at the top of his lungs, "Charlie meets any challenge," as if he'd just landed on the moon.

He slurped down his coffee, and I gave him a refill. He stuffed my dollar in his pocket and gave me a big creamy smile with sugar on his nose and in his hair.

"You should see your face," he said. "You should've known I'd do it."

"Don't you feel sick or anything?" I asked. "The least you could do is puke."

"I feel great. I can do anything. I'm fucking immortal. Did you know I quit school today?"

"What?"

"Yeah I quit. No more fucking Julius Caesar."

"But you only got two months."

"I don't care, man. I talked to one of Donaghy's people, and I'm getting a job down at the factory."

"But you're not eighteen."

"It don't matter. They said since our old man's been there so long, they could make an exception, as long as Dad signs a paper."

"He'll never sign it."

"He already did."

"I don't believe you."

"He did, Itchy. I told him I quit and there was nothing he could do. I told him I was going to Vietnam, and forget about stopping me. Then he got...well, you know how he gets, wheezing like his car, and the hair standing on his neck. He just said Charlie real loud a couple times, then he bent down and signed."

Charlie burped. His eyes were red, and he wrapped his huge hands around a sugar shaker.

"Know what, Itch? He walked out of the room real fast then, and I think he was...I think he might've been crying or something."

Charlie poured some sugar into his hand, then licked it off. I checked the coke syrup and all the other sodas, making sure they were filled to the brim. When I started talking again, it was only with half a heart.

"They'll give you some shit job," I said.

"Oh, man, it's just for a while."

"And then what?"

"Then the war."

I looked at the stains around the brim of his cup and the powdered sugar all over, but it was hard to look at Charlie.

"When you start?"

"Next week."

"A lot of guys are dying over there," I said.

"That's what happens in wars."

"Do you really..."

Before I could finish, the door between the doughnut shop and the bar flew open. Robin stood in the light with a beer in her hand. Some make-up had smeared around her eyes, and she looked scared. The bar was dark and silent behind her.

"Itchy, shut out the lights," she said.

"What?"

"The lights."

"Hey, man, I won't be able to see," Charlie said. "I was just about to eat fourteen jelly doughnuts."

Robin pointed to Irv. "Get him out of here. Eat your doughnuts later, Charlie. I already locked the bar. Close up, Itchy."

"But it's only..."

"Jesus," she said. "Some asshole shot Martin Luther King, you see? The slums are already smoking. It's coming this way."

Irv smiled at Robin. "Hey, bub, what are you driving?"

9

The strip was busy for an off-season Friday. The Club Flamingo had a show, and lots of drunks walked by, mostly local guys in their twenties and thirties, all white and staring to the southwest where the smoke rose high into the sky. It smelled good.

I kept hearing the word nigger. A door opened, and laughs poured out over newsmen with grave voices. Robin led me to her bike. There were sirens and lots of shouting and breaking glass in the distance. I caught someone watching from an alley just as I helped Robin onto the handlebars. It was just a shadow, but I was pretty sure it was Nigel. I caught a flash of his teeth.

I pedaled through the dark, with Vincent running along behind us, and soon I stood with my hands on the rail of our balcony, the ocean out front of me, and the sky glowing to my right. It reminded me of a scene from a war movie, as if the Luftwaffe had just bombed Southwest Deadwhale. I imagined Churchill making some great speech about it.

"Patrick wrote a paper about him, when he was a senior," I said. "Patrick was a good writer."

I wasn't talking very loud. I had my back to her. I held the railing and watched the sky. The sirens never stopped. There were explosions, too, that might have been guns, but I wasn't sure. The breeze from the sea tasted fresh and smoky.

"What's wrong with this country, Robin?"

It was a cool night, but I was hot. I tore off my shirt, then my undershirt and threw them over the side and watched them float toward the sliver of street that ended at the beach.

"We're worse than animals," I said. "Animals just kill 'cause they're hungry."

She stood beside me.

"Itchy," she said. "Your brother's gone."

"But he didn't deserve it. He didn't want to kill anybody, but they make you into a hero if you do. Why don't we protest? You said that's why you wanted me to stay. What happened? Ever since you started with Joe..."

"Joe's gone, too."

"Did he go there?"

"Probably. I told him something he didn't want to hear, and he left me."

"What you tell him?"

"The truth."

"What's the truth?"

"You ask too many questions."

"Robin, please? You were good, and people were starting to believe in you. Let's protest. I can't stand doing nothing. Why'd you stop?"

She smiled. "I made a mistake. For a minute, I thought I could change things. That was stupid."

"You can, anybody can. Come on. Nigel's messing everything up."

"I'm all through with that," she said. "We could never close that factory, and even if we did, it wouldn't help Patrick, and it wouldn't stop the war."

She leaned her head on me in the blackness. I looked down into her hair.

"If we all give up, it might never end," I said. "But if we protest maybe we could stop it before Charlie goes."

"You love her, don't you?" she said.

I felt something in my stomach, like a sharp knife.

"Who?"

"You stare at Suzanne with big sad eyes. You remind me of Bambi."

"I do not. It's just that you're stoned all the time. Everybody probably looks like Bambi."

"You look like Bambi, Itchy. Why don't you do something about it?"

"Charlie likes her now," I said. "Do you believe it?"

"Well, she's very pretty."

"He goes where she works and pretends he likes art. What's that jerk know about art? He goes to that frame shop and looks at a bunch of tulips by one of those Impressionist guys and says, 'Oh wow, great colors.' Next he'll be taking her pants off under the boardwalk and talking about that weird Picasso shit, where people's ears are in the middle of their faces, like it's his favorite thing."

I could feel Robin laughing against me, but she tried to hold it in.

"It's called Cubism," she said.

"It's not funny. Charlie's a bonehead football player, and Suzanne's this real sensitive person. How can he expect her to like him? Did she mention him to you?"

"Just that sometimes she dreams of his naked body."

"Oh, God. Nothing makes sense in life. He's dumber than his football helmet. He wears it to bed. Who cares about his stupid naked body?"

She pushed back her glasses and laughed into my ear.

"Come to my bed."

"Your what?"

"Bed. I want to teach you."

"Teach me what?"

"Just sex."

"You want to teach me sex?"

"Yes."

"You mean sex? S-e-x?"

"Well, at least you can spell it."

"Of course I can spell it. It's a basic three-letter word, and a famous one. Of course I can spell it."

"So let's go."

"Where?"

"To my bedroom. B-e-d-r-o-o-m."

"For sex?"

"Yes, Itchy. S-e-x. You know, where we take off our clothes and do interesting things together."

"We take off our clothes?"

"Yes, it's more fun that way."

"But I never did it," I said.

"That's why I'm going to teach you."

"But I'll mess it up. Shouldn't I read a book? I always read a book before I try something new, like when I tried to take up golf."

"You got a manual?"

"I could get one, you know, 'cause I'm a klutz, I mean, and what about if Joe..."

"Forget Joe."

"But why do you want me?"

"Because you're cute, okay, and my friend. Come on. You might like it."

"Well, I heard it was fun. It won't slow down my running, will it?"

"Speed it up, I think."

I smelled her perfume and hair and let her pull me toward her room, lay me in bed, and slide my pants off. I could barely see her. She probably couldn't see me either, but she must have heard my heart. It beat like charging horses in my chest, and when she slid in beside me with nothing on, I probably sounded like the Kentucky Derby.

"I don't know what to do," I said.

"I do."

I felt her breath on my chest and her cool hair against my chin. She was awfully warm for someone without clothes on.

"Don't be scared," she said.

"Do I have to nibble your ear or something?"

"Nibble anything. Mainly I want you to fuck me." She spit out the *f* in a way that made it sound dangerous. I could hardly breathe after she said it. "Understand?"

"Define fuck," I said.

"I'll demonstrate."

"You got a dummy, like they have in school for health? Maybe you could show me on that."

"Kiss me, dummy."

"On the lips?"

"Anywhere."

"Speaking of fuck," I said, "one time Charlie told me he saw some television show where this guy talks to his dog. I can't remember the name of the guy or the dog or anything, but it was supposed to be a show for kids, and the guy wrote an *f* on the board, and he asked the dog what it was, and the dog said, '*k*.' And the guy kept pointing to the *f*, and the dog kept calling it a *k*, and then finally the guy got pissed off, and he asked the dog, 'Hey, dog, how come every time I see *f* you see *k*?' Get it?"

"Do you want to fuck me or not?"

"Oh, God."

And it wasn't ten minutes later, she was on top of me, her face so close I could touch her nose with my tongue. There was wine and toothpaste on her breath, and marijuana smoke mixed with the scent of shampoo in her hair. She kissed me and pulled my hands to her breasts. They were small with hard nipples that I rolled between my fingers and thumbs. They were hot, too, like her legs and her back. Everything about her was hot.

"Soft hands," she said.

"You don't get many calluses from doughnuts," I said.

"Do I feel like doughnuts?"

"No, doughnuts are sugary and rough. You're hot and soft, more like Chef Boyardee pizza dough."

"My tits feel like pizza?"

"No, dough, Chef Boyardee pizza dough for making your own pizza. It's really good. You mix it with water, and then you let it sit, and it gets gooey."

She forced her tongue into my mouth before I could finish explaining about the pizza dough. I could hardly believe it, the warm kiss, her breasts like pizza dough in my hands, her legs wrapping around mine.

"Isn't this better than pizza?" she asked.

"It depends on the pizza."

She kissed my neck. She whispered, "baby," telling me to relax, don't be scared, telling me where to put my hands, and soon we were sweating, and my fingers moved inside her where she was soaked and hot and so velvety smooth I could hardly believe it, and she crawled over me and made me taste it a long time, while she reached back and squeezed and pulled at me until I thought I would scream, and then she let go and showed me in.

Robin started acting crazy then. She held her own breasts. She rolled her head on her neck. She thrashed and bucked against me, like some cowgirl on a wild horse, whispering at the ceiling, "More, more, deeper, honey, harder, harder."

She moved hard and fast and long, until it was violent, her breath coming in shrieks and heaves and then the shouts, right above me, shouting my name instead of Joe's, slamming me against the mattress, and a feeling swelling through me, until I was helpless underneath her, thrashing right and left, kissing her face, whispering her name, and freezing solid while something amazing happened.

I started laughing. I wanted to howl like a wild Indian or beat my chest like Tarzan or Charlie or some other primitive creature, and I couldn't stop laughing. I imagined this was how Charlie felt after seventy push-ups or fourteen cream doughnuts. I wanted to jump up and down and shout, "Itchy meets any challenge," but Robin clamped her hand over my mouth and stared into my eyes. She sounded like a girl.

"Was it better than pizza?"

"We could get married," I said. "And do that all the time. I'm a quick learner, and if I could get a little practice in, maybe I could make you scream louder. Wouldn't it be fun?"

"You're too young," she said. "Besides you'll marry Suzanne someday, and all the stuff I teach you, you can use on her."

"Suzanne would never do this with me."

"Someday," she said. She kissed my ear. Vincent nudged his way through the cracked door and jumped into the bed with us. Robin laughed.

"Vincent, you horny cat," she said.

And we lay naked for a long time with our legs wrapped together and Vincent running his tired motor between us. The southwest slums were burning still, and I could taste the smoke in Robin's bedroom and hear the sirens wail.

"It's so awful," she whispered.

"We've got to protest, Robin."

"Jesus, Itchy, will you drop that? I promised Joe I wouldn't. I never break a promise."

"So where the hell's Joe?"

"He's gone. Forever."

"He'll be back."

"No, it's happened to me before." She pulled Vincent against her. "Poor Vincent. Come here. Come to Momma." The cat crawled between our faces.

"People disappear on me," she said.

Vincent's fur tickled my ear. I didn't like having a cat in my face, especially a wet one. I wanted to touch Robin again, but didn't know if there was some proper interval before we could start the next lesson. I didn't want to seem any more naive than I had to, but I wanted her bad again already, almost as bad as I wanted that cat out of my face.

"My father left me with his parents and his brother when I was thirteen," she said. "Before that, was Texas. He sold our trailer, and I had to move in with my mother's parents on the ranch after he drove her away."

I tried to see Robin's face in the darkness.

"Who drove who away?"

"Well hell, Itchy, my mother. My father drove her away, and I had to move in with her parents. Why do you think I'm so fucked up?" She pushed Vincent out of the way and kissed my forehead. She squeezed my hand for a second, then slid it through the hairs onto the soaked spot between her legs. She guided my fingers. Her other hand played with Vincent.

"She was twenty-four, and it was my fifth birthday. I don't remember much, except that she left on a train, and my grand-mother cried in bed with me."

She rubbed my hand. "Go easy," she said. "It feels good. I can do it all night, but not long at a time. Can you do it again?"

"I can force myself."

"You're in your sexual prime."

"I nearly wasted the whole stinking thing. I guess I'd better do it a lot to make up lost time."

"No need to panic," she said, and she laughed, but only a second.

"My mother painted, but my father used to set her work on fire. I guess he wanted her to paint clowns with red noses, but she did these poor Mexicans down in Waxahachie. Her father had a ranch in Dallas, and she took me on the horses, and once she showed me a dead snake. That's my oldest memory, my mother's hand with paint on it pointing to this snake and saying it's worse than fire ants, but not as bad as my father."

Robin kissed me. "Joe broke my heart," she whispered. "But I told him I wouldn't protest, and I won't." She took a handful of my hair and yanked me against her. "Let's do it again. Let's just do it and do it and never think about anything else."

"Do what?"

"You're kind of an asshole, Itchy."

"Oh, yeah? Well how come every time I see *f* you see *k*?"

10

My only choice was Nigel. He was all over town with his ragged band of weird and fanatical followers. He spoke on corners in his huge coat with a bottle of whiskey sticking out of a pocket and a cigarette glued to his mouth. He shouted. He pointed. He punched walls and broke bricks over his head to emphasize his points. He swore he would destroy that factory or burn Deadwhale to the ground.

He lived in Little Brooklyn, not too far from the factory and right on the border of the southwest slums, on one of those few streets that actually had black and white people in the same row of houses. It was a bad week to be in that part of town. Blacks rioted in Baltimore, Washington, Chicago, and dozens of other cities all over the country. They broke and stole and burned and fought. They killed and died, and Deadwhale was no exception.

The southwest slums burned for three days. Whole streets went up. Fires that started in old warehouses, abandoned homes, and wooden shacks that leaned against the bay spread to the crooked brick rows of the inner streets. Docks went up, along with the fishing boats and the run-down sailboats in the southwest marina, and I was scared when I slipped up Nigel's smoky street that afternoon.

He lived on the top floor of a big old row house, and he didn't seem surprised at all to see me. He even smiled.

"Well, my good man," he said with his English accent. "What a pleasant surprise."

Nigel had his coat on and nothing else, except a jockstrap. The coat was wide open, and Nigel's chest was huge and hairy with a tattoo right in the middle, a tiny one, just what looked like an eye, maybe a fish eye, and a cross underneath it. He asked me in. I wasn't very eager, but I was determined, and I followed him inside.

There was no furniture, just glaring studio lights that made my eyes throb, a bottle of whiskey, a bowl of peanuts, a black and white television on the hardwood floor, blaring about the riots in Washington, and what looked like a sculpture of a girl. The sculpture was all white, tall, and beautifully shaped, and when my eyes adjusted, I saw it was wrapped completely in toilet paper and smoking a cigarette through a crack in the paper. Beside the sculpture, on a pile of soggy books, stood a fishbowl, the kind you put goldfish in, and inside the bowl was a big fish with its head cut off. The fish barely fit in the bowl.

"Art," he said.

"Oh," I said.

"You like it?"

The sculpture moved a little and said. "Who's that, Nigel?"

"There's a girl in there," I said.

"Of course," Nigel said. "It wouldn't be art if there wasn't a girl in there. It would just be toilet paper."

"Of course," I said. I was thinking I should get out of there fast. I pictured myself rolled in toilet paper and smoking a cigarette beside some dead fish.

"Nigel, my back hurts," the toilet paper said. "Are we almost finished?"

She sounded about fifteen, but she was tall, taller even than Nigel, who towered over me.

"Soon, love," he said. "We have a guest."

"But Nigel, it's been all morning. Can't I have some whiskey?"

"Soon," he said. "Please, love, be a good object, and stand perfectly still." He took the cigarette out of her mouth and sat across the room from her, leaning up against one of the walls.

That's when I noticed the walls. They were covered with photographs, gigantic photographs that were hard to see in the glare of lights aimed at the girl. The photographs were all of a nude girl, a young, pretty girl. Every inch of wall was covered. The girl was always naked. In some she kissed another girl or lay wrapped around a man, a skinny man, a fat man, a Chinese man with tattoos all over his body. The girl was young and beautiful and defiant. She was Robin, and it made my heart race.

"Beautiful, wasn't she?" he said. "Have a seat."

I leaned against the wall beside him. The girl in toilet paper stood motionless in the middle of the empty room. The television blared and filled the place with echoes. It showed torn-up streets in Chicago and federal troops on the steps of the Capitol. The speaker rattled.

Nigel fixed his eyes on the girl and took long swallows of whiskey. He took a peanut and put it in his nose. At first I thought I'd imagined it. He'd loaded it in there casually, and I thought maybe it was some drug thing. I just hoped he wouldn't offer me one.

"Perfect, yes?" he said. He pointed to the girl and the fish corpse floating in the bowl and the bright lights and the pictures of Robin on the walls. I didn't know much about art, and I didn't want to offend Nigel.

"I like the fish," I said.

"What fish?"

"In the fishbowl."

"That's not a fish."

"It's got gills. It's silver with fins and all kinds of other fish features," I said.

"Resembling a fish doesn't make it one."

"What is it then, a horse?"

"It's an object," Nigel said.

"It's a dead fish," I said.

Nigel shook his head. I was pretty sure the peanut was still in his nose, unless he'd sucked it into his brain or something, and I was awfully curious about what he was going to do with it.

"Ah, my poor, blind man. Perhaps it's a former fish, if we must label it, but all that made it a fish drained out of it when I took the axe to it, just as all that makes you a boy would drain out of you were I to slice off your skull, unpleasant a thought as it is. There's no fish in death, only the emotion a semblance of a fish inspires in the observer."

He was getting on my nerves, but I didn't want to argue. I saw a dead fish and figured if he cut off my head I'd be a dead boy, but I didn't want to dwell on the subject or put any ideas in his head. He had a peanut up his nose. A girl in toilet paper stood in the middle of the floor. He may have been more powerful than Charlie. I didn't want to annoy him.

"Are you painting her, or taking her picture, or what?"

Nigel laughed. "I've gone beyond that," he said. "My art is temporary and transcendent. It's a fixed sequence of moments in my mind.

I merely create her, watch her, unwrap her, and then make love to her. It's a sexual process really. Perhaps you could call this phase the foreplay, but it's wonderfully fulfilling to fuck your art."

He pressed a finger against the opposite nostril, made some incredible snorting sound, and blew the peanut out his nose so hard it whizzed by the girl and slammed off Robin's cheek on the far wall. The floor was covered with peanuts.

"Isn't that a nice trick?" he asked. "Took me years to master it. Care to take a shot?"

I inched further away from Nigel.

"No thanks," I said. "I have a weak nose."

"Pity," he said. "It's quite stimulating."

"Yeah, I'm sure." I had a sudden violent urge to get out of there. Nigel stuffed another peanut up his nose.

"So, my good man, you haven't told me how I might help you."

"Nigel," the girl said. "My back hurts."

He hit her in the face with a peanut.

"Don't bloody move," he said.

The toilet paper started turning dark where her eyes must have been.

"I want to protest," I said. "Robin won't do it anymore, so I thought maybe I could help you. My brother works at the factory, and he's taking me there today."

"Yes," he said. "Wonderful." He shoved another peanut up his nose. "Find out everything you can. Everything, but mainly, where do they keep the bloody guns? Where do they keep the bullets? Remember how the place is laid out. Look for any weaknesses, but make sure you find the guns."

"I don't think I want to blow it up like you keep saying," I said. "I think we should just try to get it closed or making something else."

"I don't care what you think," he said. He blew the peanut out his nose right into the girl's face again. "You want to help me, you do it my way."

"But you're not serious are you? I mean, you can't blow the place up. It's impossible, and think of all the people who'd get hurt."

"I can bloody well do what I want," he said. "I work at the college. I've got friends with the necessary skills, other professors as wonderfully inspired as I, who'd gladly lend me their talents with bombs and fire, and as far as people getting hurt, fuck them. Anyone who works there deserves what he gets."

"I just want to protest," I said. "My dad works there, and my brother, too, and I don't want to hurt anybody."

"As you wish," he said. "But vengeance requires violence, and if you want vengeance for your former brother, I suggest you do things my way."

I got up. "I'll think about it." I walked over to the toilet paper. The face was soggy. I whispered. The television was loud, and I didn't think Nigel could hear. "Do you want to come with me?"

"Fuck you," she said.

Then Nigel had hold of me. He forced me across the room and banged me off the other wall. He was so strong, I didn't have a chance. He whipped me around, slammed me back against the wall, and pushed his face so close to mine, I couldn't see anything but his eyes. He reeked of whiskey and peanuts, and he had dropped his coat behind him. He was naked, except for the patch over his crotch and the straps that held it on, and his left hand slid slowly, firmly, and completely around my balls.

"I know you're fucking my Robin," he said. "That's all right. You like it. You make it good for her, but you understand, someday I'm coming home, and nobody, not you, not Joe Waters, not Robert Waters, not God, is going to stop that. You understand?"

"Yes," I said.

He eased off a step. His left hand stayed where it was. It didn't hurt, but it was very convincing, and I wasn't going to argue.

"Very good," he said. "Now get me the information, and we'll get revenge. Okay, my good man?"

"Yes," I said.

He squeezed tight for a second, but still it didn't hurt. It was almost gentle, almost as if he wanted me to like it. He smiled like my best friend. His smile was warm and affectionate and made me feel better, but just when I thought it was okay, he jammed a huge hand behind my head and pulled hard on my hair. The other hand jumped from my crotch to my face and forced something up my nose so hard and fast I thought it would shoot out my ear. Then he let go, stood back, and smiled.

"It's a pretty face you have," he said.

I moved away from him along the wall. He didn't watch me go. I took a last look at the pictures of Robin everywhere, then I slinked to the door, grabbed hold of it, and took one last look. Nigel was slowly unwrapping the girl in toilet paper with his teeth. I squeezed the peanut out of my nose and ran into the street.

11

Charlie and I took the bus to the factory that afternoon. He wanted me to take a job there, but I went in to spy. I doubted I could work with a guy who shot peanuts out his nose and wrapped girls in toilet paper, but I had to do something, and with Robin out of the picture, Nigel seemed like the only choice.

Charlie worked three-thirty to midnight, and we got there just before his shift. The factory was gray and ugly on the outside and cold and dark, with ceilings way up high, inside. We headed straight for the cafeteria to buy peanuts. I'd made the mistake of telling Charlie about Nigel.

"He could blow it right out his nose?" Charlie asked, for the fortieth time, while we wound our way through a long aisle of machines.

"Yeah," I said. "At the speed of light."

"I'll bet I can break glass with one," Charlie said. "I've been building my lungs up to kick Donaghy's ass."

There were no windows, just dim lights and a shower of sparks from blades shrieking against steel and spitting hot chips that piled on the floor and stuck to the bottoms of my sneakers. I held my ears, but Charlie walked through it like he owned the place. People watched us. Our dad was a big shot there, the chief inspector, the guy who decided whether a gun could go kill people, and we were famous because of Patrick.

The cafeteria was small and ugly and empty, but there were some vending machines from the same era as Robin's phone, and one had peanuts. Charlie rushed over to a table, ripped the bag open with his teeth, and immediately shoved a peanut up his nose. He tilted his head back, squeezed a nostril, and blew with all his might. The peanut dribbled down his chest. He scooped it up and tried again and again, but his best shot barely hit the table, then rolled two feet before it stopped dead.

"Shit," he said. "If you made this up, I'm going to kill you, Itchy."

"Charlie, can we go look at where they keep the guns? You've got the rest of your life to shoot peanuts out your nose."

"Yeah, in a minute," he said. "There must be a trick to it."

"Try another," I said. "That one looks like nuclear waste or something. We ought to bury it in the bottom of the sea in lead."

He poured the whole bag on the table and started poking through them, looking for the peanut with the best aerodynamic qualities.

"I'll bet he's using trick peanuts," he said.

"Yeah, maybe they got little propellers on them," I said.

"You're a wise-ass."

"You're making excuses."

"That's what you think." He poked himself in the chest. "Charlie meets any challenge. Push-ups, peanuts, football, beating Donaghy's ass on the Fourth. It don't matter. I just got to make some adjustments in my style. Sometimes technique's more important than power."

Finally he settled on a peanut and stuck it in his nose. He blew so hard his face turned red. All kinds of stuff flew out his nose, but no peanut.

"Robin got one stuck in her nose, and they had to perform surgery," I said.

He blew again. This time the peanut squeezed out his nose and stuck to the top of his lip. I laughed. I pumped my arms in the air and pranced around with my lips puffed out, like Mick Jagger. I did Charlie's chicken walk, and said, "Charlie meets any challenge."

"Shut up, Itchy. I'll be putting peanuts on the moon. When them astronauts get there, they're going to say, 'Wow, there's peanuts here,' and all the scientists will be scratching their heads."

"You can't even shoot one across a table," I said.

"You try it then, you think it's so easy."

"I'm not sticking a peanut in my nose. Come on, wipe your face, and show me the stinking guns."

Charlie scooped his peanuts up and dropped them in the pocket of his flannel shirt. He was scowling. He took out a peanut and gave it a dirty look.

"I'm going to put one in orbit," he said. "You'll see."

I didn't see any guns. There were guys all over the place running big loud machines. There were carts full of pieces. There were lubricants gushing through tubes onto whirling blades and splashing into puddles. There were sparks and smells, but I wanted to find bullets and guns. I was a spy.

"Where they at?" I asked.

"Where's what?" We had to shout at one another to hear over the hissing and grinding.

"The stinking guns, man."

"Beats me. You hardly ever see a finished gun, but I can show you where they test them."

"Yeah, the rest of this shit's boring."

"I thought an intellectual like you would like to see how they make them. Come on."

Charlie led me by tables of women with curved backs and rotten teeth sitting on long benches, filing the edges off failed parts, and smoking cigarettes. Their faces were ugly and wrinkled. There were young girls, and they smoked, too, but they looked fresh, and one was very pretty. Charlie gave them all big smiles and waves. They all seemed to like him, like he was real handsome. I couldn't understand it. I wanted to tell them he was a big goof who was just sticking peanuts in his nose, but they were smiling at me, too, so I just smiled back.

Charlie took me to the test shack where they fired the guns and introduced me to a guy named Gino who didn't have any hair on his head but had a bare chest covered with it. We shook hands. Gino's was soaked and greasy. He wore a bandanna and blasted bullets through a hole in the wall all day.

The room was hot and cramped and reminded me of a tomb, like you'd see Christ raising Lazarus from during some Easter movie. It reeked of smoke and Gino, who handed me headphones without chords and shoved a gun through the hole in the wall. He jammed a strip of bullets in place and stepped behind the gun.

"Care for a little demonstration?" he asked.

He gritted his raisin teeth and fired. The room rocked. A tattoo of a mermaid with gigantic breasts trembled on Gino's bicep. Charlie popped a peanut in his nose. He faced away from us, and I figured he was taking target practice at the far wall.

The bullets traveled through an underground tunnel into a chamber of water. In town, you could hear the firing during the quiet hours of night. Gino fired five seconds, turned with a big smile, and took a bow. He was an artist.

"You do good work," I said.

"Fucking right, I do," he said. "Ain't a gun comes out of here ain't been fired by me."

"You should be proud," I said.

"Fucking right, I should," he said. "There's other ways to kill fucking commies besides eye-to-eye. Want to try her?"

"Try who?"

"A shot of the gun," Charlie said. "Man, you're thick."

"What's in your nose?" I said.

"A peanut, what do you think?"

Gino stared at Charlie with this confused expression, but didn't ask any questions. I stepped behind the gun. Gino got real close to show how it worked. He smelled like he hadn't had a bath in a couple years, but he was gentle and very concerned that I enjoy the experience completely.

"Just squeeze and fire off little bursts," he said.

I fired a burst. The handle was hot and soaked from Gino. I fired another. The power of the machine surged through my arms, but I couldn't see the bullets hitting, and it wasn't any fun. It was just loud and hot, and it made my stomach flip over and burn.

"Where do you take them from here?" I asked.

"They picks them up," he said. "Beats me where they takes them."

"So you don't keep them here?"

"Just till we fire them."

"Quit being so nosy," Charlie said. "If you want to see a bunch of guns piled in boxes, ask Dad. He knows everything, but this is the main thing, seeing how they look and shooting one off. Someday I'll use them for real, man, and I won't be shooting through no hole in the wall."

I dragged Charlie toward the door. "Keep up the good work, Gino," I said. He winked and gently touched the machine.

My eyes throbbed in the sun. I felt like I'd just returned from Mars. Charlie frowned into a handful of peanuts.

"I need skinnier peanuts," he said.

I looked around, figuring out where the test shack lay in respect to the rest of the plant. I figured they had to store the finished guns somewhere before they sent them off. They had to store the ammunition somewhere, too, but maybe all that was in the test shack. The factory didn't make bullets.

I hadn't picked up any good information, except that I was sure I couldn't help Nigel blow the place up. The people in there were nice. I didn't want to hurt them. Still, I'd fired a gun. I'd gotten some sense of the power, and I definitely didn't want the people I saw in their nice clothes in church on Sunday making them. They probably didn't make the connection with dead bodies and blown-off legs, but I did.

"Charlie, I'm going to help close this place."

Charlie bounced a peanut off my head.

"What? I thought she gave up on that shit."

"Maybe she did," I said. "But Nigel..."

"You're going to join up with that bulge-eyed, peanut-blowing, fucking freak? He's crazy, and so are you if you think you're going to close this place. There's nobody in town who don't have a brother, or a mother, or somebody working here."

He looked at the ground. There was a bottle cap melted into the tar by his safety boot. He reached into his pocket for another peanut.

"Itchy, we got to stick together. We got to beat Donaghy in that race. We got to win this war. Don't be against us. The war's good, and so's the factory."

"It was something else killed Patrick," I said. "Not the communists, but a bad way of thinking, and this factory has something to do with that bad way of thinking. I know Nigel's crazy, but I've got to do something."

"It's going to make us enemies," Charlie said. "I can't let you do it."

"You can't stop me."

"Yes, I can." He tapped me on the cheek. "Charlie meets any challenge."

"Except shooting peanuts."

"I'll shoot one to Jupiter," he said. "You'll see."

We both laughed, but then it ended, and we were staring at each other in the parking lot, and Charlie's face looked scared, and I imagined mine did, too. We'd never been on opposite sides of something important before.

12

Robin and I didn't sleep in the same bed, but every night she slid into my sleeping bag. She took endless showers first and came with wet hair, shiny cheeks, and powder thick on the hairs between her legs, so that it puffed like a sugary doughnut when I touched her. Her skin was always moist. Her muscles were hard. Her breath was full of toothpaste and marijuana. Her tongue tasted of wine. Her lips were thick and wet and smeared with lipstick. There was no place they wouldn't go. They were explorer's lips, and I was uncharted land.

She drank a lot. She ran the hotel by day. She held meetings with the staff, figured out the finances, lectured the maids on being thorough. The maids called her Miss Robin. They called me Mr. Itchy, or Itchy honey, and giggled when I went by.

At night Robin managed the bar. Sometimes she served drinks. Others she just drank. She would come to the doughnut shop late with some guy who looked too old for her, or too young, or stupid, or ugly. She liked men with scars and strange sideburns and twisted noses and broken veins in their cheeks. She would drink with them, tease them, then leave them.

Sometimes she met Suzanne there. Those were my favorite nights. Suzanne would sit with her eyes wide open, shaking her head at all Robin's adventures, and I would love Suzanne so much it hurt, but I would love Robin, too.

She told Suzanne about wandering London and Liverpool and Hamburg and other places that sounded dreary and dangerous and romantic after she left Nigel. She told about moving on when Nigel showed up, like he always did, and heading for New York and Greenwich Village, and her years of tequila and artists and drunken saxophone players. She told about roaming the streets with Vincent, and then the time in 1960 when she was a prostitute for a while.

She talked about having sex in doorways and lofts and alleys and limousines and dirty back seats in Harlem, and her eyes glazed over with memories, while Suzanne held her hand.

They were supposed to meet there the night of June fourth, the night of the primary in California between Bobby Kennedy and Eugene McCarthy. It was exciting now with both against the war and Johnson deciding not to run. Robin liked Kennedy because she thought he could win. Suzanne liked McCarthy, and I didn't care, as long as one of them made it.

Suzanne was late, though. Robin kept staring at the clock and frowning, and it didn't cheer her up any when Nigel walked in and sat beside her.

"Hello, love," he said.

"It's arrived," she said.

"Yes, love, and it had a wonderful rally in the park today. Over two hundred people, and they're all asking about you."

Robin sipped on her tea. She'd poured something in it, but I didn't see what.

"Nigel, I'm meeting Suzanne. There must be a circus somewhere in need of a geek."

Nigel sat as close to her as he could. He dwarfed her.

"Listen, love, people are on my side on this, but I don't seem to get more than the most radical and absurd from this pathetic town. Perhaps I'm too intellectual for them."

Robin laughed. "Yeah, you're so intellectual, with all that whiskey drooling down your chin, that you alienate the normal people."

"Exactly," he said. "But you, love, have the power to explode this town. I've heard you. I've seen these kids watching you. They're brimming with hatred, love. I can't quite tap it, but you could set it blazing."

Irv walked in and took his normal seat. He immediately pulled out a dime, laid it on the counter, and gave me his best smile.

"Hi, Irv baby," Robin said.

Irv positively beamed. "Hey, what are you driving, bub?"

"I've still got my bike," she said.

"Used to drive a bike myself."

"How nice," Robin said. "Itchy, give Irv some hot coffee and the best doughnuts you can find."

"Still driving that bike?" Irv asked.

Nigel grabbed Robin's hand. "Listen," he said. "I know you want to do this, Robin, and I need you. People say they're with me, like your boyfriend here, but then I never see them again."

"I don't want to burn the place down," I said. "That's all you ever talk about. If Robin would do something, I would help, but I'm not helping you kill people."

"Nigel, leave," Robin said. "Go to Washington. Burn the White House, but leave Deadwhale, and forget this factory. So they make a few guns? It's nothing. Why work yourself up over nothing?"

She got up. Nigel reached for her again, but she slapped his hand away.

"I'll be in the bar, Itchy. Get me when Suzanne comes. I want to watch the news."

"Let me know when you find out who won," I said.

It was a long time before Suzanne showed up. Customers sucked cigarettes and frowned at their coffee. Nigel scribbled in a notebook. Irv whispered the names of cars.

"Hey, what are you driving?" he shouted as she walked in.

"He's taking a survey," I said, and then I got a look at her face. She had two black eyes, not as much black, though, as purple and blue, just these long streaks, as if someone had slapped her under each with a dirty paint brush. The whites were full of bloody lines. Her cheeks were bruised and scratched. Her lips were coated with dried blood and swollen twice their size. It just about broke my heart.

"What happened?" I whispered.

"A football injury."

"I didn't know you played football."

"Oh, yeah." She tried to smile, but it didn't work. "I'm Joe Namath."

"Was it Donaghy?"

"You work awfully late, Shovlin. Don't geniuses need fourteen hours sleep a night?"

Her voice cracked, and a few tears squeezed through her battered eyes. She lifted her huge bag onto the counter and started searching in it. She pulled out a shoe that had lost its heel, a shot glass, and some torn slivers of the photograph of her father on the beach, but didn't seem to find what she wanted, so she put everything back in the order she'd taken it out.

"You seeing Donaghy again?"

"It's the worst day of my life. This life, I mean. I seem to recall being raped by barbarians in Rome. That was worse." She tried smiling again. I wished she would give it up.

Nigel laughed. "Looks like they caught up with you again, love." His eyes absolutely devoured Suzanne.

"They're everywhere," she said. She sat and laid her head on the counter for a few seconds. Irv shouted over.

"Hey, what are you driving?"

"Pardon me?" she asked.

"You still driving that Buick?"

"No, it's a Volkswagon, actually, but I think it needs a tune-up. It turns off at red lights."

"It needs a tuna?"

"Leave her alone, my good man," Nigel said.

"A loan?" Irv asked. "I'll leave her a loan. How much, bub?" I pushed some coffee in front of Suzanne.

Nigel slid to the seat beside her. "Who were these barbarians, my friend?" he asked.

"Her car needs a tuna," Irv shouted. "I can get you a tuna cheap. You need a loan for that tuna, bub?"

Nigel stared across at Irv with eyes that narrowed into dangerous slits.

"Did Kennedy win?" I asked her. Robin hadn't come back with the news, and I thought it might be good to change the subject. I hated the way Nigel was leaning toward her. If he touched Suzanne, I was going to pour coffee on him.

Suzanne lifted her head. "Yeah, he won, but then somebody shot him, in the hotel, I think. In the kitchen, or something. I didn't catch it all. My radio keeps blinking on and off. I think there's a loose wire."

"What?" I barely got it out.

"A loose wire."

"I used to drive a Packard," Irv said. "Good car. No loose wires. Never needed a tuna. You need a loan, bub? You let me know."

I leaped over the counter and got in the spinning chair on the other side of her. I spun her around so she faced me. It hurt to look at her, and hovering behind her was Nigel's gigantic form. A vein beat hard in his temple, and sweat had broken out all over his face.

He was smiling.

"Is Kennedy dead?" I asked.

"I don't think so. I couldn't tune it in. He's on the floor in the kitchen or something. He's bleeding. Somebody shot him in the head, or the face. I'm not sure."

"Bobby Kennedy?"

"Yeah. Somebody shot Robert Kennedy. It kind of made me think of my father. They're killing Kennedys and Waters. They definitely killed my father. It's very complicated, though, and I don't understand how they work."

She lit a cigarette. Her eyes didn't seem focused. She just glanced at the far wall at a big water stain the color of rust and sucked deep drags on the cigarette. The overhead lights buzzed like crazy. Suzanne smelled like perfume and cigarettes, and I wanted to hold her.

"I got to get a radio," I said. "Maybe he'll be all right."

"You have to tell Robin," she said. "I don't have the heart."

"She probably knows. She's in the bar."

I turned her face toward me.

"Not about Kennedy," she said. "About Joe."

"What about him?"

The door between the doughnut shop and the bar burst open. Robin stood there in the light. Her face was soaked with tears.

She shouted. "Get away from her, Nigel."

Nigel sprang out of the chair.

"Leave." She pointed to the door.

"Certainly, love." But it took him a long time, and all the way to the door, he ran his eyes from Robin to Suzanne and back, still smiling, still sweating, that vein throbbing in his skull.

"Is it true?" I asked.

Robin slammed her hand against the counter. "Of course." She took Nigel's seat beside Suzanne. She touched her face. "What happened, baby?"

Suzanne wouldn't look at Robin. She stared down at the counter. "I didn't want to tell you."

Robin held Suzanne's hand. "It's all right."

Suzanne said, "We got word today. Joe's lost in action in Vietnam over a month now. I don't know why they waited so long to tell us. I don't want him to be dead. I know it's natural and we live and die over and over, but I have to stay here without him, and sometimes it gets lonely, and sometimes no matter how hard I try to keep it in perspective I get scared that this life is all we get, and everything's right out in the open, just the way it looks."

"You need a loan for that tuna, bub? A tuna's a good fish. I like a tuna. I like a herring. You need a herring?"

Robin just looked at her for the longest time. I thought it could be a dream. I was awfully tired. Some nights I barely got two hours sleep, but I was young, and I could take it, but I couldn't take Suzanne coming in with her face all cut and bruised telling me that Robert Kennedy was bleeding on a floor in California and that Joe Waters had disappeared in Vietnam. I couldn't take the way Robin's face fell slowly apart.

"I'm sorry, Robin," Suzanne said.

Robin backed to the door. It opened, and Nigel stood there. Robin looked at him. There was something in his eyes, something like love and sympathy and triumph all mixed together and burning. He held out his hand.

"Joe's dead," she whispered.

"You're cursed, love," Nigel said. She took his hand in both of hers.

"Yes," she said.

He pushed open the door with his shoulder and led her out into the night. He stared back at me once. His face was furious, just daring me to stop him. I felt like I'd been kicked, but then I looked at Suzanne.

She smoked a hundred cigarettes and cried a million tears, and the sun was crawling out of the ocean when she finally drove me back to the hotel. The car kept shutting off at the red lights, and Suzanne said, "I need a tuna," and laughed too long, and I had to sit with a hubcap and Suzanne's bag on my lap, and the radio kept cutting in and out, but we made it and rode the elevator together, and I loved Suzanne so much it hurt in my chest, but there was nothing I could say, and she wouldn't come in, so I left her in the hall, staring into her bag, as if maybe she could find Joe in there, or something besides broken shoes, old books, and tattered pieces of her father.

Vincent stood by the door, making his noise. He rubbed up against me. I picked him up. He hardly weighed a thing, and we'd become good friends the last few months. I'd spent a lot of time trying to teach him to roll over. It wasn't working very well, but it amused Robin.

He purred in my ear. The radio blared. I heard the word Kennedy a few times. The speaker buzzed and rattled. The words came all dis-

torted through her kitchen and banged off the walls. Robert
Kennedy. California. Blood. Robert Kennedy. Serious. Very serious.

Glass was scattered everywhere. The floor was wet, and the place
stank of wine. There wasn't a sign of Nigel, except some peanuts on
the floor, no sign of Robin, except the glass and the wine. I sat in the
middle of that noise. I didn't bother to turn it down. I wondered
how long it would take him to die, and then I heard Kennedy's voice
giving his victory speech, and then I was sleeping.

When I opened my eyes, Robin was still missing. The radio still
blared. They still talked about Kennedy. He wasn't dead. Vincent
kept rubbing against me and whining. I'd never known her to leave
him behind so long, so I found him some food, and then I yanked
the radio out of the wall and tossed it out her window. Once I heard
it crash into the street, I went looking for Robin.

I thought of going to Nigel's house, but then I saw her far down
the beach. I followed her a long way. She staggered a bit. She'd been
living on pot and booze. She stopped every so often, knelt down in
the sand, and dug into it with her fingers, picking things up, holding
them close to her eye. She followed the beach north toward King's
Port, then into the streets and to the cemetery at the edge of town
where they buried the Whales.

I caught up to her deep inside the cemetery. She was kneeling in
front of a stone and arranging a pile of sea shells on top of the grave.
The sun was hardly up. It made shadows from the headstone that
covered Robin and the shells and made it hard to read the name, but
I didn't have to read. I'd come there once.

It was the grave of Mayor Waters, and Robin knelt in front of it
moving shells around, cleaning sand out of them with her shirt,
blowing dust off them, picking them up and putting them down
again. She didn't make a design, or anything I could understand, but
eventually she seemed to have them the way she liked.

She ran her hand over his name for a while, and she turned and
saw me. She didn't look surprised, or scared. There was sand on her
hands, and some stuck to her face where she must have been crying.

"So now you know," she said.

"What?" I whispered.

"Why I came to Deadwhale."

"You loved his father?"

"I killed his father," she said.

13

Robin fell into the grass. Sweat drenched her shirt, and I couldn't wake her. She mumbled things I didn't understand, and when I tried to open her eyes, she twisted and hissed at me. I carried her home on my back. I unbuttoned her clothes and laid her over the covers with a cool towel on her head. She whispered Vincent's name, so I carried the cat in beside her. She touched him. She smiled and fell asleep for a long time, and he crawled up onto her stomach and purred until he was sleeping, too.

It was Wednesday, and I had school. I thought of cutting. I was dead tired, and there were only a few days till graduation, but I decided to go. I wanted to hear everyone's reaction. Robin was asleep, and I wanted to get away from her and think about what she'd said at Mayor Waters' grave. Of course, I didn't believe it.

It was a terrible day. We waited for word, but Kennedy made it through Wednesday. Our teachers seemed sad. Some of the students cried. Some didn't care. Some made jokes, and I remembered hearing about how down South, kids in school cheered when President Kennedy got killed. It made me furious to remember that.

When I got home, I found Robin on the bathroom floor. Vomit spread from the toilet. Her face was down in it. Her hands were thick with it. I cleaned it off her cheeks and out from under her hair. I held her face under the spigot. She could hardly stand.

"Passed out," she said. "Throwing up so hard. Everything spinning."

When I got her clean, I undressed her. Her underpants were

bloody. Her skin was soaked.

"Is he dead?" she whispered. "Is he dead?"

"Not yet."

I got her back in the bed. She was having her period, and I didn't know what to do about it, so I just put some towels under her and sat there wiping her down and forcing her to drink water. She kept spitting it out.

I didn't go to school Thursday or Friday, or open Hot 'n Krispy all weekend. I handled the calls from Robin's bartenders and told them to close the bar till they got word.

Kennedy took twenty hours to die. An Arab named Sirhan Sirhan had shot him. I stared at the picture in the *New York Times*, Kennedy down on the floor of the hotel, his shirt open, his head turned to the right, a man feeling his pulse. His brother had been shot less than five years before.

I called Suzanne over and over to see if she'd heard anything about Joe, but all I got was her mother, and when I mentioned Suzanne, the phone went dead. I sat beside Robin. I tried willing Suzanne to come over, but I couldn't, no matter how hard I closed my eyes and concentrated.

I set Robin's television up in her bedroom and stayed with her. Her fever went up and down. Sometimes she would talk, and sometimes she would whisper and squirm on the bed. She threw up constantly. There wasn't much to it, just the water I kept pouring into her, but she heaved and twisted and hacked out the spit.

I carried her to the bathroom once or twice an hour. I stayed in there with her, so she wouldn't fall on the floor. She called me "Nigel." She called me "Momma," and "Joe," and once she smiled and said, "I love you, Bob," and started crying. She cried so hard, she choked. I held onto her. I'd never felt anyone so hot in my life.

I was afraid to leave her or call a doctor. I was afraid she would tell him she'd killed Mayor Waters. She kept whispering about rain and lightning. She said something about a flood. Once she bolted upright and shouted, "Robert," at the top of her voice, then fell off the bed and started crawling toward the bathroom, whispering, "Vincent. Vincent. It's falling. The wheel. It's going to kill us all."

And then she started with the neighbor. The last day, all day, she kept whispering, "The neighbor's coming. He's calling me. He wants me, Itchy. The neighbor wants me."

"Who's the neighbor?"

"The man with white hair, the neighbor, he wants me."

Saturday night she cooled off awhile. She rolled up against me. "I promised Joe I wouldn't protest," she said. "He said if I protested he wouldn't see me, and I promised." And she drifted off again, and soon she was soaked, and her eyes moved fast under the closed lids, and she whispered, "Who's the neighbor? I'm not ready."

I couldn't get food into her. I hardly ate. I just lay beside her, staring at the television. I couldn't believe Kennedy was dead. I couldn't believe Joe was lost. I couldn't believe that Robin had known Mayor Waters and claimed she'd killed him.

I remembered it well. He was the kind of hero I liked, a man like John Kennedy, handsome and smart and loved, who died young. I was convinced Mayor Waters would have transformed Deadwhale and gone on to become president, and I'd read all about him.

There were rumors, lots of rumors, but no evidence, none whatsoever of murder. It's true, his head was smashed, and his body was battered, but he'd fallen off the wharf, and the raging water had slammed him against the boards underneath. It was the kind of damage Robin couldn't have done. The case was closed. The mayor had made a mistake. Maybe he was drunk, but he hadn't been murdered.

I wouldn't ask her about it. She didn't know what she was saying, and I didn't want to know. I had few illusions left. One was that Mayor Waters was a great man. Another was that Robin was good.

On Sunday morning, she was gone when I woke up. I bolted upright and saw her in the middle of the room, naked, staring at her palms with this shocked look, as if she'd just landed here. Her eyes were hollowed out and dark. I could see her ribs.

"Is Kennedy dead?" she said.

"Yeah. He died Thursday."

"And Joe?"

"Missing in action."

Robin looked old and tired and so sad I could hardly stand it.

"How long I been in bed?"

"It's Sunday morning. You feel better?"

"Like I've been to hell and back."

"Are you cool?"

"Listen, Itchy. I don't know what I said. I was having bad dreams, but you got to forget. Everything I said, everything from when Suzanne told me about Joe until now. I was in a bad state. I was drinking too much. I was smoking. Nothing I said meant anything."

Then she narrowed her glance and stared at me.

"You understand? Nothing."

"You didn't say anything," I said.

She picked up a towel and wrapped it around herself. She got beside me in the bed and started talking. It was a long story, and it was sad, and when it was over, I thought I might be falling in love with Robin.

She talked about June of '52 when her mother was gone over ten years, and Robin was barely fifteen, and her father had just returned from his second war. His name was Paul Debussy. He had joined in '41, three days after Pearl Harbor, and fought hand to hand with Japanese on the tiny islands in the Pacific. Now he was a major, just back from fighting Chinese in Korea. He was in his late thirties now and a hero, and he had come to his father's big house a few miles outside Newark to celebrate.

Her voice trembled when she mentioned him. Her breath smelled like tears.

"He thought he was hot," she said. "He wore his uniform to the party and all the crummy medals for having the shiniest shoes on earth. Ben and I, that's his brother, called him Major Spit Shine because all he ever did was spit in his can of polish, spread it on his boots, and blow his boozy breath on them. He drank like a pig.

"God I loved Ben. He was at the party. He was only eighteen, but he was mature, like you. He made up stories about my mother for me, love stories about her and a Mexican who posed for her, and he taught me about jazz, and he read poetry by Dylan Thomas and watched birds and made calls just like them, but he was skinny and terribly shy and clumsy beside my father.

"He thought he was ugly 'cause he wore glasses, but he had beautiful blonde hair and this little beard, like some beatnik poet."

Robin smiled while she talked about Ben. She smiled and stared at the ceiling and held tight to my hand. She talked about school and the kids who made fun of her accent, Jersey kids from the borders of New York City, tough kids who smoked cigarettes too young.

The boys liked the Yankees and the Rangers, and Robin hated the boys. They made her feel like a hick. She practiced talking like a Jersey girl, picking up the tough, east-coast lingo with hard, short, spit words instead of the slow, singing drawl of her grandparents. She tried talking like her father. She tried talking like Ben.

By the time her father got back from Korea, Robin had the talk down. She had her own accent, mostly New Jersey, but with some Texas thrown in. She still hated the other kids and liked ignoring the boys now that they were paying a lot of attention to her. Ben was her only friend.

He had a tent by the lake a few hundred feet from his father's house, and during summer and most of the spring and fall, he lived out there, reading, burning a fire at night, watching birds.

She noticed he wouldn't spend time with her like he used to, and he seemed nervous. She wondered if she'd gotten ugly, or if she smelled bad, or if he had a girlfriend. She worried about him, and she got jealous, and before long she was thinking about him all the time. One day she realized she loved him, and not like an uncle at all.

A paperback book bulged from his back pocket that night while he tried mixing with the old friends, the neighbors, and drunken uncles who swarmed around Robin's father calling him Major, getting his opinions on the war and Eisenhower and all the crap he seemed to be an expert on.

Ben was old enough to enlist now, and people expected it, but he didn't know what to do. He liked reading and watching birds. His grades weren't very good, and he didn't really want to go to college, but he would have to decide something that summer. Robin was going to him when one of the relatives asked when he would join up.

"Time's running out," the man said.

"I was thinking I wouldn't," Ben said. "Eisenhower's going to end it. No point in getting shot now."

"If you're a coward, just say it," Major Debussy said.

"I ain't a coward. I just think it's stupid."

The major said, "You sit around carving ducks while the red chinks chew up guys your own age, then you have the guts to call it stupid. That's great, Benny."

"You think we'll win if I join, Paul?"

"That's not the point, Benny. The point is you're either a coward, or you're not. If you're not, you go to Korea and prove it. If you are, you shut up."

Ben stood up straighter than usual and imitated his brother.

"The point is, Paul, you're either an asshole, or you're not. If you're not, then shut up and quit proving you are."

Major Debussy threw a glass of whiskey into Ben's face. Ben took a wild swing and missed, and the major slammed him against a wall. Ben slipped down along the wall. Robin got to him first.

"Keep your hands off him, little girl," the major said.

"I ain't no little girl." Her father pulled her away, then picked up a chair and threw it. She ran, looked back once, and saw Ben stirring on the floor, her father's face all twisted and red, the guests watching in silence, the chair broken on the floor.

A while later she watched from her window as Ben headed for the woods. She wanted to follow, but didn't dare, not yet. She slept a little. She dreamt of trains and burning beds, of Mexicans sobbing by the tracks, of a snake throbbing and hissing and spitting up blood and insects.

Her father chased her through battlefields. She ran over arms and eyes and clumps of hair, and her father threw her to the dirt in a field of bursting shells. He ripped at her clothes. He tore her with his teeth and nails.

She saw her mother painting on the tracks, the train bearing down on her, Robin's father driving the train. It hit. Her mother shredded like canvas.

She woke freezing in sweat every few minutes and imagined Ben alone in a tent, hacking on wood with his penknife. And she felt lonely. She had always been so lonely, except with him.

That morning she got up early. It was warm, and she took the path toward the lake, beyond her grandfather's backyard, that hid behind a patch of woods about a hundred yards from the house. She found his tent with the sleeping bag pulled outside onto the dirt and grass. A book by Charles Darwin lay on the sleeping bag.

At the lake, she found Ben's sneaks, his tattered dungarees, and his underwear in a pile. His glasses lay on top of his T-shirt. She laughed when she saw him floating naked on his back thirty yards out. She heard him splashing and making duck calls, and she thought about his body under the water and felt sick and nervous, and something tingled high between her legs.

He still hadn't seen her. He was too busy flipping over and diving to the bottom. She pulled off her shoes and sweater.

"Well hell, Ben. You sound like Daffy Duck, honey."

He stared to the shore.

"Who's that?"

"Marilyn Monroe."

"Robin? What are you doing out here?"

He squinted and paddled.

"I'm fixing to come in."

"Don't be crazy. I ain't got clothes on."

"So what. I'll take mine off, too."

Robin undid her bra.

"It wouldn't be so terrible if somebody saw you, would it?" she asked.

He swam closer, but stayed far enough so she could see only his head through the murky water.

"At least get my pants. Then if you get lost a few minutes, I could meet you. I got books I could show you."

"You'll run away," she said. "You always ignore me."

"I'm just busy," he said.

"You were never so busy before."

Ben didn't answer. He flipped over, went under, then swam in the opposite direction. Robin unbuttoned her shirt. She dropped it and slid off her bra and everything else.

"What do you think, anyhow?" she shouted.

"About what?"

"About me?"

"What about you?"

"Am I okay? I know they're not that big, but compared to some girls my age, they're not so bad."

He swam in, stopped, then swam in the other direction, kicking like crazy, raising a storm of water. Halfway across, he looked back.

"You want to get me arrested? Put your clothes on and get my pants. If your father caught you like that, he'd..."

"I hate him," she said, "And I'm fixing to come in."

"Robin, please."

Robin ran into the water, fell under, and started swimming. After a few feet, she splashed and called for help. She laughed when he caught her and started dragging her toward shore.

"I tricked you," she said.

"Oh, hell."

"It's freezing."

She tried to kiss him. He threw her away, but she swam back and pressed her lips all over his face until he couldn't help laughing, and they were laughing and dunking each other when Robin's father called from the edge.

"Come on in, Robin. You too, Ben."

Ben threw her away from him. Robin walked slowly onto the stones at the edge of the lake, trying to cover up with her arms.

"It wasn't his fault," she said.

Her father kept his eyes on the water. Ben stayed in, about ten feet from shore.

"You getting out, Benny?" the major asked.

"I ain't wearing no clothes."

"Put your clothes on, Robin," the major said.

As she bent for her shirt, she heard splashing and saw him wade out to his brother like MacArthur returning to the Phillipines.

She shouted, "He didn't do anything."

But her father pulled Ben by the hair. Ben was as tall as Major Debussy, but skinny and not very strong, and Paul Debussy dragged him to the shore, then hit him in the face with an elbow. Ben fell into the water. His brother waded after him. He made Ben stand. He hit him some more, then led him to the shore again. Ben coughed and spit water and said please once and glanced at Robin, and Robin's father lifted Ben to his feet, kicked him between the legs, then kicked him backward as he fell.

Ben collapsed in the shallow water at the edge and lay quietly moaning, clutching his groin, blood and mucus pouring from his nose, his face half-buried in mud and ooze.

Robin's father pulled her by the sleeve toward the house. She had to run to keep up. He stopped and looked into her eyes when they cleared the woods.

"It wasn't his fault," she said.

"You're a whore like your mother," he said. "She fucked Mexicans, and you'll fuck niggers before you're old enough to drive."

"If she was such a whore, why'd you marry her?"

"Because she was pregnant. She was a little Texan slut who came to New York looking for museums of art. Museums my ass. First college boy she hooked up with, she dropped her pants and moaned like a fucking cat.

"Her mother was a whore, too, and I don't mean your grandmother in Texas. That wasn't her mother. Your grandfather came to New York once, just like his stupid daughter. It seems to attract certain types, and he got himself some half-Irish, half-Chinese bitch from the streets, and being the hick he was, he fell in love. She was a prostitute, and she had his baby and broke his heart, and he went home with the baby and married his high school sweetheart, and they raised your mother.

"Who knows what the hell happened to her real mother? I'm not interested in your family tree. All I know is your mother was a stupid woman with big dreams who got herself pregnant with the wrong man."

"So how'd she get pregnant?" Robin shouted. "By an act of God? You pig."

"Shut up," he said. "Maybe I felt sorry for her. She didn't have any money. She didn't have nice clothes, and she gave me this line about looking for her mother and looking to study art, and she had that pretty face and that little accent that makes me puke when it comes out of your mouth, and I didn't know any of this crap about your mother's tainted lineage until long after we were married."

"Tainted lineage?"

"That's right, honey. Bad enough she was a slow-thinking hick from Texas, but at least you couldn't see the chink, but I can see it in you, and you're just as big a whore as your grandmother was. I've been fighting Chinese and Koreans, and before that it was Japs, and to have a daughter with slanted eyes splashing around naked with my faggot brother makes me sick.

"You're my daughter, and I'm an officer in the U. S. Marines, so I have no choice but to provide for you, but stay out of my sight, so I don't have to hear your shitty Texas twang and remember what a slant-eyed whore you are."

"I don't talk like that anymore," she said.

"It's there," he said.

"You should have died over there," she said.

He spit on her. Robin sat on the curb while the spit rolled off her nose and down into her mouth, and she watched her father walk away. She wiped off the spit. She wanted to go back to Ben. They'd left him bleeding in the water, and he'd been making duck sounds just a few minutes before, and she was an eighth Chinese. She was a quarter whore. That sounded funny. A quarter whore. She almost laughed.

That night, she couldn't sleep. She felt hot all over, all anger and adrenaline. She rolled around. She lay on her stomach and felt the sheets like skin up against her. Her heart wouldn't slow down. There was something beautiful about him. She saw him lying on the water, holding onto himself. She wanted to touch him. She wanted to hold him. She wanted to press his skin like the sheets against her. She felt that tingling high inside her. She touched herself, and she was wet and warm, and it felt good, so good she could hardly believe it. She had to find Ben.

She slid on one of her mother's old nightgowns. She fit all her mother's clothes. She put a long sweater over that. She tied her sneakers and headed out. It was late, but she smelled his fire, good and sharp. The woods glowed around the flames.

He stared at her when she stepped into the clearing. She saw the fire in his glasses. He sat outside the tent with his legs folded on the sleeping bag. The fire cracked and flicked sparks and turned his skin orange.

"I thought maybe you'd be lonely," she said.

He just stared. Shadows jumped on his face as the fire rose and fell. His right eye was swollen under the glasses, and his lip was cut.

She stood at the edge of his clearing on the other side of the fire.

"Why don't you take off your glasses, Ben?"

He kept staring, his face blank, silent. He threw the glasses into the tent. She stepped closer to the fire. It flashed in his eyes.

"You're handsome," she said. "More handsome than him. He thinks he's great 'cause he's killed people, but you're better. I hope he didn't hurt you."

"What do you want?"

"I couldn't sleep. I'm sorry. I didn't mean to get you in trouble. I felt funny and lonely, and he says my grandmother was a whore."

Ben shrugged. "He's an asshole."

"Well, maybe I'll be a whore, too," she said.

"Go home."

"No."

"You're just a kid."

"Is that why you hardly talk to me?"

"I talk to you."

"Not like you used to."

"I'm out here a lot."

Robin looked at his eyes. They were fires now. She wondered if he could feel what she felt. She wondered if he could hear her heart. Only the fire stood between them. It hurt her legs. She was burning up.

"Don't you like me anymore, Ben?"

"Sure I like you."

"Don't you think I'm pretty?"

"Yeah, sure. You've been around so long, I'm used to you."

She dropped the sweater, then started on the nightgown. Her fingers trembled over the buttons. She unbuttoned it to her waist.

"We can get even," she whispered.

Ben stood. "You're crazy."

Robin stepped backward. Ben looked at her for a long time before he kicked out the fire. Dirt flew into the air. Sparks and twigs and stones hit her legs, and he crossed the fire and dragged her. He threw her toward the sleeping bag, then pushed her down on top of it. She hit hard. She gasped when he came down.

"I hate his guts," he said, and ripped the frilly cloth from her breasts.

"Don't hurt me," she whispered. "Don't." His hand ran up her leg, and when he kissed her, his mouth bled from his beating, and the blood came into hers with his tongue, and she could taste it, and everything changed inside her.

She was lost, and when he pulled the nightgown over her legs and left her naked except her sneakers, she begged, "Don't stop, never stop," and she gasped at the night with her mouth open, sighing and calling his name and staring at the black sky, and it hurt, and she didn't care, and she heard a rustling and saw a dark figure move over Ben. She heard a thud, and Ben twisted away from her.

She rolled to her side and saw her father push Ben's head against a tree and keep hitting the head against the tree, and it happened in seconds, Ben falling with blood running from his ears, Ben unconscious and her father kicking. Robin threw herself at her father. She hit him so fast and hard and unexpectedly, that he tripped over Ben, and they fell to the ground.

She grabbed his hair and bit down into his ear and all the way through it. Her mouth filled with blood. Her teeth clicked. He hit her stomach. The ear came loose. He threw her across the darkness at the tent. Her nose and eye hit together, the nose breaking against the hard dirt and a tent spike rising through the eye into her head.

Robin looked at me. I held her wet body close.

"That's how I lost my eye." She was whispering. "That's why my nose has this bump."

"You have a beautiful nose," I said. "And a beautiful eye."

"Ben wrote me a letter from Korea," she said. "I guess he joined the army to prove something. Who knows, but it was a love letter. He fell in love with me when I was fourteen. That's why he avoided me so much."

"Did you see him after the war?"

"Oh, no. Ben disappeared, too, just like my mother. Maybe he's with her now, but I never heard from him again. Now Joe's gone."

She kissed my cheek. "You're a good friend."

"You, too," I said.

She smiled. "It's so hard to surrender."

"Don't," I said.

"No," she said. She lifted her cat to her face. "Of course not."

14

So it began again. She was on the streets that afternoon, pale, thin, weak, and furious. By the end of the week, she'd been to every corner of Deadwhale. She didn't eat. She hardly slept. She ignored the bar and the hotel. She left the doughnut shop to me. She drank wine at night. She studied papers and magazines and everything she could find about the war. She memorized maps of Deadwhale. She smoked pot before bed. She came to my sleeping bag and made wild love, grunting and screaming, grabbing my ears, pulling my hair, slapping my shoulders. Sometimes I thought she was trying to kill me.

She could hardly speak. She could hardly walk. Instead, she shouted, she hissed, she ran. She ripped buttons putting on shirts, smashed the tops off bottles of wine rather than mess with a corkscrew. She pulled a knob off her television, broke the handle on her toilet, dropped a bottle of aspirin and left the glass on the kitchen floor.

She knocked on doors in Fishtown and Little Brooklyn with Vincent purring and drooling on her shoulder. She told housewives and sleepy factory workers we had to close the factory. When they slammed the door in her face, she banged again. If they didn't come back, she shouted through open windows, pressing her face against the screen, blackening her nose with tiny grids of dirt.

She stood on benches in the parks, Nigel right beside her, shouting at passing crowds, cursing with the men who tried to shout her down. She used filthy language. Women slapped her. Kids pumped their fists and said, "Yeah." Men spit on her, then had to face the wrath of Nigel, who came close to killing a few.

She visited Southwest Deadwhale and King's Port on the same day. She made friends. She got promises. She got slapped, punched, doused with tea, circled by dogs, lectured, chased, knocked over by a car. She limped out of King's Port only to go back the next day and the day after.

She rode a bike with fat tires from neighborhood to neighborhood. She walked the crowded streets of the southwest slums, banging against the black people, shouting at them, giving speeches on corners while they swore and laughed at her. The men whistled. Women yanked her by the hair, but slowly she won them over.

She formed an alliance with Coke Phillips. He was a lawyer, but he'd quit his practice awhile back and set up an organization called The Black Whale. It was dedicated to the liberation of Deadwhale's black population. He told her seven blacks from Deadwhale were in Vietnam, two had died there, and none had been written up in the paper. She told him that was another reason to shut the factory, to fight the war, to oppose the Donaghys. He agreed to give her his full support.

I graduated in mid-June. The next day, *The Deadwhale Lighthouse* published a letter by Robin Debussy and Dennis Shovlin. It was a furious letter, mostly by Robin, but I'd done the actual handwriting, and I'd helped her clean it up and make it more coherent.

It attacked Mayor Donaghy for exploiting the war, the people of Deadwhale for complacency, *The Lighthouse* for editorial cowardice and racism. She claimed to represent an organization called Whales for Peace, and on the top of the letter, she drew a whale balancing a dove on a spout of water.

The final paragraph appealed to the people of Deadwhale to "turn against this filthy war," to get behind Robin, to march on the factory with her on July third.

Next she printed circulars with an attack on Donaghy's failure to hire black workers, on the low wages he paid, the long hours he required, the guns he turned out. She told me to get them into the factory through Charlie or my father. She didn't ask.

When Charlie told me to stuff it, I had to try my father. He worked sixty-eight hours a week. He'd come to Deadwhale for fun in the summer of '45, leaving behind his friends, his family, and his Phillies. He'd come skinny and short-haired, with a year of high school left, and he was still here, two wars on and one son down.

He'd never finished high school.

I'd only been home three times since moving out. My father had been working or sleeping every time, but one Sunday near the end of June, I sat in the kitchen with my mother.

She looked tired and old and much too thin. I'd seen pictures from the wedding, my mom and dad getting out of some shiny old car in Philadelphia. I'd seen pictures of her on the beach the summer they'd met. I'd seen pictures of her in the middle row with lots of other girls in Catholic high school with her hands folded on the desk and September 1943 written on a blackboard at the back of the room.

She had big white teeth. She was the prettiest girl in the picture, but now her hair was thin and slashed with gray, and I couldn't imagine her as a girl in a desk or in a bathing suit. I couldn't see it at all.

We talked in the kitchen where Patrick and I used to wash dishes. She talked while she cooked. She looked at me too much. She was thinking I looked like Patrick. We both had blue eyes and thin faces and hair the color of wet sand and freckles on our noses and clefts in our chins, and now I was nearly as old as when he'd died. I couldn't look in the mirror without thinking of Patrick.

"You running?" she asked.

"Of course, Mom. How else am I going to beat Donaghy?"

"You think you can do it?"

"I don't know. He's so good, but I've been using a stopwatch, and I'm not too far off his times."

"Charlie says he's going to beat him."

"Charlie's too big and clumsy. Plus he doesn't have any strategy."

"Maybe your father should run," she said. "He's lost sixty pounds since you left."

"That's good," I said. "He can get through doors without turning sideways."

"It's not good how he's losing it. He barely eats."

"So you'll save on groceries. Maybe you can buy a new car."

Silverware clattered on the linoleum.

"Shit," she whispered.

"Watch your language, Mom. That's a venal sin."

"Venial," she said. "And don't be telling me about language, Itchy. I've heard that girlfriend of yours."

"She's not my girlfriend. Where'd you hear her?"

"Everyone's heard her. She's famous. Daddy's even gone to see her. He came home and broke things." She laughed. It was a nice musical sound that I hadn't heard in a while.

"Does she make you mad?" I asked.

"She makes me sick," she said. "Sick of this lousy war, sick of this lousy government. I don't care about her mouth."

"You think we should close the factory?"

"I like to eat, Itchy, but sometimes you have to think about other things. Maybe your soul."

She pointed an empty pot at me.

"Don't get me wrong. I'm not against her, and it's a shame we make our living off the war that killed Patrick, but I'm not marching in demonstrations, and I'm not letting Daddy know how I think the girl might be right, but if you get past her silly clothes and the make-up around her eyes and that poor sick cat, she makes sense.

"I don't know why she don't wear shoes, or why she has to be so rude, but when I hear her, I feel strong. I feel like she understands, and she helps me know who to hate."

"You didn't know who to hate?"

"No, and your father still don't, and that's why he's losing weight. He's a big man, but inside he's a boy who lost a best friend, and he's scared to lose another."

"You mean bonehead?"

"I mean Charlie. They can't talk, and when they do it's a fight."

"I can't get through to him," I said. "His head's full of muscle from all those push-ups."

She pulled up a chair. She laid the pot between us, a big old rusted thing with a screw coming out at the handle.

"I found these," she said. She laid two pills on the table. They were tiny and orange.

"What are they?" I asked.

"I found them in Charlie's shirt along with a bunch of peanuts. He's acting strange."

"What's new about that?"

"He's always doing weird stuff with peanuts. I caught him putting one in his nose once. He acted like he didn't, but I know he had a peanut in his nose."

I laughed, but my mother didn't think it was so funny.

"Your brother's putting peanuts in his nose, Itchy. I don't see the humor."

I explained about Nigel and Charlie's tragic failure to shoot a peanut more than six inches.

She smiled. "Well, he's always been one for a challenge, but there's other things bothering me. That's the second time I found pills. I thought maybe they were for football, to make his muscles big, and didn't say anything.

"Sometimes he's up all night. Sometimes he talks to himself. Sometimes he talks to Patrick. His eyes look funny, too, and he looks at me like he don't know me, and other times he's too affectionate, and once he called me Suzanne. Does he have a girlfriend named Suzanne?"

"He's got this thing for Suzanne Waters, but hell's going to freeze before she's his girlfriend."

"Could it be LSD?"

"Come on, Mom. Charlie's no hippie. I mean, at most he might smoke some grass."

"He smokes marijuana?" Her eyes were huge. She squeezed the broken pot handle.

I shrugged. "A little, I guess. Everybody does."

She stared into my eyes.

"And you?"

I looked down at the table. Her fingers around the handle were chapped and red. I thought about lying, but I'd never caught her lying to me, and it wasn't such a big deal to smoke it anyway. It wasn't like murdering people with an axe, or dropping napalm on them so their skin fried.

"I've tried it," I said.

"Oh, Jesus, Itchy."

"I don't do it anymore."

One tear rolled from each of her eyes. I just sat there, wishing I'd lied.

We ate lasagne with salad and garlic bread, but I hardly tasted the food. We took our old seats, except Patrick's was empty, and it left a gigantic hole. I remembered the day he told us he was joining the marines, and nobody talked the whole time we ate. Patrick was almost a man. Charlie was huge, and the table could barely hold us. But that was all past, and now I watched my father eat. He'd lost an awful lot of weight. He might have looked good if his face didn't sag so much. His hair had turned nearly white, but he still had his crew cut, and that made me happy.

"Your hair looks awful," he said. "Like Paul McCartney."

"So does yours," I said. "Like Westmoreland."

"He's a good man," Charlie said.

"Who?" I asked.

"General Westmoreland."

"He's a moron," I said.

"Don't fight," my mother said. "You both don't know Westmoreland from Adam."

"Who's Adam?" Charlie asked.

"The first man," I said.

"Oh. He had that Eve chick, right?" Charlie said.

"Right," I said, "But then he ate an apple, and God kicked him out of heaven."

"Was it God's favorite apple or something?" Charlie asked.

"You're both very funny," she said.

My father poked some lasagne with his fork. He'd hardly eaten a thing.

"Listen, Itchy," he said. "When you're done making fun of the Bible, I got to talk to you."

"He's a heretic," Charlie said. "We should burn him at the stake. I could get some wood from the yard."

"You're no better," my mother said.

"Burn us both at the stake," I said.

"I want my own stake," Charlie said.

"They're both smart-asses," my father said. "Now listen, Itchy. We got invited to something on July fourth, and I want you to come."

His eyes were small and gray, like tiny animals staring out of holes in the ground. I was afraid I would scare them off if I looked back too long.

"What is it?"

"They're having a service for Patrick," my mother said.

"Not a service, a ceremony," my father said. "And not just for Patrick, for that Keating kid, too, the one who got killed last month. They're putting their names on the monument because they're the first boys from Deadwhale to die in the war."

"There's two others," I said.

"There ain't no others," he said.

"Didn't you read Robin's letter?" I asked.

"No I didn't read that damned letter, and I understand your name was on it, too."

"She wrote it," I said. "I don't know why she put my name on there. Besides, what's it matter?"

"It matters 'cause I work with people who didn't appreciate that letter."

Charlie had a cheek full of food the size of a football and another gob on his fork, but he managed to say, "It was a stupid letter anyway. What's that little freak know about the war? She dresses like that Charlie Chaplin guy. All she needs is a little mustache."

"At least she doesn't look like a goon from outer space, like you," I said.

"Cut it out," my mother said. "Nobody looks like a goon from outer space."

"Except Charlie," I said.

She looked at my father. "Two colored kids from the southwest slums died over there."

My father swallowed a glass of wine. His face got red in a hurry.

"So what? I didn't plan the damned thing. If some colored kids got killed, they should let their parents in the ceremony, too.

"But that's not what we're talking about. We're talking about Mayor Donaghy calling me himself and saying he wants us on that stage with him. The Keatings will be there, too, but since Patrick was first, they want me to say something, some little speech, and I want you there."

"Oh, man," I said. "It's going to be some big all-American show."

"It's the least you can do," Charlie said. "Besides, think of all the chicks that'll see us. They like guys with dead brothers."

"Is that all you ever think of, Charlie?"

"Yeah, mainly, and football. What do you think about, Einstein? Equations, or something?"

"You'll go, won't you?" my mother asked.

"I don't know, Mom."

My father shouted. "What do you mean, you don't know?"

"I just don't know," I said.

"Well you better know," he said. "This is for Patrick."

"This ain't for Patrick. It's for the Donaghys," I said. "They make machine guns. They want the war to last forever, so they put this July fourth crap on, and get everybody behind the war, and he keeps selling guns.

"Where was he when Patrick got killed? Did he call you then? Did he stop by? Mayor Waters would've, but Donaghy waited till it was to his advantage. He's using Patrick to turn people against Robin. Don't you see?"

He slammed the table with his fist. "All I see is they're going to honor Patrick, and you won't come because you've let this little Robin creep turn your head. What the hell's wrong with you? You know that factory means a lot to me. You know what it means to this town. I asked you to stay away from that woman, and the first thing you do is move in with her and try to cost me my job, and now when they try to honor Patrick for doing his duty, you act like they're asking us to spit on his grave."

"Oh, so now it was Patrick's duty to die in Vietnam," I said. "Well, where is it, Dad? Where's Vietnam, and why the hell was it Patrick's duty to die there?"

His breath came in heavy jerks. My mother laid a hand on his wrist.

"Sit down, honey."

He wouldn't take his eyes off me.

"All right, Dad," I said. "I'll make a deal. I'll stand there and let Donaghy make fools of us. I'll let him use us to sell guns and make himself look real good and holy and patriotic and win lots of votes, but you got to do something for me. Robin had some stuff printed, and she wants to get it in the factory. It's against the war, and it's against the factory. You take it in..."

"No." He slammed the table again. My mother held his arm, but he yanked free.

"I'll have nothing to do with that woman. Nothing. She's stupid, and I won't help her steal my job."

I closed my eyes. I took a few deep breaths.

"Did it ever occur to you maybe just for one second that she might be right?" I asked. "Could it be that just maybe it's wrong to make guns to kill people we don't even know just 'cause somebody tells us to? Isn't it possible the war's wrong?"

"No," he said, trying to hold his voice down, but still red and standing with his fist clenched.

"Why?" my mother asked.

He turned at her. His eyes flared up. His breath came in hard wheezes. He grabbed his glass of wine. He stared at it. His hands shook so much the wine sloshed over the side. He tried to take a sip, spilled it on his face, then threw the glass against the wall.

"Because, Anna, I will not, I will never believe, until the day I die, that Patrick died for nothing. Never."

"He did," I said. "He died for nothing." And before I could move, before I could turn or try to avoid him, Charlie lunged across the table. He pushed me backward, then threw the table on me.

The back of my chair broke. I fell on the floor with the glass and the food and the dishes that shattered and spilled around me. He grabbed my hair and pulled me across the floor. I shouted, "He died for nothing. He didn't know any better. Nothing. Nothing."

My mother screamed at Charlie, but he didn't let go until my father said, "Stop," and then I was free. I stared through tears at my brother. He stared through tears at me.

"Don't say that, Itchy. Okay? Don't say Patrick died for nothing."

His lips were shaking.

"Okay," I whispered. "Okay, Charlie."

He looked into his hand. It was full of hair. He pulled me up.

"Take him home," my father said. He tossed Charlie the keys.

"I'll walk," I said. I headed outside. I heard my mother sobbing through the windows. I walked.

In five minutes I heard footsteps. Charlie ran my way. I stopped and waited. I wondered if he was going to knock me over like somebody on the football field. He came fast. I held my ground. He stopped in front of me.

"I'll do it," he said. "I'll take them stupid papers in the factory."

Then he dropped into the street and started doing push-ups.

"How many?" he said. He was up to twelve in no time, pumping up and down like some crazy, pointless machine.

"Eighty," I said.

"Shit, Itchy, nobody on the team can do eighty straight out."

"Eighty," I said. "Be the first."

Charlie shut up and got to work. I counted. He broke fifty without a sweat. He went slowly through the sixties, and I was getting worried, but I carried a peanut in my wallet now for just such occasions, and I figured if Charlie actually made it to eighty push-ups, I would just toss him the peanut and say, "Charlie meets any challenge," just to remind him there were some things even he couldn't do.

By seventy-two he was going real slow and breathing hard. He was in the middle of the street, and cars had to stop on both sides, and some drivers beeped their horns, but then they got out and watched, and I shouted, "Seventy-five," and Charlie went down and up and down.

He never stopped, but it took awfully long to get off the ground after seventy-eight. All the veins bulged in his neck. His face was purple. He wheezed hard. His arms trembled, but he went down again. I said it, and the people who had gathered around said it.

"Seventy-nine."

I didn't think he would get back up. It seemed to take forever. I bent down beside him. "Come on, Charlie. A little more. You can do it."

He was up again. One more. Water rolled out of his eyes. He was drenched. His arms just shuddered. They were swollen huge. Veins throbbed in his temple. They throbbed in his biceps. He started down. I put the peanut back in my wallet. It wasn't going to be funny if Charlie didn't make that last push-up.

"Eighty," I said. Somebody laughed. Somebody said, "Jesus Christ, look at this kid." There must have been fifteen people out of their cars and standing around Charlie.

Charlie's chin touched the street. He didn't move. He was perfectly straight against the street, only his chin touching. I thought he would collapse. It seemed impossible he could get up. He made some noise, half a whimper, half a gasp.

"Come on, Charlie." I shouted it. Everybody in the street shouted it. More cars stopped. Charlie was coming up so slowly. He kept making that noise. It chilled my blood. I bent close to him. "Come on. Come on."

"Itchy," he whispered. "I can't. I can't."

"Yes, you can. Think of Patrick, man. Think of Patrick on that hill."

Something horrible came over his face then, and he let out this tremendous roar. He sagged, like he would hit the street, but stopped himself inches away, then threw himself up, finishing the last push-up with one incredible thrust of his arms, shrieking, "Patrick," then falling so hard he cut his head.

Everybody cheered. Charlie lay there panting, hardly able to move, blood rolling down into his eyes. So I did it for him. I raised my hands over my head and shouted at the top of my voice.

"Charlie meets any challenge. Charlie Shovlin meets any fucking challenge."

Charlie just lay in the street, laughing and crying and wheezing all at the same time. It just about broke my heart.

15

The first march on the factory was set for Wednesday, July third. That morning I found Robin slumped on a wicker chair with a glass of wine in her hand and Vincent on her lap. Her face was pale, and the skin under her eyes had turned some ugly color. A pile of newspaper stories about the war was all jumbled up by her feet, and her glasses lay on top of the pile.

"I don't like this war," she said.

A few hours later, a gigantic crowd met us at the memorial, and when Robin stepped onto the concrete stage beside our fifty-year-old bronze doughboy, they roared. They shouted her name and pumped their fists. She stared over them with her tired eyes, pulled off her glasses, then smiled.

"Well hell," she said. "Glad to see you could make it."

A huge flag drooped under the hot sun, and Robin stood on the stage where my father would talk the next day. A tarp covered the wall of names and dates behind the statue, and there were ropes and Keep Away signs, and I figured they'd chiseled Patrick's name into the stone. The tarp made my stomach churn up.

Robin wore a white dress, the first dress I'd ever seen her wear, and it covered her knees and hung from straps over her shoulders. She'd stuck a flower behind one of her ears and put her make-up on nice for a change, but her hair was as wild as ever.

The crowd shouted every time she moved. They were mostly white and young. There were some bums and old women, a few housewives, some teachers, a priest or two. There weren't any cops. There weren't any factory workers. Mostly there were kids and guitars and flags and lots of big signs on sticks.

"Stop the Killing." "Vote McCarthy." "Make Love, Not Guns."

I spotted Suzanne and, not far from her, squeezing his way through the crowd with his baseball glove on, his tongue drooped over his chin, smiling at all the pretty girls, my buddy Irv. I imagined him nudging Suzanne and offering her a loan for a tuna.

Nigel pranced around the stage with a bullhorn. He was dressed like an Indian, two feathers in a band around his hair, shorts and bare feet, his huge chest exposed in all its hairy white glory, and his cheekbones painted with savage swipes of white and deep red. He kissed Robin's cheek and ate her with his eyes. There was something wild and hungry about him, like he'd been roaming the jungles too long without any luck.

He had a following of emaciated women who fixed him in their eyes and followed him silently through the streets, and young girls who went in groups to his house, and the worst of Deadwhale's violent boys, tattooed battlers with bashed-in faces and causes all their own. Nigel was a force.

He introduced Robin as "Joan of Arc, the woman who will save this putrefying country." He handed her the bullhorn, and her voice came through shaky and hoarse over the amplified hiss of her breath.

"We're at war," she said, and the kids shouted and waved their signs. "But not with the Vietcong, not with the Russians or the Chinese, not with the American soldiers, like Patrick Shovlin, getting ground up like shredded meat for a hopeless cause.

"We're at war with the murder machine. We're at war with the Pentagon and the White House and all the American men who spit out the lies, who swallow the lies, who perpetuate the lies that keep the machine feeding on our young.

"Stewart Donaghy is a cog in the machine, small, but vital and dangerous, and we must destroy him."

God, how they roared. Nigel threw himself into the air. He pumped his arms in every direction at once. He kicked and twisted and screamed at the sky like some spastic martial-arts madman, and down in the park, down in the grass and the walkways and the streets that stretched around the memorial, the kids shouted her name.

"We don't need a lot of bullshit," she shouted. "We've got a long walk ahead. This afternoon we'll close the factory for a while to demonstrate our strength. Tonight we'll meet here to celebrate our victory. Don't be afraid. We can't lose, because no matter what they tell us, no matter what they write and shout and broadcast, no matter how hard they try to convince us otherwise, we know without doubt that this summer in Deadwhale, we are the patriots, we are the truth, we are the conscience of America."

Her voice dropped to a whisper. "Let's go."

I got up front with Robin. Nigel was there, squeezing her shoulders, fixing her under his bulging madman's eyes. He slammed his hands together. He walked backward, shouting at the crowd, red-faced and painted, jumping and pointing, two feathers erect on his skull, a cigarette hanging, ashes pouring down his chest.

He took the bullhorn and shouted, "No guns, no war. No guns, no war." The crowd joined him. We walked ahead of hundreds of people, maybe thousands, Robin sweating and pale, rubbing her eyes, with the sun beating down and not a cop in sight.

We walked the main road that headed west from the beach and across town. It had been Roosevelt Boulevard, but now it was Waters Boulevard. It straddled South Deadwhale and the slums, winding through the southern portion of Little Brooklyn before crossing into Fishtown, then shooting north at the point where the houses ended and the wasteland of marsh leading up to the bay and the factory complex began.

People lined the sidewalks to cheer and curse. They spit from cars. They called us hippies and punks. Nigel taunted them. The boys in his private army shouted back and waved sticks and pipes. They were dressed like pirates and Indians and soldiers in foreign armies, and all had their faces painted like Nigel's. They drank hard liquor and waved the North Vietnamese flag, and when Nigel raised his arm, all their arms went up, too, and marching along with them were the girls and women of Nigel's harem.

We blocked every street along the way. I expected cops to charge from some side street swinging their clubs, like they'd done in April in the slums. They'd killed two people then.

We marched the miles up that road, and at the border between Little Brooklyn and Fishtown, I heard distant singing and saw a few hundred blacks moving up an adjoining road toward us, walking slowly behind a huge man in a white shirt with suspenders and a tie, working their way through Little Brooklyn like some tattered army, decked out in black armbands in honor of April's dead, waving more flags and banners, singing some old song that might have been from the Civil War.

They walked tight together, walking in sandals and sweaty shirts, while hundreds of people shouted from sidewalks. They came on behind Coke Phillips until they fell in alongside us. Coke smiled and said, "Lovely day, Robin redbreast."

"Well hell, Coke," she said. "You're three minutes late." And they both laughed while Nigel shouted into his electronic horn, "We don't need your fucking guns. We don't need your fucking war."

We turned left on Industrial Drive, the southwest road that cut through the marshes toward the bay and ended at the gate to the machine gun factory. A cop car sat at the mouth of the road beneath the sign that said Private Highway, but that was the only sign of cops.

There were two lanes, one in each direction. There was no sidewalk, just weeds and mud. The marsh stank and grew as far as you could see, back beyond the machine gun factory and Donaghy's chemical factory behind that, with its stacks spewing into the air and pipes crisscrossing in the sky, its waste gushing into the bay behind it, making it foam and stink.

The industrial complex had been carved out of the marshland in the fifties. There were some office buildings in small lots off to our left, a couple smaller factories where a few hundred people worked, and Donaghy's factories at the end of the road, where more men worked than in all the others combined. Most of those men made guns.

We walked beside the swampy stretches of weed and squishing mud while sea gulls swooped all around. The road ended at a fenced gate that lapped about ten yards over the marshes on both sides. Behind the fence, the road continued for a hundred yards before it fanned out into the lot full of shining cars and then the factory. If not for the marsh, we could have walked around the gate to the factory, but, instead, the only way in was through the gate and down that long road.

Guards with German shepherds patrolled behind the gate. They stared at us, and the dogs growled, but there weren't many, just a few old guys strolling around. It all seemed too casual.

Robin, Coke, Nigel, and I stood at the gate with the crowd clogging the road behind us, shouting, waving flags and signs, a long line of white faces, with a black stretch down the side. Not a car could pass. The next shift should have been arriving behind us, and when they didn't show, I got nervous.

Guns fired in the distance, muffled bursts that echoed through the marshes. I pictured the mermaids throbbing on Gino's arms.

A few cops came by about ten minutes before shift change, just three guys on horses. Nigel shouted at them, and the crowd joined in, but the cops guided their horses through, and the horses were so beautiful that the kids let them pass.

Robin pulled us together. She sat in the street, and we dropped around her. She looked awfully tired.

"I thought they'd head us off on the boulevard," she said.

"It's a stinking trap," I said.

"So I guess we should bloody well run away," Nigel said. All day he'd sounded American, but now he had an English accent again. He looked like an Indian with his stupid feathers and paint, and it was awfully strange talking to an Indian with a British accent.

"Where's the cops then?" I asked.

"I don't give a bloody damn." He looked at Robin. "Robin, love, sooner or later, they must open those gates, and that's when we strike. They can't stop us."

Robin stared at Nigel. She didn't seem able to believe her eyes.

"Nigel, what the hell are you supposed to be in that get-up?" she asked. "You look like an idiot."

"I am an idiot, love. I married you, didn't I?"

Robin looked at Coke. "I married him when I was very young and stupid."

Coke nodded. He wasn't saying much, but I'd noticed him looking Nigel over. He didn't seem able to believe his eyes, either.

"Perhaps," Coke said, "we should discuss the business at hand."

Coke had an accent, too, but there was nothing phony about it. He was born in New York, raised in London, and graduated from Oxford before coming to Deadwhale to practice law.

"Yeah," I said, "like the fact that we're trapped."

"This is not a trap, my young friend," Nigel said. "This is an opportunity. Let's try it in terms you might understand. We've got the bases loaded, and our best hitter's at the plate. Do we bunt, or bloody swing away?"

"What the hell do you know about baseball?" I asked. "They don't play baseball in England."

"Nigel's a half-breed," Robin said. "He lived here in the country he despises till he was twenty. His father was American."

"That's right," he said. "And the bloody fool knew all about baseball."

"Then you know people don't usually get killed in baseball," I said.

"No, but they do in wars, my young friend, which is what we're trying to stop, and they do in revolutions, which is what we're trying to inspire. Yes?"

He'd dropped the British accent. He talked American. It made him tougher and less amusing.

"Oh, really?" I said. "So we're going to kill the czar and all that?"

Coke laid a hand on Robin's shoulder, a huge shining hand with long fingers that wrapped around her tiny white bone.

"Robin redbreast," Coke said. "If I understand correctly, today's march was merely to prove a point. I believe you've done that. Now let's not blow it the first time. We sit for a while, then we go home. You didn't hope to close the factory today, and surely you didn't want to get people hurt or arrested."

"Surely, she did," Nigel said. "We've taken this fucking road. The opportunity's here. Let's exploit it."

Robin looked from one to the other, then at me.

"I say we leave," I said. "We got tired people who just worked all day and want to go home coming out in front of us. We got another shift that didn't show. That means they were cut off by the cops, or Donaghy gave them off. If they were cut off, the boulevard's probably full of cops waiting for a signal. If Donaghy gave them off, it was probably to get them out of the way so the cops could get at us.

"It's a trap, and that means they plan to hurt us. Why else let us in? And don't forget what these missing cops did in Southwest Deadwhale a few weeks ago. Let's get out."

She reached for her shoulder, but Vincent wasn't there. The sadness flashed over her face. She was sweating. It seemed to get hotter by the minute.

"The goal's to change it ultimately or shut the place down," she said. "But today I just wanted to express my disgust, maybe delay work, piss people off, get more people on our side, and scare Donaghy."

"That's very nice, love," Nigel said. "But we might never get this far again. I say your bleeding Deadwhale cops fucked up. I say you pull out now, the kids will want to know what the point of it all was. You'll lose them.

"Those old guards can't stop us. Let's bust the gate and smash the place. I've got the people. Yeah, we'll get hurt, but people always get hurt in revolution."

"We're just trying to make a statement, not overthrow the king," I said.

"What's the fucking statement?" he asked. "That we can stop the bloody traffic? A dead skunk can stop traffic. Robin told them we would close the bleeding place."

"Where are the cops?" she whispered.

Nigel smacked the street. "It doesn't matter, love."

"Jesus, Nigel," she said. "Quit calling me love. Surely one of your little girls would like to go somewhere and experience your genius. Say something intelligent or get lost."

His fanatic's eyes blazed, and a smile crawled over his face.

"Now," she said. "The mayor's not stupid. Like Itchy said, he knew we were coming. He should have stopped us. I wanted him to stop us."

"They let us in here so we'd do just this, sit on our asses until they're ready to hurt us," Nigel said. "They're fascists. This is America. America's at war. Ask Coke what they did in Southwest Dead-whale."

"They did that to rampaging niggers," Coke said. "They won't do it to nice white boys and girls."

"They don't care who they do it to," Nigel said. "Remember Sherman's march? Remember Hiroshima? Remember Wounded Knee? They use nice words, but in the end they'll burn down your cities, destroy you with atomic bombs, get drunk and slaughter you wholesale."

Robin jumped to her feet. "You're paranoid, Nigel. We're all Americans here. Our quarrel's with the government, and our immediate concern is this factory. Save your propaganda for your goons and old ladies.

"Let them make the next move, because if we go forward, assuming Nigel has some ingenious plan for breaking down that gate, we're risking a slaughter, and if we go back, I'm humiliated. Let's sit, then get out of here. If we can hold the factory up an hour that's a good start. So don't start anything. If I've led us into a trap, I'm going to lead us out. If the cops move in, let's see them carry a couple thousand of us away."

"Christ," Nigel said. "We don't need this Gandhi shit. King tried that, and they blew a hole through him. Isn't it obvious yet that non-violence begets violence? We've got to strike with brutal force. They don't have enough bloody cops to arrest half of us. Who cares if some boys and girls get their heads broken?"

"Do what I tell you, Nigel."

He flinched. He opened his mouth, gave her a long sideways stare, and hissed, "Remember, Robin, you have no secrets from me." He picked up his bullhorn, and the whistle blew for shift change. The factory doors swung out, and workers poured into the light.

"Here they come," I said.

Panic crossed Robin's face. "They won't let them through the gates," she said. "It would be war."

"Let them bloody come," Nigel said. "We want war."

The factory gate slid open, but only enough for a fat guard with a gnarled nose to waddle through. He asked Robin to follow. She called me along, and we followed this slow guard with the baked potato nose through the gates to the forbidden road to the factory. Robin leaned on my shoulder, and we heard Nigel over the bullhorn.

"You have no secrets from me, Robin."

"What's he mean?" I asked.

"He's crazy," she whispered. "Help me, Itchy."

"What's the matter?"

"I'm tired. Confused."

"You're doing good," I said.

She put her arm around me. She was drenched under her dress. We followed the guard.

Factory workers jammed the road in their cars. Traffic stopped at the gate. Fumes stunk up the air. Horns blasted. Some of the drivers shouted at Robin. Some whistled.

"Don't laugh at me," she said.

"What is it? This is no time to get nervous."

"It's Vincent," she said. "The vet says I should put him to sleep. He's been with me since I was seventeen."

"Everyone's depending on you."

The guard led us along the road to the brick shack where the guards hung out. He showed us in. Stewart Donaghy sat there in a beautiful blue suit with pin stripes. His brown shoes were up on a table full of coffee cups, spills, and papers. The shoes were shiny. So was his hair and his teeth.

He smiled. "So you're Robin."

"And you're Donaghy," she said.

"Stew," he said, and he looked at me. "And this must be your anti-war poster child."

"This is my friend," she said.

"He knows me," I said.

"You running?" he asked.

"A little."

"Good. Good. And the big guy? Charlie?"

"He's running, too."

"Great. Maybe I'll get some competition. Any of you as good as the dead guy?"

"Maybe," I said.

"I hear they're honoring him before the race tomorrow."

"You could call it that," I said.

"What do you call it?"

"Exploiting him."

"What a cynical boy."

Nigel's amplified voice drifted through the clamped windows.

The shack was cramped and cooking, with just a bench to sit on. Flies slammed the windows, fell, and buzzed on the floor. The windows were filthy. There was a calendar on the wall. Miss April 1966. She had red hair.

Donaghy kept smiling. He was amazingly dry in his suit. He shoved a Tootsie Roll Pop in his mouth. He had a pocketful.

"Care for one? I prefer the grape."

"No thanks," Robin said. He didn't ask me.

"Have a seat," he said, and Robin dropped to the bench. She took it too fast. A strap had fallen over her right arm, and the dress was soaked in back. Her make-up had smeared around her eyes.

"Seen any cops?" he asked.

"Five," she said. "Two in a car at the end of the road, three on horses."

"Odd they're not all here," he said.

"I suppose they know what they're doing," she said.

"And do you?" he asked.

"Of course," she said. A bead of sweat rolled down her forehead. I wiped it off. Donaghy sucked his candy.

"So you walked into the trap willingly," he said.

"We'll see who trapped who," she said.

"Believe what you like," he said.

"How kind of you."

"No," he said. "I'm not kind, and you are trapped. The question is whether I'll let you go."

"Maybe you'll explain the nature of this trap," she said. "So I can tell you why it won't work."

"It's already worked," he said.

"Your father's cops can't hurt us without hurting you," Robin said.

Donaghy smiled. The stick jutted from the corner of his mouth. He pulled it out and stared at the purple ball at the end.

"They're my cops," he said.

Robin waved at a fly. "You've elected yourself mayor?"

"The mayor's sick," he said, "and just a little drunk most of the time. Poor man's still mourning a dead man's frigid wife. You ever hear of Mayor Waters?"

Robin reached for her shoulder. The words seemed to stick in her throat.

"Of course."

"Yeah, well, my father's been fighting Robert Waters' ghost for Eleanor drunken Waters since the man died. He was smart before he married her, and tough. Now he's silly, and I've got my foot on his throat. When I move, he wheezes. Those are my cops, and you're in my trap."

He jammed the candy back in his mouth. He unbuttoned his jacket. I saw the gun across his chest in a leather strap. Robin saw it, too.

"The boulevard's full of cops, every cop in the city and then some. We cut off traffic a few minutes after you moved in."

Robin leaned back against the wall and crossed her legs. The sweat rolled down her face.

"The cops can't hurt us," she said.

"That's right," he said. "My father wanted to head you off on the boulevard, use a little tear gas maybe, look tough and all that, like he did with the niggers, only without killing anybody. That's what you were hoping. No real harm, but good propaganda. Unarmed Robin fights the cops."

He moved closer to Robin. He folded his arms and stared.

"But I convinced him we should really break you, just like we did in the slums. That was my show, and it worked fine, and this is my show, too."

"You call killing innocent people a good show?" Robin asked. "Okay, maybe you think it was, but try killing some of these kids, and see what happens to your factory."

"That's right," he said. "I lose if kids get hurt, and it looks like my fault or my father's, but I'm not going to let that happen, and if it doesn't, Robin, these people won't let you close down their factory.

"They don't care about how many little yellow commies we kill. They care about money, Robin—their cars, their mortgage payments—and they'd be glad if I brought them your fucking head on a platter, as long as I don't mess with their kids."

He slammed the table with his fists. A cup fell and broke. Robin reached for her shoulder again, then looked at me.

"What is it you want?" I said.

"I want to bring the cops off the boulevard and fill the swamps with your broken bones. That's what I want."

He licked his lips, tossed his candy stick on the floor, then ripped open another and stuffed it in his mouth. He was sweating at last.

"But I can't do that," he said. He stared out the window. We could hear the muffled horns. We could see workers along the road, then the gate, the marchers waving their flags and signs, and Nigel leading them on.

Donaghy snatched a fly out of the air, shook it in his palm, then threw it to the floor. It hit the concrete, buzzed once, then went silent.

"These men are getting angry," Donaghy said. He whirled and pointed a finger at Robin.

"All right, baby, this is it. I can get your army out of here safe, but you got to promise to leave my factory alone. Protest all you want. Burn your bra, your panties, the flag. Burn draft cards. Burn your fucking hotel if you want, but leave my factory alone. That's all, and you march away without a bump. Your protest is a small success, and you never do it again."

"And if I don't promise?"

Donaghy looked at me. He was handsome, frightening. His eyes were dark gray. There was something familiar about them, something familiar about his whole face, but I couldn't place it. "Is Suzanne out there?" he asked.

I shrugged.

"She's out there," he said. He banged the table with his fist again. Crumbs of spilled sugar stuck to the hairs. He turned away from us and stared out the window. He wiped the sugar off on his expensive pants. Sweat beaded below the perfect line of his hair.

Most of the workers were out of their cars now, standing in the road, squinting at the afternoon sun. A few tired women scattered about, but mostly men with hairy arms, lunch pails, and droopy eyes. They gathered up at the fence. They peeled off their sweaty shirts and shouted at the kids on the other side, and the kids shouted back.

"My father expects me to keep the gate shut and call in the cops if you turn down our offer. He's got a letter he plans to print in the paper about how we made you an offer, and you chose war. He's got school buses. I convinced him if we beat some of you up and hauled a few hundred to jail, it would scare you off, but I don't think you're the type that's scared, and I don't want to chance these people turning against me because they saw some cops hurt their kids. No, the cops aren't getting any call. The cops are going to be late."

He touched Robin's shoulder. "You're very wet." He moved the strap back over her shoulder. "You're very pretty."

"Don't touch me," she said.

He laughed. "But I like you."

"Yeah, I like you, too," she said. "Close your factory up, and I'll take you out for pizza."

He looked out the window again, calmly, but just a little nervous, tapping his fingers on the glass. The noise kept getting louder. He looked at me.

"Where's Suzanne?"

"Somewhere out there," I said.

"The front, the middle, where?"

"I don't know."

"Jesus," he said. "Okay, fine. What would happen if I opened the front gate, if I left the cops out on the boulevard, and just let these men and kids at one another?"

Robin jumped to her feet. "They'd kill each other. It's hot. They've been waiting."

"Yeah," he said. "The front gate opens, and here you are safe and sound with Stewart Donaghy. We'll tell the press you refused to cooperate, and we had no choice but to let our workers free. After all, this isn't a prison."

Robin whispered. "You can't. Nigel's got them all worked up. They're shouting at each other through the fence."

"They'll kill one another," I said.

"Exactly. That will keep the fathers on my side, and who knows, if the kids see you were in here with me, safe and cozy."

She closed her eyes, and a tear squeezed out and mixed with the sweat that streamed down her face.

"It sure is hot in here," he said.

"Let me out," she said. She stepped toward the door, but he jumped in front of her.

"What's the matter, Robin?" he asked.

"Let's go, Itchy."

"Now just a minute," he said. "Let me get us some air." He cracked the door. Not much air came in, but plenty of noise. The kids were chanting behind Nigel, "No guns, no war," and the factory workers jammed up against the fence, sweating in the hot sun, shouted back.

"Just march them out of here," he said. "You can keep protesting. I don't care about the war. When this stops, there will be others, and between them, we'll just keep the fear up. The fear's just as good for selling guns. Leave my factory alone. That's all."

"I'd rather die," she said.

"I don't want anyone to die," he said. "I just want to keep my factory open. Okay? I like the money. I like being in charge. Isn't there something else you can do with your free time?"

"What if we protested the factory without coming on the entry road anymore?" I asked. "What if we promised to stay out on the boulevard?"

"Shut up about the factory completely. Protest something else. Who cares about machine guns? Most of the killing's done other ways."

"No," Robin said. "It's all the same. I don't care if you supply bread for the soldiers. You're supporting the war. Do what you will. Maybe you'll win this battle, but before it's over, you'll wish you never saw my face."

"It's a nice face," he said. "Even your crooked eye."

She shoved past him. Donaghy stepped through the door behind her, grabbed her arm, and before she understood, bent close to her and kissed her on the mouth. She spit back into his face and ran up the road. I stepped in front of him.

"Don't do it," I said. "Someone will get killed. Maybe it will be Suzanne."

He stared straight into my eyes, and I saw that familiar thing again, something in his eyes, something that made me sad and confused and worried, something that made it harder for me to hate him.

"Tell Suzanne I'm sorry," he said. "She won't understand. She never understood me, but I'm going to do this, and I'm going to win. Good luck tomorrow. You'll need it, and Shovlin, if you see her, get her out of the way. She's soft in the head. She doesn't deserve to get hurt."

He nodded at the old guard with the baked potato nose. The guard stepped into the shack, touched something, and the gate between the workers and the protesters jerked.

"Tell Suzanne I love her," he said. He headed toward the factory without a look behind.

I ran after Robin. Hell had broken loose past the fence. The workers charged straight on, whirling their lunch pails over their heads. The protesters gave ground. Some ran. Some fell under the blows. It looked like they might all run, but then Nigel's voice roared over the bullhorn.

"Kill the mother fuckers. Take no prisoners."

He ran straight ahead shouting into the horn, his roughnecks swinging chains and sticks behind him, swinging signs that said, Peace and Love. They slammed into the workers.

I ran into the thick of it, nothing but arms, sweat, blood, and men and boys swinging. I heard sirens, and cops charged, high on their horses. And the cars came, too, the lights whirling, the sirens squealing, the cops pouring into the street in riot helmets, pulling out their sticks, unbuckling their pistols.

They hit the protesters from behind, cutting a swath through them in their rush toward the battle at the gate. People fell, sliding into the swamps, trampled underfoot, just pushed and rammed by the cops swinging sticks from their horses.

Kids blocked them. Bodies fell. The cops threw people into the swamps. Kids swung their signs at factory workers. I was shouting. I hardly knew it. I shouted for Robin. I heard a bullhorn. It was chief of police Heller trying to control his cops, but they were worse than any of us, crazy like they'd been in Southwest Deadwhale, hitting anything that moved, men, women, boys, girls, just clearing the street, and nowhere to push us but into the marshes or back toward the factory.

Kids fell into the crowd. Workers dropped. I was sucked under twice. I burned my hands on cement. Each time I got up, I pushed and fought, shouting Robin's name.

And then I saw Nigel running at a cop. The cop was on horseback, and Nigel gripped his arm, ripped him off with one hand, then flung himself onto the horse in the same motion. He grabbed the horse's neck, righted himself, and yanked the reins so the horse reared high in the thick of it all. And there stood Nigel, the feathers straight up, blood smeared over his face, shouting into the bullhorn, "Kill them all. Rip out their fucking eyes."

And the cop he'd knocked off pulled out his gun. Nigel kicked the horse into a gallop and tried to run right through the crowd, but the cop fired twice. The horse reared again, kicking high into the air with Nigel clinging to its back, and then went over into the swamp with blood pouring from two wounds in its neck. Nigel was gone, and I stumbled upon Robin.

A cop had her wrist. Blood matted the hair to her face and streaked from her mouth over her cheeks. Her nose was gashed and bent. Her dress was soaked to her with muck from the marshes. Her elbows were black. The cop kept banging her against his car.

"Stop," she said. "You're going...kill...me."

He flung her again. She folded against the car. Her face hit the metal. She crumbled toward the street. He aimed his stick for the back of her skull. I dove on him. We hit the street. His helmet slammed. He threw me over. He tried to hit me with his stick, but Robin hung on his arm.

"Don't hurt him," she shouted. He tossed her off. The stick came at my head. "No," she screamed. Someone grabbed it. I heard Charlie's voice.

"Drop it or I'll break your arm."

Charlie held the cop's arm behind his back and banged him hard into the street. The helmet slammed. Charlie kept banging the helmet into the street until the cop stopped moving.

Robin pulled herself against my leg. I was in shorts, and I felt the blood and tears against my thigh. I tried to help her up. She wobbled and fell. Charlie caught her.

"Jesus Christ," he said. "Let's get her out of here."

He handed her to me. I held her like a bride going over the threshold. She didn't weigh a thing.

"Follow me," he said.

Robin sobbed into my undershirt. Tears rolled down my stomach.

"Is Nigel dead?" she asked. "Is Nigel dead?"

"I don't know," I said.

People ran everywhere. Some crawled and scrambled through the marshes. The cops had pulled in a school bus and were shoving kids in. Charlie sniffed something back.

"That cop nearly killed you, Itchy."

I couldn't talk. I nodded once. Charlie led on, shoving everyone aside. He led us up the road, then off to one of the side parking lots that housed the few buildings on the road that didn't belong to Donaghy. There were six or seven buildings spread between three small complexes. Each complex was tiny compared to Donaghy's.

Charlie led us into the largest of the three, an island of concrete and macadam in the middle of the marshes. It was full of protesters and workers, panting, sitting, dabbing at wounds. The men and boys helped one another.

We saw Suzanne on a grassy spot, bent over someone who'd fallen on the hot macadam. Charlie led us toward her. We laid Robin in the grass. Suzanne threw her arms around Charlie. I nearly jumped out of my skin when she did it.

"He's hurt," Suzanne said.

Robin crawled toward the body. He was thin and twisted. I recognized his clothes and hair, all black and dusty. It was hard to tell where the clothes ended and the hair began. Robin rolled him over. She bent her ear to his heart. Irv looked up at her and smiled.

"You okay?" she asked.

"You okay?" he said.

"He got kicked by a horse," Suzanne said.

"He got kicked by a horse," Irv said.

"He keeps repeating everything I say," Suzanne said.

"He keeps repeating everything I say," Irv said.

Robin smacked his face and said, "Hey, what are you driving?"

Irv's eyes lit up. His smile got huge. "Hey," he shouted, "what are you driving, bub? Still driving that Ford? Good car a Ford."

"Itchy, I want this guy in the empty apartment next to us from now on. Understand? I want..."

And then her eyes rolled up in her head, and she fell.

16

I was too busy taking care of Robin to fall apart completely, but the sight of Suzanne throwing herself into Charlie's arms had just about killed me. I tried to convince myself it was a hallucination from all that adrenaline, but it wasn't working. There was something going on between Charlie and Suzanne. It was a miracle. I could see Charlie doing a hundred push-ups, scoring four touchdowns in a game, getting a scholarship, making the pros, even shooting a peanut out his nose all the way to the moon, but I couldn't see him getting Suzanne.

I wanted to talk to Robin about it, but she could hardly open her mouth or move, and I didn't think she wanted to hear about my love life. She lay naked in bed. The street was full of noise. A crowd was gathering by the memorial, and there were sirens and shouts, but Robin didn't seem to hear. She sipped whiskey through a straw. She'd taken four aspirin, smoked two joints, and still her face hurt. All around her nose and under her eyes had turned purple and huge. I killed a roll of toilet paper on her bloody nose.

But she refused to go to the hospital. She had to get back on the streets or everything would fall apart, and so she moaned and spit blood while I dabbed her face with toilet paper and massaged her banged-up bones. She drank herself numb on her empty stomach.

Vincent lay beside her. He kept drooling and licking. He was soaked. His heart beat too hard from the hopeless cleaning. He would collapse into heavy breathing, his sides throbbing, then rouse himself and clean some more. The more the tumor made him drool, the harder he licked at himself. Robin held him against her side.

"Itchy," she said.

"God, Robin, don't talk. That idiot might've broke every bone in your face."

She squeezed my hand.

Her voice was weak and drunk. "When it's time, will you take Vincent?"

"It's time now."

"He can last another month, maybe two."

"But he's not happy."

"He won't be happy dead."

"He's suffering."

"So am I," she said. "You going to put me to sleep?"

"You'll get better. Please shut up and let me call a doctor."

"That cop tried to kill me," she said. "Why do they hate me?"

The cop would have killed her. That final blow would have smashed her skull. I'd saved her life, and Charlie had saved us both. No one had died, but hundreds had been hurt. There weren't enough doctors to take care of the wounded or enough ambulances to haul them away. There were mostly just breaks and gashes, but a girl was nearly trampled to death. Three police were hurt, but most of the casualties were the boys and men who'd fought outside the factory gates in that first mad rush.

I hoped Robin would sleep. Her eyes would flutter, but then she'd snap back. She'd downed an awful lot of whiskey. She hadn't slept in a long time, but she refused to give in.

"Did you bring him home?"

"Who?"

"Irv."

"I'm working on it."

"Does he have anybody? He's my friend, and...You think I'm a loser, don't you?"

"What?"

"You can tell me. I know I'm not nice."

"Robin, don't talk."

"It's not hurting anymore." She touched her nose and flinched. "I don't know why my father didn't love me."

"Maybe he did."

"No. After I left, he never tried to find me and, you know, one time I thought I was a fast runner, and I was going to try for track in high school, and he laughed at me.

"He said, 'You can't run on those stubby legs, girl.' He always called me girl. I cried, and I didn't try for the track team. You think I have stubby legs?"

I laughed. "Quit being ridiculous."

"They're stubby, and I have ugly hair and a crooked eye that doesn't work. It just sits there, and it got scraped today."

She sipped the whiskey through the straw too fast now.

"You're going to get sick," I said.

"But my legs ain't stubby, right?"

"They're skinny," I said. "And nice."

She tried to smile, but it looked awfully painful, and she gave up on it. Then she shook her head. "Why's that kid got a gun?"

"I'm afraid he'll use it," I said.

"It's got to be illegal."

"Who's going to arrest him?"

She reached for the burnt-out joint in the ashtray. I lit it. When she finished smoking, she didn't open her eyes. She was quiet a long time, but just when I thought she was sleeping, she squeezed my hand, and her other hand found Vincent's head.

"I always wondered what my mother was like," she said. "I wondered why she'd marry a guy like that. He's very handsome, but that's not enough. Maybe she just wanted to get out of Texas." Her head fell to the left. "Irv looked so dirty and small."

Finally she slept. I watched her and had this horrible feeling I was really falling in love. It was the most confusing thing. I still ached when I thought of Suzanne. I still fantasized about Suzanne when I made love with Robin, and the thought of Suzanne throwing herself into Charlie's arms made me want to jump out the window and flap my arms like Hubert Ditzlow. They looked like lovers, and that was impossible. Charlie was a football player who blew peanuts out his nose and stuffed fourteen doughnuts down his throat in four minutes. Suzanne was a delicate flower. And I was falling in love with Robin, and that was impossible, too.

But watching her sleep, listening to her soft breathing, staring at the marks all over her face and the bruises on her sides and arms and legs, almost broke my heart, and I forgot about Suzanne for a while, and I couldn't stand the thought that someday I would have to leave Robin. I had a scholarship for the University of Pennsylvania. My grandparents were looking for a place I could stay, and I was supposed to leave in the middle of August for Philadelphia, but Robin needed me.

Just as I touched her face, Nigel burst in. He rushed to the bed and shook Robin hard. She barely opened her eyes before the shouting started. He shouted it straight into her face through his bullhorn. The room roared and echoed with his distorted shouts.

"You fucking bitch, Robin. You betrayed us. You made a deal. He kissed you. You don't have any secrets from me. Remember, I made you, and I own you, and when I'm ready, I'll break you."

He punched the wall. His fist went right through. He yanked it out all covered with plaster, then set his burning eyes on me. His face was smeared with dirt and paint and dried-out blood. His chest, his hair, his legs and arms were coated with grass stains and mud.

"Leave him alone," Robin said.

I swallowed. He could have knocked off my head with one swat. I wasn't about to open my mouth unless I had to.

"Leave him alone," Robin said.

"I could break you with two fingers," he said. "You ever hurt her, I will."

Then he stormed out. I took the deepest breath of my life.

Robin whispered. "Itchy, it's time you leave me." She spit blood into her hand.

"Robin, maybe you're bleeding inside."

"I'm all right. Just another broken nose."

"But..."

"Itchy, you've got to leave."

"Go back to sleep."

"I have to go out there. Joe's coming. The neighbor said."

"No. You're drunk. You're sick. You were dreaming."

"But Nigel will ruin everything, and Joe's coming. I saw it in my dream. He's so dark."

"Robin, please."

We could hear the streets through her open window. People shouted into bullhorns. They cheered and booed. There were sirens and whistles, the honking of horns, then another bullhorn, this one louder than the rest. It was Nigel's voice floating up into the window, clear and cold and vicious.

"You have no secrets from me, Robin."

"Shut the window," she said. "Then make love to me."

"I'll hurt you."

"With your tongue. Please. Please do it."

I shut the window and got into the bed. She pulled me toward her.

"I'm going out there," she said.

17

She sat in the tub with the shower pouring down and bloody water swirling around her. She threw up and sat in it until it drained away. She spit blood. She took coffee and marijuana and tried to powder over the bruises. Her nose had swollen nearly twice its size. Her eyes were puffed slits. She couldn't get her glasses on.

I led her around by hand. I dressed her and dried her. She could hardly talk. I had to hold my ear to her mouth. She fell three times, and each time it was harder to get her up. She was stoned. She was virtually blind. The blood dripped from her nose and filled her mouth.

"You want to die, don't you, Robin?" I shouted it while I led her to the door and out into the hallway in her shoeless feet and argyle socks.

"Is that the goal? Blood's leaking from your stinking brain. Your nose is broke. You haven't eaten in hours. You're full of whiskey, coffee, and pot."

She mumbled something and dragged me toward the elevator, and pathetic as she looked, I had to smile.

There were thousands in the street. The crowd swelled from the memorial into the park behind it and back in the other direction all the way to the doors of Robin's hotel. Nigel dominated the stage with his bullhorn, shouting into the falling darkness about the police, calling them fascists, calling Donaghy another Hitler. People screamed at him, shouted along with him, threw things at the stage.

Thunder rumbled, and there were faint flashes over the sea. Huge clouds rolled over Deadwhale, blotting out the dusk. The cold breeze came hard off the beach. Ropes slapped the flagpole, and the slapping amplified over Nigel's horn.

No one recognized Robin. She wore her unmistakable clothes, rolled up men's trousers and a white shirt buttoned to the neck, but her face was so swollen and discolored that she looked like some alien creature.

I led her toward the stage. Her legs wobbled. I held my arm around her. The streets were packed, and we had to force our way through. She looked hideous in the falling darkness with her blackened face and her wild hair flapping in the breeze.

Nigel shared the stage with anyone who had something to say. Some made sense. Some just wanted to shoot off their mouths. Opinion was divided between those who wanted to shut the factory and those who didn't, but everyone condemned Robin. Some said she sold out. Some said she went too far, but only Nigel defended her. At first he ripped into her for blowing the opportunity, for not listening to him, but then he called her an angel and said her only weakness was that she wasn't tough enough.

"Don't doubt it," Nigel said. "I've known Robin Debussy since she was a kid, and she'll learn from this, and I'll be there with her, and next time, that factory is going to burn."

I helped Robin onto the stage. It was packed with furious people. They argued and shoved at one another. They cursed and spit and fought for their chance to speak.

Down beneath us, the people in the crowd argued, too. There were thousands, and they weren't all on our side, and I knew it could break loose again.

I spotted Charlie near the front with his arm around Suzanne. Our eyes met, but I pretended I didn't see. I felt like I'd been kicked. How the hell had he managed it? Maybe he'd impressed her with his peanut trick. Maybe they'd eaten doughnuts together. Maybe she had a thing for pathetic muscle-bound jerks. Maybe she wasn't so smart after all. I wanted to pound Charlie. I wanted to give him a trick peanut that would blow up in his nose. I wanted to poison him with a cream doughnut, or stomp on his head in the middle of his eighty-fifth push-up. I wanted to cry.

The clouds moved closer. They were low and huge with lightning dancing and flashing between them, followed by sharp cracks. It was going to rain hard. The police were out in force, but they were scattered around the periphery. I didn't trust them. If anything they would make things worse. I wished the rain would come. Robin whispered in my ear.

"Tell Nigel talk next. I need talk before rain."

She stopped to spit blood.

"You can't talk," I said. "You sound like a baby."

"Tell him."

"But, Robin, you'll make a fool of yourself."

Someone shoved me aside. I pulled Robin to my chest and watched six gigantic goons cross the stage with Stewart Donaghy in the middle, like some king among his bodyguards. A goon ripped the bullhorn out of Nigel's hand. Nigel took a swing, but two others grabbed him from behind. They threw him off the stage. He disappeared down into the crowd, then scrambled to his feet and fixed his ferocious eyes on the men who'd done it to him. I didn't see his band of thugs, though. I wondered where they were.

Donaghy stood at the edge of the platform in front of the bronze statue, just a few feet above Charlie. He addressed the crowd in a clear and powerful voice while the daylight faded out and the sky turned pitch black above him.

"How many of you want to close my factory?" he asked.

There was a huge cheer and lots of shouts. "No guns, no war."

Robin hissed into my ear. "Donaghy?"

"Yeah, it's him."

Thunder cracked and boomed, roaring through the bullhorn in distorted waves.

"How many want to keep it open?"

There was another incredible noise. He held the bullhorn toward the crowd and let the noise blast through it. The men who supported the factory didn't like Donaghy, but they needed their jobs. He'd let half the night crew out early so they could be there.

Then Donaghy launched into a speech that was short, vicious, and brilliantly sarcastic. He explained how the town would collapse without his factory. He defended the war. He defended his father. He defended the workers who turned out his guns.

He attacked the radicals who were against him. He mocked Nigel as a babbling nitwit in an Indian suit, and finally he laid into Robin. He called her that little communist tramp. He claimed he'd offered her a way out today, a way out with honor, and that she'd said she would rather die. He blamed the whole thing on her, claiming he'd warned her the police were going to strike, that he'd begged Robin to leave while she had time, but that she'd refused, leaving him no choice but to open the gates and let the workers go home, in the hopes the police could prevent the disaster he feared.

"I don't run a prison," he said. "When it's time for my men to leave, I let them leave. And if there's trouble waiting out there for them, I'm confident they can handle themselves."

He said Robin was a power seeker and a coward who sat the whole battle out in a brick shack with him. He claimed she expected to benefit from the bloodshed. And she slipped out of my grasp, squeezed through his bodyguards, and bumped right into him. Her shouting came through on his bullhorn, but none of it made sense.

"Here she is now," Donaghy said.

He handed her the bullhorn, stepped back, and laughed while Robin shrieked hopeless sounds. The crowd went silent, but then they booed, and the harder she tried, the more they booed and hollered, and when I heard her sob amplified through the night, I forced my way beside her. I grabbed the bullhorn and shouted into it. Thunder crashed overhead, and lightning sizzled in the black sky.

"Look at her face," I shouted. My voice echoed back to me through the darkness.

"Does it look like she hid with Donaghy? They did this to her. A cop nearly killed her. I was with her when she talked to Donaghy, and he's lying. He had it all planned."

He ripped it from my hand.

"Thanks for enlightening us," he said.

"You're a hypocrite," I said. "You're a..."

He hit me with the bullhorn. He threw it down and slammed me with his fists. He knocked me against a bodyguard, punched me in the stomach, then swung me by the hair. He tried throwing me off the stage, but I slammed into Robin, and we fell together. She moaned. She cried. Donaghy came after me, but something hit him, and fighting broke out around us.

I pulled Robin aside. We leaned against a wall of carved names covered in canvas. My hair might have brushed Patrick's name for all I knew. The fighting was vicious, and Charlie stood beside Nigel in the thick of it, trading blows with Donaghy, flailing around among Donaghy's bodyguards.

Nigel was content to fight the others, but Charlie wanted Donaghy. I never saw someone get hit as many times as Charlie did. They hit him in the stomach. They hit him in the face. They hit him in the neck and the ribs and the head, but he wouldn't go down until he had Donaghy in front of him, and then Donaghy hit him hard and fast, three times in the mouth. Charlie staggered, dropped to his knee, righted himself, then knocked Donaghy over the side with one vicious swing.

And when Donaghy fell into the crowd and the darkness, Charlie stood at the edge with his fists at his sides and his nostrils flaring, looking down into the riot he'd started, looking down where Donaghy scrambled to his feet, looking down with his teeth clenched and the veins bulging in his neck and the anger so deep in his eyes I realized maybe Charlie was a killer after all, maybe Charlie belonged in a uniform with a gun destroying people in Vietnam, and I was proud of him.

And it was just like that afternoon at the factory, the fights rolling through the crowd, the men and boys shouting and swinging, but this time the cops stayed put. Charlie found us.

"Get out of here," he said. He looked down into the crowd. "I got to find Suzanne. You all right, Itchy?"

"Yeah."

"How about Orphan Annie?"

Robin mumbled something.

"She's half dead. Nothing unusual."

"Be careful," he said. "Everybody's going crazy around here. Look at this shit." He pointed down into the fighting. "Twice in one day. It's her fault."

He dove down into the center of the riot. I watched him grab hold of Suzanne and try to lead her out. I held onto Robin. She trembled and whispered things I couldn't understand. Blood poured from her nose. I wished Charlie hadn't gone. I wished someone would do something, but it went on, just like that afternoon, but without the cops, and I thought we would all die there among the fighting men and boys by the memorial for dead soldiers.

I thought we'd all die, Robin and Suzanne and Charlie and I, but then I heard a voice over the bullhorn, a firm and gentle voice, a voice I knew well, a voice that sent a chill so hard and fast up my spine, it was like the crack of a whip against my back, and the voice said, "My friends. My friends."

Robin squeezed my arm. She whispered. "Joe."

But no one else understood, because it wasn't Joe Waters' voice they heard. It was Mayor Waters' voice they heard, a voice they'd heard many times before, but hadn't heard in years, an unmistakable voice, the voice of Deadwhale's greatest hopes and dreams. He had always begun his speeches with those very words.

"My friends." And although the voice didn't really sound like the mayor's, amplified as it was, distorted in the night, and delivered in that slow, deliberate, and kind style, it was easy to make the connection, and that was all it took. The fighting stopped almost immediately. Everyone looked at the stage. Lightning flashed, a quick burst, and there stood Joe Waters, the bullhorn in his hand, his hair long and uncombed. He wore army fatigues, and before that brief burst of light shut off and brought back the darkness, I realized that Joe Waters no longer had a right arm, just a sleeve that hung there in the night.

"Love one another," he said.

The rain came in sheets, and Joe hadn't said another word, and everyone was running, and Robin was dragging me toward the center of the stage. She fell and crawled, calling his name, but Joe had come and gone in one burst of lightning, and Robin, blind as she was, had only heard his voice. She found the bullhorn where he'd stood. She picked it up. She smelled it. She kissed it. She rubbed it against her face.

"We got to get out of here," I said.

She started talking fast, all these mumbled grunts and shrieks that I could barely understand. It might have been funny if it wasn't so awful.

"I told you," she said. "You saw him. Did you? Tell me you saw him?"

The rain slapped around us. It whacked against the canvas over Patrick's name. The thunder cracked, and in another burst of light, I caught Robin's face, all swollen, black, and desperate, the blood washing off her nose. She held the bullhorn tight against her chest, the same way she held Vincent.

"Yeah, I saw him, Robin."

"He's home," she whispered.

But Joe had vanished into the darkness and the rain, and people ran, and others stared in confusion toward the stage and bumped against one another, trying to make their way home in the storm.

18

I was tired on the stage next morning. Suzanne and Charlie and I had been all over Deadwhale in Suzanne's sputtering Volkswagon, staring through rain-smeared windows for Joe. He'd vanished, and by two, Charlie and I had gone home to sleep for the race, leaving Suzanne to search the morning alone. Charlie kissed her right in front of me, like it was the most natural thing in the world. If the sight of it hadn't made me so dizzy, I might have jumped on him and started squeezing his neck until he killed me, but instead I just turned away, like I couldn't care less. It wasn't easy.

Now we sat in folding chairs. The flag flew. A few hundred people watched. The Deadwhale High School Band played patriotic songs, making them all sound amazingly similar to the school fight song, and the Keatings and Shovlins sat in a row in their suits and ties, all except me.

I'd come late, just beating the "Star Spangled Banner." I was barefoot with frayed jeans and a sleeveless shirt. I felt like a creep when I saw everyone else, all the Keatings in new suits, Charlie bulging out of a suit that was Patrick's, my father with his only suit draped over him, and my mother with earrings, a new hairdo, a dark blue dress, and so much powder on her face, she looked like the main attraction at a wake. I had this urge to clean off her face and tell her I loved her.

"Oh, Itchy, is that what you're wearing?" she said.

"I guess so, Mom." I felt like some horrible, grungy outcast, but it was too late.

"You look like a disgrace," my father said. "Like you spent the night in an alley."

"I thought it would be casual," I said.

"It's not a stinking barbecue," my father said.

"He's a hippie," Charlie said. "That's how they dress. I'll bet he's got dirty underwear, too. Show us your underwear, Itchy."

"We don't want to see his underwear," my mother said. "The outerwear's bad enough."

It was a long ceremony with lots of boring patriotic speeches that made you feel more like taking a nap than defending your country. It was all this old stuff about freedom and democracy, like instead of great ideas, freedom and democracy were used cars, and every speaker was a bad salesman with a quota to meet.

But sometimes it got good, sometimes, when some of the old veterans talked about friends they'd lost, or brothers, and something deep and true came out in their voices, and you knew this was the real thing, this was the pain of war, and these were men who knew freedom and democracy were powerful things, great things that people bled and died for and not a lot of empty words shallow politicians and failed generals could hoist on us to sell their dirty war.

The Keatings were crying soon enough. Their son had fallen out of a helicopter with a bullet through his throat, and my mother cried, too, and when they unveiled Patrick's name, and a fat kid from Little Brooklyn played a deep, slow, spine-chilling taps, I stopped worrying about Charlie and Suzanne. I dropped my head and felt a chill that started in the back of my skull and ran down my neck, through my back, and all the way through my legs, like some cold bolt of lightning, and then I was crying, too.

My hair was long, and my feet were bare, and I probably looked like a fool. I was a rebel, and I was as committed to closing the factory as anyone. I hated the war and had no doubt it was wrong. I hated their ceremony. I hated the flag waving. I hated the way they used my brother to make themselves look good, but when that fat kid blew the last notes out of his shiny horn, the tears ran down my neck. They ran down my chest. I imagined whole forests growing in my stream of tears.

When the music stopped, everyone sat for Mayor Donaghy's speech, except me. I could hardly move. I just stood there with my eyes closed until Charlie got up and gently lowered me into my folding chair.

"It's all right, Itchy," he said. And he held my hand.

Mayor Donaghy didn't exploit my brother after all. He gave a short speech, a quiet speech, in a voice a father might use with a young son who did something wrong because he didn't know any better. He talked about loss and healing.

He was fifty, but he looked much older. He spoke without notes into the microphone they'd set up, but stopped often to collect his thoughts. His face was filled with wrinkles, deep ones, all connected together, and sometimes his face looked so sad, you could imagine he might have lost a son himself once.

He talked about the riots at the factory and the fights the night before and promised he wouldn't let that change anything. The race would go on today. Work would pick up on Monday, but he asked that we stop it all. He defended the factory as vital to the town's economy and promised to speak to his son about diversifying the business and someday moving away from the guns.

"But you must not think that it's wrong to make these guns," he said. "It is distasteful, but it is necessary. Whether the war is right, and I believe it is, or whether it's wrong, and you have a right to believe that, it does exist. It goes on, and it will go on, and as long as boys from Deadwhale and all over the country must fight, it's our duty, it's our honor, to supply them with the tools they need to defend their lives."

No matter how hard I tried, I could not hate Mayor Donaghy that morning. I wished he would speak forever, because somewhere in his words, there was a sanity, and even a goodness, that I would never have expected from the man so many blamed for Mayor Waters' death. His voice was sad, soft, and slow, and I wondered what had really happened between him and the mayor, between him and the mayor's wife, but these were things I would never know.

And he was finished, and it was time for what I'd been dreading for days. My father would have to thank them and speak about the death of his favorite son. He walked slowly to the microphone. All was silence now, and I could hear the ocean far in the distance. I could hear an airplane overhead and my father breathing hard into the microphone.

He looked lost inside his suit now. He was losing weight by the day. His face was thinner than mine, and I saw Patrick in it. His hair was nearly white, like his father's. It was an eerie combination of my father, my grandfather, and my brother all in one face.

He thanked the mayor. He thanked us all for coming. He dabbed at the sweat on his forehead and cheeks and rocked from side to side. The microphone amplified his every breath. The bottoms of his pants were bunched up against his shoes.

"It wasn't so long ago, I had three sons," he said. "But now Patrick's dead, and that's why I'm up here. I was proud when he went to Vietnam. I didn't know where it was or have much idea why we were fighting, but we're all taught from the time we're little that it's an honor to fight for our country and an honor to die for it, too, and so I was proud.

"I just missed World War Two by a little, so maybe I felt like Patrick was doing the fighting I should've done. I don't know, but we're honored now that his name's in this wall in his hometown, and that he's a hero. I'm proud of him, but I wish he didn't go."

He stopped. He looked back at my mother for a second. When he coughed, it came out loud through the microphone. Everyone was silent and staring at him. I thought of Joe Waters the night before, appearing in a lightning bolt, like something blasted out of hell. I remembered the day I'd heard about Patrick's death. Taps ran through my mind.

"Anyway," he said. "I got two other sons. My youngest, Charlie, he wants to go to Vietnam. My middle son, Dennis, he's got himself mixed up with this Robin."

He stopped again. He kept rocking from side to side.

"It causes a lot of strain having sons on different sides. It makes me think a lot. Maybe if I didn't have these other boys, I would just forget it all, but I don't want to go through this again, and I was thinking, if we had to fight in Korea and Vietnam, does that mean we have to fight in every little country in the world, no matter how far away, every time the communists make a move? Will we be having these little wars forever?"

He shrugged. He looked back at my mother, then Charlie, then me.

"I'm not a smart man," he said. "I don't understand why we're fighting. All I know is, I don't want my other sons to go. There's something wrong inside me now, something I can't quite put in words.

"My wife, Anna, she writes letters to Patrick and puts them under the door to his bedroom. She don't go in the bedroom ever, but I do. I go in and dust off his bureau and pick up the letters and throw them on his bed. The bed's all covered with them now. They've got stamps and that address we used to send to. I don't have the heart to read them, but there's something I do in there.

"There's a picture of him when he was pretty young, and sometimes I talk to it. Maybe I just ask how he's doing, or tell him some things that are happening around town. Sometimes I talk to him about baseball. He liked the Phillies, and so do I, so sometimes I tell him how Johnny Callison's doing, or Tony Taylor."

He smiled at my mother. He looked at Mayor Donaghy.

"I don't think she should have to write them letters, but she does. I...well, nobody can understand unless they know, I guess. It's just like having your heart broke forever.

"Thank you, Mayor, for honoring Patrick. I...I can't stand to lose another son, to watch him fly out with a duffel bag, then go sit back in Deadwhale and wonder if I'll ever see him again, wonder every morning if he's going to make it through the day. It's awful hard to sleep at night when your son might be in a battle on the other side of the world while you're having dreams, and you know there's a pretty good chance he's going to die before you wake up."

He stopped for a long time. No one moved. No one whispered. The mayor stared at my father.

"Anyway," he said. "I guess if I keep making guns, I'm helping keep that war going, and I don't like that war. No, I don't like it. So, I won't be working at the factory anymore. I don't plan on causing any trouble or marching in the streets like some fool. But I can't make them guns anymore. I can't, and I won't."

He nodded at the mayor. He turned and sat down. There was the longest silence. It seemed like it would go on forever, but then I was out of my seat and shaking my father's hand. His eyes met mine for a second, little wet darting gray things that shot away, then came back to mine, shot away again, then settled on mine a few seconds, before finally, for the first time since Patrick's death, he looked at me and smiled, and I heard the cheers rising up from the seats around the stage, and soon everyone was standing, and they were cheering for my father.

19

There was a big crowd for the race. It was noon, and the sun blazed on our necks. About two hundred runners clumped in the middle of the street. An airplane puttered overhead, trailing a streamer with some important message.

The runners joked and stretched. Charlie touched his toes, and his huge muscles shined with sun tan lotion. Stewart Donaghy stood near the front, squinting against the sun in white shorts and a sleeveless shirt that said Columbia.

I was sleepy and scared. I'd never raced before, but I'd been practicing for months against my stopwatch. I knew every landmark along the way and how quick I had to get there to beat Donaghy's best time. I'd never done it, but I'd come close. If he'd slowed any since setting his record, I had a chance. He was twenty-eight, and he looked good, and I had my work cut out for me.

Right before the gun blasted, Nigel showed up in his coat with his eyes glazed over and red and practically popping out of their sockets. He walked to the starting line with two of his goons, pulled a bottle from his pocket, took a long swallow, then nodded at his buddies. They ripped off his coat, like they do with wrestlers or kings, and Nigel turned to face us in the tightest pair of bathing trunks I ever saw in my life, and nothing else.

Charlie blurted out, "The guy's got a bazooka in his bathing suit. What a man." Even Nigel smiled, and all the runners laughed.

Nigel had shaved a peace sign through the hair on his chest and painted it orange, and when he turned around, there was another peace sign on his back, and when the gun fired, he charged forward like a racehorse, just flying out in front of the crowd with his peace sign glowing in the sun and his bare legs and feet churning, his arms pumping like crazy, a pace I figured would kill him in a minute, or else he was going to break the world record. He ran a hundred yards faster than any man I'd ever seen, turned, and came charging back the other way. He cut a line right through us and kept on running. Lord knows where. I looked back once and saw him heading the other way, a charging bull with a sweaty peace symbol on his back.

Then Charlie took the lead with a big smile on his face. He tapped me as he went past.

"What a guy," he said.

Charlie wore a shirt with a six and the name Callison, the shirt Patrick won the race in. In '64, the Phillies lost ten in a row and blew a six and a half game lead with twelve left. Patrick loved those Phillies, and Johnny Callison was his hero that year. Now the Phillies were awful, Johnny Callison was nothing like he used to be, and Patrick was dead, but seeing that shirt, all stretched on Charlie's back, brought the memories back, and my heart ached for the Phillies and Patrick, who would never see them win a World Series.

I'd hoped to wear that shirt myself. I'd gone home after the ceremony, but Charlie already had it. My mother suggested one of Patrick's other shirts, but I didn't want that, so she gave me a present. She'd bought us each a sleeveless T-shirt with USA ironed on the front, like someone in the Olympics.

"I thought you might like this," she said. "Stewart Donaghy always looks so nice when he runs."

"I'm not Stewart Donaghy," I said.

I didn't want to wear it, but when I looked at her face, I changed my mind. I slipped the shirt over my raggedy gym pants. My father frowned.

"The kid's skinny as hell," he said.

"But I'm fast," I said.

"Charlie says he's going to win," my father said.

"I don't think so, Dad."

"How about you?"

"I might. You coming?"

"I don't think so. I can't stand to watch Donaghy win."

The first mile passed well. Charlie'd taken a big lead, but I doubted he would last. He'd explained his strategy before the race at the memorial. I'd come back to look at Patrick's name, but Charlie'd beaten me there. He sat in front of the stone wall, running his fingers over the numbers and letters. Suzanne stood smoking beside him. Her hand rested on Charlie's neck. She didn't say hello. She just asked the question in her tired voice.

"I guess you haven't seen him?"

"No," I said.

"But you saw him last night. It was him, right?"

"No doubt about it."

"You're the only one who saw him so close."

"Lots of people saw him."

"But you were right there, and you knew him. You saw him, didn't you?"

"Yes."

Charlie started tying his shoelaces. He didn't want me to know he'd been touching Patrick's name.

"Hi, Itch."

"So what's the strategy?" I asked.

"Easy, man." He jumped to his feet in Patrick's Johnny Callison shirt. "I'll just get out front and hold on."

"Charlie, it's five miles. The last two are over sand."

"So what? If I get out front and refuse to give in, how's that asshole going to catch me? Huh? If I just refuse, he can't catch me."

"Your body will give in," I said.

He laughed. "Oh, come on, Itchy. What are you going to do, track him down with your stupid stopwatch?" He put his arm around Suzanne. She fell back against him. I clamped my teeth down on my tongue. It hurt.

"Itchy's got to be scientific," he said. "He don't understand about will power. I'll just get out there and hold on. Five miles is nothing, man. Charlie meets any challenge."

"You still can't blow a peanut out your nose," I said.

"I swear I'm going to put one on the moon just to shut you up."

"I don't understand why he doesn't come home," Suzanne said. "I mean, if he's in Deadwhale, why doesn't he come home, or why doesn't he visit Robin? I called the police, but they won't do anything. It's like talking to monkeys."

"He'll show up when he's ready," Charlie said. "Here, put this junk on me." He handed her the sun tan lotion. "I'm going to be a greasy streak of lightning."

"Good luck," I said. I didn't think I could stand watching Suzanne run her hands all over his body, but he pulled me back.

"This is for Patrick, Itchy. Don't forget."

The greasy streak of lightning was far ahead, but I was more worried about Donaghy. I didn't want him too far out when we reached the sand. He was ahead of his pace. Whenever I looked at my stopwatch, I was amazed. I'd never run so fast. I was beating his record, and he was seven seconds ahead.

The sun blazed. I was used to the cool beach at night. I was surrounded by pounding feet and stinking men in sweat-stained shorts. They panted and plodded along. I ran barefoot, as usual, and felt the stones and glass cutting at my feet.

Faces lined both sides of the road, faces and voices shouting at us. Someone threw a coke in my face. Ice and soda rolled down my chest and into my shorts. Someone said, "That's her faggot boyfriend." I felt sad, but kept running.

When we hit the beach, Charlie was still far ahead. The drenching rain had hardened the sand, but the sun was hot, and the sand was nearly dry already. Donaghy had me by about fifty yards. I glanced back and saw the others stretched out behind us and the spectators swarming onto the sand.

I could hear the waves pounding in and whooshing out. I squinted. My hair stuck to my neck, and stinging sweat trickled into my eyes. The sand sucked me in. It was like running in a nightmare, but I was used to it. I took long strides and coasted over it before it could pull me in and suck away my strength.

I tasted the sweat with my tongue. My throat was parched. Donaghy was smooth. His arms were tan and lean and powerful and full of flexing muscle. His legs were thin, endlessly pumping and striding and kicking up sand. I just stared at those wonderful calves, sucked in that hot air, and ran.

The race went far down the beach, turned at a lifeguard stand, then headed back over the mile we'd just covered, and on up to the finish. Charlie made the turn first, and when he came back on my right, I saw the agony in his face. He'd done incredibly well. He'd held the lead for four miles on his tight end's legs at an inhuman pace, but he couldn't possibly last. He was heavy and clumsy, and his feet went deep into the sand before he pulled out and pushed on.

Donaghy turned at the lifeguard stand. Our eyes met for a second. He smiled. He looked strong, much too strong. When I made the turn, I couldn't believe my watch. I was five seconds ahead of his best time, eight seconds ahead of mine, and still trailing. I tossed the watch away.

My side split. The sweat ate into my cheeks, and he lengthened his lead. No one was close. He was way out there and going after Charlie. He was going too soon. Charlie had slugged him off a stage the night before. Charlie had stood up to his gun. He was spooked by Charlie, and now he was making his first mistake. He had underestimated me and overestimated my brother.

I saw the others on my right, a long line stretching way down the beach, some crumpled into the sand, some purple and wheezing and gripping their sides, others plodding along comfortably, but no one in striking distance.

I couldn't let him get too far ahead. My face burned. My ears rang. My back ached. My side ached. My lungs begged for oxygen. But the worst hit my stomach. My legs could last as long as that gut fire held off. I could ignore the rest, just keep moving, one foot in front of the other, over and over like the waves. Ignore the fear. Ignore the pain, the heat, the exhaustion.

It was all will. My body could go forever if I could deal with the pain. A question of will. Mind over matter. Determination. The body said stop. The mind said go.

I thought of Joe, one-armed in the lightning, just a flash of him. Where'd he come from? Where'd he go? Where'd he been all these months?

I thought of Suzanne. Poor, miserable, chain-smoking Suzanne. What was she doing with Charlie? I wanted her so bad. I wanted to win for her. I wanted her to know I loved her, but I couldn't tell her, and now Charlie had her. It was unbelievable. It was the worst dream ever dreamt, next to what happened to Patrick.

I thought of Patrick buried in pieces in the earth, his name etched below the monument in the center of town, his wonderful laugh gone, and I looked ahead to his old shirt, and just as I did, Charlie lurched.

His legs banged together. His knees dipped. He almost went down. His right hand grazed the sand, then his left, then he was up and running, but crookedly, weaving left and right. Donaghy didn't pick up speed. He knew he had him. He just kept coasting on while Charlie fought against the sand, his huge body slumping and fighting, and I realized how brave he was and how incredibly well he'd done. He hadn't trained like me. He couldn't run like me. He was huge and clumsy and ruined by the sand, but he'd held the lead over four miles, doing it all with the power of his heart, and I shouted up to him.

"It's okay, Charlie. I got him."

Donaghy glanced back over his shoulder.

"That's right," I shouted. "I got you."

I came on harder. Charlie lurched again. He fell. He got up. He fell again. He got up again, and Donaghy breezed past him.

I came alongside Charlie just as the speed faded out of him. His eyes were glazed. He looked at me, and tears poured down his face.

"I can't," he said. He wheezed and choked. His face was pure red.

"You okay?" I asked.

"Itchy, can you catch him?"

"Maybe."

"Take it." He yanked the shirt over his head. "Wear the shirt. It's for Patrick. Patrick."

He handed it to me, then fell, hitting the sand face first, letting loose a horrible moan, and shouting, "Go. Go."

I looked back once and saw him crawl a few steps, then stop, face down and still in the sand, only his horrible sobs telling me he was alive. I slid Patrick's stretched and drenched shirt over mine and began the final chase with tears and sweat eating into my skin and Charlie down in the sand behind me.

And on I went. Step after step. Pain upon pain, straining to match his stride. God, I hated him. Every elusive dream of my young and uneventful life ran out there ahead of me. Why didn't he struggle? I huffed. My legs knocked together. Tears stiffened on my face. Twenty yards back and running out of time, over and over, one foot in front of the other.

But there was hope. He'd spent himself chasing Charlie. He'd been far past his record pace when I threw my watch. He couldn't have improved that much. He was running an Olympian's pace, and he wasn't an Olympian. If he was, he would have been heading to Mexico. He'd failed at that, and I knew he had to slow down. I had time. There had to be time.

I wished Patrick could see me chasing his enemy, the person who'd humiliated him just two years before, turning at the finish line to run through backward, turning and taunting Patrick, who fell ten feet behind him and had to crawl over the line.

I wanted to win so bad, but I couldn't hold on much longer. My body refused. I kept seeing Charlie stumbling into the sand, thudding down in a cloud of dirt, twisting and rolling and crawling until he finally collapsed.

I could never win. My stomach was on fire. Every step was a chunk of heart swallowed in the flames, and I kept digging at it, and I knew I would run out. What could I give then? I had to break stride. I had cut his lead, but I was sick. I could faint. I could die. Half a mile left.

I surrendered. I got ready to shift, and then I heard a voice, just one lone cracking voice from the sand to the left. We'd reached the far end of the crowd.

"Come on, Itchy." It was my father. "You're catching up. Don't let him beat you."

I looked. They were all blurry, my parents, in the outfits they'd worn to Patrick's memorial, out front of the line of cheering people, and not far from them, Suzanne, smoking and shouting at me, and beside her, amazingly, stood Robin, all bruised and swollen, holding hands with Irv, waving at me with one of her battered arms.

And people I had never met were shouting "number six" and "Callison" and "Itchy."

I laughed. I could hardly breathe, hardly think, hardly see, but I laughed and ran after Donaghy with tears blowing off my cheeks.

I saw the tape, the finish, the faces. I was five yards back and closing. He was slowing down. Less than a quarter mile. Another minute. A minute forever. An endless minute. My heart had burnt up. I ran on insanity. I had to move, had to catch him. I'd been sprinting down this beach all year, burning myself for that last burst. I could fly at the end.

I roared and sliced the gap, wheezing at his shoulder, and I saw his surprise and horror and hate and determination, and for one split second, I loved him. I was right behind him. It was all there. Every ounce of guts and heart, all right there, and if I lost, I would lose it all forever.

"I'm with you." I wheezed it out. "Every step you take."

"I beat your brothers. I'll beat you."

I saw black and green and a shimmering flash of orange. I decided to go. I shouted. The crowd wavered, diffused through heat and delirium. I pushed. I stretched, glided, and passed him. Nothing between me and victory. I felt the joy, and he passed me right back. My heart broke. I pushed harder. I pulled alongside. Tears streamed. Sweat poured, rolling down my chest, greasing my pumping arms.

And something snapped inside me. I felt like I'd hit a wall. I expected the blood to come pouring down my face. I felt like I was falling, falling forever, deeper and deeper into an endless tunnel, a black hole that spiraled down forever. I thought I'd died and that I would fall for a million years, and I saw them far ahead on a patch of sand under a streak of sunlight deep within the hole, and they were waving. They called me on.

My body had taken its last breath, but I was falling and still running, and waving me on were the three of them. Joe was out front, dirty, old, and bruised, shouting for me to fall faster, and Patrick was there in a uniform and with no hair, and beside Patrick stood Mayor Waters, taller than the others, huge, glowing in that beam of light. His eyes had been plucked out. His brain leaked through a rip in his skull, but he was calling my name, and I continued to fall, and then it snapped again.

I was out. I was swallowed in flames of unbearable sunshine and pain. I saw the finish, people jumping and shouting on both sides. We sprinted full out. Full, wild, furious sprint, side by side, like the ocean, like the wind, our legs and arms pumping up and down, the veins throbbing in our necks, hair flying, eyes hooked to the tape, pumping and pumping and pumping.

And Donaghy cut right a little, just enough to push against me, throw me off, nearly trip me. His elbow hit my chest once, twice, a third time. I stumbled, almost went down, moved right, and he kept coming, forcing me over, trying to cut me down, forcing me to work harder than ever.

I saw the tape, the finish. Only yards. I saw Donaghy. Side to side. I hurtled toward the finish. I pumped. I cried. I wheezed. "Jeeez Christ. Jeeez Christ. Jeeez Christ." People shouted and jumped all around us, and then I made my mistake. He came at me again, gently but irresistibly, mixing his legs with mine, beating his arm against me, and I swung out hard with my elbow, just slamming his shoulder. He backed off, but we were close to the finish, and people saw.

And Patrick's eyes appeared before me and pulled me through the pain. The pain. The noise. The leaping, shouting crowd, and we charged over the final yards without an inch between us, and Donaghy lunged for the tape, his arms spread, his head out. He was diving. I was dying. He would touch. I would lose. He'd tricked me. He'd beaten me. I was dead. He went down. He missed. He fell too soon. I grabbed the tape and crossed and rolled and blanked out in the sand, but I'd won. I won. I beat him. I swirled through that deep and endless tunnel into Patrick's arms and didn't wake up for a long time.

20

Ah, the fireworks were fun. Charlie kept bringing people over to shake my hand. He kept walking around our blanket on the beach and pointing to me and shouting, "Itchy Shovlin's over here, fastest runner on earth." He would sit for a few minutes, maybe drink some beer, then jump up and do it again. I expected him to build a tent around me and sell tickets.

Of course, it would have been more fun if Suzanne was with me instead of with him. He kept kissing her. He made these sickening smacking sounds and whispered sweet stupidities into her ear, probably stuff about peanuts and football, but I was getting used to it. I would have to until Suzanne came to her senses or I figured some way to have Charlie bumped off. I tried being philosophical about it. Charlie was my brother and I loved him, but he was an idiot, too, and I figured Suzanne would catch on soon enough, or else I just didn't understand how life worked.

The air was full of pot, and there were parties all along the sand around wine and beer and joints that circled and flared like fireflies. Everyone cheered and laughed, and no one argued about the war or the factory.

It was a peaceful night, the eye in the hurricane, and even with Suzanne squeezing Charlie's fat, ugly hand, and Robin's face so bruised that Charlie'd nicknamed her the space monkey, I felt happy. I'd beaten Stewart Donaghy across the finish line, and Robin held my hand, and the colors blazed against the sky.

Of course, I'd lost the race. When Donaghy'd nudged and tripped

me to cut off my final charge, he'd done it with skill, but I'd lifted
my elbow and slammed it across his chest, like somebody knocking
down a tree, and they'd disqualified me.

When they announced the winner, the crowd booed, and all night
on the beach, people told me I'd been cheated.

The protesting didn't start again right away. First was the healing.
Whatever they'd broken in Robin's face, they hadn't shut her up.
Her determination got more vicious, but instead of just going nuts
with fury, she got smarter. She was determined now to outthink
them, then destroy them.

Within days she was on the streets again, hobbling along all bandaged and swollen, but healthier than I'd ever known her. She'd
slept and eaten like a normal person and cut the booze and pot. Her
face was finding its old shape, but it would never quite look the
same. It wasn't just the added twist to her nose. It was a change of
expression.

She didn't look so young anymore. A look of permanent serious-
ness mixed with a lot of fear in her only eye, made her look a little
desperate, a little dangerous, like someone running out of time.

She spent that week when it hurt to talk or move, searching the
back streets and alleys with Suzanne, haunting the police and the
papers and all the contacts she'd made in the neighborhoods, in a
hopeless attempt to find Joe.

They were two hopeless lunatics that week, but Suzanne was the
worse, chain smoking, drinking, never sleeping, scouring the
beaches, bothering the police at all hours, asking me the same questions until I shouted at her.

"Yes, it was him, Suzanne. I know it was him."

"Where did he go?" she would ask. "I just want to see him so
much."

I was splitting apart. It drove me crazy to see her with Charlie. I
couldn't hold the idea in my head. It was like trying to understand
the theory of relativity or imagine men evolving up from fish. It
kept me awake at night with a puzzled look on my face that hurt
after a while, but there was something good in it. Maybe she would
keep Charlie from going to Vietnam. Nothing else was going to. His
thick head was set on it. Maybe she would save him.

There were times I wanted to step between them, tell them they
looked stupid together, like a French poodle and a German shep-
herd, tell them how little they had in common besides the fact they
breathed air and walked on two legs, but then I would think of

Charlie hunched down in some rice paddy with mortars crashing all around him, or Charlie's name on that wall beneath Patrick's, both brothers shrunk to little scrawlings in stone that would fade in the rain and the years like millions of other names on monuments all over the earth, and I would throw myself over in the sleeping bag and hope Suzanne could keep him home.

I was eighteen, smart, supposedly smarter than anyone in my school, or even in my town, and I didn't understand a thing. I didn't understand my country, my family, or my friends. The world seemed crazy. The only thing that kept me going was my anger and Robin's blazing body in the night.

Sometimes I felt strong. Sometimes I was scared, but I didn't know where I was going, what I wanted, or what could possibly happen next. Then I got the most amazing phone call.

It came around seven just a couple days after Robin hit the streets again. She and Suzanne were in the kitchen. Suzanne was drinking and smoking, as usual. Robin was explaining how everybody knew her now, and how people were always grabbing for her hands and kissing her, and how even the ones who hated her listened. Everywhere she went, they cheered and cursed, and Deadwhale went crazy all around her.

Downtown and all along the beach, the streets were packed with summer tourists. Her hotel was jammed. Every No Vacancy sign in Deadwhale burned. The beaches overflowed, and hippies swarmed the park behind the memorial with their guitars and their hair and their pretty girls. They gathered by the hundreds on the wharf and dangled their bare feet over our half boardwalk, smoking marijuana and singing. They held huge parties under the Ferris wheel at night, and they talked about Robin as if she were God or Bob Dylan.

They camped on the beaches against the law. They made love in their tents and their sleeping bags and right out on the sand. They did LSD and walked naked by the water in the early morning. They slept in tents in the parks, and when the cops chased them from one spot, they rolled up their sleeping bags and moved to another.

And there were Nazis, too, and grown men in sheets who marched through the center of town with swastikas and burning crosses at night or in the middle of the afternoon, fighting with the crowds that turned out to attack them. There were veterans against the war holding sit-down strikes on the roads to the factory. There were beatniks, evangelists, Hari Krishnas. There were factory workers marching in support of their jobs. There were veterans of other wars who thought this one was just fine. There were always lines of people marching through the streets and waving signs, and hundreds of others shouting from the sidewalks.

The stores were filled, the bars, the clubs. The strip was packed. The doughnut shop was a madhouse. Money poured into town. The factory cranked out guns. I cranked out doughnuts. Rock music blared into the night.

Coke Phillips gave speeches on the steps of city hall. Small groups of blacks staged sit-ins for jobs. Black Power guys set off bombs. The violence of April never really ended in Southwest Deadwhale. Sirens seemed always to blare from that direction. Smoke rose every night into the sky. Southwest Deadwhale was like a war zone and another world. I'd never been in there in my life. It was a place you just didn't go.

Every day Nigel led his growing band of radicals to the factory, never making it again to Industrial Drive, always throwing themselves against the line of cops that came out to stop them with clubs and tear gas somewhere in Little Brooklyn then cart half of them to jail. The jails were always packed. The cops were always tired. Nigel walked the streets shouting into his bullhorn, his face painted, and his eyes shooting fire.

He organized protests on the steps of city hall to correspond with Coke's. He organized draft card burnings and flag burnings and all kinds of violent desecrations of city property. His boys and girls waved North Vietnamese flags, Vietcong flags, Russian flags with the hammer and sickle. They charged the police with sticks and rocks and crazy helmets.

He dropped by once a night to fill Robin in. He marched around her living room stinking of tear gas, sweat, and whiskey, raving about the cops, the war, the fascists, burning me with his eyes, touching Robin on the shoulder, the hands, the face, pointing and shouting, shifting from his British to his American accent, then charging out the door like a tornado that had come in through the window and shot out again, leaving just a stink, a chill, and a memory.

Compared to Nigel, who'd taken to writing her letters about how much he wanted her, compared to the Nazis and the Ku Klux Klan, tiny Robin, with her foul mouth, her men's clothes, her argyle socks, and her battered nose, was a moderate. But still, police in uniform and men in suits attended her every speech. They waited across the street from the hotel. They followed her in her endless search for

Joe or down to the strip to check on her places.

They trailed her in police cars when she rode by bike into South-west Deadwhale to meet with Coke. Once they warned her about going in. Southwest Deadwhale had become more dangerous than ever. The Black Power guys turned over cars in the night. They fired guns, started fires, and broke windows. Coke couldn't reason with them, but Robin went in and gave speeches by his side.

She was straight. She was determined. She was calm, but when she got home those nights, it looked like her face would crack off and fall in little pieces if I snapped my fingers.

I was listening to Robin and Suzanne when the phone rang. It had rung twice in the past hour, but Robin had answered, and it had clicked silent. I hated answering the phone. Usually it was some heavy-breathing patriot who wanted to shout into Robin's ear. Something like, "Love it, or leave it, bitch." This time I knew the voice right away. It was Joe's.

"Don't let on," he said. "Understand?"

"Yes," I said.

"Is she there?"

"Yeah."

"Lie to her," he said. "Take this number and call it as fast as you can. How soon?"

"Ten minutes."

"Okay."

He gave me the number, and the phone went dead. Robin and Suzanne looked at me for a second. I shrugged.

"Another weirdo," I said.

"It never ends," Robin said, and Suzanne lit a cigarette.

21

Joe's directions led far to the west end of town, out where the marshes, the bay, and Fishtown all came together near the very edge of Deadwhale, a point where no one lived, no lights burned, and the crickets scraped up the air with their noise.

The sun was nearly down. I had one of Robin's bikes, but the road was lumpy and cracked, and I was walking now. A house slumped off to the side where the road vanished into the weeds. It was a wooden house raised on stilts that collapsed in back, tilting the house almost into the mud. A set of broken planks led from the back out over the shallow puddles. There must have been more water once, but the bay didn't come in this far anymore.

The paint had peeled away. The windows were long broken out, but there was a ripped screen in one, all shredded and dangling, and the house was half-hidden and choking in the wild grass that swarmed against it.

I waited for the longest time, while mosquitoes sucked up my blood. Joe'd made me promise not to come in until I saw a flash of light, and the flash didn't come until complete blackness had settled over the house.

I was scared. I'd never seen it so dark. I could hardly see the house. I couldn't see the road. I tripped once over the bike, but what scared me most was Joe.

He'd hardly said a thing on the phone, just giving the directions and making me swear to keep it secret. His voice had been low, calm, but hard-edged and cold. My hand sweated on the receiver.

"Do you understand?" he'd asked.

"Yeah."

"Itchy." And then his voice was barely a whisper. "I died." The phone clicked, and then I didn't hear anything.

There were a few stars, no moon, lots of clouds, and then a flash of fire that sent up strange shadows and vanished, just the flick of a lighter, or a match. I laid Robin's bike in the road. I'd been holding the handlebars, standing beside it in the dark. It made me feel better, ready for a getaway. Now I felt naked, groping along, the steps creaking underneath me. I climbed them toward the black hole behind the doorway. Weeds swished between my legs. The railing nearly broke in my hand. I stepped through that black mouth into the house. It was hot in there.

"Joe," I said.

I waited a long time. Spider web brushed my face, and something scraped across the floor, maybe a mouse or a rabbit, maybe worse. I squinted into the black, but couldn't see a thing, absolutely nothing. When I couldn't stand it anymore, I reached for my matches. I always had matches because Robin hardly used electric light in the apartment, only candles.

The second I struck it, something slapped against my hand, and the match went out.

"Give me them."

He snatched them away. I smelled the smoke. I smelled Joe.

"No light," he said. "Ever. Sit."

I felt like he had a gun on me. I found a spot on the dusty wood. My heart beat too hard. I thought of his words. "Itchy, I died." I thought of the scratching I'd heard a few seconds before and expected something to run across my lap, bite my hand, or lay cold fingers on my neck.

He spoke. "You didn't tell anyone?"

"No," I said. "God, does it have to be so dark?"

"I see better in the dark," he said.

"Well, I can't see shit."

"Then you'll have to learn," he said.

I slid back against the wall. I felt safer with something behind me. There was spider web on my hand, spider web in my hair. Something shot across the floor.

"How's Robin?" he asked.

"Okay now, I guess. Are there rats in here?"

"She's lost," he said.

"Joe, what's running around in here? I'm not sitting here if some stinking rat's going to take a chunk out of my hand."

But he just ignored me.

"I'm watching her," he said. "I'm watching Suzanne."

I heard something digging at the far wall. My eyes weren't adjusting much. I couldn't find Joe.

"How long you been back?" I asked.

"Just before your march on the factory."

"We were worried about you, scared. I was afraid you died."

"I did," he said. "But only for a while."

"Did what?"

Wings fluttered deep in the house. They stopped, then fluttered again. The night was full of noise. I couldn't see, but I could hear every sound, every strange bird, frog, and cricket.

I wasn't sure I understood him. I tried to let it pass. I was scared. All the humor was gone from his voice, all the personality and charm. I imagined his face as a blank. I imagined his eyes off-center, glazed, and far away.

"Are you all right?" I asked. "Man, we were so worried. Why didn't you contact anybody?"

"I was lost, too," he said.

I couldn't figure out where he was. His voice came from different spots in the room. He must have been pacing, but I couldn't hear him move, and his voice was so soft and clear, it seemed almost unreal.

"You're Robin's lover," he said.

It wasn't a question.

"What do you mean?" I whispered.

"I saw it."

Something slammed way back in the house. I wanted to move. I wanted to run. I wanted to see Joe so bad, but no matter how hard I strained, I saw nothing.

"I saw everything," he said. "Only I didn't know who you were, and I didn't understand it all. I've been away so long, and there were so many dreams. I mean, not just away from Deadwhale, but away, away from my body, from consciousness, from earth. I died, Itchy."

I felt sick when he said it.

"Come on, Joe. Quit saying stuff like that. It's getting me spooked."

"It's true."

"You telling me you're some kind of ghost?"

"No," he said. "My heart beats, and I take food from the forest, but for a short while in that Viet hell, I was dead, and after that, well, after that I'm not sure."

"What do you mean, you were dead?"

"I was dead in the grass. I saw my arm hanging off and my face burnt and the whole squad around me, all dead. We were together, though, dead together, just sort of hovering above it all, watching the NVA pick over our bodies, pump rounds in any that weren't stiff enough for them, rip away our boots, stack up our weapons. I could feel the others with me, only somehow I knew they were farther gone. They were going on, but for me, it hadn't been decided."

He was closer now. I could hear him breathing. I could smell him again, a mix of things, like grass and dirt and sweat. I had a feeling I was smelling the war.

"I used to love that body," he said. "I worked so hard on it, two hundred push-ups a day, two hundred sit-ups, like Charlie, combing that silly hair. I used to stare at myself in the mirror. I thought I was beautiful, and there were always girls saying so, and there it was, my body, me, all burnt and bleeding, my face black, and I just didn't care.

"I was happy to be away from it. I had no feelings, just curiosity, while they sliced off my arm. Who knows why they did it? Maybe they didn't like half-finished work. There wasn't much left of it anyway, just some splinters and melted skin, but they hacked it off with a knife and threw it in the trees. I didn't hate them. I didn't give a shit about the arm. I felt sorry for them, really, and just a little sorry for my body, and I was confused why the stump didn't pour blood. It's funny what you wonder when you're dead."

"You saw all this? You didn't dream it? I mean, when they gave you morphine or something?"

"That's what I'm telling you. I was dead, and all my friends were dead, and the men who'd ambushed us were taking our stuff. They were quiet, nervous, very businesslike. They just butchered six men as casually as you brush your teeth, and I wanted to know them, get to understand why, and I had the feeling I loved them and we were all the same, and I realized, in some higher way, some way that had nothing to do with reasoning, that the war was wrong, and then I died."

"What do you mean you died? How'd it happen?" I asked. "Your arm, I mean, the whole thing?"

"I don't know. I remember something hitting some sergeant in the neck. I can't remember his name, but I remember how he blew up, just disintegrated, except for his head, and that floated up into the air, and there were screams, fire and shots, and pain, and then nothing. There's blank spaces, weeks, even years gone from my memory, but mostly I can't remember what happened that day or how I ended up where they found me, and even, for a long time, months I guess, I couldn't remember my name.

"They found me miles from where I should have been. My arm'd been bandaged and my face. I'd been fed. They told me this in the hospital, and when they asked my name or my unit or where I'd been, I couldn't tell them. I couldn't tell them anything. I could only remember my dead body and dying, the peace, the light, and meeting my father, and then there were just dreams, days and days, an eternity of dreams.

"I died, but they let me come back. I have a mission, you see."

"What's that, Joe?"

"To die again," he said.

"But why? What good's that?"

"Please, Itchy. I can't explain. I get tired when I think about it. The doctors say there's no damage to my mind, but I get so tired, and I have this terrible pain in my fingers, the missing ones.

"Come back. Every night if you can. I know how to live in the jungle in the dark. I was a good soldier. I believed for a while, and when the VC came, I was ready to kill, ready to die. Yeah, I believed, but when it was over and we counted the dead, I wanted to be counted, too, and then I didn't believe so much, and later, I didn't believe at all.

"Being lonely doesn't hurt. There's nothing lonely like combat, but I need to know what's happening in the town and with Robin and Suzanne. I need to know when it's time."

"So go home. Visit Robin. She's looking all over for you, and Suzanne's even worse."

He was quiet for a long time. Something buzzed off my face. I swatted at it longer and harder than I should have, but it was gone. I heard a scuffling sound in the corner behind one of the walls. I imagined Joe heard it, too. I imagined he knew every sound in that house, maybe every sound for miles around. I imagined he knew how to live with rats and every kind of bug and spider. He was at home in the darkness. He was part of it.

"I'll see Suzanne when I'm ready," he said. "Tell her that I'll find her, but don't let her find me. Don't let anyone find me."

His voice was stern.

"But what about Robin?"

"I'll see her at the end," he said. "At the factory."

"Joe, she's hardly holding on."

"Tell her I'm with her," he said. "Tell her not to doubt herself. When the time's right, I'll be there, but she'll never find me, and the harder she looks, the harder it will get.

"And tell her this, Itchy, so she'll believe in me. Tell her she shouldn't feel guilty, that what happened was my father's fault and that he forgives her. My father forgives her, and so does the neighbor."

I heard my breath hiss out. I reached for him in the darkness. I wanted to touch him bad, to prove that he was there, that I wasn't dreaming. He was close, but I couldn't reach him.

"Who's the neighbor?" I asked.

"The light in Robin's dreams," he said. "The light of my death. The one Suzanne calls the keeper."

"But, Joe, I don't understand any of it. You didn't tell me where you've been, or what happened to you, or why you won't see Robin. And what's all this shit about your father and this neighbor and..."

I stopped. I heard the shuffling in the wall again, the sound of claws against wood, like something trapped and scraping like hell to get out. Something fluttered against my face, and I stabbed at the dark, but all I got was air. The shuffling stopped. I whispered his name, but there was no one there. I was alone in the black night.

22

It was hours later. Robin and I had just made love in her bed, and I was trying to figure out how to tell her about Joe without ruining the mood. A candle dripped on the bureau and made shadows, and our hearts pounded together. The dark reminded me of Joe, and I knew I had to tell her.

She pulled a bottle of water off the floor and poured some between us. She rubbed her chest against mine to spread the water around so we wouldn't stick. She gave me a big kiss.

"What about a hunger strike?" she said.

"Huh?"

"I was thinking a hunger strike might help close the factory."

"You think about the factory while we're doing that?"

"Yeah. What do you think about, the Pittsburgh Phillies?"

"Pittsburgh Pirates, Robin. I hate them. The Phillies are from Philadelphia."

"Pittsburgh, Philadelphia, what's the difference? You still didn't tell me what you think about."

"You, mainly," I said.

"I think about you, too. I was thinking you'd go on a hunger strike."

"You do it. It's your stinking idea."

"I'm too skinny."

"Then get Nigel to do it. He could lose some weight."

She threw herself out of bed. She brushed her teeth, put on Coleman Hawkins, and checked on Vincent. She was always checking him over, kissing his face, and cleaning him up. She was trying to wish away his tumor. It was a trick Suzanne taught her. She put her hand on the cat's neck three times a day and concentrated on curing him. She said he looked better already, but he looked like he'd been spit out the back of a lawn mower to me, and I'd given up on teaching him to roll over. It was a trick just to get him to move now, and I got sad whenever I looked at him.

"Nigel's insane," she said. "He sent me flowers today and a drawing he did when I was seventeen. My face, with horns coming out the skull."

"He's crazy."

"Yes, but he's useful. He distracts them and makes me a lesser evil. I wish he wasn't doing it to get in my pants."

"Everybody wants to get in them, Robin. Those old guys playing checkers in the park do."

"Nigel's more insistent. He's tasted blood. He used to devour me. I thought that's what sex was, getting ripped up by wolves and left for the vultures."

"What's it like with me?"

"Oh, I don't know. Getting nibbled by rabbits maybe."

"What do you want me to do, claw off your face?"

"No, it's good. I like rabbits. They're hairy and cute and gentle, just like you."

"Oh, great, Robin. Somehow I get the feeling you prefer being ripped apart to nibbled."

"Well, it is exciting."

"Great. Come here, I'll bite off your head."

"Oh, Itchy, you could never be wild. You're too civilized."

"Maybe I should grunt and beat my chest like Charlie."

Then the singing started. I buried my head under the pillows.

"Isn't it beautiful?" she said.

"No. It's driving me crazy."

It was Irv. We'd moved him into the next apartment, and every night, he sang with the most awful voice in the history of mankind. You could hear it through the walls. I'd begged Robin to move him, but she liked Irv's singing. She liked Irv. I couldn't understand it. She helped him shave every morning. She washed him and combed his hair. She had him over for dinner, and he would sit there spewing out the names of cars and ruining my appetite, and now he was singing, and I was seriously considering moving home.

She stood by the window, her beautiful body small and curved and delicate in the candlelight.

"I should sleep with him," she said.

"Who, Nigel? I'll bet you already did. Didn't you, the night Kennedy got shot?"

"No," she said. "I came to my senses after I kissed him. It wasn't like being kissed. It was like getting sucked into a fire. I meant Irv. He sings so nice, and he's lonely, and I'll bet he's a virgin."

I ripped my pillow. I had to let go before I tore it into pieces. I spoke as slowly and clearly as I could.

"Robin, the man cannot speak English. He repeats the same three sentences over and over."

"I like that," she said. "Articulate men can be so boring. I hope that doesn't bother you."

"Oh, no. Sleep with anyone you want. Maybe you could go to the zoo and get a nice gorilla, you know, sort of savage like Nigel, yet inarticulate like Irv. What a great combination. He could tear you to shreds and grunt stuff about Studebakers."

"You're so funny when you're jealous."

"I'm not jealous. I'm merely pointing out that your taste in men is just a little bit weird."

"That's why I'm sleeping with a boy."

"We can stop any time you want."

Irv hit a high note. I threw the pillow over my head again. I couldn't believe it. I was jealous of this opera-singing mental midget who knew seventeen words, each of which described a motor vehicle. I was jealous of Nigel. And worst of all I was jealous of Joe. I didn't want to be in love with Robin. It was bad enough dreaming about Suzanne all day long. I didn't need a woman who was twelve years older, and probably out of her mind, breaking my heart and running off with the first wild beast who came along, but I didn't want her sleeping with anyone else.

She squeezed her face under the pillow and kissed me.

"Itchy, don't be jealous. I'll sleep with anyone I have to. I'd sleep with Stewart Donaghy if it helped, and I don't want to worry about your little feelings getting hurt."

"Great, Robin. Go sleep with the Phillies. Fuck the fucking army, or those guys playing checkers in the park. They like you, or how about Westmoreland?"

Irv was absolutely screeching.

"I'm just telling you," Robin said. "You're eighteen. I love making love to you. It makes me feel young, but it's going to end."

I lifted the pillow off my head and stared at her eyes.

"Okay," I said. "I don't care, but if you have to do it with somebody else, at least let it be Joe."

She reached down between my legs, and I closed my eyes.

"I don't think I'll ever have that chance," she said. "I see him in my dreams. I see Joe and fire, and I know he's coming, but I don't think he's coming for me."

The candle had burned to a stub, and the flame barely flickered above the wax all around it.

"Robin, who's the neighbor?"

"I don't know."

"But you talk about him in your dreams."

She kissed my shoulder.

"It's something about dying and then a bright light, and a voice says, 'the neighbor's ready now,' and something comes out of the light, like a hand that's burning."

"Did you ever tell Joe?"

"I never had the dream before Joe left."

"You never told him about the neighbor?"

"There was no neighbor then."

"I talked to Joe tonight."

She didn't move. She didn't make a sound. Irv's horrible singing filled the room. It was the end of his song. It always ended the same, this long, painful squeal, as if he'd smashed his toe with a hammer. It stopped. I heard Robin breathing.

"And he said he won't see me?" Robin asked.

"Yes."

"Because he doesn't love me anymore?"

"He loves you."

"Where is he?"

"I promised not to tell. Robin, he got hurt."

She grabbed hold of my hand.

"He lost his right arm, and maybe he was burnt. I'm not sure. He's hiding in the dark, but he told me he loves you and forgives you."

I told her what I could remember. She didn't cry or ask questions while I talked. The candle burned down to nothing, and the jazz drifted on the darkness.

"He told me to say that the neighbor forgives you and that, well, his father forgives you, too."

Robin started trembling so hard, the bed moved with her.

23

I brought Joe the paper every night, a newspaper, a sandwich, and a bottle of beer, and sat with him in the dark. He could unwrap the sandwich, chew it, wash it down, lay the bottle down, all with hardly a hint of noise, all with his left hand.

Robin spent a long time on the sandwiches and kissed the bread before she wrapped them. She put letters in with the newspapers, but Joe never mentioned them, and Robin pretended she didn't care.

So every night I sat like a blind man listening to the spooky sounds of Deadwhale in the swamps, sounds that only bothered me when they stopped. I felt safe with Joe. He'd mastered the dark, and I loved those visits.

Joe was just a voice, a mystery, almost something holy. When he talked about the war, I felt like I'd contacted something beyond a single person, like a great spirit, the giant spirit of the scared kids who'd have to run or fight and maybe die in a war they didn't understand but couldn't avoid.

You saw them on the news at night, guys from Brooklyn and Philadelphia, guys from California and far down south, farmer's kids, or the sons of factory workers and bus drivers and men all over the country who'd never gone to college or even read a book, big kids, nice kids, and stupid kids, smart and poor, black and white, from dusty streets and tiny towns in Missouri and Nebraska and immigrant neighborhoods in Boston and Baltimore, the cannon fodder. America.

He talked about the war even when he didn't talk about it. He couldn't say anything without fitting it into what the war'd done to him. He called the place Viet hell or just hell. He made it abstract, like a place that didn't really exist on earth, and sometimes I wondered if he'd been there at all, or if he'd just had a bad dream.

He didn't remember how he'd gone in, or where. He didn't remember his unit, or where he'd fought. He'd enlisted in the army. He'd gone to Viet hell. He'd been wounded, and those were the details. The characters and places didn't have names.

It was a sharp memory of incredible heat, of snakes and huge bugs and men who moved in the night, a sharp memory of tears, blood, and fire, all screwed up like the frames from a horror film, cut, confused, then projected, a messed-up string of pictures with no story to tie them together. He saw moments, a flash of an NVA soldier's eyes in the night, a lizard on a dead friend's face, a severed hand on the forest floor, his own body stretched and burnt on the dirt while someone hacked off his arm.

And he talked to me. He talked out his fears and lost memories, and when he got his mind away from the jungles and the helicopters, he talked about the war in another way. He talked about the politics in a way Robin could never talk, not with her fire and hatred, but with a slow, analytical, almost mystical reasoning.

He let me write down some of what he said, and I carried the words to the *Lighthouse*, and in a couple minutes I was alone with Neil Funk, the most important man on the paper. The next day there was a huge headline. Joe Waters In Hiding. There were lots of quotes from me, the same photo they'd showed when Patrick died, and there was Joe's letter.

He condemned the war, but his solutions were far from Robin's and so sharp and graceful that it made her look crude and foolish, like Nigel. While Robin walked the streets passing out pamphlets and shouting her throat raw about another march on the factory, a showdown, a sustained show of physical, emotional, and psychological resistance, a disruption of everything from the bus system to the postal service, Joe sat in the darkness and dictated a single letter with more power than anything she'd ever done.

He said the war broke his heart and shattered his faith in America. He said he was ashamed of what the government made our soldiers endure and what our soldiers were forced to do to the Vietnamese under orders from civilized men in suits far from the battle. He said the United States disgraced itself in Vietnam, that our crimes were worse than Hitler's because they were carried out by sane men who insisted against their heart's judgment on the worthiness of their cause.

He called it a sin against the higher powers. The sin was that the Christian nation facing totalitarian, atheistic communism had adopted methods that would make Christ weep. He quoted the New Testament. He laid out Christ's philosophy of nonviolence and pacifism and claimed if America wanted to fight in the name of Christ, or even dare to invoke Christ's name, or God's name in association with the war, then America would be condemned by Christ forever for adopting all He despised as the means of perpetuating His honor.

While Robin screamed about murder, insanity, hypocrisy, Joe just said we'd betrayed Christ. But he took it one step further. He said anyone who used violence to oppose the violence of the war was just as guilty as the war makers, and that the only way to close the factory was to appeal to the conscience of its workers, even if that meant making a sacrifice so painful they couldn't help but understand.

"He wants us to roll over," Robin shouted when she read the letter. "He wants a bunch of Kings and Gandhis, but where did they end up? Shot dead. He goes to Vietnam and comes back a prophet, but he's wrong. Tell Joe I'll fight fire with fire, and I'd rather lose fighting beside Nigel than making sacrifices with Joe."

24

It rained the night I took Suzanne to see him, one of those low, salty rains that swirled off the bay and the ocean. It made everything cool and slippery. This was our third try. The first two the weather was fine, but Joe never showed. This time he promised to be there and gave me the directions on the back of a paper bag. They were crazy directions that led all over Fishtown and didn't seem to end anywhere, but I hunched over them in Suzanne's Volkswagon while she squinted through the rain with the wipers slashing back and forth.

Suzanne couldn't drive in good weather, but with the rain falling, the roads slick and dark, and her nerves shot wondering whether he would be there this time, she drove like a mad blind woman, swerving around corners, running up the curb, slamming the brakes at red lights.

Somewhere along the way, with the rain whipping through and her face practically touching the windshield, she shouted to me louder than necessary.

"Charlie doesn't want to go to Vietnam."

She tried to light a cigarette. It wasn't easy with a hand on the wheel and one or the other rubbing the fogged window every few seconds, and I had to light it for her.

"He thinks he has to," she said. "Like it's a mission from God, or if he doesn't, he's not a man. It's his stupid ego. It's gigantic, like Jupiter. It even has gravity. Once we went bowling, which he was very bad at, and all the balls started circling around him, like little moons."

She looked to see if I was laughing. I was. Her face was wet and pretty, and I could hardly stand it. It was always strained and scared and squinting into the darkness, and there were cuts and scrapes all over it, as if she'd been in a fight with some vicious cat. I knew Charlie wasn't doing it, so it had to be Donaghy. I couldn't understand why she was seeing both of them.

"All he ever talks about is your brother," she said. "About how great he was and how brave. Sometimes I wish he'd shut up about it, but he says he never talks about it with anyone else. He says he can't stop thinking about it and nobody understands."

"I understand."

She yanked out her ashtray. The car whined and skidded along. Streetlights streaked across the soaked windshield. The ashtray spilled all over and sent up a cloud.

"He thinks you don't respect him," she said. "Because he's not smart like you, but he is smart, you know, in his own stupid way."

"He said I don't respect him?"

"Sure. He says it all the time."

I squeezed the directions and stared at her face. She wasn't sexy like Robin. She wasn't the kind you looked at and just wanted to undress and put your hands all over. She was the kind who made you feel clumsy and stupid, an untouchable type of girl, the kind you just wanted to look at and maybe in a million years get to hold hands with.

I loved her then in the rain and darkness on those narrow streets. I wanted to touch that beautiful black hair. I wanted to kiss her cheek and smell her perfume and stare into her eyes, and it was hopeless, and I felt it sinking into my bones. I could never have Suzanne, any more than I could ever play third for the Phillies or run on the beach with Patrick and Whitey. I could only hope to ride with her now and then, talking about Charlie and Joe and trying to keep her on the path toward where we headed.

"I respect Charlie," I said. "We're just different is all."

"Charlie's nice," she said. "He always tells me to stand straight and not worry about being so tall, and he never does some of the wrong stuff other guys used to. The smallest things will turn me off. I remember one guy. I really liked him for about ten minutes, and then he ordered this awful sandwich full of pickles and lunch meat.

"Before Charlie, I never had more than one date with anybody, unless you count Stewart, but we didn't have dates. He was a lot older, you know. One day he came over to visit, and there I was, fourteen, his new sister, the parents off drunk. He knew how to take advantage of a situation."

"Take a left," I said.

The car skidded, but she got us around and sucked her cigarette.

"Nice road," she said. "It improves your driving skills."

The road was mud. No lights, a lot of trees hanging low on both sides.

"Maybe we should walk," I said. "Your driving's too exciting for me."

"Is this it?"

"No. It says go up about half a mile, take another right, and then get out."

"I'm not walking till I have to," she said. "There might be alligators or something."

"There's no alligators in Jersey."

"How do you know? You ever see any?"

"No. That's how I know."

"Maybe they're so smart nobody knows," she said. "Maybe there's millions, and one day they're going to take over while we're sleeping."

She slammed on the brakes. A tree was down. The car skidded up against it, turned sideways, and stopped. I got out. The tree was straight across the path. We were in the woods now. The mud was a few inches deep against the wheel and sucking on my sneaks. I went around to her side.

"We got to go back."

"What?"

"This road's a mess. We got to..."

But she was out of the car, and I had to run after her. She was slipping, and twice she went down to her hands. When I finally caught her, she was soaked and moving fast through the mud. Her jeans and red sneaks were drenched, and the further we walked, the darker it got. I had to strain hard for the second dirt road Joe had promised.

"What about the alligators?" I said.

"There's no alligators. Don't be ridiculous."

She held my arm, and I didn't care that rain dripped down my face and neck or that my sneaks were full of mud. We were into some heavy woods now, one of the small patches mixed in with the marshes at the edge of town. The trees were thick wet things that swooped all around us and jostled huge drops on us in the wind. The thunder was still far away, but it made me nervous.

We'd left the car running and the headlights on, but couldn't see them anymore. All was black until we saw some lights on the left, and far down a hill out toward the bay, we saw the factories, the chemical factory strung up against the night with its thousands of twinkling lights wired from one smokestack to the next and wrapped all around the pipes that crisscrossed the sky, and the machine gun factory, dark and spooky in the rain, like a big gray warship cutting through the Atlantic in some movie.

Suzanne squeezed my arm, and we stared toward the far-off lights, and I realized you could make your way through the woods straight onto the middle of the road where we'd held our march that day.

"Are we lost?" she said.

"Of course we're lost. We're in stinking no man's land."

"Well, it's your fault. You've got the directions."

"You're the one who drove us into a tree."

"I was following your directions."

"The directions didn't mention any tree, Suzanne."

"Well, they're not very good directions."

"Maybe he'll be up a little ways, but shit, I don't know if he'll be out in this rain."

"He's not coming," she said. "He's been letting me down all my life. Sometimes he's just like Stewart, so selfish and disappointing, but this time I'm not falling for it. Come on. This is fun. I love the rain."

She unbuttoned her shirt, then wiggled out of it. She reached back and popped off her bra.

"Hurry up," she said. "I don't want to be undressed all by myself. It's bad, like drinking alone."

"You want me to take my clothes off?"

"How else you going to get undressed, wait for lightning to hit?"

"Yeah, right. How else?"

In just a few seconds, her clothes were piled on the floor of the woods, and she was drinking rain drops. I tried not to stare, but it would have been easier to stop my heart from beating, and it was beating hard.

"God, it's great," she said. "This must be what it's like to be wild and free like an animal. Do I look like a giraffe? Charlie says I do. Oh, poor Charlie. I'm afraid I don't love him anymore. His whole life's peanuts and push-ups, and all these silly challenges he's trying to meet. Would you put your arms around me?"

I'd had dreams like this, but I was pretty sure this wasn't one of them. I was shivering a bit and soaked and naked, and I imagined Robin could hear my heart pounding all the way back in town.

"Don't you want to?" she asked.

"Yeah," I said. "I was just thinking."

"Sure," she said. "It's a big decision. Why don't you think about it over here?"

"Yeah. Okay. I'll think over there."

I crossed the few muddy feet between us, and Suzanne pressed her soaked body against mine. I was afraid my heart might knock her unconscious, but she didn't complain, and I could feel hers, too.

"Itchy, why's Charlie so determined to shoot a peanut out his nose real far? Is there something I don't understand, maybe something in his past?"

"It's a challenge. Nigel can do it."

"Nigel's an idiot like no one's ever been since the time of dinosaurs. Does Charlie have to do everything every idiot on earth can do?"

"It's a challenge."

"You already said that."

"Sorry." How could I help repeating myself? She was pressed tight against me. She was slippery and soft and breathing into my face. I was trying to be cool, but I was starting to hyperventilate.

"You're not like that, are you?" she asked.

"I never once had a peanut in my nose, except against my will."

"Did Charlie put it there?"

"No, Nigel."

"How come?"

"Because I tried to get the girl in the toilet paper to leave with me. I was trying to help her."

"Oh, of course. Nigel had a girl in toilet paper."

"Yes."

"And you tried to help her."

"Yes."

"So he put a peanut in your nose."

"Yes."

"You were wonderful in that race."

"Thank you."

"Joe doesn't love me," she said. "He won't come."

The woods were dark, and the rain poured, and just as Suzanne moved her mouth toward mine, there was a flash of light, and Joe's voice floated on the air.

"Don't move," he said.

Suzanne's breath hissed in my ear.

"One move I'm gone. Back up, Itchy."

I stepped away from Suzanne. She groped along the ground for her shirt. She knelt and slid into it fast and started grabbing for the buttons.

"Joe, where are you?" she said.

"I just wanted to see you," he said. "It's been so long."

"I...I...don't have...my pants," she said. She was slapping her hands in the mud now, feeling around for her pants. Then she had them. She turned away from Joe and pulled them on. The rain slapped hard all around us.

"Joe, come home," she said.

"I am home."

She was dressed now, covered with her drenched, muddy clothes, and I was slipping into mine when she shouted. It was a terrible shout, and I imagined it carried through the trees and the rain all the way to the factories a mile or two in the distance.

"This is home, out in the rain where it's so dark you can't see your hand?"

"Where's home then?" he asked. "Back at the house? That place was never home after he died."

"You mean after they killed him?"

"He killed himself."

"No." She shrieked it. "Donaghy had it done. Stewart even told me. Mom was having an affair with him, but she broke it off, and that man, that disgusting man, had Daddy killed."

There was the longest silence. The rain swarmed over me. Thunder moved just a bit closer, and in the far sky way beyond Deadwhale Bay, the night glowed with flashes of lightning.

"You always took her side," Suzanne said. "You thought she was this angel, this victim, and just because Daddy wasn't as wonderful as everyone thought, just because he took every woman he could get, we had to forgive her for everything, but she's no angel, Joe, and you never should have left me with her.

"You've been hollering all these years about Stewart's no good for me, but it's not him who scratches my face. Can you see my face?"

"It's her?"

"Yeah, it's her. Please come home."

"You let her?"

"What am I going to do? Kill her? I'm all she's got."

"Why does she do it?"

"She's always got some reason."

"Like what? Why this time?"

"I was smelling Daddy's coats."

"What?"

"His coats. There's a closet of his coats. Sometimes I put my face in them because you can smell him, but she says it's sick and I have to be tough. She hits me to make me tough, but I'll never be tough. Maybe in my next life I'll be a boxer, or a bulldog, but this time I'm just a girl, and I want you to come home."

"I can't," he said.

"Why?"

"Suzanne, do you believe in God?" he asked her.

"What?"

"Do you believe in God, a higher power?"

"Of course, I do, but not this crummy little Christian God you write this shit about. What do you know about Jesus? Shit, Joe, people think there's this stupid guy with a beard up there who wants us to fight this war. It's so much shit."

I sat down in the mud. I was drenched. I could see Joe now for the first time. I could see his dark figure, but I couldn't make out his face.

"I've seen God," he said. "And he's not crummy, and he's not little, and he's not anything like you could imagine, and this summer, I'm going to die."

"No, you're not," she said. "What the hell's wrong with you? You've suffered enough. There's no reason to kill yourself."

"I won't." His voice was quiet and calm and confident, but just a little sad. "They'll kill me."

Suzanne shouted at him. "You saw this in a dream, or did God appear in a bush?"

"I just know," he said. "Most of me died there. I saw myself dead, and what's here now, this part of me you hear, will just stay for a while."

"Joe, you had a dream. You were hurt. You didn't see God, and you don't have to die."

"I never came back from the war," he said. "I never will."

Suzanne started crying into her hands. Joe reached for her, but his hand stopped far short of her face, and he faded backward and kept going backward until he'd faded from view. Suzanne looked around her, saw that he was gone, and ran into the darkness, but she never found him.

25

A couple days later, someone from the mayor's office called and arranged a meeting with Robin. He asked for me, too, and at three that afternoon, we rode to city hall in a police car. It was the only way to get Robin through town without people grabbing at her.

City hall was a big building, all huge stones, marble, pillars, and gigantic windows with black grating over them. It used to be white with a dome, and a light shining on it all night, but the stone was all worn and gray now and covered with pigeon shit.

The inner corridors were cement with offices behind glass doors. Some of the offices were locked with huge chains. Some were just dark. Others were bright and dingy, and we walked far down the concrete hallway with two cops. I smelled urine and rotting food until we entered a door into a nicer area, a hallway with rugs, some music playing, antiseptic smells like you might get at a hospital, and soon we were in the mayor's office.

I didn't recognize him at first. He sat behind a huge desk with a vase of flowers on it, rubbing his eyes with one hand and squeezing the petal of a flower with the other. His eyes were pink, and his smile was tired, but it was a real smile, and I smiled back. Robin didn't smile. She looked scared, or nervous, and looked over her shoulder a couple times like she might make a run for it. A tear ran down her face, and she wiped it off so fast and hard, I thought she might scrape off her cheek.

An air conditioner rattled in the window, and pigeons shuffled behind it, cooing and scratching against the metal. The mayor whacked the air conditioner, and it stopped rattling, but not long.

"Coffee?" he asked.

"No thanks," I said, but Robin just kept staring at him. She seemed to be in some kind of sudden trance, and she was shaking, like she was cold or scared to death.

I looked at the mayor. He didn't scare me. I felt sorry for him. I'd always hated him. Most Whales did, but they voted for him anyway. The competition was weak, and Donaghy had a certain competence about him. He had a reputation as a smart guy with a lot of money, a guy who always had a tan and a woman or two and didn't care too much about anyone but himself and maybe the city, but now, even though he was over six-foot, he seemed kind of shriveled and beat.

His hair was parted on the left and all streaked with gray and stiff with some kind of oil. His eyes were gray, too, and his face was white and wrinkled with a few yellow blotches and dark spots under his eyes. Once he'd been handsome. Once he and Mayor Waters had both been young and handsome and in love with the same woman while they battled for control of the city.

A cigarette burned in a mound of them on his ashtray, and whenever he took a drag, his hands shook. The scar stood clear on his neck from that long ago day when they'd rushed him to the hospital. He never explained. There was no investigation, no charges. The mayor lived, but he'd left Eleanor Waters after that, and everyone knew she'd cut him.

"Things have deteriorated," he said. "Have a chair."

I had to pull Robin down into a couch beside me, and the mayor got to look down on us. Robin snapped back then.

"They'll get worse," she said. I'd never heard her so vicious.

"Care for a cigarette?" the mayor asked.

"I hate them," Robin said.

"I hate them, too, about forty-five times a day."

Robin crossed her legs. A toe showed through one of her socks. She wore a white shirt, a tie, no shoes, gray argyle socks, and gray pants, and she faced a man in a white shirt and suspenders.

"I won't let them get worse," he said.

"You couldn't stop us so far," she said.

"I haven't chosen to, but now you're pushing things."

"It's not just me."

"You're at the fulcrum."

"My influence is waning."

It was true. Robin could inspire people, but she couldn't control them. They marched all over, down the alleys, the streets, and the beaches. They took drugs out in the open. It was all fighting, blaring rock, drunks, endless shouting, breaking bottles, wild laughter in the night, and the marches, the street-corner debates, the sit-down strikes, the flag burnings, the draft card burnings.

"What are you trying to achieve?" the mayor asked.

"The end of western civilization," Robin said. She spit it out like she really meant it. Something about the mayor or his office ate at her. She kept looking at the furniture, the floors, the ceiling, even that old air conditioner.

"You won't be serious?"

"Of course, I'll be serious. We want to close the factory. That's all."

"And you'll ruin the city to accomplish that?"

"We'll disrupt it as necessary. I'm not advocating vandalism or violence."

"But those are the by-products of your efforts."

"No. Those are the by-products of this society. You live in King's Port, where the trees are huge and the streets are clean. You see the world from there or from this dark office. You don't know the pissy fucking alleys of Deadwhale or the people who live there. What you see is the by-product of hatred and deprivation."

The mayor smiled. He sucked on his cigarette and stared at Robin a long time.

"I see. And what alternative are you offering?"

Robin stood. She started walking around the room. She didn't look at the mayor. She looked at his window, his carpets.

"It's not my job to offer alternatives."

"If you destroy the factory, which I understand as your goal, you'll gut the economy. King's Port will survive. It's the people you express sympathy for, the Whales in the pissy fucking alleys of Fishtown and Little Brooklyn, who will suffer."

He smiled again. "Do you care about these people or are you using them? Do you have a vendetta against me, or my son, or is it the society as a whole?"

"The war's immoral," Robin said. She stepped up close to the mayor. He leaned back in his seat and drew slowly on his cigarette. "By contributing to it we disgrace ourselves. By closing the factory we purge ourselves."

The mayor stuffed out his cigarette and pointed a shaking finger at Robin.

"Do you care about these people or not?"

"Of course."

"And you'll employ the thousands who lose their jobs?"

Robin picked a flower from the mayor's vase. She stared at it a second, held it close to her nose, then clasped it against her breast.

"Are you suggesting, Mayor Donaghy, that I place economics above morality?"

"Is it moral to steal the livelihood from hard-working people?"

"If they've become parasites on the war, yes," she said. "Let them lose their jobs. Let them worry a little, then let them learn something new. I have no sympathy for people who can't make the connection between their work and the havoc it wreaks. You don't have to drop the napalm to incinerate a child."

"Then everyone's guilty," Mayor Donaghy said. "The farmers that grow food to feed the soldiers, the truck drivers who deliver it, the letter carriers who bring them news. Is a mother guilty because her son goes to war?"

"A mother's guilty if she doesn't try to stop him."

The mayor stared hard at Robin. His face looked tired but alert and full of concentration.

"The factory doesn't have to make guns," he said. "Why do you insist on its destruction?"

Robin slid the flower back in among the others.

"The factory's a symbol of what's wrong in this country. The factory's the common people enslaved to an illegal war. If the factory converts to making hubcaps, that's small news and a small victory. If the factory burns, it's news, maybe national, maybe international. It's not just a question of economics. We're trying to strike a blow against the war machine, and not just a symbolic blow, but a physical and violent and frightening blow, something they can understand."

I whirled on Robin. She had never talked about destroying the factory before, but her face was hard, and she glared at the mayor as if she wanted to kill him.

"So you admit you want to destroy it physically, like your friend Nigel."

"Yes. Now. Just this minute, I realized," she said.

"You've come a long way, but I won't let you go any further. By striking down the working people, and that's what you're doing, you're not sacrificing a factory, you're sacrificing a city."

I jumped in then. I was shocked by what Robin was saying.

"Mayor Donaghy, are you willing to stop making guns in Deadwhale?" I asked.

"The factory's privately run," he said.

"Your son runs it."

"I've divested myself of all interest in the factory," he said. "It's Stewart's now."

"You don't influence your son?" Robin asked.

The mayor took a long drink of coffee. I figured it was very cold.

"For too long I've put up with the legacy of Bob Waters. Okay, he was a Whale, a Democrat, the son of working people. I'm a King, a Republican, a rich boy who came by everything easily.

"He gave a good speech. He made stirring promises. He made people feel good about themselves. I don't do these things, but when I took over, the city's finances were a shambles. People claim I killed all his projects, dismantled his miniature Great Society, but I did the best I could with what he left me.

"This is my city now, and I won't let you destroy it. I don't understand..."

Robin cut him off.

"You don't understand that it makes me sick to drop fire and death on this poor country and that it's men like you, old rich white men running the fucking thing, men whose sons don't lose their arms or come home in bags? You don't understand that?"

She pounded the mayor's desk. He watched her hand slam down on the wood, rise up, then slam down again.

"Do you support the war, Mayor?" I asked.

He smiled. He looked at Robin, then me, and nodded slowly.

"Yes, I support the war. We're running it badly. We're losing it, but just looking at it on a map and thinking strategically, it's certainly no foolish war. Show me a communist nation where someone like Robin wouldn't be dead or locked up?

"Certainly the war's ugly, disgusting, maybe even disgraceful, but what alternative do we have? Can you deny that the communists are sworn to defeat us? Can you deny for a second that every country that falls takes us closer to the time when we're surrounded and strangled? This isn't a moral cause, and those who try to make it into one are fools and hypocrites. This is a matter of survival, and to survive you sometimes have to kill. It's kill now, or die later."

He lit a match and held it up. I hated the way his hand shook.

"At the risk of being corny, I want you to think of a country, a free country, as a small fire, like this match, or maybe a candle. It's an old analogy, a cliché. But freedom burns. Communism snuffs it out forever."

He squeezed the match slowly between his fingers.

"No communist nation has ever lit the flame again. We fight to keep those flames burning. Look at the Czechs. Do you really think the Russians will let them have a little freedom? Isn't it noble to fight a war like this or Korea or any war for the freedom of people who can't defend themselves? What's so..."

Robin hit his desk so hard the vase shook, teetered, eluded the mayor's grasp, and crashed on the floor. The flowers lay there among the glass, and Robin shouted.

"Not when the bleeding's forced on poor kids with no hope, kids who haven't been asked, kids who die for your silly version of what's good and noble. The peasant Vietnamese do not threaten us, and if it were your son over there doing the fighting, you'd probably see it a lot more clearly, Mayor Donaghy. It's easy to practice cold politics with other people's blood."

She kicked the pile of glass at her feet. It scattered and bounced. The mayor came around the desk. He towered over Robin. She took a backward step, but he didn't even look at her. He just gathered flowers. When he had them all, he sat again with the flowers piled on a blotter in front of him and just a few stray petals on the floor.

"I can shut you down," he said. His voice was quiet now, emotionless. "We've documented a lot of drug use and underage drinking in your bar. Your doughnut shop's roach infested. Your hotel's a fire hazard."

Robin dropped down in the sofa.

"It will be easy," he said.

"That's the oldest and nicest hotel in Deadwhale," she said. "People come just to stay there. You'd damage the economy as much shutting me down as shutting the factory."

The mayor played with a flower. He smoked. The room was full of smoke. I hated breathing it.

"Of course, I could have you arrested," he said.

"On what grounds?"

"There will be curfews, a ban on public speaking, a ban on gatherings of over five people. I'll make rules. You'll break them. You'll get lawyers. I have lawyers. I'll slow you down, tie you up, break your momentum, and the summer will pass."

"It will go on without me," she said. "There's Nigel, Coke, Itchy. There's even Joe Waters writing his stupid letters."

The mayor flinched at the mention of Joe. He dropped his eyes and acted very interested in the flower.

"You're planning another march," he said. "You've made no secret of it. I realize there are factions and that you've got competition now from black radicals and this Nigel character, but I think you're in control, whether you care to admit it, and to stop this march, I've got to stop you. I'm asking you to stop, but I'll take the necessary measures if I have to, and if all else fails, I'm in contact with the governor. He'll send in the guard."

"You'll bring your army of freedom to Deadwhale?" she asked.

"If necessary."

"Those are all threats, Mayor Donaghy," I said. "I had the idea you were going to offer something more."

"Of course," he said. "Making guns is shortsighted. We've got to look at alternatives. We can't depend on endless war."

"Yes, we can," Robin said. "As long as the rich boys don't have to fight."

"No," the mayor said. "This war will end badly, and after that, there won't be the stomach for it, or the political will. There might be some cheap quick and easy public relations wars that make the president look like a hero, but this is the last of these."

"There will be others," Robin said. "Until the end of time."

"What's your offer?" I asked.

"We don't want to hear his offer," Robin said.

"Come on, Robin," I said.

"No," she said. She pointed at the mayor. "Carry out your threats. Snuff the candle, Mr. Mayor."

"There's a difference between freedom and anarchy," he said.

Just then the door flew open. A noise and a breeze rushed in from the corridors, and Stewart Donaghy rushed in with them.

"What the hell you doing?" he asked.

"Stewart, I'm conducting a meeting with these people."

Stewart sneered at his father. His father glared back, but his fingers had begun shaking almost out of control.

"I told you no compromise," Stewart said.

"I'm holding a discussion."

"You can't discuss with Raggedy Ann and her boy. All they understand is this."

He wore a double-breasted blue suit, like some gangster in "The Untouchables," and he reached inside the suit and pulled out his gun, that long revolver. He flashed it at Robin. She jumped back against me.

"See that," Stewart said. "The little bitch isn't so tough."

"Stewart." The mayor's lips shook. The muscles in his face twitched. "I asked you to get rid of that."

He whipped the gun on his father.

"You going to arrest me?"

He extended the gun at the end of his right arm, maybe a foot from the mayor's nose. The mayor sat back in his chair and stared at the gun. His eyes were straight and steady, and they dared Stewart Donaghy to pull the trigger, and when he finally did, just so slowly squeezing it, the mayor didn't flinch, and Robin's hands dug into my arm, and there was a click, and Donaghy turned and fired into Robin's face and then mine.

He laughed. "Don't worry, Robin, baby. When the time comes, the gun will be loaded."

And he was gone as quick as he'd come. The mayor stared straight ahead, his eyes fixed somewhere above the flowers. Robin's grip slowly eased off my arm.

"I would like to talk to you alone, please, if it's all right," the mayor said. He looked at me, then at Robin, as if he wanted permission. "I've got a car waiting for you, Miss Debussy, and I'll send your friend home separately."

26

The mayor locked the door, drew a shade over the glass, and settled into his chair. He didn't say anything for a while. I didn't mind. He was waiting for his nerves to calm down, and I was waiting on mine. I didn't like guns. I didn't like men who carried them or collected them or thought they had some God-given right to own them. I especially didn't like them right in my face.

I settled into the couch and waited. My arms stuck to the leather. The air conditioner hummed and rattled and blew like crazy, breaking strands of hair from the plastered mass on the mayor's head and shaking them around, but the air it blew was barely cooler than the mayor's cigarette-heated breath.

I heard the pigeons again, making those silly cooing sounds. I noticed the clock behind his head, a big white thing, a schoolroom clock. The clock moved in jerks, as if the minute hand had to wrench free of some invisible power every sixty seconds.

"I'm sorry," he said. "About your brother."

I dropped my head like I always did when someone mentioned Patrick.

"He must have been very brave."

"Brainwashed, I guess."

"But brave, nonetheless. Aren't you proud of him?"

"Yeah," I whispered. "I'm proud of him."

"And you should be proud of your father. What's he doing now?"

"He drives a taxi. He didn't know how to do much else, except what he did in the factory."

"I'm sorry to hear that," he said.

"He's all right. They have a car and a house."

"You've had a lot of attention lately," he said. "Smartest kid in Deadwhale, Robin Debussy's right-hand man, and of course, Patrick, and the race, and your father quitting like he did, and now this stuff with Joe Waters."

His eyes rose up from the desk and settled on mine for a second when he mentioned Joe, but they dropped back down, and then I knew what he wanted to talk about.

"I never knew Joe," he said. He had trouble saying Joe's name. "Of course, he hated me. I suppose he blamed me for Robert's death. That is the general perception, isn't it, that I'm involved in Mayor Waters' death?"

"A lot of people think so," I said.

He rested his chin on his chest and stared at the floor. Something popped then with a loud snap, a burst of light, and then darkness. The air conditioner wound down. All the sounds in the room changed. The lights vanished in the hall behind me. The whole building must have gone dark, but it was over in a flash. Power surged on. The air conditioner rattled louder than before, but the mayor and I were in a darker room now. The light on his desk had blown dead, and just streaks of daylight from a window far up by the ceiling kept the room from going black, and in the changed light, I could see the scar on the mayor's neck much better than before.

"I doubt that anyone knows the truth," he said. "I've often wondered what he was doing on the wharf on a night like that. It's a dangerous place, but he was fond of it. Eleanor's fond of it, too, something to do with their early days, I guess.

"I've wanted to rip it down. There's that gang of kids up there, and it's irresponsible of me to let them risk their lives, but then I think of Eleanor and Bob and how it meant something to them. That damned wharf and that damned Ferris wheel. I should rip them down."

He rubbed his eyes. He wasn't looking at me. He was looking far away into something I could only guess at, but it wasn't a pleasant thing. I thought it had to do with the scar on his neck. I imagined everything did.

"I guess we'll never know," he said. "Eleanor begged me to prevent an autopsy. She thought there was something holy about his body, and I didn't care if he was drunk, or drugged, or beaten to death. He was gone. I was glad of it. We didn't need an autopsy."

He tugged at his suspenders a little. Sweat had spread dark all around them, and the sweat glistened on his neck and rolled over that thick tissue that had sealed over the wound.

"Yes," he said. "It was over."

He just stared at the floor. He seemed to be shrinking behind the clutter on his desk, the flowers and papers and cigarettes, and I wondered what had happened.

I imagined Eleanor Waters, or was it Donaghy now, his new wife, stalking him in the dark, roaming down the halls at night with a candle in her hand like someone in a horror movie, her gorgeous, crumbling face, maybe tears in her eyes, maybe drunk or drugged, slithering down the hall with a knife, a razor, maybe the blade from a hacksaw, her nightgown swishing on the floor, and then throwing herself at the mayor while he slept, burying the blade in his neck, the blood running over the pillows and sheets, and the mayor reaching up from his dreams and grabbing hold of her wrist, meeting her eyes in the darkness, and wrenching free.

I imagined her crying in the corner while he shouted directions into the telephone, gripping a towel to his throat, watching her, wondering if he was going to live or die.

"You're the only one who's talked to Joe," he said. The scar moved up and down as he spoke. "I was wondering. The things he writes. They're so different from the way he used to be. They're brilliant. A woman like Robin, with her ranting, no matter if she's right, could never turn me against the war. But Joe. He makes me wonder if we're all fools."

He touched the scar, running his hands mindlessly across it, like Robin reaching for Vincent on her shoulder.

"But, you know, there's something fanatical in his writing, something suicidal, or deathlike. It's as if he's already dead, as if he's writing with the wisdom of the grave. He lost his arm, they say. Is it true?"

"Yeah, it's true."

"And is he damaged in other ways, mentally or emotionally?"

"I don't know. Sometimes I think so, and sometimes I think he's just hiding because he's scared."

"He would never talk to me," the mayor said. "I wanted so much to talk to him about the weather or Princeton. I tried, but he would hang up the phone or walk away, or of course, the one time he attacked me. I didn't want to defend myself.

"He was crazy about his mother, but after she married me, he was through with her. She was so proud of him. She used to show me the things he'd written in school. He wrote great essays. He thought we needed a philosophy as a nation, something positive to counter communism. He said anti-communism defined itself by what it opposed and that a true national philosophy defined itself by what it represented.

"I can't do it justice, but I read his words, and I thought, this is a kid with genius. I wanted...Oh, it hurt Eleanor when he stopped talking to her. I think that's what pushed her over the edge."

He looked at me then. His eyes were bright and shining. They were pleading. His whole face was pleading.

"How can I help him?"

"I don't think you can."

"But I can find him a place to live, get him a job, some medical treatment, whatever it takes."

"But he's gone," I said.

"What?"

"He's gone." It was true. I'd gone looking for him just the night after he spoke with Suzanne, but he hadn't turned up that night or the next, and I was afraid I would never see him again.

"Where'd he go?" the mayor asked.

"I don't know. He just disappeared."

The mayor grabbed a handful of flowers, and I started talking about Joe, telling him everything I could, and while I talked I started to understand what it was in Stewart Donaghy that was so familiar that day in the guard shack. It wasn't so much the way he talked or looked. It was his eyes. They were the mayor's eyes, and they were Joe's eyes, too, and when the mayor looked up again, the eyes were full of tears, and then I understood. He just nodded.

"Yes," he said. "Eleanor Devine was my great weakness." He smiled. "Joe was conceived in a hotel room over one of those pissy, fucking Deadwhale back alleys your friend's so fond of. We thought it was fun to do our cheating in the sleaziest of environments. We showered in brown water when it was over."

I just stared. I was too shocked to do anything else.

"Of course, we kept it from Bob. I had to watch my rival raise my son. I had to accept the fact that Joe would always love him and never love me. Yes. And it was foolish to marry her. She was beautiful, but she was never what you'd call stable. She always preferred Bob, but I loved her much more than he ever could."

The far away look snapped off his face, and he got up.

"I want him to know," he said. "I want to tell him I'm his father. Find him. I'll do what I can to help. I'll give you some phone numbers. Call every day. I don't believe this stuff about him seeing his death, but if he believes it, he can make it happen. You've got to help me stop him. All my powers are at your disposal. He has to know that his father's alive."

"But if there's a march on the factory…"

"There won't be any march."

"But it might be a way to flush him out. You couldn't miss him. He'd have to come down the main road with the rest of us. You could have the police pick him up."

I could see him thinking about it, his eyes fixed hard on the wall behind me, the way they'd probably looked in the past when he'd dreamed of stealing Mayor Waters' wife away. He led me to the door and handed me a slip of paper with some times and phone numbers.

"I have to think," he said. He grabbed my wrist. His hand was soaked and hot. "No one knows this, just me and Eleanor, and now you. Understand? No one. Not Suzanne, not Stewart. I trusted you because you're my only hope, you've got a good reputation, a sincere face. I've had police and detectives searching for weeks.

"I've never murdered anyone, or condoned, or plotted, or any way involved myself in murder, but if this secret gets out, I honestly believe that you will die."

He stared into my eyes, and for the briefest of seconds, it was like looking into the face of Stewart Donaghy, the face I'd seen the second he pulled the trigger with his gun three inches from my nose, but then the mayor's face turned soft again, and I saw Joe Waters there. He showed me the way out and told me there would be a police car waiting outside.

27

I was shaking when I walked out of there. As soon as I cleared the government wing, past the rugs and nice hallways and out in the concrete passageway of broken windows and shut-down offices where cats wandered in the pissy air, I leaned against a wall and soaked the sweat off my forehead with a hanky.

I wanted to get out, to run and never stop. I took a step, and two guys came at me. Daylight flashed at the end of the hallway, and they were silhouetted against it, two huge figures. When I tried to step around, they stepped with me. One spoke. His voice was soothing and polite.

"Follow us, Mr. Shovlin."

They got on either side of me.

"Did the mayor send you?" I asked.

They got tight against me, and I had a feeling the mayor hadn't sent them. I smelled aftershave on one and onions on the other. I preferred the onions. I knew there was a police car out there, fifty yards ahead where the sun shined. I thought of running for it. The path was clear. The hallway was empty. We walked past an adjacent alleyway, and they pushed me that way.

"Where we going?"

One grabbed my right elbow. The other grabbed the left and flashed a knife in my face.

"We're taking a detour," he said. "One word, this hits your chest. It will hurt."

I followed along as politely as I could. They were giants, and I didn't want that knife in my chest. My heart was in there, and I remembered a story about Martin Luther King. He got stabbed once, and the knife stayed in his chest, and the doctor who took it out told him one sneeze, and he would have died. I figured I might be a sneeze or two away from dying, and I wasn't going to argue.

We didn't go far down the hall when a door opened, and they pushed me inside. The door slammed shut. I squinted in bright light and made out Stewart Donaghy on a green chair against the far wall. The chair had wheels, and the room was full of boxes and more chairs on wheels. A naked bulb swayed off the ceiling and moved our shadows up and down the walls.

"They used to give lie detector tests in here," Donaghy said. "Now they store office chairs." He smiled and sucked on a Tootsie Roll Pop. "Have a chair."

He kicked one of the chairs toward me, and his friends made sure I sat. They weren't polite about it. They wheeled me under the light. I could feel it, maybe two feet overhead, the brightest bulb on earth. I had to squint to see Donaghy.

He looked comfortable, the chair bent way back, his blue jacket open and that leather holster across his chest. I thought of some old movie. I was a criminal. Donaghy was a cop. They were going to smoke a lot of cigarettes, and I was going to talk.

His friends took the walls to my left and right, a couple young guys, sort of handsome, like tackles coming out of the lockers after football. They wore suits like Donaghy's. They wore blank faces. They didn't carry machine guns. They didn't have bent noses or scars.

Donaghy lit a cigarette as slowly as he could. I was surprised to see him smoking, but figured he was doing it for effect. The room was piping hot, and I was sweating already.

He sat four feet away and blew the smoke toward me in long streams.

"You think I'm stupid, don't you?" he said.

I decided it wouldn't be to my advantage to agree with him.

"I think you're very intelligent," I said.

"You think I'm stupid," he said.

"What do you want? Your father said a cop was waiting."

"He'll have a long wait."

He smiled. Smoke swirled around his head. He blinked away the smoke and stared at me from behind folded arms. He sucked his candy.

"Do you think much about life?" he asked.

"What do you mean?"

"You've been hanging around with Joe Waters, haven't you? The great philosopher."

He practically spit the name.

"Joe Waters," he said. "You like Joe Waters?"

"I like everybody."

His chair squeaked. He kept switching between the candy and the cigarette.

"You believe that crap?" he asked. "That Jesus crap?"

"No."

"You against the war?"

"Yes."

Something clicked behind him. I looked up. Another clock. Just like the one in the mayor's office, jerking a minute from that invisible force, but the clock had only one arm, just a minute hand working its way toward the three.

"The war's a great thing," he said.

He flicked his cigarette at me. It buzzed past my ear. He lit another and started walking around the room. I could hear him breathe. I could hear his friends breathe, and piano music, a faint tinkling of keys like early drops of rain before a storm.

"I'm twenty-eight years old," he said. He stopped behind me. I wanted to turn, but I was afraid. I thought of Martin Luther King, one sneeze from death. I stared toward the wall and all those office chairs. Smoke drifted in the light.

"I made one hundred thousand dollars in 1967. Think I give a fuck about some peasant on a water buffalo that's smarter than him? I love this war."

The light beat over my head. The sweat ran down my back. Then his hand was in my hair down around my neck.

"Your hair's too long," he said. "Hey, Rick, get out your knife and give our friend a styling."

I whirled around. I tried to get up, but one of his thugs knocked me back, then flashed the knife. Donaghy smiled.

"It's only hair, Itchy."

I swallowed. I stared at Donaghy's eyes and something yanked at the back of my head. It went on for half a minute, the jerking and pulling and the pain. My head rocked back and forth. I closed my eyes. It had taken a long time to grow that hair.

Finally Donaghy reached across my head, nodded at his friend, then threw a handful of hair in my face. I wiped it out of my eyes. The tears started coming. Hair stuck to them.

Donaghy crouched in front of me. I smelled the smoke on his breath. I saw the little holes in his face, the sweat pouring out of them now, glistening in that terrible light. He stared at his Tootsie Roll Pop for a second, then touched the sticky thing against my nose. He put it back in his mouth.

"Don't you love this war?" he said. "Don't you love a country with the money and the power to travel to the moon, feed its niggers, and stomp on another country like a giant on a hill of fucking ants all at the same time?"

He tossed the candy away, stuck the cigarette in his mouth, and slammed his fist into his open palm. The piano tinkled far away. I tried to picture someone, maybe a little girl, pecking at the piano and drinking a coke. I tried to picture it nice and innocent, like a Norman Rockwell. The girl had pigtails and a nice white dress.

"And there's nothing they can do, and there's nothing in the world can hurt us."

He slammed me across the face with the back of his hand. My head rocked. I couldn't believe it was happening. I listened for the girl in the pigtails, but she'd stopped playing, and the only sound was that clock wrenching a millimeter from its tired springs every sixty seconds.

Donaghy put his face up to mine. His gray eyes were inches away. His voice sounded like Joe's.

"Nothing can stop us, except you and Robin Debussy and Joe fucking Waters. Why can't you people let us be?"

The light buzzed overhead, casting a dome that trailed off near the walls.

"What do you want?" I said.

"It's all about power," he said. "You ever think about power, Itchy?"

"No."

"Ah, but it's such a great thing, power." He kept circling my chair, looking at me all the time. A clump of hair sat in my lap.

"The country has no power without men like me. Only evil can defeat evil. Principles are a weakness. Joe Waters had principles, and now he's a cripple. You need the power of evil, Itchy, evil to give the orders, and the ignorant masses to execute them. We've had that power, and people like Debussy and Waters, they drag it down."

He knelt in front of me. He smiled.

"Would you like me to demonstrate about power?"

I just looked at him.

"Get down on the floor," he said. He pointed at me. "Lie face down, and do it immediately without a word and without a second's delay. Do it now."

I lowered myself onto the dirty linoleum, pressing my face into the grit. The tears rolled onto the floor, and I was happy to get away from that light, away from his eyes. The floor was cool, and there had been no point in resisting. He had the gun. He had the look of a killer. He had the two big men. I lay on the floor and waited.

"You see," he said. "You're learning about power. Now lick the floor."

"What?"

"Just lick the floor, Itchy. It's pretty simple."

"But it's filthy."

I saw a shoe, his wing-tipped black shoe, the heel a few inches from my nose, a beautiful, thick rubber heel.

"Lick the floor. Pick up your head and lick it with the front of your tongue, like an ice-cream cone."

"No," I said.

The toe of his shoe kept moving closer until it was touching my nose. I watched it lift, then slowly come down until it pinched my nose against the floor. He only did it for a second, but that was long enough to make the point.

"Lick the floor."

I wondered if I was going to die. He could get away with it. He was the mayor's son. I promised myself I wouldn't die. I got up on my arms. I lowered my face. I stared at the floor. It hurt to focus so close. I looked left and right. The floor was covered with dust. There were dead insects and pieces of old food. There were streak marks from the chairs. A spider went by, and with my eyes only a foot from that spider, I stuck out my tongue, and I licked the floor.

I licked it slowly. I didn't want to do it again. I didn't want him stepping on my nose anymore. I licked it humbly. It tasted like dust and plastic, and I coughed and swallowed the dirt, and I sobbed once or twice.

"Very good," he said. "You're a quick learner."

He sat on the floor. His gun came down beside my face, and he dropped a bullet alongside it.

"I like your friend Robin," he said. "I understand she was Joe Waters' lover."

He picked up the bullet. I couldn't see what he was doing. I heard something spin on the gun. I heard a clicking. He put the gun down, but the bullet was gone. I noticed his hand. It was shaking bad. That didn't make me feel any better. I didn't think he would be shaking if he was just trying to scare me.

"And I like your brother," he said. "He's got balls. If it hadn't been for him, you wouldn't have won that race. I let him psyche me out."

His hand came down on my back. It was a gentle touch.

"But you're a great runner, my friend. I've never seen anything like you. Maybe if things were different, and you weren't on Waters' side, we could have been friends. I haven't had too many friends in my life. Even my father was never my friend."

The piano started up. Someone played good now, a song I recognized, something Robin played for me once. I couldn't remember, though. It seemed there should have been an orchestra, but I couldn't remember the name. The taste of dirt had worked its way down my throat. I couldn't see through the tears, but as long as that piano played, I knew this would end. I imagined a man with white hair at the piano. I imagined Beethoven. I imagined he was deaf and could only hear the notes in his mind.

"But I want you to tell your brother to stay away from Suzanne. Okay? Just tell him that. Maybe you could explain about power. Do what you have to, but Suzanne's mine. She doesn't believe that now. She's playing at being a Whale, or a hippie, or some kind of fucking gypsy astrologer. But I've got a hold over her. Tell your brother that. Make sure, Itchy, because if he's with her a month from now, you'll be down on the floor again, and next time, you won't get up, and that would be sad."

He patted my back.

"Come on. Roll over."

I did what he said. The light was straight above me. It was like looking into the sun. I shut my eyes.

"Open them," he said.

I opened them. I tried looking left or right, but it hurt just the same. He pulled up the chair I'd been sitting in, nudging it right up against me. The wheel pinched my skin. He stuck the barrel of his gun on my nose.

He was sweating now, just covered with it, and he wasn't sneering, or smiling, or trying to look tough. His face was open and honest. I'd never seen it that way before.

"I would kill you," he said. "If I had to, and maybe before the summer's over, I will. Maybe it will be you, maybe Robin, maybe Joe, maybe all of you. We're in our own war here, and I'm going to win, but I don't really like it. I didn't like hitting you with my elbow in that race, but I couldn't let you pass me, and I can't let you close down my factory.

"Ever since I was a kid, Joe Waters and I have been enemies, always on opposite sides, fighting over Suzanne, fighting over...I don't know, my father always had some thing about the bastard. I never understood that. I'm going to beat him. Where is he, Itchy?"

"I don't know."

He fell off the chair across my chest with a knee on either side of me and cracked the open barrel against my mouth. It smacked my teeth.

"Where's Joe?"

I spit blood, but I swallowed more than I got out. He held me by the hair and pushed the gun against my mouth.

"Don't make me hurt you. Just tell me where he is."

"I don't know. I swear."

He spinned the chamber on the gun.

"Open your mouth."

I opened. He forced the gun in, barely sliding it between my lips. It was cool. His head blotted out the light. I stared into his eyes.

"Know anything about Russian Roulette?" he asked.

I closed my eyes.

"Where the fuck's Waters?"

He pushed the gun in farther. I listened for the piano. *Rhapsody in Blue*, I thought. George Gershwin. That was it. He wrote it in the twenties. Robin played it for me. *Rhapsody in Blue*.

"Suck on it," he said.

I pictured Gershwin with slicked back hair, all soaked and parted in the middle, playing in a tuxedo in a room down the hall, banging at the keys, lost in the music, no idea that a room or two away, separated by walls and space, a kid lay on the floor with a gun in his mouth.

"Suck it," he said.

I sucked the gun. I sucked my own spit and blood off the metal. It tasted worse than the floor. He forced the gun until I choked and tried to throw him off. He yanked it out then and tapped it against my nose, right on the bridge. God it hurt. I threw up, and he let me turn my head and spit it to the side.

I cried so hard, the tears choked me. He just stared down at me. He ran his fingers through my vomit and smeared some on my face.

"There's one bullet," he said. "Five empty chambers."

He gave it a spin then pressed the gun against my temple. He leaned close, his nose almost touching mine, his eyes inches away, his breath all full of smoke and some horrid old booze.

"I count to three. Then I pull the trigger. Or you tell me where Waters is."

"What do you want him for?"

I'd never been so close to a man. Our eyeballs almost touched. I wanted to pull his out of his head. I wanted to squeeze them between my fingers until they popped.

"He's dangerous."

"You wouldn't kill him."

"Why not?"

He spinned the chamber.

"One," he said. The piano stopped. Everything stopped. There was just Stewart Donaghy sitting on my chest with a gun against my skull. "Two."

"I don't know where he is. I swear to God I don't. I could help you find him, but..."

"Three." He pulled the trigger. It clicked. Something hot ran down my leg. I started praying. Please, God, get me out of here. Please get me out of here.

"One more time," he said. "One bullet, four empty chambers left. The odds are in your favor, but life's not always fair."

"If I knew I'd tell you. I swear to God."

He didn't count. He fired twice, two more clicks. I closed my eyes. I thought I would explode. My pants were soaked. My heart thrashed, and I talked. I shouted, telling him how to get to the abandoned house, just shouting it at the top of my lungs, and he kept making me slow down and repeat things, and then it was all out, and he jumped to his feet, fired three more times at my face, then tossed the bullet out of his hand, where it had been all along. It clinked on the floor beside me.

"Don't kill him," he said. And he was gone. Something smashed out the light. Glass sprinkled on top of me. There was silence, and piano music, and I thought I'd better say something in a hurry, maybe crack a joke or invite them for dinner on Thanksgiving, but I couldn't think of anything except to say, "So, do you guys like the Phillies?" There was laughing then, and pain.

28

They came from the distance, from out where something rumbled like thunder and flames stretched far into the sky. They walked in single file up a dusty road. At the end of the road stood great hills all shrouded in clouds and filled with trees, and the line of people stretched deep into the hills, before it vanished under the clouds.

Some wore those cone-shaped hats like the Vietnamese on the news at night. Some wore the clothes of European peasants and reminded me of people from paintings by Vincent van Gogh, or of the people in black-and-white photographs of the Soviet Union after the Nazis came in, finding their dead strewn across a field in some Ukrainian town. Some looked like the Jews from that same world, peering through the doors of trains just before they closed. Others had black faces, African faces, and hardly any clothes, and the children had big heads and crooked stick legs.

They all looked peaceful and patient. There were lots of soldiers, young German boys and old German men who'd gone to war during Hitler's last days, Russians from Stalingrad with frostbitten faces, and American marines from the Chosin Reservoir in Korea. There were French from Verdun and tired British who'd washed onto the shores at Dunkirk. There were soldiers from all the books I'd read and all the movies and documentaries I'd seen, all the soldiers mixed together and marching.

They were refugees, the peaceful dead, marching toward distant hills, and I was just feet from the path, watching their faces, when Joe Waters walked by.

"Itchy, there's peace." He pointed toward the trees in the mountains. "Just over those dark hills."

And then, from farther down the line, someone shouted my name, and it was Patrick, and we ran toward one another, and I came just so close to falling into his arms.

But I never fell into his arms. That day, it had been the pain that woke me, and today, it was Suzanne touching my back. I jumped a bit. We'd arranged to meet, but I was far gone in the memory of the dream and hadn't heard her. The sun was going down, and I was at the very end of her father's boardwalk with my feet hanging over the edge. I tried to hide my eyes.

I always cried when I remembered the dream. I'd wanted to reach Patrick's arms so bad, but instead I'd fallen awake in a heap in the darkness, drenched in piss. Donaghy's handsome friends had bounced me off walls and boxes and chairs for five endless minutes, tossing me around like a ball with legs, taking extra care just to keep knocking the wind out of me, jarring me with slaps, backhands, and palms, leaving no bone unbruised, but never actually breaking anything. They were pros, all right. They'd topped it off with a couple kicks to my battered ribs, and finally, one pissed on me while *Rhapsody in Blue* played through the wall. I passed out. The last thing I heard was that clock.

Suzanne dropped her bag between us. She'd sewn a pink peace sign to the side. The bag was getting awfully ragged. It cheered me right up.

"You look pretty good," she said. "Last time you looked like a bad boxer. Of course, you've still got that ugly haircut. You should sue your barber for malpractice."

"My body still hurts," I said.

"Oh, that's just pain," she said.

"I know it's stinking pain."

"Well pain always hurts," she said.

"You should be a doctor."

"I was a doctor in Babylon thousands of years ago. All my patients died. Even the ones who weren't sick."

She stuck her head in her bag and reached in to her elbow. She was always pulling something out of there, like some magician. I imagined her pulling out a lion's head, like Bullwinkle trying to get a rabbit from his hat.

"Wrong hat," I said.

"What? What hat?"

"Nothing."

"How about your lips?" she asked. "They okay?"

"Why, you going to kiss me or something?"

"If I get the urge. Here. I finally got that harmonica I didn't tell you I was thinking of getting you. I hope it's the right color."

She handed me a new harmonica. I liked the way it felt in my hand.

"It's the right color," I said. "But what am I supposed to do with it?"

"Use it to catch fish."

"Don't I need bait or something?"

"Come on, Itchy, just play the stupid thing."

"I don't know how."

"Let it come to you."

She grabbed it from me and ran it across her mouth a few times, blowing random notes that drifted toward the water.

"Play 'Love Me Do,' " she said. She forced it back in my hand and smiled. "Come on, this cost me five dollars."

She started singing. Her voice was scratchy, but it was good, and she could carry any tune.

"But I never played in my life," I said. "You might as well give me a violin."

"So what? You're a genius. I saw it in the paper. Just poke around till 'Love Me Do' comes out."

"Nobody said I was a musical genius. Patrick played the harmonica, not me."

"You've got the same genes. Just play."

She sat right beside me. Our legs touched, and I smelled perfume in her hair. I felt nervous and happy.

"Play," she said.

I blew into it a few times. She tapped on my leg and sang it again, but I couldn't find a single note.

"Some genius you are," she said. "I should get my money back."

I tried to hand the harmonica to her, but she acted offended.

"Maybe if you practice," she said. "In about twenty years you'll be able to play 'Love Me Do.' "

"With a lot of practice."

"A very lot. Maybe in another life. You know what?"

"What?"

"I don't know," she said. "What are you going to do with your life this time, anyway? I mean, you're not going to be a musician. Are you going to fix toilets, or teach poetry, or what? How about an astronaut? You could be the first Whale on the moon. I'll bet you'd look good in one of those helmets. They're very stylish.

"Do you think they're really going to walk on the moon? I have a friend who's an artist and never paints soup cans, and he thinks they stage the whole thing. He says they film it all in Hollywood, and when they go to the moon, it's really going to be the Sahara Desert. So what are you going to do with your life?"

I shrugged. She dug in her bag again. I was afraid she would pull out another musical instrument, maybe a tuba, and insist I play "Eleanor Rigby," but she had this nervous look she got, and I realized she wanted a cigarette. I hated the way she smoked all the time. It reminded me of forest fires, the way you'd see them on the news, all this beautiful forest burning. I hated to see something beautiful get ruined.

She got a bent one out and lit it. She closed her eyes for a second.

"God, they're so good," she said. "Too bad they're stunting my growth and taking twenty years off my life. Plus, they make me smell awful, but I'm an addict, you know. It's built into my spirit. Once in Turkey I was addicted to opium, many lives ago, of course."

She gave me this crazy addicted look, opening her eyes real wide and spinning them around.

"Want to go to Turkey? There's a bazaar in Istanbul, and it's huge and ancient, and they sell everything known to man. We could buy exotic pipes and harmonicas and a lamp with a genie in it. What are you going to do with your life? Huh?"

"I don't know. Maybe I'll go to Turkey."

"Come on, Itchy. Be serious. You're never serious."

"I don't like anything more than everything else," I said. "Except maybe history, especially twentieth century stuff, but there's no future in history."

"Maybe there's no history in future," she said.

"Huh?"

"Oh, nothing. I think you should be an artist," she said. "All the most interesting men are artists. They're all crazy, of course, and drunks, and you'd be miserable all the time, and you would have to take up cigarettes and maybe get addicted to opium, but you'd lead a romantic life, and you'd have a beard. You should lead a romantic life, Itchy, not some dull life where all you do is go to work every-day or talk about a lot of books you read. You should die young, like with tuberculosis or something."

"I could be a writer. Some of them get tuberculosis, but I don't think I can grow a beard. I don't have many whiskers."

"That's a good idea," she said. "Writers are artists, except most of them, and you don't have to have a beard. Besides, you could glue one on. Why don't you be a writer? Why don't you be Jack London and travel to the Yukon and sleep with Eskimo women? You know, if you visit an Eskimo man in his igloo, he'll expect you to sleep with his wife. If you don't, he'll be offended."

"Thanks for the tip," I said.

"It's true, and they smell very fishy. You could be Jack Kerouac and ride across the country in cars with some madman."

I tooted the harmonica.

"Writing's probably easier than playing the harmonica," I said. "Now how about you?"

"Me?" She shrugged. "I'm already what I'm going to be."

"You're going to be a stinking picture framer?"

"No. A tragic heroine."

"Do they make good money?"

"Well no, but they get in great books, and they get great men."

She dug into her bag again and came out with three paperback novels. For some reason, they reminded me of Robin's cat. She handed me one.

"You see, this is *Madame Bovary*. She cheats on her husband because he's a bore, and she has a very sad, romantic life. I want to be like her."

"So what happens to her?"

"She dies. All the best tragic heroines die, of course. Look at this one. *Anna Karenina*. She throws herself in front of a train."

"Well, now that I know the ending..."

"Who cares about the ending? From the very start, you know she's going to throw herself in front of a train. It's in the atmosphere of the book. The author became a mystic, you know."

"Robin's mother left her on a train."

"Are you going to marry Robin?" She laughed. "Boy, your face turns red fast."

"Well, it never crossed my mind to marry Robin."

"Why not? She's pretty, and she's very brilliant and tragic."

"I don't pick girls by how tragic they are, and she's twelve years older than me, or thirteen, depending on the time of year."

She took the harmonica away. She tried to get something out of it, but she was no better than I was, and the whole time she played, she stared at me.

"I think you love her," Suzanne said. "And she loves you, and who cares about age? When you're twenty-eight, she'll be in her sexual prime. Won't that be fun? Better than an Eskimo, I'll bet."

"Are those my only choices, Robin or some Eskimo?"

"You never know."

I could feel myself turning redder and redder, but I didn't know how to change the subject.

"And everybody knows what goes on between you two," she said.

"Nothing goes on between us."

"Oh sure. Robin oozes sex. Don't tell me she's keeping you around to tell her jokes."

"You don't like my jokes?"

"I'd like them better if they were funny."

She stuffed the books in her bag. I never saw the third, but had a feeling there was a tragic heroine who died at the end.

"Sometimes I feel like we're at the end of time," she said. "You ever feel like that, like you can't imagine anything more happening? I don't think we'll ever get through our lives. They've got all these nuclear weapons, and they're always having wars, and the men who have them are really stupid. It's just a matter of time, but that's not it.

"I mean, I don't think we'll have a nuclear war for a few years. I just feel like everything's moving so slow, and we're not going anywhere, like time's just going to stop any day now. Know what I mean, like maybe how you'd feel on that Ferris wheel the very last second before it stopped for good? You know?"

"I don't think so."

"You're not a very good genius. Now just shut up and listen for a second, and you'll see."

"Listen to what?"

"Shhhh."

She clamped her hand over my mouth, and we sat with our legs dangling over the edge of the boardwalk her father had never finished. We sat for a long time without a word. The breeze blew cool and perfect off the water. The sun set behind us. The water turned dark and gloomy and beautiful, and Suzanne sat close beside me, blowing smoke into the night, breathing softly, and listening to the waves roll in.

"Do you hear him roar?" she asked.

"Hear who?"

"The keeper."

"You mean the Ferris wheel guy?"

"Yeah, except I've decided he's more than the Ferris wheel guy."

"Oh yeah? What is he?" I asked.

"I can't say for sure."

"Have you seen him lately?"

"I see him all the time. Do you hear him?"

"All I hear is waves."

"It's more than waves. You can hear him roar anywhere. You could hear him good the night I saw Joe."

"That was rain and thunder."

"Yeah, and everything all mixed in the sky and vibrating kind of. It's his voice in the wind, and in it, you can hear people crying in China and worms crawling under the earth, like birds can, and you can hear space dust burning in the atmosphere and bombs falling in Vietnam and a billion hearts beating and even the earth spinning on its invisible axis. It's all mixed together, but sometimes he's quiet, and you have to listen hard."

"You're crazy," I said.

"Yes, I think so."

She grabbed hold of my hand.

"Do you ever have memories, maybe because you smell something from when you were a kid, or because the wind feels a certain way, or you hear part of a song, and it makes you so sad you can hardly stand it?"

"Yeah, I guess, I mean, sometimes I'll hear a dog bark and think about Whitey."

"Well, I feel that way all the time," she said. She whacked her feet together, and sand fell off and sprinkled the air. She blew a few more notes into the harmonica, mashing her lips around it and closing her eyes.

"You see, because everything reminds me of something bad. Like when I look at you, I remember what you told me about how Stewart put that gun in your mouth and how he said I shouldn't see Charlie anymore, and I remember some of the times when he was nice to me, like this one time when he bought me a heart full of chocolates two days after Valentine's Day because I cried when he didn't get me anything."

She laughed. "They were on sale, and he made a joke out of it, and it was the first time I thought he really cared about me, and I thought someday we would get married.

"You know, emotions don't make any sense. Sometimes I wake up in the night and wish Stewart was there so bad. Sometimes I think I love him, even though he's so horrible, but I remember a time, just maybe two years ago, when he wasn't so bad, when I thought he really cared about me. He never once hit me, you know, not like people think.

"And sometimes he reminds me of Joe, and I get so sad. I get so sad when I think about Joe, but anyway, did you know Charlie's been taking a lot of drugs, and I have, too?"

She played the harmonica again, staring at me with those huge black eyes. I was madly in love with her by now.

"What do you mean, drugs?"

"You know, like acid. We did some the other night, something called orange sunshine or orange wedge or something. There's different kinds, like purple haze, and we did this orange stuff and just sat on the beach all night without any clothes. It was so great, but it's scary, too, and I don't like it, but Charlie, he keeps wanting to do more and more stuff."

"I don't believe it."

"Believe it. And he talks right out loud to your brother. He talks to him just like he's there, and if I'm doing acid, too, I can almost hear your brother answering. I mean, Charlie's part of the conversation is so real, I almost know exactly what your brother's saying to him."

She squeezed my hand. She lifted it to her mouth, stared at it like she'd never seen one before, then kissed it.

"You're so nice," she said. "Charlie's nice, too, but he's not the kind of guy I wanted to end up with. I always thought it would be some kind of artist or something, if it wasn't going to be Stewart, but anyway, Charlie asked me to marry him."

Her eyes drifted out over the dark sand. My heart had just about broken by then, and I didn't know what to say. I wanted to ask her to marry me instead. I wanted to tell her that I would be an artist and die of tuberculosis if it would make her happy, but Charlie would never be any more than a football player.

"What did you say?" I whispered.

"I said no. I can't marry him. He's going to Vietnam. He's dead set on it. You know, when he talks to your brother, they argue about it, and Charlie kicks sand and shouts, and there's nobody to shout at. I can't stand it, and I'm not marrying him unless he promises he'll go to college and stop taking that stuff and then maybe if he gives me a box of old chocolates or a used diamond or something."

My eyes were on the boards underneath me. I still had that good feeling, that excited happiness she stirred up inside me, but now I was miserable, too, weighed down with the thought of Charlie doing drugs, of Charlie going to the war, of Charlie asking Suzanne to marry him.

"I've got to find him," I said.

She folded the harmonica back in my palm. Our eyes met for a second, and she tried to smile, but it didn't come out. Finally, she got beside me on her knees and squeezed my head against her breasts. She kissed my wounded hair.

"You don't mind if I love you, do you? I mean, not like a boy-friend, I guess, you know, with you having Robin, and all, and me dating your brother, but in a different way, you know. You don't mind, do you?"

I couldn't think of anything to say.

"Let's do an experiment," she said. "Close your eyes. Okay, now don't jump or anything. This is for science."

Her mouth closed over mine. She held my head with both hands and kissed my lips just long enough to nearly kill me.

"Talk to him, Itchy. You're the only person he respects, and listen when he talks about Patrick. I think you can contact him."

She kissed me hard once more, grabbed up her bag, and ran down the boardwalk, leaving me all excited and confused with my heart pounding away.

29

I hunted for Charlie that same night. When he wasn't with Suzanne, he usually smoked cigarettes with his friends on the wharf, talking about cars and the Phillies and whatever else those guys talked about during their endless nights of beer drinking and sitting in the dark.

They were having a peanut blowing contest when I walked up. I couldn't believe it. They were all stoned and drunk and laughing like madmen and taking turns blowing peanuts from their noses. It was turning into a fad. Charlie called it peanut snorting, and he couldn't do it to save his life.

"Hey, it's Itchy," Charlie said. He threw a peanut at me, and all his clever buddies did the same thing. They must have hit me with a hundred peanuts before they didn't think it was the funniest thing in history anymore and finally stopped.

"Come on, Itchy, snort one," Charlie said. And they all started yelling at me to snort a peanut, and when I wouldn't, they started pelting me again. Charlie rolled on his back laughing, and I just stood there with peanuts in my pockets and stuck in my hair, while Charlie and his friends hooted and drank and yelled, "Snort one, Itchy. Snort one."

"I'm not putting a peanut in my nose. It's ridiculous," I said.

"You're just chicken," Charlie said, "because you can't do it."

"You can't do it, either," I said.

"I'm going to put one on the moon," Charlie said. "Soon as I build up my sinus muscles."

"Yeah, you doing nose exercises?"

"That's right, Itchy. I'm doing nose push-ups."

One of Charlie's friends asked when we would burn down the factory. Another asked if I was screwing Robin. They loved to hear about Robin, what she fed me, what we talked about, what she wore to bed, and they wanted to hear about Nigel, too, especially about the time he put the peanut in my nose and the girl in the toilet paper. It was a famous story now, and I was famous, too, and it took an awfully long time to get Charlie out of there.

We walked onto the beach and headed toward the Ferris wheel with its cars creaking in the late summer breeze. Charlie climbed in one of the cars and started rocking. The Ferris wheel hadn't turned in years, but I remembered it lighting up the sky and a long line waiting to get on. I remembered music and colorful lights and young girls shouting. Now it was all rusted and crumbling.

"Man, I'd love to see it go around again," he said. "Imagine having a beer up there on a windy night with your hair blowing, and you could see for miles?"

"It ruins your liver."

"What?"

"Beer. It ruins your liver."

"Oh, man, you're like some old fucking lady."

He chugged the beer. It swished and gurgled in the bottle.

"Remember Patrick talking about the Ferris wheel?" he said. "He was so full of shit, but you had to laugh. He'd get that serious face and say this ridiculous stuff, like about florescent whales and all."

Charlie rocked, and I sat in the sand with my hands around my knees, looking toward the black water and remembering Patrick.

"I remember the night Whitey escaped," I said.

"Good old Whitey," Charlie said. "I'll bet he swam to England. I never knew a dog could swim like that guy. He was a fucking fish with a tail, man."

"Fish have tails," I said.

"Oh, man, you just know everything, don't you?"

"Well, they do."

"Not long furry ones, egghead, not like Whitey."

"I saw you guys in the yard that night," I said.

Charlie shut his mouth and squinted at me. The chair squeaked.

"When?"

"The night Whitey got away."

"In the yard?"

"Yeah, I saw you dig the hole. It must've been cold."

Charlie climbed off the seat. It banged and rattled. He lifted the empty bottle straight up, so that he faced the sky. He drank it empty, then hurled it as far as he could. When it finally landed, I heard the thud, and then Charlie's voice.

"Coldest night ever," he said. "My fucking nose kept running. Fucking Patrick wouldn't let me stop digging, kept saying we couldn't let you find out and all this shit about how it would kill you. He thought you were real fragile, like a cracked egg or something. He would never let me beat you up for being so smart all the time. Boy, you were an annoying kid. So many times I wanted to pound your head in. But I never figured you knew about Whitey."

He walked ahead of me. I stayed in the sand and stared at his huge figure in the darkness. The ocean swished, and Charlie waved at it like he was saying hello to somebody.

"Hey, Whitey," he shouted. "You out there? I got some peanuts. Come on in, Whitey."

"Maybe he's not hungry," I said.

"He's always hungry."

"How come you're acting so weird?" I asked.

"Because I'm weird. Did you talk to the giraffe?"

"Yeah," I said.

"What she tell you?"

"She said you wanted to get married."

"You don't mind, do you?"

"Why should I mind?"

"I don't know. I got the feeling you might like her, too. Do you?"

I wanted to tell the truth, but it seemed impossible.

"I like her, yeah, but not the way you do. I just want to be friends."

"Well, you deserve her more than I do. I don't know what she sees in me anyway. She's a million times too smart, and I swear, Itchy, I'll give her up if you want her."

"You're drunk," I said.

"I'd give her to you, though, man, and you could give me Robin, that little freak. I'll bet she's fun. She reminds me of some vicious little dog."

"Suzanne doesn't want me," I said.

"She doesn't want me, either. She wants somebody who's sensitive and doesn't do push-ups all the time, some boring painter or piano player or something. Maybe if I learned to play one of them cello things. Could you see me in a tuxedo on a little bench with all these orchestra guys?"

"I can see you running for touchdowns with five guys on your back and safeties biting your legs and nobody stopping you, like against Wood last year, man. Don't worry about joining an orchestra, just be like you are. I think she likes you that way, and maybe if you really want, you could get her to marry you."

"Oh, man. Sure. If I promise not to go."

"Yeah, well if I loved Suzanne and had a choice between her and the stinking war, I know what I'd pick."

"Would they let me back in high school?" he asked.

"Of course they would. Why not?"

"I don't know. Oh, what the fuck's it matter? I'm going. I knew the day I heard about Patrick I was going. I know it's all fucked up. I'm just going 'cause he died, and I feel bad and want to get away."

"Is that why you're doing drugs, 'cause you feel bad?"

"I knew she told you."

He threw a handful of sand straight overhead. It came down on top of him. He brushed some out of his hair.

"What've I got to lose?"

"Her."

"She's not going to stay with me, and I like that stuff. When you get it right, it's like a whole other world you can find in your head. It makes you smart. I imagine it's like being you, only not half as boring."

"She said you talk to Patrick."

"Nothing like blabbing my whole life to you."

"What's he say?"

Charlie sat on the Ferris wheel again. I waited, but he just rocked, so I asked him again.

"You won't believe me," he said.

"So you have hallucinations about Patrick? Maybe it's natural."

"They're not hallucinations."

"What are they?"

"When I take that stuff, Patrick comes."

"And what do you talk about?"

"You're just making fun of me, or maybe you think I'm crazy, but I don't care. If I do enough acid, Patrick shows up, and we talk about when we were kids and stuff."

"She said you fight."

"Yeah, sometimes he gets mad about the war. He don't think I should go."

"What are you telling me, Charlie? You talk to Patrick's ghost?"

"He's not a ghost. He's just Patrick."

"Patrick's dead."

"No he ain't, man."

"How much beer did you drink tonight?"

Charlie banged the seat.

"So I'm a little drunk? I still know he ain't dead."

"So what is he?"

"He's just in another place, and when I take that shit, it's like I go through something, like a door, only there's no door. It's like there's another world and things holding us out, like things you believe, but when you're tripping you forget all that, and you can pass through to places you can't most times, and I pass through and see Patrick."

I felt cold. I joined Charlie on the Ferris wheel. We sat side by side with our legs touching and the waves swishing in the distance. I remembered Suzanne talking about the guy on top of the wheel and how you could hear him roar. I wondered what the hell she was talking about. I wondered if birds could really hear worms moving underground. I wanted to put my arm around Charlie, but I was embarrassed.

"Maybe you get through to another part of yourself," I said. "The part that knows it's stupid to go."

"I'm going," he said. "Not even Patrick can stop me."

"Charlie, if you die, too, Mom and Dad..."

"If I die, you can marry Suzanne. She just went out with me because she felt sorry for me anyway."

Finally I put my arm around him. It was a thing Patrick used to do, and I could tell Charlie liked it.

"Itchy, it's great to see him, and he keeps asking me to bring you. He says he can explain about the neighbor, and all that."

"I told you about the neighbor?"

"No, man, Patrick did. I don't know what he's talking about half the time. Who's the fucking neighbor?"

"Charlie, don't play around."

"I ain't playing around, man. Who is he? I mean, we got the Monteiths on the left and that deaf lady on the right. Is that the neighbor, that deaf lady who plays cards with Mom?"

"No. It's somebody Robin dreams about. I must've told you."

"You never told me, man. Why's your mouth hanging open?"

30

Robin smeared her mouth against mine as soon as I walked in. Her tongue tasted like wine, and her breath was full of it. We'd been fighting ever since our talk with the mayor, and it was good to feel her lips and taste her tongue after a week of hating each other.

I couldn't understand why she sounded like Nigel all of a sudden, all this stuff about fire and destruction. Joe had published three letters, and after each, she sounded more violent, and now she was giving speeches with Nigel. I hated it. I didn't mind protesting, or even putting men out of work if we had to, but I wasn't out to blow anything up.

Her face was just inches from mine. Sweat soaked through her shirt.

"I thought you quit drinking," I said.

"I got problems. They get any worse, I'm canceling the march."

"Are you crazy? Cut the shit about blowing it up, but don't cancel it. Half the town's ready to jump off bridges for you."

"It's getting complicated," she said. "The mayor's had inspectors in here three times, and at the stores, too.

"And Nigel's in trouble, something about a girl. He wouldn't give the details, except she's fourteen, and he needs ten thousand bucks. Her father's blackmailing him or something, and he wants me to pay. He says he was in Deadwhale long before I realized and knows all my secrets."

"What stinking secrets?"

"There's more." She handed me a paper. It was crumpled and wet.

"I found this on your sleeping bag. I don't think the mailman left it."

"Who's it from?"

"Joe. It's a letter to you."

"How'd he get in here?"

"He walked through the wall, I guess. Read it to me."

Robin squeezed Vincent against her. She kept the place dark, and the handwriting was awful, so I had a hard time seeing, but I held the paper close to my eyes and read Joe's words.

"Itchy, don't ever let them forget this war. Don't ever let them make it look pretty and heroic, or try to bury its memory in the glory of other wars, or blur its lessons with clichés and glib misinterpretations of history. No matter how many wars we fight, this will always be the war we grew up on, this will always be the war that corrupted our innocence and spoiled our youth, and don't let them make you forget. Don't let the wound heal. When they talk of reconciliation, when they try to justify it all, when they say forget, it's behind us, rip open the wound, and stick their faces in the pus and the blood. Don't let them forget this war, because this is the lesson America must always refer back to when charting its future. This is the lesson we must never forget. This is the wound that must never heal.

"Give Robin my deepest love. I cannot change what she's going to do. Tell her I'm with her and that when all seems lost, that's when it all begins. I've seen the flames in my dreams, the flames she's seen in hers, but it will take my death to spark them. Tell her I've seen the neighbor, too, and that it's for me he's waiting. Good-bye."

I dropped the letter. It floated softly to the floor, and Robin took a candle to it. We watched it burn and curl to black ash on the wood.

"What's it mean?" I asked.

"It means if we march, Joe's going to die."

"Then we can't," I said.

"There's still more, Itchy. Nigel does have something on me, and it could ruin my reputation and Robert Waters', too."

"What's stinking Nigel know about Mayor Waters?"

"Close the windows. Lock the doors."

I did what she told me. The apartment was already hot and black, but it got worse. I heard her in the kitchen. The refrigerator light stayed on awhile, and I watched her shadow opening bottles of wine. She came back with the bottles and some clothes on her arm.

"Undress," she said.

She gave me orders a lot. Sometimes I argued, but this time I didn't. After I dropped all my clothes on the floor, she handed me a white shirt and a tie.

"Wear these."

The shirt drooped over me. She buttoned it up and helped me get the tie on. She wasn't wearing much herself, just a shirt like the one she handed me, buttoned all the way to her neck. The tail covered her ass and halfway down her legs.

"Pour wine into me," she said. "And don't touch me."

I held a bottle over her mouth. It was freezing, and she let it pour down her throat and over her face and down her neck and soak the shirt to her. The bottle was half-gone before she pushed it away.

"Pour the rest over my hair."

She lowered her head. Her arms hung at her sides, and the freezing wine drenched her hair to her face and spilled down onto her shoulders.

"There's initials on your tie," she said. "Guess whose?"

"I don't know. Who cares? Nigel's? Joe's? Why you acting so weird? You're getting the whole apartment wet. Aren't you cold?"

"RSW," she said. "You've heard those initials."

I swallowed some wine. Robin stood soaked in front of me, her bottom lip shaking just a bit.

"Robert Samuel Waters," I said.

"Take off my shirt," she said.

I reached for the buttons, but she shouted.

"Rip it. Rip it hard with two hands, down the middle."

"Robin, I don't like this."

"Do what I fucking say."

"Robin..."

"Do it."

I grabbed the collars and pulled. The fabric split. The buttons popped, hit the floor, and rolled. Robin's breasts were white, soaked, pointed. She slid her arms free and let the shirt fall.

"I met him in New York," she said. "He was at some conference for mayors."

She closed her eyes. Her breathing picked up, and she smeared wine across her breasts, slowly, her head dropping back on her neck.

"Get behind me," she said. "Close as you can. I want your breath in my hair. I want to feel your body's heat. But don't touch me."

I got behind her. I stood as close as I could without touching her skin. I smelled the wine that dripped off her hair onto my feet. I smelled the perfume. I wanted to touch her.

"I saw him leaving a hotel. He had a briefcase. I was drunk. Vincent and I were hungry, so I asked if he wanted...I offered him my mouth for fifteen dollars. He liked my work."

She reached behind her, sliding her fingers around me, just like Nigel that crazy afternoon, only it felt a lot better, and I didn't expect a peanut up my nose when it was over. Her hand was cool from the bottle. It was an expert's hand.

She made me pour more wine on her. I poured it over her shoulders and breasts. I poured it into her mouth and all over her face. She swallowed some and let the rest splash off her skin. She slapped her feet up and down in the puddle, and then I was behind her again, and her hand was back, and I was sweating.

"I spent that week between his legs," she said. "He didn't talk to me. He didn't kiss me. He tore off my clothes and drenched me in wine and made me do things in front of him, but he wouldn't touch me. I hated him, but when he left New York, I left with him."

Her hands slid up and down my legs. She rolled her head back against my shoulder.

"Bring your hands around," she said. "Squeeze my nipples hard."

I did what she told me. She rubbed back against me. She shuddered. "Yes. If only he would have touched me like this."

One of her hands wrapped around me again, but the other moved down inside her.

"He set me up here," she said. "He got me a job cleaning his office, but his office never got clean. It was the same office we were in last week. Seeing Donaghy there made me want to destroy everything on earth.

"I spent the worst moments of my life in that office, and the best. He hardly talked to me, except to tell me when to come and how to get in and how much he was going to pay me. I would crawl under his desk. He would take phone calls and write letters. He ran the fucking city with my mouth scraping against his zipper and my hand soaked with my own cunt, like it is now. Feel it."

She took my hand inside where she was drenched and hot. She pushed my fingers in and rolled her head. Her soaked hair brushed my face, and I could smell the wine, and I could smell what I was touching.

"It got risky," she said. "He got addicted to my lips. He started coming here. We started talking. I fell in love listening to him talk. I fell in love like you wouldn't believe, and still he wouldn't kiss me. He wouldn't fuck me. He just stood there in his shirt and tie and watched me fuck myself. He never took off the shirt, never took off the tie.

"I begged him to make love to me. It was killing me, and finally, one night, when it was pouring rain and the ocean was spilling over the wharf, he opened the windows and let the storm in. He took me over by the window."

She grabbed my hand, the one that was inside her. She kissed it and dragged me to the window. She threw it open wide. The cool air blew over us like a great splash of water. She sucked from the third bottle of wine. She poured some over my head.

"Take off the tie," she said.

She planted herself against the window, leaning forward, her hands on the wall on either side of it, her head out in the night, her legs spread wide, and her ass pushed back at me. She glistened with wine.

"Get behind me," she said.

I got close again. She stretched the tie between her legs and made me hold it on both ends so she could straddle it, like a swing right through the middle of her, or like the hard center of a bike.

"I thought I would die that night. Do it, Itchy. Pull that tie inside me. Pull it hard, like he did."

I hated what she was making me do. I hated the desperate sound of her voice, the way it shook on the edge of breaking down, the tears in it and the anger. I hated the picture in my head of Mayor Waters humiliating Robin this way, but I couldn't resist her commands. I knew that she wouldn't let me stop, that she was teaching me something and that I was doing something for her that had to be done. I knew, too, that I was excited beyond my powers to resist.

I pulled the tie from both ends. Robin twisted and rocked on her heels and slid up and down on the tie, pressing her face against the wall, her hands closing into fists, her mouth open wide, a string of spit sliding onto her chin. At first the tie hardly moved, but soon it was slick, and she rode it, shouting at me, "Tighter. Tighter."

She reached back with one hand, stretched her neck, and found my mouth. She sucked my tongue into hers. She bit and pulled and sucked, while that hand slammed up and down between my legs.

She panted out her breaths between kisses.

"He never fucked me," she said. "All he gave me was this, a fucking tie, his fucking tie with his initials on it, and I loved him so much. I would have…"

Her whole body heaved. She sobbed and pulled my hands so the tie jammed high and tight inside her. She grunted against it with her eyes shut and her forehead wrinkled. She buckled from the waist, throwing her body back and forth, twirling her neck with her tongue out, moaning, long soft deep moans.

She twirled around against me. I lost the tie, and Robin came down on top of me, down on her knees. I slipped in wine, and we fell to the floor, and Robin clawed at me, sucking so hard, I grabbed hold of her hair and tried to pull her away, but she was too strong, and it was over fast, and she held me against her face while it ended, sucking and licking and letting it soak her until she crawled across me and kissed me with her soaked face, smearing it over my lips, sucking my tongue in again so I tasted the wine in her salty mouth.

She cried and moaned and thrashed against her own hand. She jammed the tie inside her and whispered his name, "Bob, how could you do this to me? How? How?"

She rolled away from me and cried on the hard floor, crying and throbbing against it and whispering his name, and finally she shrieked it out, "He died that night. He died, and I knew he had a son."

I sat beside her. She kept crying.

"If he would have kissed me," she said. "Just once. He was starting to love me. It was in his eyes. Why'd he have to die?"

Robin pulled the tie out from between her legs. It was bundled up and soaked. She squeezed onto it, holding it close to her mouth in both hands, like some old Catholic lady with her rosary. For a second her face was peaceful, but then it twitched with a violent spasm of hate and disgust, and she threw the tie across the room and pulled my head against her chest. Her hot breath filled my ear.

"I don't care about the National Guard," she said. "I don't care about Joe. I don't care what Nigel tells them. I'm going to close that factory or die."

She kissed my hand. "I've loved you, Itchy. I'm sorry it has to end. He wouldn't even kiss me."

31

All my illusions were cracking, and I didn't know what to do. The thought of Mayor Waters humiliating Robin made me so sad I could hardly stand it. It was almost time for the next march, and I didn't know whether I was for it or against it. I was confused and scared, and so, I tried to reach Patrick.

I knew it was crazy, but I was young and pretty sure life had big plans for me, something better than dying of some silly overdose before I'd even gotten out of Deadwhale. If there was a chance I could steal a glimpse of Patrick's soul, no matter how strange and unbelievable it seemed, I had to take it.

We did it under the boardwalk, not far from where Mayor Waters' new boards met the old boards of the wharf where Charlie and his friends wasted their nights. Suzanne was late, and while the sun dropped and the water slowly darkened, we started without her.

Charlie handed me a milk bottle of orange juice, tequila, and LSD. He claimed he had the perfect mix and for every two glasses he took, I should take one. We drank from shot glasses. Charlie took two shots, I took one. Charlie took two more, and I took another. Then we started sipping. If nothing else, I would surely get drunk.

Soon it was cool and spooky under the boards, and Charlie and I were disappointed that Suzanne hadn't shown. It was the first time we really talked about her.

"It's her eyes, man," he said. "Without them eyes, she'd just be the fucking girl next door."

"The girl next door? Shit, Charlie, if she was the girl next door, I'd never get any sleep."

Charlie laughed and drank straight from the bottle. We'd finished half, and the boozy taste didn't bother me anymore.

"Such great eyes," he said. "It's so cool how dark they are and how they curve up at the edges, and those long lashes."

"Yeah," I said. "But her mouth's the main thing."

"Her mouth's all fucked up, Itchy. Her lips are too fat. They don't line up, and she's got those gigantic front teeth."

He handed me the bottle. I lay on my side in the sand with my head propped up on my arm. I'd forgotten about the acid and why we were there, and I felt awfully good.

"It's her eyes," he said.

"Her mouth, man. All the great women have screwed up mouths and big lips. Look at Brigitte Bardot. Shit, Suzanne's sexy like her, and I love the way her mouth won't close and those big teeth are always showing."

Charlie threw a handful of sand up off the boards. I heard it hit far too well.

"Sometimes they close, and then did you ever notice how her lips kind of stick together?" he asked. "And how like the top one kind of breaks loose and flaps up like a shade that was stuck, and there's a string of spit between them?"

"Yeah. Yeah. I love that spit."

I pictured Suzanne's lips. I saw them so well it scared me. They were perfect in my mind, and I wanted to kiss the spit off them. I wanted to kiss them so bad, I thought I would cry. I reached for the bottle, but Charlie pulled it away.

"It's pretty strong," he said.

"It won't work on me," I said. "I'm immune. Hey, isn't the sand cool? Just dig under a little. I want to put my face in it."

"Don't put your face in the sand."

"I want to bury my head like an ostrich. You know how fast an ostrich can run?"

"Who cares, Itchy?"

"Faster than Suzanne's car."

"Nuns run faster than Suzanne's car. Remember Sister Elmira?"

"Yeah. She's dead."

"She was dead when we had her. They used to prop her up in the morning and wheel her out in the afternoon."

"I wonder what it's like to be dead?"

"Probably boring," Charlie said. "No challenges. No chicks."

"Maybe it's fun. Maybe Sister Elmira's surfing in the afterlife."

"That would be a good name for an album," Charlie said. "Surfing in the afterlife."

"How's the peanut snorting coming?" I asked.

"Shot one two feet the other day."

"Wow, that's halfway to the moon."

"You'll see, pal, once I get my technique down, I'll put that Nigel freak to shame."

His voice echoed strangely in my head, and I could taste the salt in the air like I'd never tasted it before, and I could hardly believe how good the sand felt when I touched my cheek against it. And when Suzanne's voice came down along the boards and echoed past me, I felt unbelievably good and happy. Charlie hollered back to her, and in a minute she'd found us. She took one look at me and laughed.

"He's gone."

"I'm not gone. I'm right here."

She brushed sand off my face. Charlie handed her the bottle, and she took an endless drink.

"Sorry I'm late. I got in another fight with my mother," she said. She lit a cigarette and sat with the bottle between her legs. I stared at her mouth.

"She's possessed by dead fascists or something. I think Hitler and Mussolini share her soul."

"What's that supposed to mean, Suzanne?" Charlie asked. "You say the weirdest shit. And what's a stinking fascist, anyway?"

And I saw it. I saw Mrs. Waters answering the door that day. I saw crazy things in her eyes, horrible bloodshot fears and hatred. I saw her coming down the hall with the knife in her hand. I saw her crying blood. I saw Hitler and Mussolini playing poker in her soul, and her soul was a tent in a desert, and all the cards had skull heads on them.

"Does her breath smell like tanks?" I asked.

She smacked Charlie on the arm. "You gave him too much."

"He's immune," Charlie said.

"Suzanne, I saw a painting once of some sunflowers by Vincent van Gogh," I said.

"That's nice, Itchy."

"They were your lips. I can see them, beautiful like your lips."

"He has a thing about your lips," Charlie said. "He thinks they're Brigitte Loren's."

"Sophia Loren's?"

"Brigitte Bardot's," I said.

"What's that have to do with van Gogh's sunflowers?" she asked.

"All the great women have messed-up mouths," I said. "Perfection's ugly."

"Robin has a good mouth," Charlie said. "Except it's kind of foul."

"She talks like a boat full of sailors," Suzanne said. "It's neat. I saw her today with this huge crowd around her. All the girls are dressing like Robin now, and every time she opens her mouth, about a million people scream and wave their fists."

"She's a dangerous little freak," Charlie said. "If she pulls off this next march, it's going to be like a war."

"Robin's an angel," I said. "No. She's the Holy Ghost. She's a burning fire that floats over the earth."

Suzanne laughed and poured the stuff down. She lay beside me in the sand, and we stared up at the dark boards.

"Itchy, you have too much imagination," she said. "You don't need drugs."

Charlie grabbed hold of the edge of the boards and started doing chin-ups. He did thirty of them.

"You're a monkey," Suzanne said.

"Watch me," I said. I did three and fell and twisted my ankle. It hurt, but the pain was fascinating. I thought about it for a long time while they laughed and made fun of me, and then Charlie started making guitar sounds, the introduction to "Satisfaction." It sounded great. It roared under the boards.

"Well, I'm driving in my car..."

He shouted his version of the lyrics. I limped onto the sand and played guitar beside him. The boards barely cleared my head. Charlie stooped under them and sang. He sounded just like Mick Jagger, and I was Keith Richards, and I danced, and Suzanne laughed on the sand, and time did funny things, and Charlie kept playing, and it seemed I danced forever, and I felt wild and free, and I sang, and Suzanne kept laughing, and time went far along, and finally Charlie shouted something, and everything got real quiet.

"He's coming," Charlie said.

Suzanne stopped laughing. The bottle sat empty, buried to its neck in sand. A cold wind whistled through the boards. It swirled the sand under my feet. I'd taken off my shoes and socks and shirt a long time ago. My heart beat clearly in my ears. I saw the chambers opening and closing like I'd learned in biology.

Suzanne pulled me down into the sand. She squeezed my fingers. "I'm scared," she said. "Why's he bring that ghost around here?"

"Look out there," Charlie said. "He walks in off the water." Then he shouted. "Patrick, I got Itchy."

Suzanne curled up against me. We watched Charlie. I felt Suzanne's breath on my face. I smelled the cigarette on it, the clearest I'd smelled a thing in my life. I saw tobacco plants. I saw farmers and the sun. I saw an army of hooded men in black tearing at Suzanne's lungs with picks and shovels and skeleton claws. I saw the fat smiling face of a sweating businessman.

I squinted. Everything was black under the boards, but out toward the sea, I could make out the white tops of the waves.

"I hate it so much," Suzanne said.

"Is Patrick coming?" I whispered. "I have my harmonica."

"Kiss me," Suzanne said.

"He's under the boardwalk," Charlie said.

Charlie was out on the sand, not too far away, but far enough so I could hardly make him out.

"You want him to come out?" Charlie shouted.

Suzanne's tongue touched my neck. Her breath roared in my ear, a blast of water and heat, of tequila and orange juice.

"Kiss me."

I turned my mouth toward hers, and she banged against it. Our teeth clacked together, and her tongue rushed inside me. She tasted all smoky and boozy and wet. She grabbed my face with both hands. Flecks of sand broke loose on my skin. Tears brimmed out of my eyes.

"I'm burning," she said.

"Do you love Charlie?"

"I don't want to see this."

"Itchy." He was shouting. His voice echoed up and down for miles under the boards. It jumped out of my head.

"Itchy. Come out. Come. Oh, man. I got to sit down."

Suzanne pulled at my pants.

"Everything's coming at me," she said. "I'm burning." Something snapped. I heard her zipper. "Put your hand on me." She moaned. The moan cut into me, and I felt so weak and hot, I was afraid I couldn't pull away.

"Zippers rust," I said.

"I'm touching myself," she said. "I'm so hot. Robin says you can make yourself feel better than any man can. Oh God, I'm soaked. Give me your hand."

She bit into my chest.

"I'm dying," she said. "I'm dying. Taste my finger."

And then something had me. I shouted. I was lifted out of the sand. Everything turned bright. I throbbed inside my pants, but I was in Charlie's arms, and he carried me away from Suzanne toward the water, carrying me like a baby, and the water rose louder and louder until it roared in my ears, and Charlie waded out into it and dropped me, and I fell. The water froze my hands and knees. I tasted the salt splash over my face.

He pulled me up, and we stood face-to-face with the water sloshing over our bare feet. I heard Suzanne crying, but far away, and the water was cold and beautiful, and Charlie had his face right up to mine, like he was going to kiss me, only he wasn't Charlie anymore.

"Hello, Itchy," he said.

"Hello. Patrick?" I whispered.

"Yeah. Are you sad?" he asked.

"It won't go away."

"But I'm all right," he said.

I trembled so hard, I could hardly stand up, but Charlie's hands were clamped on my shoulders, and he held me against his face, so close I could only see the bright glow of his eyes, only they weren't Charlie's eyes, and it wasn't Charlie's voice. I didn't doubt for a second that I was staring through Charlie into my dead brother, and it seemed as natural as the water that washed over our feet.

"Where are you?" I asked.

"Over the dark hills."

"From the dream?"

"From the dream."

"And you know the neighbor?"

"We all know the neighbor. We are the neighbor."

"I don't understand anything. What's happening to me?"

"You can't understand. To not understand is why you live. Only the neighbor understands."

"Will I ever understand?"

"When the neighbor comes."

"What should I do?"

"Don't interfere. Your friend will die, but your other friend will live."

"Who's going to die? Is Charlie going to die? He wants to go."

"Charlie won't go."

"Why not?"

"Because of the flood and the Ferris wheel."

"What flood?"

"You'll know when it comes."

He hugged me against him then, so tight I could hardly breathe, and then he let go, and Charlie stared into my eyes.

"I don't know what I'm saying," he whispered.

"I don't know what I'm hearing."

He left me there. He walked up the beach by himself, a sad, huge, mysterious figure, and his voice echoed in my mind, and I was sure his voice had changed for a while and that his eyes had, too. I was sure of it, and I ran the conversation through my mind, over and over and over, and it went through fast, and the words all ran on top of one another, and Suzanne came to me out of the darkness.

She didn't say a word, and I didn't either. She pulled me back to the edge of the beach. She was beautiful beyond anything that could be said or imagined, and we dropped to the sand together, and the water fell over us a thousand times, and I made love to Suzanne for millions of years, and I didn't think it could end, and I didn't want it to end, and during an ecstasy my body and mind held with all their strength, I broke into terrible tears and realized I'd hit the peak second of my life, the peak of ecstasy, and nothing would be this good again, and even this wasn't good enough because ecstasy was a limit, and I had touched it for the last time, and I had cheated, and I didn't understand a thing.

Hours later, the sun slipped out of the water. The sea gulls walked along the beach and bobbed in the waves. They swooped high above me. My head hurt. I was naked and alone and so scared it was all a dream, that I could hardly move.

32

It was September. I should have been in Philadelphia by now, but I'd delayed my entry into Penn until the next semester and enrolled full time in Deadwhale Community College to stay draft-exempt. Robin said I was stupid, but I could tell she was glad. The march was coming up, and she was going to need me.

She kept on drawing huge crowds around town. Sometimes she talked about burning the factory. Sometimes she just wanted to close it. She didn't seem to know what the hell she wanted. It changed with her mood. But she was determined to do something, and I didn't try to stop her. I had plans of my own.

Then one warm afternoon, Nigel stormed by. Robin and I were sitting on the floor. Vincent lay in a streak of sunlight beside her, soaked and panting, while we discussed strategy and the best route for the march she was planning for the following week.

Nigel stunk of booze. His hair was dirty. His beard was long and oily. A half-empty bottle of whiskey stuck out one of the pockets of his long coat, and he fixed his red eyes on Robin and drank.

"Well, love," he said. "I've saved you."

Robin closed her eyes, reached out for Vincent, and pulled him in.

"What did you tell them?" she said.

"Ah, my cynical friend."

"Nigel, what did you tell Donaghy?"

He paced, and when he passed the window, the room went black. The plants seemed to shrink away in his shadow, and the smell of whiskey followed him around.

"What couldn't I tell them if I wanted, love? I know everything."

"I thought you were on my side," Robin said. "I thought in your freakish way, with your feathers and paint, you were finally someone I could count on."

"You can count on me, love."

"If you told about me and Bob, they'll hate me around here."

Nigel swallowed more whiskey. He stared at Robin while he paced. Sometimes his eyes would burn across me like the sun shooting between clouds.

"I don't follow your logic quite, love," he said. "So you had a bloody fuck or two with their mayor?"

Robin petted the dirty cat.

"You never saw that," she said. "You're guessing."

"I saw him coming here three nights a week. It's nothing to be ashamed of. It certainly establishes your credentials with me. You're as sleazy as you look. It's your incorruptible sluttiness that kept me on your bloody path year after year, despite all your elaborate gyrations to lose me."

He finished the bottle with one long swallow, three inches of whiskey gurgling down his throat. He smashed it against a wall. Robin didn't move. Glass sprinkled her hair and sparkled in the sunlight. She pulled the cat against her. Nigel held the neck of the bottle and flashed the jagged edges at the air. Vincent let out a feeble hiss.

"I did not betray you, Robin. I made it possible to cleanse yourself before your spirit's corrupted with your cause."

Nigel blotted out the window now. His shadow swallowed the two of us on the floor, and when he flashed at the air with the chunk of sharp bottle, shafts of light cut this way and that from under his shoulders and behind his head, as if he were throwing light at us.

"Nigel, you've been amazingly persistent this summer. You've always been persistent, but this summer you've helped me in your way. I thought you liked this mayhem. There was fire and death and blood, all your favorite things. Why ruin it now?

"I thought maybe you'd changed, maybe you'd found a new cause, but it was just the same shit in a different form. It's not far from your butcher's art to your new-found love of anarchy."

"Yes, love. Yes, but it's not new-found. I've dedicated my life to the bloody truth, from art to action, and what is the truth but death and corruption? The purpose of society, the purpose of everything ever done and built is to deny that.

"It's a world of lies, constructs, sculptured illusions contrived to hide the laws of entropy and rot. This American government is a construct, and this is a war to defend that construct, to defend this pitiful idea of democracy.

"Donaghy's a puny construct within the construct, and even you, Robin, are a self-made construct, a set of lies, foolish hopes, and silly morals to define yourself as more than blood and shit, even a glass eye to fill a hole in the construct, but what are you really, besides a sex-crazed fool bleeding for a dead cat and sucking the cock of a little boy? You're shit, Robin, and that's why I love you."

His eyes absolutely blazed. The light danced behind him, climbed over and around him, shimmered at the edges of his form, but couldn't get through. He shouted, panted, waved the bottle. His breath stank of whiskey clear across the room, and he stayed in the window, huge and dark, a hulking silhouette.

Robin didn't move, flinch, or hardly seem to breathe, but her face turned bright red, and she stroked Vincent fast. He kept hissing.

"My art was a celebration of anarchy, a celebration of decay, of corruption and truth. I've given it up, but not the cause. Sure it galls me that because of you I'm wasting here, teaching photography and drawing to draft-dodging Jersey illiterates with the talent of cockroaches in a school with the academic prestige of shit. The only thing worth a bloody fuck in this town is its name."

"If only you could find a dead whale for your studio," Robin whispered.

"Yes. A dead whale. A dead buffalo. Remember the lamb's heart? Remember the day I ripped the ear off your cat? Anyone can show you a pretty flower, but I'd rather give you a sheep's heart drenched in black and white than a pretty lie, and that's why I've loved you, because there was nothing silly or sentimental about you, and even your beauty, your disgusting sexuality, wasn't the least bit pretty.

"Your only weakness was that wretched cat, but you don't love that cat. You love the horror it conjures. You love the memory of the blood and the screaming and the pretty pain of your deprived youth. Swallowing its ear was an inspiration. You've never looked at that cat without a little pain mixed with those softer sentiments. Still, I've failed, or you wouldn't be torturing the damned thing now. You're weak with your pathetic miscomprehension of love for that ragged piece of fur and breathing death."

He stepped away from the window. The light burst into the room. He knelt on the floor in front of Robin. He reached slowly across the space between them and touched her cheek. His hand was thick with hair. It looked like a paw on her face. She shuddered, but didn't move. Vincent bared his teeth. His heart pounded at his side, and he hissed again, a long sharp hiss, the hiss of a wild animal.

"And you've been soft in your approach to that factory, love. Now it's going to take balls. No more idealistic crap. No more good intentions. Just destruction. It's you or the factory. You can back down and preserve your reputation, or you can say 'fuck it all.' "

"What did you tell them?" she asked.

"I've made you, love. I've dedicated my life to your corrupted soul. I've tried everything to catch the truth with film and light and chemicals, but I've failed, because in the end I've got something dead and structured, something that can't possibly grow or turn against me. The closest I've come to perfection is you, and I won't let you go wrong. I made you. I forced you into the streets full of bitterness. I crushed your wings so you could fly."

Robin settled her gaze on Nigel then dropped her head back, exposing her throat.

"Then finish it," she said. "Slash the canvas." She grabbed his hands and pulled the glass toward her throat. He held it steady at her neck.

"Come on, Nigel. Cut me. I'm tired of hanging on the walls in your perverted mental gallery. Cut me."

"Don't," I said.

"He can't," Robin said. She pushed away his hand. "What's the matter, Nigel? Aren't you corrupt enough to make me bleed, or is it that you are corrupted, corrupted with a love you can't stand or control, a love that makes you crazy and refutes everything you've just said?

"You haven't made me. My mother made me when she took a train out of my life. My father made me when I was sixteen, and he came to my room every night until just before you found me crying in the rain in Amsterdam. And I made it good for him. I thought it made the sin that much worse. I thought I could bury his doomed soul in hell.

"Yeah. I never told you that, did I, Nigel, love? You couldn't corrupt me any more than you can flood this town by throwing a bucket of water in the ocean. You're nothing.

"But you're right about my weakness. I don't oppose this war or this factory solely out of spite, blindness, stupidity, or some frustrated desire to battle the ghosts of my father's memory, the way you would want it. I have a vision of America that's good and open to the lost souls of the world, and this war offends that vision. War's desperate and primitive, and when it's waged without moral justification and supported with lies and false appeals to patriotism and buried fears of man-made demons, we have to fight against it.

"It's true. I've stated my case in negatives, what I'm against, instead of what I'm for, just like they fight wars against communism, instead of wars for justice and democracy. I've made an error of tactics but not an error of heart. You've helped form my cynical exterior, but you haven't touched my soul.

"So yes, I'm weak to your warped perceptions. My intentions are a little more than destruction, but if you told them something about me and Robert Waters, it's over. I won't have Suzanne suffer that."

She ran a hand across her throat as if she were slicing it with Nigel's whiskey bottle.

"Maybe I'm finished, Nigel, but I'm not corrupted, and you'll never control me."

Nigel smiled.

"Yes, love. I'm afraid I will." He tossed a pile of money on the floor, nice clean bills. The top was a hundred. I figured they all were. "This did not come cheaply," he said.

"They can't hang me for having sex with a married man."

"No," he said. "But perhaps they can for killing one."

Robin's mouth opened, closed, then opened again. She accidentally spit on herself and wiped it off her chin. She laughed, but it wasn't really a laugh.

"I never killed anyone," she said.

"I suppose it's a question of perspective," he said. "I was on the beach that night, and I was proud of you."

Robin's head rocked back as if she'd been slapped. She let out three long, slow breaths.

"I don't know what you're talking about," she said.

"You have no secrets from me, Robin."

Robin looked at me. "Itchy, don't believe him. He's insane."

"I don't," I said.

"But Donaghy believed me," he said. He pulled a watch from his pocket. It hung at the end of a chain. I smelled the whiskey again. He picked up Robin's phone and dialed. He waited a second. A look of pure disgust passed over his face.

"Yeah, I've got her," he said. He handed the phone to Robin. "It's Stewart Donaghy."

Robin took the phone to her ear. She listened for a few seconds with her eyes closed and tears squeezing through them.

"Yes," she said. "Yes. I understand. Of course. Good-bye."

She laid the phone on the receiver, then took it off the hook and let it lie on the floor. The light streaked across the room. It hit her face. Her face looked tired and older than ever before. I touched her hand.

Nigel stood. He stuck his head out the window. When he looked back, his face was covered with tears.

"I needed that money, Robin, and going to that lollipop-sucking fuck tore me apart, but you wouldn't help, and I saw how it could fit my plans for Donaghy and for you, and now I want to destroy that man, and you are going to help me. The people will march with you. They will march with me."

"No," she said. "You told him I killed Bob. He believes it."

"You fool," he said. "Who else is going to believe Waters would sleep with a tramp like you? I conned Donaghy out of that money. I told him how much I hated you. I gave a great performance, but there's no way in hell, without a witness, they can pin a goddamned thing on you, love.

"I've got the fool's money, and he has nothing but promises I have every intention of breaking. If he spreads the story, they'll think he's lying to discredit you. It will backfire. Now forget your fucking guilt. We know what happened that night, and the only way anyone else will ever know is if you back down now. I've been planning this for months. I've got men with skill and dynamite and just enough insanity to pull it off, and I need you to make that fucking march go so we can burn that construct to the ground and strike a blow against this war that they'll hear all over the world. The end is near for America."

"America will survive the fury of your onslaught, Nigel, thank God. But I'm finished."

"You don't understand," he said. "I'm the artist, and I'll decide when the work is done, or I'll make sure everyone knows what happened between you and that man."

He rushed out of the room, threw open the door, stopped for a second, then shouted back.

"You'll make the right decision, or I will talk, and they will listen. There's your choice, love."

"It's over," she shouted. "Your masterpiece is complete."

"No, love. It's barely half-finished." He slammed the door.

33

That night Robin called me into her bedroom. She was curled around Vincent and staring toward the window. The room was black, and I got in bed beside her. We hadn't talked since Nigel left, and I could tell she was suffering. She was a hero now with the kids and war haters who flocked into the streets to hear her speak. She'd divided Deadwhale, and she'd promised a huge march on the factory and a sit-down strike, a long occupation of the road that wouldn't end until the factory shut down or they stopped making guns, and I knew how desperately Robin wanted that march.

And Mayor Donaghy wanted it, too. He called every night to see if I'd heard anything. He had private detectives and half the police force searching. He drove the streets himself, the main roads, the back alleys, the dark wooded paths on the edge of town, and there was never a clue.

We made a plan. The mayor would fight the march with everything he had, but when the time came, he would let it happen. I would tell him our route and the time and anything else that might help him spot Joe, and he would have the whole way monitored, every side street, every lane and alley, every step of the way, and sooner or later, Joe would join the march. Joe would be out in the open, and the mayor wouldn't let him disappear this time until after Joe found out who his father was.

The mayor didn't care about Stewart's factory. He promised to force it closed the day of the march so we wouldn't have another war outside the gates. He promised we could sit in that road until the end of time if we wanted, as long as we didn't try to go on the grounds. It would be Stewart's problem to get his workers back in after the first day. The mayor didn't believe we would stick with it. He figured we would get bored and go home. He figured even Robin would get tired after a day or two. She could make her point, declare herself a hero, and forget it. We were gambling that her occasional talk about blowing it up was just talk.

I liked the plan. We could get on the factory road unmolested. Robin would have a chance to do what she'd planned all summer. Joe would come out into the open, and I would see Patrick's words come true.

And that was the main reason I wanted the march. Sure I wanted to bring Joe out. Sure I wanted to see Robin victorious, to see Stewart Donaghy humiliated, to strike a symbolic blow against the war, but mainly, I wanted proof that Patrick lived. I wanted that march because a friend of mine had to die or everything that had happened that night between me, Charlie, and Suzanne had been a dream, an LSD illusion. Charlie couldn't remember any of it. Suzanne wouldn't talk about it.

But it was seared into my brain. I remembered the look in Charlie's eyes, the change in his voice, not so much the sound, but the way he used it, the way he said words and emphasized his points. I remembered it, and I believed it, and I had to prove it was all true. Otherwise, Patrick had died for nothing and disappeared forever.

It meant that somehow Patrick lived on, that somehow Patrick had communicated with me. I didn't understand all this stuff about the neighbor, these psychic mixed dreams between Robin and Joe and Charlie. There could be an explanation. I couldn't come up with one and didn't really want to, but I didn't doubt there could be an explanation.

But Patrick was dead, and he had spoken to me through Charlie. If I could prove that once and for all, then none of it would hurt anymore. There was hope in Patrick's death. There was hope in Joe and Robin and even in the war if I could prove that Patrick lived on. He'd promised a death and a flood, and I needed that march because I knew that was where my friend would die and fulfill part of Patrick's prophecy, and I knew it was going to be Robin or Suzanne, and I made myself believe it didn't matter, because if Patrick lived on, then we all did, and if I had to lose Suzanne or Robin to prove that to myself, I was more than willing.

"It's cold," Robin said.

"You want me to shut the window?"

"No," she said. "It comes from inside. I want you to take Vincent tomorrow."

"Okay," I said. "It's better."

"I'm thinking I'll sell the hotel," she said. "I'll sell everything. I'll get a lot of money and go back to Europe. I liked Amsterdam. I was only there a night when Nigel found me. It's a whole life that didn't take place.

"I won't read papers. I won't learn the language. I'll get a cat. We'll drink wine in dark bars. We'll listen to the music. I want to see Venice. Maybe you can visit. I don't think Joe's coming back anyway. Could you put your arms around me?"

I moved close to her. I heard Vincent wheezing and purring. I heard Robin's heart.

"Nigel's right," I said. "Nobody's going to believe that stuff about you and the mayor. Everybody knows he fell off the wharf. Why do you let him scare you?"

"We were lovers of a sort," she said. "I don't want to lie about it."

"Refuse to talk about it. Say it's beneath your dignity. Donaghy will look sleazy."

"No," she said. "I can't bear it. Suzanne would hear. I would have to confess."

"If you don't do what he wants, he'll make it public anyway," I said. "So what have you got to lose? Either way Suzanne's going to hear."

"It's over," she said.

"Then what was it all about, Robin?"

Vincent moved up between our faces. Every move seemed to take all the strength out of him. I petted his head. I couldn't imagine Robin without him, or the apartment without him licking himself on a window sill or the edge of her bed.

"I wanted to save some soldiers," she said. "Or maybe my soul." She slapped the mattress.

"Will you hold him when they put the needle in?"

"Please don't give up," I said.

She kissed my hand. "Will you hold him?"

"Yeah, I'll hold him."

"He'll know why he's there. Maybe you could talk to him. He was my friend for years and years."

Something slammed against the door to Robin's apartment. It

slammed again, and the door broke in and before we could move, men were running through the apartment. They had flashlights, and the lights ran up and down the walls and hit our faces, and dark figures charged in behind the lights. They were shouting and knocking things down. I heard laughing, whispering, smelled someone's boozy breath, and I was hit.

When I opened my eyes, everything was dark. The back of my skull throbbed, and I felt the blood leaking down my neck. I lay on the floor, and Robin was crying above me.

"I can't see," she said. "They broke my glasses. They punched me, Itchy, so many times. Are you all right?"

"Yeah. My head."

"Where's Vincent? They broke my glasses. Vincent? I thought I heard him cry."

She helped me to my feet. She held my arm, and we worked our way toward the living room. Robin kept calling Vincent. I turned on the light. It was blinding. I covered my eyes for a second. Everything was knocked over, all the plants and books. Glass and dirt lay scattered across the floor. The door had been smashed in, but now it was closed, splintered on its hinges, bent and battered, and Vincent was dead against it, hanging by the nail they'd slammed through his skull.

I didn't say anything. Robin kept calling his name. I turned out the light. I led her back toward the bedroom. I sat her down, but she felt them with her feet. She broke free, threw herself on the floor, and picked up the glasses. They were twisted and cracked, but she pushed them over her nose and ran into the other room before I could stop her. I saw the light flash on. Then I heard the screaming. I didn't think it would ever end.

34

The note stuck to the nail said, "All's fair in love and war, Robin. No hard feelings." It was signed by Stewart Donaghy, and four days later, we marched by the thousands toward his factory in a cold drizzling rain. I held hands with Robin and Suzanne, out front of a roaring crowd and scared to death.

It was a long march. The streets were clear of cops, but men with binoculars watched from rooftops all along the way. We took a different route this time, but they knew it. I'd told the mayor. Not that the plans were tricky or secret. She'd pulled the march together in the fury following Vincent's murder by charging into the streets and shrieking about the war and the factory and the man who'd killed her cat, shouting for three days from sunrise to late night, and Stewart Donaghy never said a word about her and Mayor Waters.

It could have been worse. School had started. Most of our summer guests had left for another year, and only the young kids of Deadwhale were left to march with her. She didn't even have the blacks from the southwest slums anymore. They marched in the opposite direction that very afternoon, marching on city hall to demand jobs, any jobs, even jobs at the factory. Coke and Robin had split over the black march. It had been planned for a long time. Robin asked Coke to postpone it and join her. She insisted that they make a stand against the factory, but Coke was desperate. He was losing out to the violent types, and he refused.

The mayor called in the National Guard. He'd threatened Robin with them all summer, but hadn't wanted to scare off the tourists, but as soon as the tourists pulled out and the fires in the ghetto got worse and Coke Phillips promised to bring thousands of blacks into town, the mayor requested the guard, and the governor was glad to oblige.

And so they'd come in the night on big trucks that stunk up the air and made so much noise, Robin and I heard them on the fourteenth floor, but they hadn't come to fight Robin. For all the shouting of the summer, there hadn't been much violence in the white parts of town. As long as the mayor saw no threat to white lives, he took the risk, let the money flow in, and hoped nothing broke loose. Nine blacks had died, but they were black, and the incidents were separate, blacks killing blacks in black neighborhoods. As soon as they threatened white Deadwhale, Mayor Donaghy called soldiers.

And so, with the National Guard all over town, we marched. And a friend of mine was going to die, and I thought, what if it's Suzanne? Our hands were soaked together in the drizzle.

Everything had been different since that night on the beach. She seemed nervous around me. She avoided me. She'd quit seeing Charlie, too. I stopped by the frame shop once, and she showed me a poster by a guy named Munch. It was called *The Scream*, and she laughed and said it was how she felt inside. I asked her if she remembered that night on the beach, and she said she didn't remember a thing, and then we didn't say much, and I walked out with *The Scream* fixed in my mind.

She looked at me now and smiled with her face all covered with rain.

"I wish it was the French Revolution," she said. "Some famous event, like storming the Bastille. Wouldn't it be great to get mowed down by Cossacks storming the Bastille, and they would read about us in the twenty-first century?"

"There weren't Cossacks at the French Revolution."

"I didn't say there were. Besides how do you know who was at the French Revolution? Were you there?"

"Cossacks were Russians."

"So wouldn't it be great if this was the Russian Revolution, and the czar's troops would lop our heads off into the snow?" She blew smoke in the air and smiled.

"I'd rather die of tuberculosis," I said.

Robin stared straight ahead, furious and silent. Her expression hadn't changed since she saw Vincent's head smashed against the door. Even in sleep, her face never relaxed.

"Maybe the National Guard will mow us down," Suzanne said. "Maybe fifty years from now, they'll talk about how five hundred people died in Deadwhale, and the country was so ashamed, they stopped the war."

"I don't want to get mowed down," I said. "I had better plans for my life."

"Well not me. I want to get mowed down this time and look like I died for a cause," she said. "Do you think Joe will come?"

Robin turned to Nigel. He was a few feet behind with his bullhorn, and feathers sticking up in his hair, his face painted black and red and white, his eyes all smeared over from the whiskey he sucked from the bottle in his coat. He looked tired, and the paint smeared in the rain, but he marched and shouted and waved his fist, and his Gestapo imitated his every gesture, young Nigels, all full of hate and booze.

"Get them shouting together," she said. "If they're going to be so fucking noisy."

"No guns," he shouted. "No war."

And what if it's Robin, I wondered? I couldn't imagine Suzanne dying, but I could see Robin walking into a gun. She would dare them to shoot, and one of these National Guard kids might pull the trigger. But the mayor had promised the guard would let us be. So maybe a cop would get her.

"Something bad's going to happen," Suzanne said. "I wish Charlie would come."

Nigel had the crowd chanting, pumping their signs and crazy flags. It scared me to look back. It was like looking down from a tall building. It sounded like a train behind us, or the roar of waves when you lay on the beach at night, and Robin marched fast, and down every street people shouted and men stared from rooftops with binoculars. Our shoes squished and slid, and I waited for the police to charge from some side street, or the soldiers to leap from behind a barricade and shoot Robin through the chest, and closer and closer we marched, and all along the way I looked, but Joe never came, and we marched with the marshes stinking to the left of us and the factory far down the road, and finally in the distance, not far from where we would make our final turn, I saw the barricade.

School buses, fire engines, and trucks lined the road, but we kept going, and they didn't cut off the path, they just narrowed it, funneling us inward, shrinking our width and slowing us down, but they weren't going to stop us. There was no way around without going over the marshes to our left or walking through the houses on our right, and Robin marched straight ahead.

Men with cameras and cops with binoculars watched from the tops of buses as we headed into the narrow path they'd set up for us, but none tried to stop us, and as we walked between the buses and trucks, squeezing tighter together until we could only fit three across, I realized we were being crushed together so they could slow us down and look in our faces.

It amazed me. At that very minute, Coke Phillips and most of Southwest Deadwhale were marching on city hall, but the mayor had arrayed a ton of resources on the route to the factory, not to stop us, but to inspect us, so he might find Joe.

Cameras whirred and clicked. The noise of the crowd bounced between the street and the huge vehicles to our left and right, and Robin, Suzanne, and I passed through first, coming out the other side before the left turn up Industrial Drive and onto the factory.

There were cops in the street, but they let us turn, and as we did, I noticed the mayor's black limousine off the side of the road, parked beside two ambulances, fixed so he could see everyone before they turned onto the drive, his wipers sweeping in the misty rain, a cigarette glowing in the dark car, and the mayor hunched over his steering wheel.

Our eyes met. He didn't recognize me. His mind was set for one face, and I thought how terrible it would be if that face didn't pass his eyes sometime that afternoon.

"There's the czar," Suzanne shouted. She waved a fist at the mayor, and when he saw her, his gaze snapped onto her, hesitated for a second, then flashed away.

Nigel came up beside us. "Nothing's going to stop us now," he said. "They're not searching my guys."

"Searching your guys for what?" I asked.

He didn't seem to hear me. I grabbed Robin's sleeve.

"What's he talking about?"

"He's blowing up the factory for me," she said.

"What?"

"Leave me alone, Itchy."

And we headed up that long road. The crowd trickled in through the barricade behind us, and Nigel got them shouting, and we weren't far down the road when we saw the soldiers less than a mile away, standing between us and the gate. I couldn't make them out at first, but the closer we got, the more obvious it became that Mayor

Donaghy had lied. He hadn't mentioned the National Guard in the street, but there they were, only thirty or so, spread in a line from one side of the marsh to the other, an impenetrable barrier of young men with rifles.

And Robin didn't slow down, and the crowd kept coming behind us, and Nigel kept shouting, and Suzanne's hand was soaked to mine, and none of us said a word, but now I knew I'd made a mistake, and I didn't want it to happen anymore.

I didn't care if Patrick was dead anymore. I didn't care if I'd had a hallucination that night. I didn't want anyone to die. I couldn't stand the thought of Suzanne or Robin dying because I'd made a deal with the mayor. It had all been crazy. Patrick was dead, and another death wouldn't make anything better, and the mayor had lied, and the National Guard, a bunch of wet and tired kids, stood in the path ready to raise their rifles against the mob, and Robin wasn't slowing down.

I squeezed her hand. I was afraid that after all that had happened, she would gladly march into a blaze of bullets.

"Robin, Jesus, what are you going to do?"

I had to shout it. Nigel stirred the crowd to a fever pitch, but he heard me and whirled and shoved me away.

"Leave her alone," he said. "She knows what she's fucking doing."

Robin shouted at him. "Keep your hands off him."

"Don't let this fucker slow you down again, Robin."

"Nobody's slowing me down," she said. "I'm walking through them, and if Itchy doesn't want to come, he doesn't have to. Go home, Itchy."

She walked backward and pulled me toward her.

"Please go home."

"Robin, you trying to get us killed? Is that going to solve anything?"

Suzanne came up beside us. "He's right," she said. "Let's talk. Let's drop down in the street and wait. It's not any good if we get hurt."

Robin kept walking backward. The soldiers looked bigger and bigger. They were milling around before, but someone yapped out an order, and they formed a tighter line, and some went down on one knee, and some stood behind them, and far in the distance, maybe a hundred yards to their rear, the gates to the factory road opened, and a figure moved through them and out onto the road toward us, about as far behind the soldiers as we were in front of them, and it wasn't long before I knew it was Stewart Donaghy coming to meet us.

And Robin marched on, and Stewart came the other way, and if the soldiers hadn't stood between them, it would have been like a gunfight in the old west, Robin and Donaghy with holsters hanging from their hips, and Robin walked out front of us all, and Suzanne stayed close behind her, and Nigel shouted into his bullhorn, and the crowd got thicker and thicker behind us, and I wondered if the mayor had set up some kind of massacre, and Donaghy came closer, and I started shouting at Robin that she had to stop, but she just kept walking on.

Suzanne whispered into my ear. "I didn't really want to die," she said.

"I know," I said. "And I didn't want you to."

"We're getting too close," she said.

Nigel pushed past us. "This is it, Robin," he shouted. "They ain't going to shoot, baby. Just march right through them. My boys out there got the shit, man, dynamite and everything. These guys know what they're doing, man. Chemistry fucking majors and engineers." His eyes were red and bulging and full of water. "That fucking place is going up. You and me, Robin. Keep marching. I've been waiting a long time for this."

We were fifty yards from the guns. Charlie'd run that far for a touchdown the last game of the season. I saw the faces of the boys in helmets. Half were down now, as if they would wipe out a herd of charging Indians, and the other half stood with their guns across their chests. One walked behind them, giving out soft instructions to hold their ground, and Stewart Donaghy rushed up in a suit, and I wondered if he would ask them to fire, or ask them to let us through.

I wondered if the mayor had told them to fire or to let us through. I wondered if Suzanne was going to die, or if Robin was going to die, or if I was going to die. I wondered how many were going to die, and Robin kept marching on, and we were at thirty yards, and I could see the confused eyes of those nervous soldiers, and I wondered if they would kill us if someone told them to, and I decided they would because that was their job, and finally I ran past Nigel, grabbed hold of Robin with both hands, stared into her eyes, and shouted over the roar of the crowd.

"Robin. You've got to stop."

She kept moving. The soldiers held their ground. Her dead eye was blank, but the other flared up, and I knew she wasn't going to stop until they knocked her down. I pushed her. I held onto her, but Nigel hit me across the jaw.

"Out of her fucking way, boy," he shouted.

Robin reached for her shoulder. Tears ran down her face. The Adam's apple rode up and down Nigel's neck. He ran his hand through the thinning hair. Suzanne held her head high, and Robin kept moving, and Stewart Donaghy broke through from the other side and stood there watching us. Robin stopped dead.

The crowd stopped behind her. A deep silence settled over the street and the marshes, and soon the only sounds were sea gulls, the American flag flapping on the pole way back at the factory, the beating of hundreds of hearts, and the sound of Stewart Donaghy's shoes tapping in the wet street in front of the National Guard. He was smiling, but he was shaking, too, just enough, like the day he'd put a gun in my mouth.

"Hello, Robin," he said. "I was hoping it wouldn't come to this."

"Get these soldiers out of our way," she said.

"March over them," he said. "You're a brave woman."

Robin looked past Donaghy at the boys with the guns. Not many looked older than me or Charlie. They were all soaked in the rain. Their guns were wet. Mostly their faces were blank. One kept moving his lips, some black kid, like maybe he was praying. Robin looked back at me. The crowd was silent still, except for the whispering, as word traveled about what was happening.

"You surprise me," he said. "I bought some good information off your friend there. Of course, I knew it would backfire if I used it, but I didn't figure I'd have to. I didn't think you were smart enough to know that I knew they would hate me even more if I tried to claim you had a little fling with Suzanne's daddy."

Suzanne rushed to Robin's side. "You're so full of shit, Stewart," she said.

"See," he said. "I guess I wasted my money, but I thought for sure I'd scared you off."

"You went too far," Robin said. "You didn't have to hurt Vincent."

Donaghy smiled. "Vincent. Yes. The cat. I heard about that. Of course, I had nothing to do with it. No reason to piss a crazy woman off after you beat her. It was clever, though. It had the right effect, but it wasn't the effect I wanted. Was it, Nigel?"

Nigel loomed over Robin. His hand wrapped around the whiskey bottle. He dropped the bullhorn, but didn't bother to pick it up. He looked at Robin.

"I don't know what he's talking about, love."

Donaghy stepped closer to Robin. The soldiers relaxed a bit behind him.

"Yes he does, love," Donaghy said. "Who besides that madman would kill a harmless cat? I may be a cold fucker, but I wouldn't stoop that low."

Robin whirled on Nigel. He took a long drink. He spit a mouthful of whiskey in the street. Rain rolled from his hair down over his long beard.

"It was just a formality, Robin. The cat was already dead. I knew that crucifying the thing would help you do what you wanted to do. I did it for you, love."

Her head dropped. She whispered Nigel's name and stared into the street. He touched her shoulder, drew back his hand, then held it forward again, but couldn't bring himself to touch her anymore. He sucked out of the bottle then tossed it aside. It shattered, and the whiskey mixed with the rain and the mud of the dirty street.

"Turn around, Robin," Donaghy said. "Nigel's not the only one who betrayed you. Your boy Itchy told my father all your plans. They had some crazy idea that if we let the march through, Joe Waters would rise from the dead. It could have worked if I hadn't found out. A quick call to the governor got these brave men standing behind me, and if I tell them, I believe they'll shoot. There's no need for that. All your friends are turning against you. Who can you trust, Robin?"

She kept staring into the street. I didn't bother to defend myself. She wouldn't understand, and I didn't think she cared. The rain came harder. Donaghy walked back toward the soldiers, stopped once, and said, "You've done well. You're smarter and braver than I ever imagined. Now go the fuck home before somebody gets killed."

Robin pulled up her head, took a deep breath, and pointed at him.

"I'm coming through," she said. "Itchy, I don't want anyone following. They won't kill me, and they're not going to stop me."

"I could stop you myself," Donaghy said.

"Then you'll have to," Robin said.

Suzanne took Robin's hand.

"We'll both go," she said.

"How nice," Donaghy said. "And what will you do when you get there, break it apart with your little hands?"

"Just ignore him," Suzanne said. "He's been sick through many lives."

"Not too sick for you, though, Suzanne, not so sick you didn't drag me into your bed every chance you got."

"I should have done like my mother and stuck a knife in your neck," Suzanne said.

"Your mother knifed the wrong man, honey. She should have stabbed that hypocrite father of yours and spared us his reign of self-righteous bullshit. It was all a big seduction, Suzanne. Talk about making life nice for the Whales, have your little neighborhood committees and screw all the wives for community relations, screw the wives and the whores in the streets, and even a little slut like Robin Debussy, only it went a little too far with Robin, because Robin ended up killing the poor man."

Robin charged at him. She hit his face so hard the smack echoed over the swamps. She hit him again and again, driving him back against the soldiers until he fell among them and grabbed the gun that was hidden under his shirt and pointed it at her head.

His lips trembled. The gun shook at the end of his arm. He was white. Robin was right up among the soldiers, and I thought she might step through them right into Donaghy's gun, but Suzanne shrieked out a name, and everyone stopped, and the blood froze solid in my veins.

"Joe."

She shouted it three times, and everyone saw him at once, coming down across the marshes to our right, coming down the narrow path in the woods from way up where Suzanne and I had seen the factory that rainy night, and Suzanne ran toward him, but she slipped on the road and stumbled into the marsh, falling in to her elbows, and crawling through it toward him. The mud caked to her legs and arms, and she kept crawling and stumbling forward, but it was hopeless, and finally she stopped, drenched and filthy, and watched him come on.

And Joe walked down that path, and it led past the soldiers and emptied out behind them on the way to the factory. He came limping, wearing the uniform of a soldier, a veteran of Vietnam, a uniform not much different from that of the guard that stood between us and the factory, and the crowd pushed toward the side of the road right against the marshes, some falling in, and word rushing through that Joe Waters was coming down, and everyone started cheering. They started shouting his name, and Joe moved slowly across the muddy path, his face all twisted, huge stretches of scarred flesh swirling from his left ear down over his neck and on under the uniform, a sleeve flapping hopelessly beside him, a beard that hadn't grown over the scar tissue, and long, dirty black hair all streaked with white and gray.

Robin had pulled back from the soldiers. Her hands curled into fists. She couldn't move. She couldn't speak. Suzanne cried into her hands and whispered his name, her hair all soaked with mud, her face covered, and Joe kept coming, his crippled figure bobbing through the weeds that rose around him, the rain pouring down on him, the clouds gray and low above him.

Sea gulls circled. The flag flapped far in the distance. The soldiers turned away from us. They watched the war they'd missed walk out of the weeds, and Joe didn't care that hundreds cheered wildly for him, that his sister cried on her knees, that a line of soldiers had turned to watch him come on, and then I heard Donaghy. He pulled at the lieutenant who'd been giving orders.

"Bring them back. Cut him off," he shouted.

He yanked the soldier by the arm, but the lieutenant pulled free.

"He ain't hurting nothing," he said.

Donaghy shouted and pulled and tried to make the soldiers do something. Robin just stared, and Joe walked slowly forward, and now his face was clear, his eyes were bright and shining, and he didn't look at us, or anywhere near us. He looked straight ahead and walked onto the street behind the soldiers, who turned to watch him walk by, and Joe was behind them now, heading up the road toward the empty factory, heading toward the barbed-wire gate wide open in the distance, dragging his right leg, the full-length sleeve flapping beside him, his uniform old and dirty and coated with mud and dead leaves.

I could hear Suzanne crying and the crowd shouting behind me. Robin just stared. The National Guard lowered their rifles and watched Joe head up the road behind them. He had gone about thirty yards.

And he knew what was going to happen. He had probably known all along, and I knew, too, and I wondered why I hadn't seen it before.

Donaghy shouted, "Stop right there, Joe," but Joe didn't stop. "I'm warning you." Joe kept going. "I said stop." And then he took a step away from the soldiers and fired. The blast echoed up and down the swamps, and Joe kept walking like he hadn't heard the

shot, getting further and further up the road. Donaghy fired again.
He missed again, and someone shouted and brushed past me. I saw
a flash of black, a giant shadow, then Nigel, springing through the
line of soldiers, hitting Donaghy from behind, and crushing him to
the ground as the gun went off once more. The bullet bounced off
the road, and Joe went down, and a single shout rose up against the
rain and out over the marshes, a long, slow, chilling shout that
seemed to last forever, and time jerked and jumped and slowed and
spun, and the shout died, and there was screaming and sirens and
pushing and the mayor running.

And time shuddered back into motion, and everyone headed
toward Joe. The guard held back the crowd. Donaghy lay flat on his
back with Nigel stretched over him and pounding him with his fists.
Three soldiers tried to pull him off. Donaghy's face was a pulp. His
eyes were shut, and he was begging, but he squeezed the trigger a last
time, and Nigel's head rocked.

They tore Nigel free then. Soldiers pushed him back. Our eyes
met. Nigel's were flaming coals. A bullet had ripped through his
coat, right in the center, and the blood colored the black cloth, but
Nigel stood tall and struggled with the soldiers. I thought the bullet
must have gone through his heart, but maybe it missed, maybe his
heart was steel, but he didn't go down.

I made it to the crowd around Joe. He lay on his back with blood
pouring from the back of his skull. He faced the sky with his head
in Robin's lap. The mayor bent over him, and when Suzanne tried
to rip him away, Joe stopped her. He stared beyond us to some dark
point in the sky, and he spoke loudly and firmly with the smallest
smile on his lips and peace on his face.

"Let him talk, Suzanne."

She dropped to Joe's side. Her face was the saddest thing I'd ever
seen.

"I wanted to tell you," the mayor said. "I wanted to confess."

"You're my father," Joe said. "It's written in the sky. This is my
father, Suzanne. Love him." He reached up to Robin's face. He
touched her cheek. "And this is my wife."

Robin squeezed his head against her. Her hands were soaked and
red.

"Joe, please don't die."

"You don't need me," he said. "You have each other. Why won't
you understand that?"

"I don't understand anything," Robin said. "Won't you stay?"

"Stay," Suzanne said. "Stay and teach us."

Joe never moved his eyes from that spot in the sky. "Yes," he said. "I could teach you. The neighbor and I will decide."

"Who's the neighbor?" Robin whispered.

"I...I," Joe said. He smiled and closed his eyes, and Robin kissed his chest. The mayor touched her, and Robin let out huge, heaving sobs, and there was a tremendous roar. Three times. Robin's name. Just this unbelievable shout, and there above the scene around Joe's body in the street, stood Nigel, his eyes fixed on Robin.

He saw her crying for Joe. He saw Joe's head in her arms, and he raised both arms into the sky and shouted her name again.

"Robin."

The tears streamed down his face. He turned and headed up the road. He dropped his coat and ripped off his shirt, and I saw then that the bullet had come through him and cut a hole through his back that dripped into his pants. And he took down the pants, too, and started naked up the road to finish Joe's work.

No one moved to stop him. No one moved to help him. The mayor held up his hand, nodded first at the lieutenant, then the cop who seemed to be in charge, and I realized they were letting Nigel go.

Nigel staggered once and went down on a knee. He got up and staggered again, like a bull I'd seen late at night on a UHF station, with blood all shiny on its coat and a man slamming a sword through its back, and Nigel walked up the road, and then a few others did, and before long they were all behind him, maybe thirty of his followers, walking slowly under their foreign flags behind their bleeding leader.

And it wasn't long, maybe ten minutes, when the sirens were screaming and Robin and Suzanne were climbing into the ambulance with Joe, that I heard the first explosion and saw them all running back my way. There were three explosions, gigantic balls of smoke, and then the fire, and as I watched them running back toward me, shouting and waving their fists, I realized that Nigel was no longer with them.

I pictured him bleeding, crouched in a corner of the factory by some huge machine, staring at a far wall and blowing peanuts out his nose, while the factory collapsed all around him. I pictured him in the flames and the heat whispering Robin's name, triumphant at last.

I waved my fist high into the air one time for Nigel.

35

I sat on the balcony until the sun came up, waiting for Robin to get back from the hospital. The streets were noisy all night, full of shouts and explosions. The National Guard roared this way and that in noisy trucks that left a trail of smoke. There'd been a riot while we marched on the factory, and Coke Phillips was in jail. Hundreds of blacks had been hurt. There were sirens and fire engines, and the smoke floated on the breeze. The factory seemed to burn forever.

Robin got in around seven. She collapsed on the bed and stared up at the ceiling.

"Is he...?"

"He's in a coma," she said. "They got the bullet, but the doctor says he'll probably die."

"He said that?"

"No, but it was in his voice. He told me there was always hope."

"How's Suzanne?"

"Very brave. She brought her mother out there. They're with him."

"Maybe he'll make it," I said.

"It's my fault."

"Nothing's your fault," I said.

The smoky breeze washed in off the water and reminded me of that night with Suzanne when we rolled in the waves together.

"I destroyed the whole family," Robin said.

"Don't talk, Robin, if you're going to say shit like that."

"It was my fault Robert died, and when I told Joe, that's why he went, but I had to tell him. He wanted to marry me."

Her face was blank, but she choked on the words, and her chest heaved.

"Why was it your fault?"

"Don't ask questions you don't want the answer to."

"He treated you like shit," I said. "He deserved what he got."

She walked out onto the balcony. She looked over the side, and I thought of Hubert Ditzlow flapping his arms all the way to the street. It was an image that came to me a lot.

"I was starving when he came," she said. "I didn't live anywhere. I was drunk all the time, and he took me here, and once he said I was beautiful, and I loved him so much it was like being sick. Every second, I thought of him, nothing else, and when he died, it only got worse."

I put my arm around her. She was small, bony, hot, sweating. I'd held her so many times. I knew every inch of her body, but still it always amazed me how small she really was, and how much, deep down, when I let myself admit it, how much I really loved her.

"Yeah, he treated me bad, but he didn't deserve to die for it."

"Do you know how he died?"

"Yes."

"Tell me."

"No," she said. "I don't want you to know. I told Joe, and that's why he went to Vietnam. He was so disappointed in his father, so disappointed in me. I don't want to disappoint you, too."

A police car drove onto the beach below us. The siren blasted, and the car twisted right and left before getting traction and shooting across the sand.

"But you understand, right?" I asked. "You know that Mayor Waters wasn't Joe's father. Mrs. Waters had an affair with Mayor Donaghy. Mayor Donaghy was Joe's dad. You weren't in love with Mayor Waters' son. You were in love with Mayor Donaghy's son."

"It didn't make a difference to Joe when I told him."

"But it's true."

"So Joe died for a man who wasn't even his father."

"Joe's not dead."

"He will be, and he went because he hated the truth about Robert Waters. Vietnam ruined him. It wouldn't have happened if he hadn't loved Robert Waters and if I hadn't destroyed Robert Waters. It doesn't matter who his father was."

I held my hand against her lips. She ran into the house. I caught

her in the bedroom, staring into her bed. She pushed me away and
started throwing things around and looking everywhere. She looked
in her closets, her drawers. She ran through the room, throwing
clothes and earrings. She fell on her knees and started thrashing
under the bed with her hands.

"Vincent," she said. "Vincent."

She collapsed into the bed. She called the cat once more, and then
she was sleeping. I watched for a while. The bottoms of her socks
were caked with mud. She whispered things that didn't make sense
and threw herself over on her back. Her face jerked a few times, but
slowly it relaxed. It took a long time, but she breathed softly and
deeply. She slept like an angel. I touched her cheek, and then I went
back to the balcony.

I was so tired, I could hardly move. I wondered where Charlie
was. His eighteenth birthday was coming up. I wondered when we
would have the flood Patrick promised. I wondered how long it
would take Joe to die.

36

Then one day it started raining. The clouds hung over town for five days of gloom and drizzle. The ocean crept in on us, and a huge storm moved over the coast. Deadwhale had flooded before. Lots of wind and rain and churned-up sea, and the water could roll right through town, and I figured this was it. They weren't predicting floods, but it didn't matter. Something was going to happen to Charlie.

He talked about the war all the time now, but he wasn't looking forward to it anymore. It was something marked on his calendar, like going to have some teeth pulled out. It had ruined everything with Suzanne, and between Charlie and my father, but I was used to it by now, and I didn't believe it anyway. Patrick said there would be a flood, and Charlie would never go, just like he'd said my friend would die. Joe hadn't died yet, but he'd come awfully close, and deep down, I knew he would. He'd told me so himself.

The storm crashed in with lightning and thunder and rain that pelted the roofs of cars and slashed through the streets, blinding and vicious and cold. I had school, and it had been raining a long time when I finally carried my soaked body up to the apartment. The phone was ringing when I walked in. I'd heard it when I got off the elevator and all the way down the hall. I didn't see Robin anywhere. I answered the phone.

It was Suzanne. She was shouting. I couldn't understand a word. She just kept shouting and making crazy sounds, like maybe she was laughing and crying hard at the same time, and it took me a while to get her to calm down so I could understand.

"Joe's talking," she said. "He's awake, and he's saying Robin's name. Why did she give up on him? She hasn't been here in a week. His eyes are open."

That's when I saw the note sitting on the kitchen table. It said, "Dear Itchy, I'm sorry to leave you this way, but someone's calling in the rain."

I didn't know what to make of it. All I knew was that I was tired and soaked and that Suzanne was raving on the phone and that maybe Joe was going to be all right after all. It didn't make sense. Patrick said my friend would die. No friend had died.

"I'll find her," I said. "And bring her over."

"It's so wonderful," Suzanne said. "He's going to make it. The doctor won't say, but I just know he will."

I hung up and looked at the note again. It scared me. I was taking my clothes off when I looked out the bedroom window and saw a tiny figure way out on the end of the wharf in the downpour. Then I understood.

I ran to the elevator. Outside, the ocean rushed to meet me. The water crossed my ankles when I hit the flooded beach. I ran past the Ferris wheel with its cars rattling, and the whole thing starting to bend and groan, and the water splashing underneath me.

Salt water rose over my knees before I was halfway to the wharf. By the time I reached the steps, the water crossed my chest, and the waves pushed me back. I climbed onto the planks. They were slick. The ocean slid across them in bubbles and foam. I kept slipping. The wharf was long and jutted far into the raging water, and at the very end, Robin faced the sea.

I shouted to her. The wind swallowed my voice. I could barely push against it. I was afraid she would wash off the edge. I looked over my shoulder, but the beach was empty and black and covered with ocean.

I shouted again, but she just stared over the edge in her black clothes, soaked and tiny against the sky, no shoes, just those ragged socks soaked to the boards. The sea swelled over the brim. Rain beat against my face, but I inched closer to Robin. Twice I fell to my knees. The wharf rocked from side to side and kicked up and down. I thought it would break free any minute.

I kept shouting, moving toward her, but she wouldn't look. The boards creaked and bent against the waves again and again. The whole thing shuddered, as if something had rammed it, something huge under the water beating its head against the wharf, pounding and smashing and ramming.

She stood where Robert Waters stood the night he died. The water was black, and the storm so loud, and I remembered Suzanne talking about the keeper's roar, and now the roar rose in front of Robin. It swirled and kicked and snatched at her, and she didn't care. She stood in its mouth and waited.

And before I could reach her, there was a crash, a snapping, a twisting, a giant spray of water and smashing wood. A whirlwind behind her. She turned then and saw the ten-foot gap ripped through the wood. She was trapped.

And as her eyes rose up from that swirling hole, lightning flashed, and we stared at each other across the water. Robin wrapped her arms around herself.

"Leave me alone, Itchy."

"Robin, Joe's awake. I just talked to Suzanne. He's saying your name."

"You're not going to fool me. I can't stand it anymore."

I knelt and stared across the gap, afraid I'd go swirling away like a stick. I pictured myself on the beach in the morning in a pile of seaweed and trash.

"Get down and talk," I said. "I never lied to you."

"There's nothing to talk about. I killed them. Now it's my turn."

"You didn't kill anybody. Will you listen? Joe's awake."

A wave cut Robin's knees. She fell, catching herself with her hands and pushing against the slippery planks that urged her toward the vicious hole between us. I held out my hands. I didn't know what else to do.

"Hold onto the side planks and work yourself over."

"You don't understand," she said. "I killed Robert and knowing that killed Joe."

"You didn't kill anyone. I just talked to Suzanne. Joe's getting better. He said your name. Come on. I'll pull you up."

The wharf lurched again. Robin almost slid over the edge. She stepped toward me. She had about five feet to maneuver in. She looked into the swirling hole between us.

"Come home," I said.

A giant wave swept us. Robin fell. It knocked me down. I saw her flat on the boards, getting up slow. The wharf shook hard. Robin fell again and skidded. She coughed and jammed her fingers against the wood to stop her slide, but she was sucked toward the hole, and another wave smashed her into the wood. She gasped, swallowed, breathed, spit, and everything rocked, and I thought we would break off, but it settled a second, and Robin told me the story, croaking it out between sobs, sitting on the wharf in the driving rain with the water swirling around her, and I begged her to shut up and come over, but she talked, and as she did, I felt this horrible amazement, like all the secrets of life opening to me at once, and it wasn't like listening to her voice, it was like clawing my way out of an egg and coming out into the lightning and rain and squinting hard in the cold air and knowing I'd emerged into a place where I could never be safe again.

"I pushed him," she said. "That last night with the tie, I begged him to treat me right. I told him I loved him and would do anything, and he laughed at me. He said he liked me, liked me a lot, but could never love me or leave his wife for me. So I said I would tell it all, everything we'd done. I would ruin him.

"We were drunk, and it was pouring, and I ran out into the rain. He chased me here. I called him names right at the edge, right here, and he twisted my arm and said he could never love such a whore, and I slapped him, and it was raining so hard and the wind, and I couldn't let him go, and I tried to talk, and when he called me a whore again, I remembered my father with Ben by the lake, and I pushed him. I didn't push him hard. He shouldn't have fallen, but his shoes were slick, and he slipped and looked at me and reached out, and maybe I could have saved him, but I held back my hand. I held back my hand, and he fell.

"I called his name a thousand times, but he didn't come up, and I just stared into the waves and the dark, but he never came up. I must have stood two hours at this edge, and I should have left Deadwhale then, but I knew he had a son."

There were crossbeams on either side of the hole, holding her half of the wharf to mine, and without even realizing it, I was in the water, clinging to one of the beams, and working my way across the gap between us. If I slipped once, I would never come up, and they would find us, like they'd found Bob Waters the day after Robin pushed him, with sea gulls pulling at our brains, but I didn't slip, and Robin reached, and with my throat full of salt water, nearly blind, I pulled her down, and we worked our way across, and the broken half of the wharf started to rock and rise up, and I held Robin above the water with one arm and pulled us back over with the other.

We coughed and spit, and the waves broke over us, and when we reached the other side, Robin worked her shoulders across and helped me up behind her, just as the rest of the wharf twisted off and rushed by.

We were up, facing inland on our knees, gasping and wheezing, until a wave rocked us over. I was tired, but the sea wouldn't wait, and we scrambled along the planks, tripping and falling and holding together until another wave knocked us apart, and my face slammed the wood. I saw a flash of green, and then I was choking.

When I got up, I saw Robin fighting her way toward land, bobbing up and down and screeching my name. The beach had flooded to the street. The Ferris wheel moaned. Boards rushed past my head, and the wharf kept breaking apart.

I fought toward Robin, half running, half swimming. I saw her come out and go under and come out again. She tried to swim, and the waves pushed her toward home, but I couldn't get near her. The wind swirled around me, and I would lose her and find her and lose her again, and those big boards shot past her, and the rain fell hard and dense, and I was so tired, and I couldn't find Robin anymore.

I heard the Ferris wheel shriek, and pieces broke away and dropped onto the beach, and she's not going to die, I thought. She's not going to die. She can't die. Patrick, you were wrong, Patrick, you were wrong.

The water rose over my chest sometimes, and sometimes it was over my head, but I fixed my eyes on the sea, and when I saw Robin again, far behind me now, I tried to work my way in front of her and hold my spot. She flailed at the water. She was too short to stay above it, and I whispered between coughs, like in the race, "Jeeez Christ. Jeeez Christ," and all the time thinking, she's not going to die. Robin can't die.

But a wave knocked me so hard my skull slapped the water. It took me under and bounced me off the bottom, and I didn't know where I was. I didn't know how to get up, and water poured up my nose and down my throat.

I found the bottom and pushed and broke into the air, facing the beach, where I saw the Ferris wheel breaking apart and someone running up from the street. I whirled around, and Robin was gone, just water and waves, just rain and clouds and noise. I saw a million miles into nothing. I looked a million years at nothing, and everything seemed to stop, suspended by the stabbing shock, like when Joe fell in the street, and when I got the news of Patrick.

And I couldn't believe it. She'd been there, and now she was gone.

I thought maybe my eyes were lying, maybe I was dreaming. She couldn't be dead. She couldn't be lost forever, not like Patrick. It was impossible. These things happened in movies and wars and horrible tragedies in the newspaper, but they didn't happen to people like me, the real people who never did any harm, who tried to do their best and didn't deserve to suffer.

It was so unfair. I couldn't accept it. I wouldn't. She couldn't die. I would never die. I was a kid, and Robin and I would be together forever and never ever die, not in a storm, not in a war, never, never. I knew it and thought it all in the passing of an endless second and got off something like a prayer, just a feeling of helpless pleading, not in words, but with all my body and heart, and the prayer went to Patrick, and something rammed me hard.

It took away my wind and clung to me, and I felt her face against mine, and she was saying my name.

"Itchy. Itchy. Is Joe alive? Does he want me?"

I grabbed hold of her and kept her up and let the waves push us toward the shore, but we just couldn't make it. We were both so tired, and I gave in, and maybe she did, too, because we'd fought so long and so hard. There was nothing left, and we fell, and all I wanted to do was sleep, and the water swept over us, and that's when Charlie reached down and took Robin up over one shoulder and pulled me up over the other.

"Fuck, man," he said. "You two are amazing. If I don't pop up once or twice a week, you're dead. You got cops trying to kill you. You got Stewart Donaghy knocking you around a stage. You drown in floods. Christ. It's my fucking birthday. I came to tell you I joined the marines. No fucking rain's going to stop me, and you're up to your neck in the fucking ocean."

He kept hollering and swearing and wading through the water toward the shore, and I was whispering it out between the gasps.

"Be careful, Charlie. Remember that night. Patrick said you wouldn't go...go...to Vietnam...because of a flood...a flood."

But he got us in where the water just cleared his knees, and he was laughing, and I took huge breaths and looked up and saw the Ferris wheel breaking completely away.

"Charlie," I shouted.

He saw it. He grabbed Robin, then pulled me against him. He pushed us down into the shallow water and bent over us as well as he could, and it came down all around him, steel and wire and concrete everywhere, just flying into the storm and bouncing and crashing and twisting and blowing over our heads, and we were right in the middle of it, and it happened so fast and seemed so long and slow and horrible, and Charlie held his body over us and wouldn't let us move, and then it stopped.

I crawled out from underneath him. He stayed down on all four. His jacket was ripped. Blood ran down the back of his head. He'd been smashed by bolts and pieces of steel. There was dust and rain in his hair, and he didn't move for a long time, and Robin and I tried to help him to his feet, but then he broke free.

He stood straight and stared up into the sky where the Ferris wheel had been. He was all battered and cut, and his face was soaked with rain, and the rain slapped the water all around us, and he pointed into the sky.

"You can't hurt me," he shouted. "You can't fucking hurt me. You took away my brother, but he wasn't me. He was better than me, but he was smaller and weaker and didn't know how hard things are, but I know, and you can't hurt me. You can throw anything you want, but you can't stop me with your fucking Ferris wheels, or your wind, or your thunder, or your lightning, and I'll go to this war, and you can throw bullets and fire and everything out of hell you got at me, but you'll never hurt another Shovlin as long as I'm fucking alive, and that's going to be a long time. You understand? You can't hurt us. You can't hurt me."

Robin took hold of the huge arm that pointed into the sky and gently lowered it. She reached up and touched his face.

"It's okay now, Charlie," she said. "It's all over now. It's okay."

But Charlie didn't seem to hear. He ripped off his jacket, and he ripped off his shirt, and he tore his undershirt down the middle and threw it in the water and stared up at the sky. I could hear his heart. I could see the blood throbbing in his neck. I could see where he'd been hit and cut all over his chest, and every muscle in his body was tight and flexing, and he stared at the sky with his naked chest soaked in the rain. He stared and stared, and the rain stopped dead.

And when it did, Charlie dropped into the water on his knees and pulled me in against him.

"I saw you out there, Itchy, saving her. I was so proud of how brave you are."

"Nobody's as brave as you," I said.

Robin held his head against her chest. "It's all right," she whispered. "It's all right, Charlie. It's all right."

37

Charlie left a week later. He was going to Philadelphia first to see my dad's parents, and then he was flying out for the marines. My mother wouldn't come to the bus stop that afternoon. She couldn't even say good-bye to Charlie. She locked herself in Patrick's bedroom, and my dad drove us to the bus stop in his taxi without her. None of us said a word. Charlie just sat in the back with the smallest suitcase you ever saw resting on his legs.

When we got out, my father didn't even look at him. He just looked at the meter. Maybe it was out of habit. Maybe he was going to charge us a fare. Charlie put his bag in the street. My dad put the car in drive, but before he pulled away, Charlie came around to the window. He looked in for a second.

"I'm sorry," he said. "I've got to do it."

My father didn't say anything. He didn't look at Charlie. He looked smaller than I could ever remember. He put the car in neutral, gave it some gas, then reached across and shook hands with Charlie.

"Come back," he said. "All in one piece."

"Damned right, Dad."

"Your mother didn't mean to hurt your feelings."

"I know. She just don't understand."

"She's scared," my father said. "And me, too."

"Nothing can hurt me, Dad. You just got to believe it."

My father nodded a few times. He kept looking at that meter like it was going somewhere. He looked at Charlie for a second, but didn't seem able to for long.

"Good luck," he said, and the car pulled away. It stopped in the middle of the street for a second. It just sat there, but then it moved along.

Charlie shrugged and winked at me. He looked around, but didn't seem to see what he wanted, and we sat on a dirty bench together. Charlie got out his penknife and started poking at his palm, and I looked at the scar on his arm, the one that said Patrick.

"I wish you weren't going," I said.

"They'd have drafted me."

"But the marines do all the dirty work."

"It's all dirty work, but it's what I want to do."

"Do you believe anymore, Charlie, the way we used to believe, I mean about America and the flag and all, like when we were kids?"

Charlie snapped the knife shut and stuck it in his pocket. He ran one of his fingers over the scar, just like he ran his hand over Patrick's name on the memorial way back on the Fourth of July.

"I remember when we were kids," he said. "You were always sick a lot, and me and Patrick used to hang around together on our bikes. He always had this little flag on his handlebars. It was always falling down, and he was always standing it back up. Just this little flag and a horn, the kind with the big black rubber thing you squeeze. I can picture him straightening out his flag and honking that horn, and every July fourth, he would hang a flag out his window. Remember?"

"Yeah. Sure. He used to hum that song when he stuck it out there. You know, about oh beautiful for spacious skies."

"Yeah, and whenever I see a flag I think of Patrick, and whenever I think of Patrick I see a flag. Maybe the war's all wrong. It probably is, but it don't change the way I think about things. All them guys over there now, they got brothers and parents. Maybe someday one of them will come home who wouldn't if I didn't go, like maybe you wouldn't have come home from that riot that day or from that flood. Maybe because of me a couple other brothers somewhere won't have a year like we just did, and maybe some kid's mother won't have to lock herself in a room or write crazy letters to some dead kid.

"I don't care if the war's wrong. Sometimes I used to get so mad at Robin when I'd hear her out there yapping about the bombing and napalm and peasants and all that crap, but it used to piss me off even more when there'd be guys on the side of the road calling her a communist and shit like that. What did they fucking think all these wars were about? So what if she's a pain in the ass? If people like her can't say what they think, then what's the fucking point in fighting? We already lost. It makes me feel good to go over there and fight so maybe that little freak friend of yours can shoot her mouth off in the streets another fifty years.

"I know this war probably don't make a big difference like I wish, but if it just makes a little one, I'll always be proud that I went, and yeah, I still believe," Charlie said. "I'll always believe."

He put his arm around me. He leaned over me close and whispered. "Promise me something, Itchy."

"Sure," I said. I touched his arm where the skin was all burnt and scarred. "Anything you want."

"Promise you love America. Okay? Promise you always will."

"Okay, Charlie. I promise I love America, and I promise I always will."

"Good," he said. "I'll fight better knowing that."

And then the bus pulled up with its black smoke, its rotten smells, and all its squealing and rattling. The driver helped an old lady down the steps. She carried an empty bird cage. Her face was all grooved and wrinkled. She must have been eighty. The driver folded down the side of the bus where they kept the luggage, and he took out another bird cage and handed it to the lady.

A crowd gathered around the bus then and started filing in, mostly people heading back to Philadelphia for one reason or another, lots of young guys with long hair, lots of dirty guys and pale women crushing out cigarettes in the street, a few old men, a woman with three kids with dripping noses, and a kid in a uniform. He had bad skin and oily hair, and the uniform was green and wrinkled. His tie was wrinkled, too, and everybody ignored him. Charlie hugged me so hard he nearly killed me.

"You go to that college and break records," he said.

"I will," I said. "Tell Grandmom and Grandpop I'm coming soon."

"I will. Maybe Grandpop can get you Eagles tickets. Why do they always stink so bad?"

"Like the Phillies," I said. "Be careful, Charlie. Don't try to win the war yourself. It's not football."

Charlie smiled. "Why not?" But then he looked sadder than I'd ever seen him. "Itchy. It never would have worked out between me and Suzanne, so I'm kind of glad she didn't show up today, but if you could, maybe you could look out for her. She's kind of messy about things."

"I can take care of myself." It was Suzanne. She'd come up behind us. She threw herself on Charlie's arms. She disappeared inside them. "You're such a fool," she said. "Such a fool."

"Take care of braino," he said. "Keep him out of the rain, and try to keep him away from Robin. The woman's dangerous."

I stepped away, and they held each other, and then Charlie got on the bus, and the doors shut. The engines kicked up with an awful roar and a burst of smoke. I smelled the rotten fumes. I tasted their filth all the way to my heart, and I remembered Patrick getting on a bus once with a big goofy smile on his face. I couldn't watch the bus pull away. I could hear Suzanne shouting at him. I knew she must be waving, and he must be waving back, but I couldn't look. I just waved my hand in the air, and hoped he understood. I just sat on a bench and waited for the noise of the bus to go away, but then Charlie was calling me, and I had to look.

He'd jammed his giant body through one of the windows, from the waist up, like a monster jack-in-the-box. He waved a bag of peanuts and gave me his biggest smile. He stuffed a peanut in his nose and fired it. The peanut must have gone ten feet before it trailed off onto the road.

"To the moon," I whispered.

And Charlie shouted, "Charlie meets any challenge." He waved his arms in the sky. Peanuts scattered across the street, and the bus pulled away. "Charlie meets any challenge."

The bus went down a hill and around a corner, but I could still hear Charlie's voice getting fainter and fainter, shouting all the way, "Charlie meets any challenge." I imagined him shouting all the way to Vietnam and blowing peanuts toward the outer reaches of the solar system.

And Suzanne sat beside me in a beat-up jacket, brown leather with a brown fur collar, one of those bomber jackets, and it was Joe's, and she disappeared inside it, and her pockets were all stuffed with paperback books that were kind of yellowed and bent and probably about tragic heroines, and we listened to Charlie until his voice was just this faint thing far in the distance, and then we couldn't hear him anymore.

"It sure was a crazy year," she said, and she wiped the water off my face with her sleeve.

"It's the year everything gets better after," I said. "The war will end, and we won't have any more because we'll be inoculated, and we'll get old and forget the other stuff."

"I'll never forget," she said. "Those Russian tanks in Prague, and Robert Kennedy, and that awful picture of that man shooting that other man in the head. Wouldn't it be nice to be a bird and never feel guilty because of the other birds?"

It was cold, but we sat outside the bus station where it wasn't so dingy and depressing, and we leaned against one another on the bench. Suzanne threw her arms around me all of a sudden. The leather of her jacket crackled in my ear, and she kissed my cheek.

"Wouldn't it be amazing if Joe got better?" she said. "He's improving, and the doctor says it's possible, and he spoke his first sentence yesterday."

"Really?"

"Yeah, I walked in, and Joe said, 'Hey, what are you driving, bub? You need a loan for that tuna?' "

"He did not."

"Okay, but he's getting better anyway, and the doctor said there's a chance he might get back where he was before he got shot. Of course, he can't grow his arm back. He's not a starfish, but at least he could walk and think and laugh."

Suzanne kissed me again. "Robin says she wants to marry him when he gets better."

"She didn't tell me that."

"She asked me to. Come on. She was too old for you anyway. Why you looking so sad?"

"No. It would be great," I said. "But I got so used to being with her, it's hard to imagine. Well, I'll be leaving soon anyway, and I guess it wasn't very natural."

"You did so much for her," she said. We didn't say anything for a while. My emotions were going crazy. I couldn't imagine Robin marrying Joe, but it was a good thought, and there was hope. I'd been to see him. They'd shaved his skull and wrapped bandages around it, but his eyes were clear, and he smiled when I came in, and Robin got him to say my name.

"Nothing came out like I figured," I said. "I really thought I was talking to Patrick that night on the beach. He told me one of my friends would die and Charlie wouldn't go to the war because of a flood, but it didn't work out. It was close, but nobody died, and the flood didn't stop Charlie. Maybe I imagined it all. Maybe it was just a close guess."

"I remember," she said. "That night on the beach. I remember how cold the water was and how warm your mouth. You didn't imagine the part with me. It was wonderful," she said.

She leaned her face against my arm.

"Suzanne," I said. "Sometimes I used to think I would do something great with my life, you know, like maybe be famous and change the world. Sometimes that seems like the only reason to live. I know I'm smart, but maybe I don't have anything great in me, so I was thinking maybe you could be a great man in a quiet way, you know, a way nobody knew about, not changing the world, but just getting one person with a lot of troubles through life as well as you can.

"I was thinking maybe I was supposed to do that for Robin, but I guess I was wrong."

"I have a lot of troubles," she said.

Our eyes brushed together for a second, and my heart started beating fast.

"Remember a long time ago?" she said. "When we first met, and you were real sad about Patrick, and I told you about how life works? Remember what I said?"

"You said it was like a war we put ourselves through, and we were all the soldiers."

"Yeah," she said. "And you're the best soldier of all."

"I didn't do anything so great. Charlie's the one."

"No, I think it's you, and I was thinking what if I'm wrong about everything? If this is the only life we get, I wouldn't want to make too many mistakes with it. I already made lots of big ones, and I was thinking maybe when you find the best soldier of all, that's where you stay, unless he doesn't want you around."

She brushed some hair out of my eyes, and stared into them, and I could tell she wanted to know whether I wanted her around.

"So, want to hear a funny thing?" she asked.

"Yeah."

"Promise you won't laugh?"

"You're going to tell me a funny thing, but I'm not allowed to laugh?"

"It's not that kind of funny. It's like embarrassing funny."

"I won't laugh if you don't."

"Okay. Well, I was thinking maybe I knew you from another time, like maybe we went through hundreds of lives together and get to go through hundreds more, but I get so scared this is the only one, and we've got to make the most of it, and you know, the funny thing is, I don't care about the other lives, because I love you in this one. Yeah, the funny thing is I love you, and it took me so long to realize."

She smiled. "Isn't that funny? I know you don't love me. It's okay."

"I do," I said. "Ever since that first night."

"You do?"

"Yeah."

"Oh my God," she said. "Wouldn't it be great if Robin and Joe got married, and we went as a couple? You could play the harmonica at the reception. You stink at it. Let's get a present for Robin. How about a cat, a special cat with two ears, and a cane for Joe? You really love me?"

"Sure, like I want to jump off a bridge." I started laughing.

"Don't jump off a bridge. Let's sit here all day. This is the happiest day of our lives, and we're not even old yet. Isn't it strange to be happy? Isn't it amazing? Maybe life's wonderful, and nobody told us."

"Maybe with you," I said.

"Let's sit here all day," she said. "Let's just sit here and watch the Ferris wheel spin."

And she laughed, and I laughed, too, and I didn't bother reminding her that the wheel lay flat and broken on the beach. I didn't bother because I knew she didn't care.

"There," she said, and she pointed into the distant sky, where the Ferris wheel used to stand. "I see him. Way up high. I see him."

And I followed her hand toward a spot in the distance. The sky was empty and bare, and for the first time, it really hit me that the wheel had fallen and how sad that made me feel.

"You might have to close your eyes," she said, "and concentrate."

"Should I click my heels and say 'there's no place like home'?"

"Don't be silly, Itchy. This isn't Oz. This is America."

So I closed my eyes to make her happy, and I concentrated hard, and it wasn't more than a second or so, when somewhere in the far darkness deep at the end of my mind, I saw a blazing sky of purple and black, and dark black water, deep and frightening and glistening orange in an invisible sun, and rising from beneath it, crawling up against the sky, cutting out of the water like the fin of a giant shark, I saw the Ferris wheel slowly rise, until it conquered the horizon, huge, black, and unreachable like the shimmering steel ghost of countless forgotten summers.

And spread against the wind at the very top of the wheel, his arms stretched wide like a prophet's, stood a man with fire in his eyes and hair white like the moon, howling at the empty sky like a million hungry wolves, and somehow my imagination had gotten away from me, and it just about broke my heart when I realized who it was on top of the wheel.

"I see him, too," I whispered. "On the very top. It's Patrick."

Suzanne squeezed my hand and whispered softly into my ear.

"That's not Patrick, Itchy. That's the Keeper of the Ferris wheel."